EVERYTHING TO LOSE

EVERYTHING TO LOSE

Jennifer Bacia

HarperCollins*Publishers*

HarperCollins*Publishers*

First published in Australia in 1999
by HarperCollins*Publishers* Pty Limited
ACN 009 913 517
A member of HarperCollins*Publishers* (Australia) Pty Limited Group
http://www.harpercollins.com.au

HarperCollins*Publishers*
25 Ryde Road, Pymble, Sydney, NSW 2073, Australia
31 View Road, Glenfield, Auckland 10, New Zealand
77–85 Fulham Palace Road, London W6 8JB, United Kingdom
Hazelton Lanes, 55 Avenue Road, Suite 2900, Toronto, Ontario M5R 3L2
and 1995 Markham Road, Scarborough, Ontario M1B 5M8, Canada
10 East 53rd Street, New York NY 10022, USA

National Library Cataloguing-in-Publication data:

Bacia, Jennifer.
    Everything to lose.
    ISBN 0 7322 5986 X.
    I. Title.
A823.3

Typeset in Sabon 10 on 13.5
Cover photograph: The Photo Library/Reza Estakhrian
Printed in Australia by Griffin Press Pty Ltd Adelaide,
on 50gsm Ensobulky

5 4 3 2 1
03 02 01 00 99

This book is dedicated to
Carole Bartholomew and Jill Marshall
with heartfelt thanks

ACKNOWLEDGEMENTS

With thanks again to Selwa Anthony who has always been so much more than a literary agent to me, and to John, my precious husband and soulmate.

PROLOGUE

The committal hearing was set down for ten a.m. before Magistrate Adam Geddes.

The morning was unusually hot, but that didn't deter the long line of the curious, eager to find a space in the public gallery. In an age where the media did its best to dull public sensibilities with its daily diet of sensationalism, there were still some events that could cause genuine shock.

Among those waiting to enter Court Seven were three women who knew the accused. They had come today, taken time out from their usual routine, to offer their support. For each had wanted to prove that the past had counted for something.

Yet, if each were honest with herself, she'd have admitted that her presence there that morning had as much to do with guilt as with friendship.

But they made their silent excuses: how could any of them have guessed what the end result would be?

Which of them, on that summer evening just ten months ago, had seen any sign of the tragedy to come? That night, when their lives had interwoven again after a quarter of a century, it would have been beyond their wildest imaginings to have envisaged such an appalling outcome.

Only now, when it was too late, did all three of the accused's friends face the fact that each could stand accused of her own deception on that momentous evening.

Would it have changed things if they'd been honest with each other then?

None of them would ever know.

CHAPTER ONE

She was going to be late. It was six forty-five when she finally escaped the hell that was Military Road and turned into the suburban street that led to home. Why, today of all days, did bloody Marcia have to call a last-minute meeting?

As she drove too fast through the narrow, winding side streets, Rory Hudson prayed that Ian had managed to get home on time. The nanny left at seven and she had to shower, change, get ready and be back in the city by seven-thirty.

Tense with anxiety, she jerked to a stop outside the double-fronted cottage — with a mortgage so large it frightened her to think about — and cursed softly. No sign of Ian's Audi.

Grabbing her laden briefcase she slid out of the car, slamming the door angrily behind her. Damn Ian! She'd *told* him how important tonight was. Why the hell couldn't he have made the effort to get here on time? Just for once.

As she let herself into the house, a curly-haired young woman appeared at the end of the hallway.

'Hi, Rory.'

The girl smiled as she jiggled the baby on her ample hips. 'Look, darling, Mummy's home. Give her a great, big kiss.'

Setting aside her impatience for a moment, Rory strode down the hall, dropping her briefcase by her study door and shrugging off her jacket before she reached out for her baby son. She'd learned the hard way what baby dribble did to an Armani jacket.

'Cam ... my sweet, sweet pet ...' Rory kissed her son's soft hair, then smiled as she dropped him backwards into her cupped hands. 'So tell me, have you been a good boy for Deb today?'

'He's been fine. A little grumble over an afternoon nap, but we got over that.' The girl gently pinched the baby's rosy cheek. 'We did, didn't we, you little devil?'

Rory couldn't help thinking to herself that at the exact time her nanny had been trying to get her son to sleep, she had been at lunch with Scott Dorvane, one of the authors she was most proud of having signed. As always she said a silent prayer of thanks for the young woman whom she knew she could trust with her most prized possession.

She glanced at the hall clock. 'Oh, hell, I'm going to be so late, Deb.' With her baby son still in her arms, she made for the bedroom at the back of the house. 'Ian was supposed to be home by now. I made him promise he'd be here on time tonight. I've got to be out of here by seven-fifteen at the very latest.'

She left the implication hanging in the air.

The young girl hesitated as she stood at the bedroom door. Her normal hours were seven to seven, and this evening she'd arranged to meet a friend to see a movie. But she couldn't avoid the plea in her employer's face.

'I — I don't mind staying till he gets here.'

Rory's face brightened in relief. 'Oh, Deb, that's so good of you! You're wonderful. We'll make it up to you, I promise.' What's another few dollars on top of the fortune they were paying already? she asked herself.

Cam was starting to grizzle and squirm in her arms and gratefully Rory handed him over.

'I'll give him a bottle and put him down.'

'Thanks, Deb.' Rory was already fumbling with the buttons of her blouse, stepping out of her skirt. 'I'm sure Ian won't be too long,' she called out as she twisted on the shower tap in the ensuite.

She had less than ten minutes to get ready. A great impression she was going to make.

Then something made her think of Leith. For a night like this, Leith would probably have started getting ready a month ago.

❋

Wearing only a bra and pants, Leith Arnold sat absolutely still and gazed at her reflection. The soft lighting around her dressing room mirror bathed her in a warm and flattering glow.

Slowly her lips parted in a satisfied smile. Great. An absolutely first-class job. It was three months since the op and no one would ever guess.

Her timing had been fortunate rather than deliberate. She hadn't known about the reunion when she'd made a date for the surgery. Her decision had been prompted by the fact that at forty two she had been faced with the first real signs of aging. The facials, the sun blocks, the expensive creams — none of them alone or together, she had realised, were able to fight the pull of gravity. With increasing anxiety she had noted the subtle hooding closing in her once large green eyes, the lines that were becoming more noticeable across her high forehead, and had known the time had come for her first bit of 'reconditioning'.

The brow lift and eye job had achieved the subtle result she had hoped for. If she'd waited any longer, it would have made it easier for her friends to guess that she'd had something done. Not that she was changing nature, she reminded herself, merely preserving the good looks she'd been blessed with in the first place.

From the time she was very young, Leith had realised she was more than ordinarily pretty. It was a message reinforced not only by her own extended family but also by the strangers who would stop her mother in the street to exclaim at the beauty of her curly-haired daughter.

But, unlike some children whose youthful good looks blur into ordinariness with age, Leith's beauty had grown with her. At sixteen, when many of her contemporaries were still round-faced and lumpish, Leith had often found herself being compared to someone as stunning as Farrah Fawcett. The tumble of honey-blonde hair, the lustrous green eyes, the sensual delicacy of her facial planes. Her figure —

slim, high-breasted, narrow-hipped — was yet more evidence that the gods had been prepared to bestow on her an abundance of their gifts.

Leith was pleased, of course. What young woman wouldn't be? However, what she hadn't realised at first was that beauty brought more than its own reward. It gave a woman power, too.

She could see how interested boys were, and was self-consciously aware of their eyes following her, watching her on the beach, on the street, in shopping malls. Only when she started going out with them did she come to see how much physical beauty in a woman meant to the opposite sex. Not merely as a stimulant, but also as a signal to the world of their own worth: 'Look what I can get . . .'

Leith didn't find such knowledge altogether comforting, for how, she wondered, would she know when she was liked for herself rather than as a trophy? And there were other drawbacks too, she soon discovered. All too often she was left an outsider with her own sex, envy being no basis for close friendship. When the rejection and loneliness got too much, she'd often cry herself to sleep. She so longed for even one close girlfriend, someone to confide in, to share her hopes and dreams and fears with.

In the end she'd finally figured out a way to break down the barrier that stood between what nature had bestowed on her and her ability to make friends. Where previously she had been quiet and attempted to make herself as unobtrusive as possible, she now began to adopt a self-deprecating humour, come up with witty put-downs of her effect on the opposite sex, make it clear that she didn't take herself or her looks too seriously.

Her strategy worked. When her surprised peers realised that she wasn't stuck-up or captivated by her own beauty, they slowly began to thaw. As they got to know her, they also learnt that beauty did not always provide a guaranteed protection against vulnerability or lack of confidence. Once they viewed her as one of them, Leith was able to form the sorts of friendships everyone else took for granted. It was at that time she'd grown close to Rory and Judith and Cate.

Now, as she buttoned up the slim-fitting, red silk suit she had bought in New York a few months before, Leith wondered why she'd let those friendships slip. The first year out of school they'd all kept in touch, excitedly recounting to each other the joys of their newly found freedom, their work and studies, their first real boyfriends.

Leith's eyes suddenly clouded. The way she'd always thought of it, her father had been her first real boyfriend. The first man who had always been there for her. And she'd been certain he had adored her as much as she adored him. He had called her his 'little princess' and never stopped telling her how pretty she was, how she was the most important person in his life.

But none of that had stopped him leaving when Leith was just fourteen years old. She had tried not to hear the bitter arguments that had gone on between her parents, had buried her head under her pillow at night against the raised voices and angry words. Mainly it was money they fought about, or the way her father never seemed to stick with any job.

At the time Leith couldn't understand why things like that were so important to her mother. Daddy loved both of them, didn't he? Wasn't that all that really mattered?

But in the end he had gone, leaving Leith shattered. For the first year or so he'd rung to speak to her about once a month. She remembered how she'd sob and beg him to come back.

But he never had. And she'd never got over it.

Which was why she had married a man like David, a man she was sure would be able to give her everything she'd been robbed of when her father left: the attention, the love, the security of knowing she was the centre of his world.

And he had. At least for a while.

❇

Leaving the three steaks under the grill, Judith Burton hurried back upstairs to confront the jumble of discarded outfits that covered the bed.

What the *hell* was she going to wear? she asked herself in despair. When she'd pulled out the pantsuit she'd finally decided on, she'd found stains on the lapel of the jacket. Only then had she remembered that the last time she'd worn it, she'd eaten pasta for lunch. The tomato sauce had splattered on her and, of course, she'd forgotten to send the jacket to the cleaners.

'Mum! The steaks are burning!' Her sixteen-year-old son's voice resounded up the staircase.

Judith closed her eyes a moment in frustration. Then, still in her petticoat and towelling robe, she hastily made her way down the stairs and into the kitchen. Smoke was pouring out of the griller while Luke lounged on the family room sofa, glued to the sight of men dressed in white on the television screen.

'Luke!' She yanked out the griller and looked in irritation at the charred meat. 'Couldn't you have turned it down when you saw they were burning!'

Her son's answer was a shrug, his eyes never leaving the cricket field.

Judith carried the meat to the sink. She could scrape off the worst, she supposed. Luckily Greg liked his meat well done.

She could see her husband from the kitchen window. He'd made it home earlier as she'd asked him to, except that now he was busy swimming his twenty laps of the pool.

Doing her best with the overcooked meat, Judith quickly tossed a salad and set the table.

'Luke, tell everyone it's ready, please.'

No response.

'Luke! Did you hear me?'

His attention finally distracted, her son sighed heavily as he dragged himself to his feet. 'I heard you. You don't have to yell, you know.'

'I'm going out. I've got to be dressed and out of here in twenty minutes. Tell Brent and your father it's on the table. Now.'

He lurched out and Judith heard him banging heavily on his brother's bedroom door further down the hall. It was locked, no doubt, with Brent deaf to anything but the earphones of his expensive sound system.

Well, if it's cold, too bad, she thought as she quickly made her way upstairs again to deal with the ongoing problem of what to wear. She was upset about the pantsuit. The jacket did a lot to hide the kilos she'd stacked on in the last couple of years. She didn't kid herself. What had done it was the chocolate biscuits, the potato crisps, the bacon sandwiches she cooked for herself on those too frequent evenings when she sat in the house alone. Comfort food, she knew. Nothing to do with hunger. She even wondered sometimes if the whole process of eating didn't help to choke back her anger.

As she rummaged in the walk-in robe, searching for an appropriate substitute for the all-forgiving pantsuit, Judith found herself thinking how much she hated her life. It was a thought that occurred to her all too often these days. However she might have imagined her future, it certainly wasn't what she had now.

After a few more abortive changes, she finally settled on something passable, hurriedly applied some lipstick and blush and ran a brush through her newly tinted hair. It was auburn now in place of the mousey brown that had started to grey at an alarming rate since her fortieth birthday. The hairdresser had talked her into it, but Judith wasn't sure if it really suited her. Though Greg had made some innocuous comment when she'd asked him for his opinion, she doubted that he'd even noticed until she'd actually pointed the change out to him.

In much the same way that he didn't seem to notice what was happening to their marriage.

Downstairs, her husband and two sons were eating the burnt steak, their eyes still skewered to the night cricket match.

Greg, at least, made an effort when she said goodbye.

'Enjoy yourself. What time do you think you'll be back?'

'Shouldn't be too late, I imagine. We'll probably all just check out each other's wrinkles and go home.'

But he'd missed her attempt at humour, his attention caught by another roar from the TV.

She'd just picked up her keys from the hall table when her eldest son stuck his dishevelled head around the door of the family room.

'Mum, I need my whites for tomorrow and there's a seam needs fixing — right leg, I think.'

Judith merely nodded. That meant taking out the sewing machine at whatever time she got home. And she had an early meeting tomorrow with her supervisor. Seven-thirty. But then, she could cope with it all, couldn't she?

As she let herself out of the house that so impressed all their friends, Judith wondered if instead of her Honda she should take a cab.

She wasn't really a drinker, but the way she was feeling at the moment, tonight might be an excellent excuse to take on a skinful.

❊

Cate Tremain felt a familiar sense of contentment as she let herself into her apartment. This is what she prized the most, she thought. Security and privacy. A place to come home to that was totally her own. A place no one could take away from her — except the bank if she defaulted and, given her present salary, that wasn't an imminent problem.

She'd had a hectic day. The worst of it was that bloody actress pulling out of the satellite link-up at the last minute. With only an hour to go to air, it had been a nerve-wracking scramble to find a half-decent replacement. Dramas like that she could live without, but they were all part of the adrenalin rush of putting together five-days-a-week live television.

Cate loved her work. She'd struggled and pushed and mouthed off in the right ears for almost two years until at last she'd landed her dream job. A producer on *Live!* — the highest-rating program on daytime television.

Live!, with host Leanna Peters, covered it all: current events, politics, gossip, the arts. Its vast audience comprised mainly women viewers, and advertisers had finally realised the power of the female. It was the woman of the family who decided where they were going to holiday, what they were going to drive, where they were going to live. Advertisers queued up for their slot on *Live!*, as did anyone with a movie, book, new CD, political party or face cream to flog. They tore flesh to appear on a show with the sort of ratings *Live!* attracted.

Cate was in charge of the entertainment segment of the program. She not only arranged interviews with visiting big name actors, directors, singers, authors and so on, but also had to keep her ear to the ground, figure out who was going to be the Next Big Thing and get them first for *Live!*

She'd been with the program over three years now and knew she'd never find another job to compare. It was tiring and exhausting, exhilarating and exciting. Every day she was flying by the seat of her pants, praying nothing would go wrong, exulting when an interview she'd arranged and researched went like a dream.

The money was fantastic, too. It had enabled her to move from a crappy, cramped box at Willoughby to her small but modern apartment with its glimpses of Balmoral Beach. It meant a longer drive to the studio, perhaps, but it was worth it. Home was her retreat, a place to unwind, a precious haven from the crazy whirlpool that was her working environment.

As she flopped down onto the sofa and clicked on the news — a TV junkie and proud of it — she didn't feel like going out. If it weren't that she'd promised Judith she'd go along tonight, she'd have given it a miss. Nostalgia wasn't her thing, it was the present, the future that excited her.

But Judith had rung her a couple of months ago with the news of the reunion. The two of them had kept in desultory touch over the years — Christmas cards, the odd phone call. God knows why really, thought Cate. They had little enough in common.

'You've got to come, Cate,' Judith had insisted. 'It'll be fun. I'm going to try to get onto Leith and Rory, too.' She'd sounded excited. 'Can you imagine it? Twenty-five years. My God, it seems impossible! But I guess at least we've all survived.'

Yes, Cate agreed silently, she'd survived.

And she'd vowed never to allow anyone to have charge of her destiny again.

With a weary sigh she hauled herself up from the sofa and headed for the bathroom.

CHAPTER TWO

Flustered and still annoyed at Ian, who had appeared ten minutes after she was meant to have left, Rory pushed her way in through the revolving door of the inner city hotel. A sign in the foyer told her that the function was being held in a room on the floor above and, heels clicking like castanets on the marble floor, she hurried towards the elevators.

When she emerged a few moments later, she was confronted by swarms of forty-something women clutching drinks, and by the buzz of noisy conversation, punctuated by squeals of recognition and bursts of laughter.

God, who would have dreamed so many of her former class-mates would have shown up? She had taken a few hesitant steps into the crush when suddenly she heard her name being called.

'Rory! We're here!'

Scanning the faces around her, she caught sight of

an overweight woman with auburn hair waving at her. It took Rory a second to realise it was Judith ... and there, beside her ... God, it was Leith and Cate ...

Face widening in a grin, she pushed her way through the crowd towards them.

'Rory!' Judith threw an arm around her and planted a gleeful kiss on her cheek. 'I knew it had to be you! You haven't changed a bit. Still as thin as a rake, you bitch!'

'Darling, how lovely to see you!' Leith, looking wonderful of course in a brilliantly cut red suit, hugged her warmly, and Rory caught a whiff of something undoubtedly French. No Liz or Estee or Calvin for our Leith.

And then it was Cate's turn to plant a kiss. Cate, with a fan of wrinkles around her dark blue eyes, but the same wild dark hair and freckles and interesting clothes. Tonight, she'd gone sort of thirties in a dress that was all soft draping, topped by what had to be an antique fringed shawl.

'Can you believe it's been twenty-five years?' Cate smiled and shook her head in awe.

Rory laughed out loud as she turned from one to the other of them, taking them in, seeing the women who had formed from the girls she had last seen as teenagers.

'This is great!' she grinned. 'This is really great!'

They had sat together at dinner, clapped the speeches, marvelled at the way their classmates had either changed so radically in looks or temperament or, conversely, remained so much the same. Later, like everyone else, they moved from table to table, catching up on the present, triggering memories with those who had shared their youth. It was fun, but it made it hard for the four of them to really talk.

'Jude! Twenty years of marriage? You've got to tell me how you did it!'

'I still can't believe it, Rory — a baby at forty!'

'God, Cate, I thought for sure you'd be married by now.'

'So tell us, Leith, what's it like to be filthy rich?'

They talked over the top of each other, firing questions, being interrupted too often by others, never able, it seemed, to finish what they were trying to say. There was just too much to talk about and too little time and peace and quiet this evening to do much more than scratch the surface.

'Listen, we can't leave it like this,' Judith protested as the evening drew to a close. 'We've got to meet for dinner sometime soon and catch up properly.'

The others were in complete agreement.

'Leave it to me,' Leith announced, taking out her organiser and noting down telephone numbers. 'I'll call everybody early next week, tie down a date and book the restaurant.'

She'd make sure it was somewhere, she reminded herself, where she hadn't appeared with any of her ... distractions.

❀

As she sat in the back of the taxi heading home, Cate realised that she'd enjoyed the evening more than she'd expected to. The friendships you made when you were young were different, she thought, more real, more intense. As teenagers, the four of them had been so open with each other about their fears, their problems, their inadequacies, their crazy, wonderful dreams. It was only when you grew older that life grew more complicated, less clear cut, and made you more wary, more protective.

Now, as she stared out into the night, Cate asked herself if she would confide in Leith or Judith or Rory about what was happening in her own life at the moment.

But she already knew the answer.

❊

Dressed in her nightdress, Judith sat at her sewing machine in the spare bedroom, mending her son's cricket trousers. It was past midnight and she wasn't only tired but resentful too.

How, she wondered, despite all her efforts over the years, had her sons turned out the way they had — lazy, ungrateful, distant, incapable of any positive emotional reaction that wasn't directly associated with some sporting win?

She had done her best to bring them up so that they wouldn't end up like so many men of her own generation: males who had no idea how to express their feelings, who were suspicious and fearful of women, who stifled their potential and killed their relationships beneath the bravura and machismo that put so many of them in an early grave.

19

She'd been so determined not to have her boys end up like their father. But already, she could see, the similarities were frightening.

I should have stayed home with them longer when they were babies, she blamed herself now, not gone back to work so quickly. Full-time mothering for those few crucial years might have made all the difference.

But Greg had made it clear he expected her to return to work. As soon as possible. Her eyes clouded as she fiercely snipped off a thread. We need the money, he'd told her, we can't manage on just one salary.

Well, she thought angrily, if we had lived in a normal house, driven ordinary cars, cut back on the wine clubs, the entertaining, the golf club memberships and everything else, we *could* have managed on what Greg earned.

It was *his* ambition that had forced her to keep working full-time. It was Greg, running hard and fast from his deprived working class background, who was driven to acquire, to impress. And she'd been forced to play the game with him.

When they'd first married, she'd imagined that she'd work until she had kids and then be a full-time mother until they went to school, maybe working part-time after that. But Greg had had different ideas and she'd ended up with a career, whether she'd wanted one or not.

Now, after more than two decades with the same employer, she was at the top of her particular tree: floor manager in a large suburban department store. The salary was good, she quite enjoyed her work as well as the company of most of the other women she worked with, but still, somewhere inside her, Judith felt cheated. Life hadn't turned out the way she had imagined it. She felt that there had to be something more. What exactly that might be, she wasn't quite sure, but she knew it wasn't what she had now.

Sudden tears welled into her eyes and angrily she blinked them away. Normally she managed to keep her emotions under control, but something had got to her tonight. Instinctively, she knew it had to do with seeing her friends again, and all those other women with whom she'd shared her youth. The evening had been full of reminders that once she'd had dreams, dreams that she knew now had little chance of coming true.

She'd been so much in love with Greg when they'd married, had been sure that the closeness they shared on their wedding day would only grow stronger as the years passed. Instead, the opposite had happened, and the arrival of children had made it worse. In the end, Judith thought self-pityingly, she had finished up sharing her life with three people who ignored her, used her, and took her for granted.

By a slow, gradual process, she had lost her own sense of identity, had become someone who merely helped to pay the school fees, the food bills, the telephone account, who was useful only to clean, cook, mend their bloody clothes and, in her sons' case, drive them around on weekends.

Fighting back her bitterness, Judith snapped the lid on the machine and carried it back to the wardrobe. As she stored it among the overflow of their winter clothes, she caught sight of a stack of old files and papers, topped by a blue manila folder. It was a sight that did little to improve her mood.

That folder had been part of her dream. It contained her writing efforts — numerous half-finished stories, jottings of ideas, notes for a novel she had been crazy enough to think she might one day write. But, she reminded herself, she *had* received some encouragement. She could still remember her utter delight when one of the short stories she'd sent to a leading woman's magazine had been accepted. She had felt as if she'd won the lottery, and had been giddy, ecstatic with joy. The acceptance letter and cheque were the first tangible proof that perhaps she did have some talent.

But that had been more than three years ago. And since then, despite all her efforts, it had seemed so difficult to find the time and energy to direct to the one and only area of her life that brought her real pleasure and satisfaction.

With a sigh, she turned out the light and padded down the hallway towards her bedroom. Later, she promised herself. Later, when the boys had left home, she'd find the time for what she so ached to do.

Greg was asleep, snoring softly, and as she slipped into the bed beside him, Judith suddenly remembered what she'd learned tonight about the two girls from her class who hadn't made it to the reunion.

Both dead of breast cancer before they'd reached forty.

Judith felt a little chill run through her. How much time do any of us have, she wondered?

Rory stood in the darkened room and stared down at her sleeping son. Even now she sometimes found it hard to believe that she was actually the mother of a child, that she and Ian had produced this tiny human being, made its beating heart, its perfect skin, its brain, its cells ... Motherhood still thrilled her ... and terrified her.

She hadn't given babies a thought until she turned thirty-eight. Before then, she'd been consumed by her career, climbing the ladder, making a name for herself. At thirty-eight she'd been a literary fiction publisher for two years with one of the industry's most respected, heavyweight companies. During those two exciting years, she had discovered new talents and seduced some of the country's biggest names into changing houses. She'd been completely immersed in her work.

Then, suddenly, some biological time bomb had gone off inside her, and almost overnight she had made up her mind that she was going to have a child before it was too late.

By then, she and Ian had been living together for four years. They both had secure, well-paying careers — Ian as Associate Professor of English at Sydney University — and an inner city lifestyle of movies, theatre, art galleries and music, that they shared with like-minded friends.

Their life had seemed complete until the awakening of her sudden intense longing for a child.

Ian, she knew, hadn't been as keen. He was two years older and worried that he'd left it too late, was too set in his ways, to become a father. And he'd made it clear he was worried about her, too. Was she sure that after all these years of living life so spontaneously, so freely, she could adapt to the limitations set by having a child? And what about her work? The hours she put in when there were deadlines to face? How did she think she was going to cope?

Driven by her obsession, she had done her best to reassure him. Of course they'd have to make a few changes, but they'd have a nanny. Other women managed and she would too.

In the end Ian had come round. Not least of all because he wanted to make her happy, but also because he accepted the strength of her desire to have a child.

There was only one point on which he had stood firm. He had no interest in marriage. He'd told her that from the very first and he reiterated it now. They didn't need to make the committment demanded by Church and State to declare themselves a couple, he'd insisted, and having a child wasn't going to change his views.

Rory did her best to hide her reaction to his rigid proclamation. When they'd started living together, Ian's aversion to marriage hadn't really worried her. Most of their friends were in de facto relationships, too, so what did it matter? But, as the years passed, and so many of the others eventually made it to the altar, she secretly began to wish for the same formal vow. Occasionally, half jokingly, she would make some reference to the fact, but it was clear that Ian's attitude hadn't changed.

Yet once she had declared her wish for a child, Rory never doubted that marriage would be part of the deal. It was the way things were done. Non-conformity was fine when you had only yourself to think about, but now there would be a child to consider. Fitting society's norms made everything easier.

But when she realised Ian had no intention of changing his mind, she had to bite back her disappointment and distress. Doing her best to rationalise the situation, she had reminded herself that Ian loved her, would never leave her. That what really mattered in the end was having a child to love and bring up together.

The physical side of things hadn't happened easily. It had taken her more than a year to fall pregnant, and her delight was short-lived when, a few short weeks later, she had miscarried. The thought that she might have left it too late, that she might be denied the child she now ached for, had plunged her into despair. But they had kept trying, and finally the tests proved positive again. This time she had been more restrained in her jubilation until her belly grew and she was convinced that this baby would go full term.

Nine months and one week later, she had produced a healthy baby boy.

Now, as she stood by her son's cot, Rory thought back on the rollercoaster her life had been over the last fourteen months. Even with the help of a nanny and part-time housekeeper, there had been mammoth adjustments to be made. These days, time had become her most precious commodity. She seemed to spend her life in a continual fever of organisation, both at work and at home. And on no front did she ever seem to be in complete control.

Ian did his best, but, because it was she who had persuaded him into this dramatic change in their lives, Rory tried guiltily to shoulder most of the burden herself. The sheer workload left her exhausted, and sometimes she felt overwhelmed by the fact that this helpless human being was so totally and utterly dependent on her.

Yet strangely, this evening she had felt the most relaxed since Cam's birth. She had a sense of some tight knot inside her being released. As if, in the company of the women she had once been so close to, who had shared her innermost hopes and thoughts, she had stepped back into her girlhood and could throw off the responsibilites and duties demanded by her adult life.

In the bedroom she undressed in the darkness, glad that Ian was asleep and couldn't see her. Once at ease with her nakedness, she'd grown self-conscious about the changes pregnancy had caused in her body. Judith mightn't have noticed, but she was painfully aware of her widened hips and mottled buttocks, the little pot that sat on her once hard, firm belly.

It might be easy for women like Madonna and Elle to bounce back to physical perfection, she thought cynically, but then they hadn't been close to forty-one years old when they'd given birth. It was tougher when you were older.

Still, she admonished herself, she'd have to do something, join a gym or hire some sort of torture rack and set it up in a corner of her study. She'd had all those good intentions at the start but it was time, as usual, that had defeated her. When she'd first brought Cam home, there hadn't seemed to be a spare moment to do anything for herself. And after that she'd been back at work, putting in the extra hours to try to make up for the time she'd lost.

During those first few weeks, alone with her baby son, Rory had imagined she'd have plenty of time to catch up on her work, organise a routine for herself. What, after all, did new babies do but sleep and eat?

Except that she'd forgotten that they eat on demand and then need to be burped, cleaned and changed. The lack of sleep had left her near to comatose, and she'd found herself turning into one of those slatterns she'd vowed she would never become. There were too many days when she'd still be in her dressing gown at midday, the beds unmade, dishes not washed, everything focused on the needs of the one tiny creature who was so utterly dependent on her.

Rory climbed into the warm sheets and tucked her body close to her lover's. Yes, it was tough. The toughest job she'd ever faced in her life. But, she assured herself, they hadn't made a mistake. Having Cam in their lives made it all worthwhile. They were a family now.

Within seconds she was asleep.

❊

As she turned into the driveway of her Hunters Hill home, Leith could see lights on the ground floor of the house. Of course, David would have waited up for her. Surprisingly, she felt a momentary disappointment. Normally she would have enjoyed the rare pleasure of her husband's company, but tonight she felt a need to be alone with the thoughts and emotions that the evening had generated.

For while she had been delighted at seeing her old schoolfriends again, there'd been a negative reaction, too — the shock of looking at faces she had last seen in the flush of youth which were now drawn and lined by the passing of the years and the vagaries of fate. At seventeen, she thought, none of them had known what lay in store. Fresh-faced innocents, they had left the confines and protection of their parents and teachers to face whatever the world dealt out to them.

But I've been lucky, Leith thought, suddenly ashamed of her earlier thought. I've got David.

They'd met when she was working as a stewardess on one of the domestic airlines, the sort of work where her looks had counted. And in true clichéd fashion, David Arnold had been one of her passengers.

Leith hadn't been surprised when he'd started to chat and eventually asked her to have dinner with him. It was the kind of thing that happened all the time in her sort of job. More often than not, with a warm smile, she would knock the invitations back. But there had been something different about David. He'd had a quiet dignity, a sort of old-world charm and good manners that had made an impression. And he'd been handsome, too, with strong features, crisp dark hair, friendly blue eyes and a wide, perfect smile.

She had quickly checked for a wedding ring. There was none, but that didn't mean anything. Half the men who tried to pick her up were married and their fingers were invariably bare.

But this time she trusted her instincts and said yes.

It was a night that changed her life. He took her to a small French place with soft lighting and first-class food and over the next four hours told her all about himself.

He'd grown up in Dubbo, come to Sydney to study and started his own company just a couple of years before. At thirty-five he was twelve years older than Leith and had never been married.

'Not that I've got anything against marriage, mind you, just that it's not easy meeting the right person.' He twirled the stem of his wine glass and added with a lopsided smile, 'I don't like to make mistakes.'

His work, of course, made it difficult. As owner of a small but expanding engineering firm, he was constantly on the move. 'I've got plans for moving into South-East Asia, too. I can see that being our next big market.'

It was clear he was ambitious and Leith admired that, but David Arnold had more to talk about than just his work. His interests were wide-ranging, from politics to travel to the arts. He spoke about the books he enjoyed, the movies he'd seen, the places he'd still like to visit in the world.

'Except that it's not much fun alone,' he said, looking at her, 'or with the wrong person.'

Leith had never before met a man who spoke so personally so quickly.

Two months later, in another intimate restaurant, he asked her to marry him. Pulling out a small velvet box, he put it on the table in front of her.

Leith opened the lid and stared at the brightly flashing diamond. Her heart raced. She had been almost certain it would come to this, only not so soon ...

Yet even in the short time she'd known him, she had no doubt that David would make a wonderful husband. She loved him and knew he would look after her, protect her, give her the life she hoped for.

'David,' she looked up at him, her eyes shining, 'it's beautiful. I —'

Quickly he interrupted. 'Leith, I — I can't let you give me an answer without telling you something.' She heard the strain in his voice, and her brows drew together in a frown. 'You have to know, darling, that I can give you almost everything in the world you could want but I can't — I can't give you a child.'

Mind racing, Leith stared back at him as he explained about the childhood mumps that had left him sterile. 'Tests were done at the time and there didn't seem much hope. I — I saw my doctor recently again and nothing, I'm afraid, has changed,'

Leith understood. He had had the test in anticipation of this moment, and his handsome face was anguished as he waited for her reply.

Reaching across the table, she covered his hand with her own.

'I can live without a child,' she said softly and gently, 'but I can't live without you, David.'

And it was true. For why did she need a child when she sometimes still felt like a child herself?

David smiled at her now as she entered the kitchen. He was wearing the silk dressing gown she'd bought him for his fifty-third birthday a year ago.

He kissed her cheek. 'So, darling, how did it go? Did you enjoy yourself?'

'Oh ... it was fun, but maybe a little depressing, too.' Unbuttoning her jacket, Leith shrugged it off.

He helped her, took it from her and draped it across a chair. Then he slid his arms around her waist and she felt the warmth of his breath as he spoke close to her ear. 'Time passes for all of us, darling. But it doesn't matter when you're truly loved.'

Leith closed her eyes as she relaxed against her husband's strong shoulder. Oh, David, David, she thought, you have the surprising gift, so rare in a man, of being able to sense a woman's mood.

It was late when they went to bed, but they were both ready to make love.

David had always been a good lover. He took the time to arouse her, not only her body, but even more importantly, her mind. He kissed her and whispered how she made him feel, how beautiful she was, how much he adored her. Then when she was ready, he eased himself into her, filling her, and slowly, expertly, brought them both to a climax.

'That was wonderful,' she said breathlessly as she laid her head on the soft mat of his chest. 'I only wish you were around to do it more often.'

It was her gentle hint. A way of trying to make him understand her growing dissatisfaction.

CHAPTER THREE

Her usual frantic schedule meant Cate had no time to think about the telephone message that had been waiting for her when she'd arrived home the previous evening.

Putting a live show to air meant there were always last-minute hitches or changes in schedules, and today was no exception. As on-air time approached, Cate shuttled between her cluttered cubby-hole of an office with its walls of note-covered cork boards, the studio, and the VIP green room, where a visiting US female singing star was busy warming up her voice.

Sticking her head into Make-up, she handed a copy of the final program schedule to Leanna Peters, the vibrant, outgoing blonde who had been the show's anchor since its inception five years before. Cate liked Leanna. She was uncompromising and demanding of her staff and crew, but also completely unflappable in the face of sometimes amazing last-minute chaos. Her quick mind readily absorbed her myriad daily briefings and she conducted each interview with the sort of rapt interest that most of her high-profile guests responded to with relish.

Cate never failed to be impressed by Leanna's prodigious energy in hosting a live show for forty weeks a year. Of course she'd heard the malicious rumours about that energy being dependent on certain illegal substances, but Cate put them down to jealousy and ignorance. Anyone who worked closely with Leanna could see she was one of those human beings who is naturally buoyant, and her high came only from her work.

At this particular moment, however, the host of *Live!* was sitting silently in her chair as the make-up girl gave a final coat of spray to her hair. These few minutes just before the start of the day's program were the only time Cate ever saw Leanna so still and quiet. Yet the instant she stepped out in front of the cameras, everything changed. As if a surge of electrical current had been switched on, Leanna Peters immediately radiated high energy, warmth and fun. It was the sheer force of her personality that made the show the success it was.

Today, thank God, everything went off without a major problem and, as the last of the studio audience filed out, Cate could finally let herself relax. Only now could she think about grabbing a quick bite of lunch, yet there were still meetings to attend for upcoming shows, schedules to arrange, details to finalise. It was a crazy pace to live at, she knew, but she loved every minute of it.

It was after four-thirty before she finally found a breathing space to think about last night's call.

Sipping a cup of black coffee, she sat at her desk, frowning as she remembered Tom Gillespie's message. A month later and he was still trying to get her to change her mind. Cate sighed. God, she didn't need this sort of complication in her life any more.

❄

She'd met Tom Gillespie three months previously at the launch of his latest book. He was a sociologist who'd found a popular market among his fellow baby boomers with works that helped to explain the rapid changes taking place in Australian society as they approached the millennium.

Cate had already lined him up for *Live!*, and his agent had invited her to the launch to meet the author. After the formalities were over, the two of them had had a short chat, and Cate had found her guest-to-be charming, witty, and clever. His tangle of greying curls told her he must be in his forties, but he still had the sort of boyish energy and enthusiasm she had always found appealing. He'd be a natural, she knew, on the small screen.

'I'll give you a ring by the end of the week then,' she said, aware of others hovering, keen to claim his attention. They would have to decide which points of the book were of most general interest so she could brief Leanna.

It was then Tom Gillespie had shot a quick glance at his watch. 'Look, I don't know about you, but I'm starving. I'll be out of here in about twenty minutes.

What about we grab a bite and get it all worked out right now?' He gave her an impish grin. 'Unless of course you're already full on the stale Jatz provided by my munificent publishers.'

With a smile, Cate had agreed to his proposal.

He took her to Marios, where they shared a bottle of Verdicchio and some excellent pasta. Cate found herself enjoying his company. He made her laugh. He was quick, irreverent — and, of course, married. First wife even, not that any of that mattered any longer to Cate. She was long past checking out the marital status of likely men. These days she was happily single. And proud of it.

What's more, even if that hadn't been the case, she wasn't crazy enough to get involved with a married man.

A week or so later he turned up for his appearance on the show and greeted Cate like an old friend. Tom Gillespie was certainly someone who knew the value of PR, she thought cynically as she walked out of the Green Room.

When it was time for his segment, she took a moment or two to watch him on the monitor. Animated and friendly, he conveyed his message in a way that entertained as well as informed. He was, as Cate had been sure he would be, a natural live performer.

There might never have been more to it than that if, a few days afterwards, he hadn't called her at work.

'You did a great job for me, Cate. I'd love to say

thank you. May I have the pleasure of your company for dinner again some evening?'

Cate was a little surprised. In most cases it was only Leanna who got the thanks. But then, she reminded herself cynically, Tom Gillespie was just making doubly sure that he was remembered for his next book.

Well, her social life wasn't exactly brimming over with invitations, she thought, so why not have a meal with a man whose company she enjoyed?

Now, a month after she'd called their affair off, she was still upset with herself for having got involved. Sure, Tom was attractive, seductive, charming, but she should never have let it happen. What really disturbed her was the way the affair, despite its brevity, had unbalanced the rhythm of her life, unsettled her in a way that she'd promised herself would never happen again.

It was a pledge she had made six years ago when things had ended so badly with Simon. She and Simon had lived together for more than five years, had talked freely about marriage, a family, and Cate had felt certain about her future.

They had met at a party. She'd come with someone else and so had he. But by the end of the evening, there had been enough sparks flying between them for them to readily exchange telephone numbers.

Simon was a talented graphic designer, confident and outgoing, with a wit and dry humour that had captivated her. She hadn't found out until later that he was living with the woman who had been his date that evening. Yet it hadn't stopped him pursuing Cate. Less than a month later, he'd walked out on his live-in relationship.

Cate had often thought afterwards that perhaps she should have read the signs right then, but at the time all she could focus on was how lucky she was that he'd chosen her. The fact that he'd cheated on another woman hadn't really made an impression.

Nor did she ever dream that the same thing would happen to her. Not until that terrible evening five years later when he'd told her he was leaving. For someone else, someone who'd been in the background for more than six months. The shock and sense of betrayal had left her feeling like one of those cartoon characters who get hit over the head and slowly crack into a thousand pieces.

Within the week Simon had cleared his belongings from the flat and, at thirty-six, Cate had had to face the prospect of starting her life again. It was then she'd begun to realise just how much she had depended on someone else to take care of her. It was Simon who'd had the 'important', well-paying job, while she'd fiddled around the edges of the film and television industries, picking up freelance work where she could, secure in the knowledge that Simon was handling the rent and the major bills. She had been as ignorant as a child trusting in a 'Daddy' to look after her.

Afterwards, she had had to face the harsh reality of coping alone with a hostile, unfamiliar world, while at the same time struggling with the tumult of her raging emotions. There had been times in those first few months when she'd wondered if she was really going to make it.

But she had. Step by step she'd made the changes that had been forced on her by what had happened. She had moved into a smaller, cheaper flat, found full-time work, begun the long hard process of learning to stand on her own two feet. And now, when she thought back to the pathetic, needy creature she'd been, Cate was sometimes amazed at how far she'd come. It was a journey that had made her stronger, more self-assured, more adaptable, that had given her the confidence to take risks and conquer her fears.

Now, at forty-two, she was in charge of her own life, proud of her independence, and could never imagine putting her destiny in the hands of any man again.

There had been lovers, of course, but as time went on she had withdrawn from risky sex indulged in mainly for the fleeting comfort of a man's arms. Sometimes when she looked back she was shocked to realise how many strangers' beds she had fallen into. With shame she remembered the spunky Czech taxi driver who had dropped her, in less than sober condition, at her apartment one evening. He'd spoken to her so kindly in the cab that, moved almost to tears by his sympathy, Cate had found herself spilling out what had happened to her, how lonely she was.

It was his kindness that had made her invite him in. No pretence about coffee, just her desperate, transparent need to feel a man's arms around her, to pretend for a moment that she had someone of her own.

Now Cate doubted that she would ever love again. She was too wary of the risks of emotional involvement, and too content with her life to make the changes necessary to accommodate a full-time lover.

Perhaps, she reasoned to herself, that was why, after so many months of celibacy, she'd let someone like Tom Gillespie into her bed. A married man would offer no risk to the stability of her life, she'd thought, nor any real disturbance to her routine.

But in the end it hadn't been quite so clear cut. For one thing she had been very uncomfortable with the clandestine nature of the affair, the fact that she was doing to another woman what had been done to her. She couldn't even console herself with the fact that Tom's wife was a bitch, for he'd only ever spoken about her in positive terms.

Then why are you doing this? she had felt like asking. But she hadn't, because at that moment she was greedily taking what Tom could give her, gorging herself on the companionship, sex and appreciation she'd been deprived of for so long, and hating herself for still needing it so much.

The turning point had come when she realised she was beginning to develop expectations, that as the weeks passed she had wanted to see Tom more often than he was able to be with her, and missed him when he had to climb out of her bed and go home.

It was then she knew she had to end it.

But to her surprise, her lover hadn't found it easy to accept that the affair was over. Was it a male thing, she wondered, the idea that the ending of a relationship should be in the man's control?

He still rang her, tried to coax her into changing her mind. I miss you, he said. I miss what we had.

And Cate missed it too. It frightened her to see how difficult it was to pull back even after so short a time. Her life had lost its edge of excitement; she missed Tom's calls, his jokes and conversation, their meals together, the heat of his body next to hers in her bed.

Worst of all was having to acknowledge to herself that while she had been so sure she'd fought and conquered her battle with loneliness, those few short weeks had shown her it was a battle that can never truly be won.

And that was the reason she couldn't give in to his pleas. The only way to survive and stay sane was to be alone. She would grow old with her girlfriends. Or at least, she thought wryly, with those who didn't settle for jerks out of fear and desperation.

❇

Despite David's protests that he was quite happy to take a cab, Leith had risen early to drive him to the airport.

Their lovemaking of the evening before had left her with a glow of contentment but David, she could see, was once more in his familiar mode of busy distraction as he dressed and did the last-minute checking of passport and tickets and business papers. The trip to Manila and Bangkok would keep him away from home for ten days this time.

'You really don't have to do this, darling,' he said again as she picked up the car keys.

'I want to,' Leith replied. And she meant it.

She had never underestimated how lucky she was to have met someone like David, and she knew there were plenty of women who would envy her her marriage. She wasn't constrained by the demands of a career, or by lack of money. She could fill her time any way she liked. Involved in his own immensely busy life, David had no objections and rarely showed any interest in how she kept herself busy — which, paradoxically, was part of the problem.

As he had become increasingly absorbed in his work, Leith had longed for him to be more available, to have the time to notice her, take her out, make her feel as important to him as his work so clearly was. Instead, she had been left to fill her empty days and nights with shopping and tennis and dinners and theatre nights with her girlfriends.

It was like living with a flatmate who was rarely there, she often thought.

On occasions she'd tried to talk to him about how she felt, but somehow she couldn't seem to make him understand. It was difficult to put into words how much she craved his attention, his total and undistracted attention, how she needed it like a drowning man craves air.

Leith often wondered if other women were as needy as she was. Or was it her past that had made her the way she was?

❋

Back home from the airport, she changed and did her daily weights routine, followed by twenty minutes of yoga. Exercise was a discipline she'd succumbed to only recently. While her body had always been naturally slim, she'd noticed with alarm the differences that age had started to make to her suppleness and tone.

Afterwards she made herself some green tea and, with the daily newspaper under her arm, carried her tray into the informal sitting room. Through the wide expanse of glass, the harbour shimmered in front of her.

Leith loved her home. When she and David had first seen it five years ago, they'd been immediately drawn to the broad, shady verandahs, the ivy-covered sandstone walls, the lush lawns with their mature pines.

It was a wonderful home for entertaining. Leith had imagined herself giving exotic dinner parties in the timber-panelled dining room, organising post-tennis Sunday lunches on the verandah and summer cocktails beside the pool.

Only it hadn't quite worked out that way. Again it was David's erratic work schedule that made it difficult to line up anything too far ahead. As it was, Leith couldn't remember the last time she'd had people over for a formal dinner.

These days she'd had to learn to amuse herself.

Now, as she sipped her tea, she spread the newspaper out in front of her and felt her usual thrill of anticipation.

She loved the whole process of making her selection, of slowly reading through each column and trying to decide which of all these men she would most like to meet. Very occasionally there was no one who interested her, and she would fold the paper away with a sense of disappointment. But usually she could count on selecting one or two who piqued her interest.

It had started off as no more than that. A game with which to amuse herself. Light-heartedly, she would read the voice mail personals and try to decide whom she'd like to meet if she were single.

It wasn't that she ever wanted to be single again. Oh, God no. She had always been the sort of woman who needed a man, who thrived on a man's protection and flattery and appreciation. Yet despite the fact that she was married, there was much about her life in the last couple of years that made Leith feel as if she were, in fact, still living as a single woman. She came home so often to an empty home, ate simple meals in her dressing gown in front of the TV, faced lonely weekends when all her friends were busy with their husbands and families and she was left to fill in the endless hours because David was away somewhere.

That was really why it had happened. Why she had taken the next step.

There were still times when she felt guilty about it but, she hurriedly reassured herself, she wasn't hurting anyone. Not David, not herself, not even the men whose company she shared for a few hours. She never considered that she was leading them on, because in reality none of them had ever really attracted her. Even if she'd been single, things wouldn't have gone any further.

Carefully she scanned this week's offerings. She preferred men near her own age, of her own generation, who could discuss the music and books and films they both could relate to.

Running her pen down the page, Leith hesitated beside an advertisement that particularly appealed.

Laze away winter mornings over a steaming latte with a tall, stylish, fit 38y.o. Roam a book store, a gallery, take a country drive or simply picnic in front of the TV

Leith smiled. It sounded so wonderful. A man who had the *time* to do things as a couple ... who didn't live to catch the next airline connection, the next meeting, plan the next agenda ...

She read the ad again and, with a sense of excitement, finally put a definite tick beside it. At least now she would have something to look forward to.

❊

Judith had had a shit of a day. There had been a confrontation with one of her department managers, stock that had gone astray, and problems with her monthly reports.

It didn't help her mood to be fighting her way around a supermarket crowded with after-work shoppers while trying to think what she was going to cook for the next three nights' dinners.

Finally she escaped the endless checkout queues, dumped her groceries in the boot and edged her way into the peak-hour traffic that had grown worse while she'd done her shopping.

Why do we live here? she asked herself. Why do we put up with it? What, in reality, did this city provide them with that they couldn't do without?

If the decision was hers, she'd leave tomorrow. But she knew Greg would never live anywhere else, even after the boys left home — if they ever did. Judith had heard the horror stories of her slightly older friends, whose twenty-something children showed no sign of ever leaving their parents in peace.

But how would it be, she wondered anxiously, as she waited for the traffic lights to change, if it were only Greg and I? What would we talk about? How would we fill our time? In recent years she'd begun to realise that the boys were their only point of common interest, a buffer that enabled them to go on pretending they weren't really leading such separate lives.

It frightened her to think of spending the next thirty or so years with the man she had married. Greg didn't need intimacy or companionship. He needed food, a clean house and ironed shirts, plus the occasional hump in bed. She may as well have been his housekeeper and done only one job instead of two.

Her own needs were so different. What she longed for was a man who would talk to her — real talk, not superficial exchanges about who was going to drop off the dry cleaning or call the pool service. She wanted a man who would share his thoughts and feelings as she longed to share hers.

But then, she reminded herself cynically, that's what all women wanted. And men like that didn't exist, or if they did, they didn't like sleeping with women.

Not that she had much of a sex life herself these days ... Mostly she was too tired but, more importantly, she knew that her most vital sex organ was rarely turned on. A woman needed to be in the right frame of mind for lovemaking, and resentment and anger didn't exactly achieve that. If what she had read was right, Greg was like most men. They had no idea it was what happened in the twenty-four hours before they took a woman to bed that made the difference to her enjoyment of sex. They didn't seem to understand that a woman couldn't catch fire from a cold start as easily or as quickly as they could.

But then, she thought bitterly, why should they go to all that bother when the end result for them was still the same? For even on those occasions in bed when she could barely disguise her disinterest, it didn't seem to make any difference to Greg's performance. Thinking about it now, she couldn't honestly remember the last time they'd had sex. A month ago? Six weeks? In reality, things had probably been as indifferent as that for the last couple of years.

As she turned into the street where she lived, the thought suddenly occurred to her that maybe Greg had found someone else.

It was the fact that the idea barely upset her that unnerved her the most.

The kitchen was in its usual after-school shambles. The boys had raided the fridge, and the litter of their snacks had been left for her to clean up before she could start the dinner.

Angrily, Judith stacked plates in the dishwasher. How many times had she asked them to make it easier for her? She may as well have spoken to the cat.

While the vegetables steamed slowly on the cook top, she went through to the laundry and began to sort out the pile of dirty washing. A moment later, Brent poked his head around the door. Straggly tufts of growth speckled his thin, pimply face. Barely looking at his mother, he mumbled, 'Gran rang. Wanted to know why you haven't been to see her.'

Judith slammed down the lid of the washing machine. She didn't know whether to scream or to cry.

Over her usual protestations, they ate dinner to the accompaniment of some mindless sitcom. Judith understood now why her sons' conversations were composed mainly of grunts. With their attention focused on the television screen, they had no interest, or experience, in conducting a real dialogue.

And their father wasn't much better.

'We're not doing anything on the sixteenth, are we? Friday week?' Greg looked at her expectantly as he finished his chops.

What did he mean by 'we'? she wondered. They rarely did anything together any longer. Most Friday nights she spent alone. The boys were invariably out somewhere, while Greg indulged in his usual end-of-week drinks with his mates.

'What did you have in mind?' she asked cautiously.

'Two guys from head office are in town that weekend. I thought I might ask them home. Have a meal here. Do the right thing, you know.'

Judith knew exactly. What Greg really meant was that he wanted to ensure his insurance company colleagues saw the tangible evidence of his success, were imprinted with the image of a winner, someone to keep in mind when the next round of promotions took place.

But she would be the one to bear the brunt, having to rush home, pick up groceries, cook something special, tidy, shower and dress all in record time.

'You sure they wouldn't prefer to go to a restaurant?'

'Melbourne's full of restaurants. A bit of home cooking'd be a real treat.'

She knew there was no point in arguing.

❋

Piles of manuscripts and paperwork sat on Rory's modern glass-topped desk and seemed to keep growing. She took as much home as she dared, but then had to face the guilt of feeling she was neglecting Ian and her son. As a result, it was an endless battle to meet her numerous deadlines.

There was a tap on the door and she looked up to see the enquiring smile of her assistant, Anita Tait.

'Okay if I disturb you a moment?'

'Sure, if it's only a moment.'

Anita had been appointed as her assistant three months before Cam's birth. She was in her early thirties, had a degree in philosophy, of all things, and an instinct for her work that had both surprised and impressed Rory. There was no doubt she'd depended on the younger woman in those first three or four months after her son was born and had been grateful for her help. But recently, certain internal changes had been made that Rory couldn't help find worrying. Most importantly, her assistant's responsibilities had been expanded beyond mere editing. Now, like Rory, she was able to search out authors as well.

'Anita'll still be under your guidance,' the managing director, Colin Rikard, had assured her. 'You'll still have ultimate veto on what she comes up with, but I think it's a good move that we let her seek out her own people, too. I know how snowed under you've been lately.'

Rory had been alarmed by the extension of the younger woman's responsibilities into her own sphere. And she was ultra-sensitive to anything that might have been a criticism of her capabilities. She, who had always prided herself on anything to do with her work, suddenly felt as if she were losing control. And it seemed to be happening on all fronts. In recent months two of her leading authors had been lured away, authors whom she'd discovered and nurtured, whose work she had fought for with the marketing and publicity people, and who, in the end, had become the successes she'd been certain they would.

Both had now moved to other publishing houses and Rory felt she'd lost them because she hadn't been able to convince her own company to pay the bigger money needed to keep them. In the end they'd managed to pull off better deals with her rivals.

She couldn't help worrying that maybe she had taken her eye off the ball, that perhaps she should have anticipated the problems earlier and worked even harder to give her authors the backing they needed. But it so often seemed as if there weren't enough hours in the day to do all she had to do.

At four-thirty that afternoon, Maggie Hayden, the marketing manager, asked her if she could stay back to have a 'quick word with her team' about a book on next month's list.

Rory hid her dismay. She knew how Maggie's 'quick word' could drag on, and she couldn't, just couldn't, beg Deb to stay late again. God, she thought, why couldn't she just tell Maggie it was impossible, that she'd deal with it first thing in the morning? But she knew how that would look. Maggie Hayden was divorced, childless. She had none of the outside demands on her time, energies and emotions that Rory now faced.

It seemed to Rory that the days when she'd been so free of such responsibilites belonged to another lifetime.

It was almost eight-thirty when they finally sat down to eat. Ian had opened a bottle of red and, for the first time that day, Rory felt herself start to relax.

'You haven't forgotten the faculty dinner this Saturday, have you?'

She looked up from her meal, a pasta dish that was simple and quick to make.

'Course not,' she said, shaking her head.

But she had. It had slipped her mind completely. She'd have to pray that one of their usual sitters would be available at short notice.

If her life had been half-way normal, she thought,

she would have remembered the dinner. She had always looked forward to them. One of the things she most enjoyed about her relationship with Ian was the continuing connection it gave her to academia. She'd loved her years as a student, had immersed herself in university life, delighted by the stimulus and challenge. When she'd landed her position in publishing, she remembered thinking how similar the two worlds were and how lucky she was to have found her niche.

There were pressures, of course. Publishing was a business where risk-taking had to be balanced with filling the coffers. The profits made by established authors helped make it possible to take on new or less commercial writers and until recently Rory had thrived on the demands of getting that balance right.

But in the last few months, she knew her focus had been distracted. She felt stretched and buffeted between her roles of mother, partner, career woman. Sometimes she would lie awake in bed and feel the flutters of panic in her throat as she wondered if she were ever going to work things out and get her life under control again.

Her reverie was disturbed by the ringing of the phone.

Ian gave her an apologetic look. 'Probably for me. Anyway, I've almost finished.' He put his fork and knife together and got to his feet.

It was for him, a student, Rory could tell. Which meant he'd be on the line for far too long. Irritated, she finished her own meal and started clearing the plates. She really wished he wouldn't hand out his home number to his students quite so readily. Didn't they have enough hours in the working day to see him? Sure, she knew all about class sizes these days, the fact that so many kids now held down part-time jobs, which didn't make it easy for them to catch lecturers during office hours, but as she stacked the dishwasher, she still felt an irrational resentment. Their time together was so precious, she hated having it interrupted.

It was late by the time she did her final check on Cam and at last called it a day.

'Everything okay?' Ian was already in bed.

'Fine.' She knew he worried as much as she did. It would be unbearable if anything happened to their child. And at their age there would be little chance of another.

Now as she slipped into bed, Ian moved towards her.

'It's not too late, is it?' he whispered, stroking her bare thigh.

It was, but if she said no, he'd think she was having trouble handling the balancing act of devoted mother, career dynamo and sex siren.

With a stifled sigh, Rory willed her tired body to respond.

CHAPTER FOUR

It was almost three weeks before Leith was able to fix on a date that suited all of them.

They left it to her to choose the restaurant, and she'd settled on a place she had eaten at a couple of times before. The menu was small but interesting, and the other positives were the carpeted floors and crisp linen tablecloths. The latest trend towards bare floors, tables and walls made the chance of real conversation a near impossibility.

The first to arrive, Leith smiled to herself as she was shown to their table. Tonight was for talking with a capital 'T'.

The others arrived in quick succession and greetings were exchanged among a flurry of kisses.

'On time for a change,' said Rory as she relaxed into her seat with a sigh of relief. 'I had a sitter lined up, but Ian did a little changing round and made it home on time.'

'He's good with the baby then?' Cate leaned back as the waiter draped her napkin across her lap.

'Fabulous,' she lied. 'Does everything he can to help. Trouble is his schedule's as crazy as mine.'

'Well, schedules are off the menu tonight,' ordered Leith as she waved for the drink waiter. 'Tonight's for fun and a good old goss!'

Yet it wasn't quite as successful an evening as she might have hoped.

They talked, of course, but perhaps it had been too much to expect that they could recapture the initial excitement and euphoria of the reunion night. For much of the evening, it seemed to Leith, the conversation had been merely superficial.

It's been too long, she told herself. Maybe we've all changed too much, got too little in common now. Or perhaps it was only that the task of trying to catch up on so many years was just too daunting — and not worth the effort.

They were drinking their coffees, finishing the last of the wine, when Cate suddenly threw the question.

'So, tell me seriously,' she said, looking at each of them in turn, 'at the ripe old age of forty-two or so, have we all got what we thought we wanted out of life?'

There was a sudden silence. Amidst the banter and anecdotes, the unexpected seriousness of the question caught them off guard.

'Jude?' Cate looked at her. 'What about you? Are you happy? Marriage and kids — is that what you always wanted?'

'I ...' The others' eyes were upon her, and Judith felt a sudden rush of warmth in her cheeks. Jesus, she hadn't come here tonight to be put on the spot like this. She wanted to forget her problems, not be reminded of them.

She shrugged. 'Yes ... I guess so.' Well, it was true enough. She had always wanted a family, only not the one she'd ended up with, she thought dryly. But she wasn't going to admit to that.

'Sure, I'm ... I'm as happy as anyone. Anyone who has teenage kids, that is,' she ended, with an attempt at humour.

'Okay, one success story.' Cate redirected her attention. 'And you, Leith? Did you get lucky, too?'

Leith's slim, manicured fingers played with the stem of her empty wine glass. 'Oh, God, I've got nothing to complain about. Great husband, wonderful lifestyle ... what more could I ask for?'

Except, she thought, the time with David she craved, the attention he had once given her so readily. But to admit to her husband's shortcomings was to admit that her marriage was less than perfect. And she wasn't prepared to reveal that.

'What about kids?' Judith put in. 'They were never on the agenda?'

Quickly, Leith shook her head. 'No. No. And luckily, David wasn't interested either.'

No need to go into the details.

And then it was Rory's turn.

A little thick-headed from the wine, Rory smiled, but her lips felt tight. 'Hell, I just wanted it all. And I got it — the career, the relationship, the child.' She gave a quick laugh. 'Too good to be true, really.'

'And marriage?' asked Cate. 'It didn't matter? Even when you knew Cam was on the way?'

Rory tried her smile again. 'Who cares these days? It's just not an issue. Never was.'

Nor would she ever admit to anything else. The same way she'd never admit to her panic about keeping all the balls in the air at once.

'Okay, Cate, your turn.' Rory was happy to divert attention off herself. 'What did you want from life?'

Cate smiled. 'Easy — freedom, independence. It took the split with Simon to make me understand that. I'm in control of my own life now, and I've got no intention of ever giving that up.'

Except that she sometimes wondered how freedom and independence would feel at sixty. Alone. Growing older. Forgetting what it felt like to be held in a man's arms ...

'Not even if the right man came along?' It was Leith who asked the question. She couldn't imagine living totally alone, deprived of male company and attention.

Cate grinned and shook her head. 'Let me tell you, darling, that the right man is a figment of Danielle Steel's overworked imagination.'

They laughed then, all of them, relieved to be rescued from the discomfort of their deceptions and lies.

56

At the end of the evening, they kissed and hugged again, called out their goodbyes, each proclaiming that now they really must stay in touch.

But as she drove home, Leith felt again as if time had won and the long-ago schoolgirl friendship was no longer relevant to any of them.

It was three days later and Leith, as always, was relishing the whole ritual of preparation: the leisurely bath, the extra attention to hair and make-up, the selection of exactly the right thing to wear. As she got ready that evening, she felt aglow with the same tingle of anticipatory excitement that she'd felt as a teenager preparing for a date. There was the same obsession with detail, the eagerness to present herself as faultlessly as possible to ensure the desired response in the opposite sex.

Over the last few months, she'd gone through this routine half a dozen times, had dressed and prepared herself to walk into some restaurant or bar or coffee shop to meet a stranger. A man about whom she knew nothing except the three or four lines in a newspaper column and whatever else he chose to offer via some brief voice mail message.

The man she was meeting tonight had had a beautiful voice, she recalled, well-modulated and cultured. On his message he'd also stated that he liked music, books, travel and had described himself as 'spontaneous' and 'adventurous', a man who liked a woman with 'longish hair and a kind heart'.

Carefully, Leith had left her reply, along with the

number of her mobile phone. And less than twenty-four hours later he had got in touch.

Their conversation had lasted about twenty minutes. Paul Houston had sounded well-mannered and educated. As on those previous occasions when she'd made contact this way, she had offered only her first name. A woman needed to be mindful of her security. A point, Paul Houston assured her, that he quite understood.

By the time they said goodbye, he'd invited her to have dinner with him the following week.

David would be in Melbourne.

She parked her red Mercedes across the street from the small Balmain restaurant at which he'd proposed they meet. It was a seafood place Leith had never eaten at before.

Heart starting to beat a little faster, she checked her face in the rearview mirror before sliding out and locking the car. She was wearing a pale pink knit dress, clinging but not too tight, its neckline just low enough to offer a fleeting glimpse of cream lace. Her wedding finger was bare of its rings.

He'd told her the table would be booked in his name, but Leith singled him out easily the moment she entered the softly lit room. The only person sitting alone. As the waiter led her to the table, he rose to his feet, smiling, and Leith caught her breath. He was so good-looking. Well-cut thick blonde hair, strong features, perfect teeth, slim but broad-shouldered in his dark suit. He was thirty-eight, but younger-looking than she'd expected.

'You must be Leith ...' With a warm smile he put out his hand and she took it in her own, feeling its slim strength.

For the first time in a long, long time, Leith felt flustered in the company of a man. *She* was used to being the one who made the impact, and Paul Houston had thrown her off balance. She hadn't expected anyone as appealing as this.

She said something in greeting, quickly trying to cover her reaction, as the waitress flipped open the napkin and draped it over her lap.

For a moment he merely stared at her across the table through intelligent hazel eyes, a small smile playing around his lips.

'I wasn't expecting someone so perfectly lovely.'

Leith felt herself relax. This was the role she knew and was used to. She smiled back, thanked him for the compliment. The evening, she knew, was going to be a success. Another pleasant interlude to fill her lonely life.

As they ate, Paul Houston spoke with appealing frankness about himself. He'd married at twenty-seven, divorced four years later. 'Just one of those mistakes you make when you're young,' he explained as the waiter refilled their glasses. 'A lovely girl, but Sara and I were just wrong together. The break-up was as amicable as these things can be, and at least there weren't kids to make it more difficult.'

Leith felt irrationally pleased that he hadn't made any negative comments about his ex. The mark of a real gentleman, she thought. A couple of the other men she'd been out with had been all too obviously embittered by the traumas of their marriage break-ups. It hadn't made them appealing.

Paul had a background in finance and stockbroking and was now the owner of a successful investment firm. 'Everyone's worried about their retirement these days,' he explained. 'The financial services market is a growth area. We've got offices in four states.'

'Must keep you busy.'

'It's better now than during the first few years. Back then I was putting in twelve- and fourteen-hour days, but now everything's more or less under control. That's why,' he looked at her over the top of his wine glass, 'I've finally got more time to concentrate on my personal life.'

'Do you find it difficult to meet women?' She could hardly imagine someone with Paul Houston's looks and charms having that problem.

'Given the nature of my work, it's not that easy. The majority of my clients tend to be men and so the opportunities are limited. As well as that, I hate bars and nightclubs. I was pretty sure the sort of girl I'd find in places like that wouldn't really interest me. Not in the long term, anyway.' His eyes twinkled with amusement. 'So, I told myself, Paul, this is the nineties. Why not try the personals?'

When, inevitably, the conversation switched to herself, Leith stuck to the story she had used before. Yes, she was divorced too. No kids. Had a wonderful job in personnel that took her throughout Australia.

Normally it was enough. Her other dates had never questioned her very deeply, but Paul Houston seemed interested in knowing more.

'Which company? Based in Sydney?'

'Uh ... yes ... with one of the airlines,' she stumbled.

'Tell me exactly what you do.' He held her gaze with those wonderful eyes. 'I'm interested.'

At that moment, to Leith's relief, the waitress reappeared with the welcome distraction of the dessert menu. She made a fuss about asking for an explanation of the various offerings and, for the first time in years, she ordered a sweet.

Not only would it serve to divert her companion's more personal questions, it would also help to make the evening last longer.

Leith could hardly believe the time had passed so quickly. The evening had been such fun and Paul such good company! Interesting, clever, funny. She'd felt herself relax to the extent that a couple of times she'd come dangerously close to slipping up on her rather flimsily constructed background. For the most part she had stuck to generalisations, but when they were sipping their coffee, he'd asked with a teasing smile if she felt safe enough now to perhaps tell him her surname. For a fleeting moment, she'd hesitated. On previous occasions she had always called herself Leith Ashton. But somehow she felt uncomfortable about lying to this man, who had been so forthright and open with her.

Nights like these were only ever meant to be antidotes to her loneliness, to feed her need for male attention and flattery, to assure herself she was still attractive as a woman. They always ended when she said goodbye at the end of the evening.

Still, for some reason, she found it impossible to lie to this man. And her surname was common enough. The risk, she decided, was small.

'It's Arnold ... Leith Arnold.'

It was almost eleven pm by the time they left. Outside, on the kerbside, he put a hand on her elbow and walked her across the road to where she'd parked her car. Now comes the tricky part, she told herself. Without exception, all her previous dates had asked if they could see her again and, as gently as possible, she'd tried to make them understand that while she'd enjoyed the evening, she would prefer to leave it at that. She knew she was safe. No one had her home number, and there was no way they could find her again.

Now, her heart beating a little quicker, she stopped beside her car and used her key to release the locks. Turning, she faced the man with whom she had spent such an enjoyable few hours.

'Paul, thank you ... It was a lovely evening.'

In the glow of the street light, she could see his attractive face.

He grinned at her. 'I think tonight's just managed to restore my faith in the opposite sex.'

She laughed, pleased, but dismissing the compliment. 'Oh, come on ...'

'It's true.' His tone and expression were suddenly serious. 'I can't tell you how nice it was to meet a truly feminine and classy lady.'

Before she could reply, he leaned over and she felt his lips against her cheek, caught the scent of some lemony after-shave, felt the soft brush of his hair against her ear. Her senses spun. Oh, God, this was crazy ... She was reacting like some dippy teenager ...

Then the moment was past and he was pulling open the driver's door for her, helping her in, closing the door behnd her. She felt his eyes on her as she slipped on her seatbelt, and for the second time that evening, she felt confused and flustered. Was that *it*? Not a word about wanting to see her again? Not, of course, that she had any intention of taking this any further, but considering how well the evening had gone, she had fully expected that he would at least *ask*.

She rolled down the window. Paul Houston leaned down, but all he said was: 'Thanks again, Leith. You drive carefully now.'

And with a final smile, he turned and walked away.

❄

For days after the evening with her old schoolfriends, Cate had felt unable to pinpoint the source of her discontent.

Unable to shrug it off, she finally managed to understand what was causing it. Subconsciously, she realised, she was comparing herself to Leith and Rory and Judith. All three of them had managed to sustain long-term relationships; two of them were mothers. In comparison, Cate was the only one who seemed to lack any real foundation to her life. Sure, she had a great career, personal freedom, but was that really an adequate substitute for children and a good relationship?

Yet the instant she arrived at this conclusion, she angrily brushed it aside. Oh, for God's sake, give it a break. She had never wanted children. She didn't have a maternal bone in her entire body. And as for relationships, well, hadn't she learned just how fickle and precarious they could be? If it had worked out for the others, then good luck to them. But just because she was alone didn't make her life any less fulfilling.

No, she reiterated firmly to herself, she felt powerful alone, able to control her own destiny. Her loneliness had gradually become a solitude in which she had found real pleasure.

Weekends no longer frightened her. At the beginning, after Simon left, they were the worst times to cope with. Work had filled Monday to Friday, but the two days in between had been terrifying in their emptiness. At that stage all she could still think and talk about was Simon.

She knew she had stretched her friends' sympathies to the limit; they couldn't be expected to rescue her every weekend, listen to her repetitive lament. So she had ended up alone in her apartment, almost comatose with grief, wondering what to do with the rest of her life.

Gradually she had started to see other men, yet found fault with them all as she compared them, inevitably, with Simon. When she admitted this to her friends, some of them were openly exasperated. How can you still care for someone who's been such a shit to you? they demanded. He was playing up on you, for heaven's sake! Where's your self-respect?

At the time she'd been hurt by their harshness, but they were right, of course. The problem was that it had taken her a long time to view the break-up with any degree of rationality. It was immensely difficult, she discovered, to learn to hate someone when you were used to loving them.

Now, at forty two, she had no expectations of ever meeting a man she could contemplate sharing her life with. This was Sydney, for God's sake. She'd given up looking at attractive men, so certain was she that they wouldn't be interested in a woman. And even if by chance she'd got it wrong, she knew that it would be a woman a lot younger than herself who'd win the game. So she wasn't playing any more, had withdrawn from the race ... however you wanted to put it.

These days her weekends were an oasis from the frantic pace of her working week. She was never at a loss for something to do. She met friends for lunch or a movie, visited galleries or bookshops, had people round for drinks and simple meals. Her friends now were mainly single women like herself. And there were a lot more of them around these days as they dumped husbands and lovers, walked out on relationships, intent on finding something more before it was too late. Of course it was different, Cate told herself, when you were the one doing the dumping.

This weekend, however, she would be out of town. Work was on the agenda. If you called getting on an airplane and heading for one of the country's main tourist spots work. The last time she'd been to the Gold Coast, she'd been nineteen, on a two-week break with some friends from college. They'd had a ball. The beaches were fabulous, the water clean, the sand soft and white, and there was plenty of talent around to keep them amused. But in the twenty or so years since, the place had changed, or so she'd read — rampant development, a city now instead of a retreat, glitz and conmen and overtanned women wearing too much jewellery.

Still none of that mattered to Cate that Friday afternoon. Her task was merely to spend the two days checking that everything was in order for when Leanna and *Live!* hit town in two weeks time. Occasionally the program relocated for a change of scene, and this time it was the Gold Coast's turn to star on national television. *Live!* would be broadcast from a major shopping complex on the Broadwater, and Cate's task this weekend was to meet with the local invited guests and ensure they were prepared for their upcoming interviews. By now, she was past being surprised at how often the most outgoing and successful people could still sometimes freeze in front of a bank of television cameras.

To save time she'd taken her overnight bag into work and was able to catch a cab from the studio straight to the airport. It was the usual Friday night bunfight but, thankfully, she already had her ticket and seat allocation.

It came as no surprise that the flight was delayed twenty minutes — this was Sydney airport after all. Making her way to the Qantas lounge, Cate found a seat among the sea of dark-coloured 'suits' and, leaving her briefcase there to stake her claim, went to pour herself a coffee from the buffet.

As she sipped it, impatient for her flight to be called, she remembered how travel had once been her obsession. When she'd finished college, she couldn't wait to work out her two-year teaching bond and head for London. It had been the mecca then for young Australians, and probably always would be.

She had walked wide-eyed through Piccadilly and Hyde Park, along the Kings Road and the Chelsea Embankment, thrilling to the fact that she, Cate Tremain, was a resident, temporarily at least, of one of the world's greatest cities, a city with a population almost the equal to the whole of Australia's, a city where history stared one in the face around every corner and down every narrow lane.

The excitement of actually being there had left her dizzy. She'd never wanted to go home. Even having to get up in the dark and freezing cold every day to teach a bunch of rowdy working-class kids hadn't daunted her. The work was a means to an end, a way of raking together the money she'd needed to see more of the world.

She'd spent almost nine years in London and, during that time, there wasn't anywhere she'd wanted to go that she hadn't been. She'd visited most of Western Europe, as well as Turkey, Malta, North Africa, and the then Soviet bloc countries. All on a shoe-string, but that hadn't mattered. It was the experience that counted.

Her decision to return home had been prompted primarily by her mother's illness, but also by the fact that she had begun to realise there *were* things she missed about home: the lack of oppressive crowds, the comparative affordability of housing and food, the clean air and sunshine, the sense of Aussie egalitarianism.

She had come home, too, with a different career focus. Teaching had been just a job, never something she had seen herself doing long-term. In London she had ended up working in all sorts of jobs but, a couple of years before her return, she had miraculously managed to inveigle herself into a position at the BBC. A totally lowly attachment to a weekly current affairs program, a go-between, a jill of all trades, the person who fetched the assistant to the assistant producer's coffee and sandwiches. But Cate had found her niche. She had kept her eyes and ears open and learnt everything she possibly could.

Television, the media, excited her. The adrenalin rush of near catastrophes. The thrill of watching a breaking story rushed to air. A darkened studio, she was sure, was where she wanted to spend her working life.

Once home, she had applied for a string of jobs in television, most of which were never advertised. But the BBC reference on her CV didn't carry much weight when she was forced to admit the limit of her hands-on experience. 'But I can *do* it. I *know* I can,' she had begged on those few occasions when she was lucky enough to reach the preliminary interview stage. 'Please, just give me the chance.'

Her chance had been a long time in coming and she was still only working casually with a smallish production company when the split with Simon occurred.

It was desperation that had driven her to apply then for a position on *Live!* She'd heard through the industry grapevine that the program was looking for a segment producer in charge of entertainment, and she was crazy enough at that particular stage in her life to give it a go.

She had a professional video made and sold her pathetic experience as confidently as if she'd just walked off the payroll at *Entertainment Tonight*. Somehow it had worked. She was offered an interview!

It hadn't landed her the job, but it did get her a position as a researcher on the program. And from there Cate had watched and learned again. And waited. Finally, almost three years later, the position she'd originally applied for had fallen vacant. And this time she cracked the jackpot.

Three years down the track, she still loved every moment of her work. The pace, the variety, rarely slackened. No two days were ever quite the same. Yet, for all that, there were rare moments when she found herself thinking of taking that next step. Film production interested her. She knew it was an even harder area to crack than where she was, but she'd got to know a lot of people in the film industry over the years. Maybe, one day, she might feel the time was right to take the risk and change direction.

Or maybe — she smiled wryly to herself now as her flight was called — she might just count her damn blessings and stay right where she was.

The plane flight was crowded. A scattering of businessmen, the usual Asian tourists and local holiday-makers.

As she inched her way up the aisle, Cate prayed she wasn't going to have to endure the overweight, the overperfumed, the overtalkative. But it was a slim, well-dressed guy about her own age who occupied the middle seat next to the one she was looking for. He spotted the travel bag in her hand and, nodding at it, advised, 'You'd be best putting that under the seat. The locker's full already.'

Vaguely aware of an accent, Cate looked up and saw that what he said was true. The adjoining lockers were packed, too.

'Thanks,' she said as she squeezed into her seat and did as he'd advised. Then, as she struggled to find the ends of her seatbelt, she accidentally jabbed him with her elbow.

'Oh, God, sorry.' She gave him an apologetic smile as she snapped the buckle closed. 'Remember when travelling was supposed to be glamorous?'

He smiled at her good-humouredly. 'Probably still is if you can afford first class.'

Cate rolled her eyes. 'Oh, come on, who the hell can stomach all that Bollie and caviar?'

He looked at her and they both laughed.

His name was Cal Donohoe. He was a GP with a practice on the Gold Coast and had been in Sydney for a continuing education seminar. The accent, she learned, was Irish.

'Emigrated from Dublin thirteen years ago.'

'But why the Gold Coast?' Cate wanted to know as the attendant served refreshments.

'Guaranteed sunshine.'

'And that's enough? What about culture — you must miss that — and the buzz of a big city?'

He turned to look at her. He had tanned clear skin and his hair was dark, curling on his collar. Thick, black lashes Cate would have killed for fringed blue eyes that gleamed with suppressed humour.

'Oh, you mean art galleries, good films, concerts, writing festivals, that sort of thing?'

Cate nodded. 'Yeah, that's exactly what I mean.'

He peeled the cellophane off two rock-hard biscuits and shook his head in mock dismay. 'Another ignorant city dweller, brain numbed by lead fall-out, nerves jangled by seething masses and macro mortgages. Pity is my foremost emotion.'

He did his best then to convince her of the Coast's various cultural offerings. 'We've got it all: film festivals, writing festivals, concerts. On a smaller scale, of course. But Brisbane's close. And the trade-off is clean air, traffic that actually moves at the speed limit, people who have time to smile and who have the pleasure of living in the bosom of beautiful Mother Nature.'

It was true what they said about the Irish, Cate decided. Cal Donohoe certainly had the dry humour, the gift of the gab.

'You sound like a travel brochure.'

He grinned again. 'Happens naturally when you live in the best place on earth. But, enough of such feuding, tell me what brings you to our el dorado.'

She explained about her work, the reason she was spending the weekend at the Coast.

'Where are you staying?' he asked.

'The Marriot.'

'Top notch. You'll love it. If I can drag you out of the place, would you perhaps be free for dinner tomorrow night?'

The invitation was totally unexpected. It had never occurred to her that a man as attractive as Cal Donohoe might actually be single and available. But then she could be jumping to conclusions. He was probably married. Breaking the boredom. Looking for some light entertainment of the carnal kind with someone he'd never have to see again. In a split second Cate's mind raced through the various possibilities.

He was watching her, waiting for a reply, that mischievous gleam again in those incredible eyes.

'No apparent serial killer tendencies,' he hastened to assure her, adding, 'well, not as yet, anyway. Single, clean and ridiculously generous.'

Amid the banter, Cate noted the 'single'.

She frowned, as if still considering. 'Hmm ... Let

me see, can I get out of my date with that Mongolian freedom fighter?'

Cal Donohoe laughed out loud, and Cate knew that the Irishman's company would beat sitting in a hotel room watching reruns of *The Bill*.

He apologised that he couldn't drive her to her hotel. His car was in the airport parking lot, he explained, but he was due to visit a patient in the nearby John Flynn hospital before going home.

'No problem,' Cate replied as they walked towards the luggage carousel. 'I'm happy to take the shuttle.'

He had no need to wait, his only luggage a suit bag and small overnight case. Amid the milling crowds, he turned to her and extended his free hand. 'Until tomorrow night then. Is seven too early to pick you up?'

Cate shook her head; his hand felt smooth and cool. 'That'll be fine.'

With a final smile he turned and strode quickly towards the exit.

Cal Donohoe was right. The Marriot *was* top notch.

Her room was on the sixteenth floor and, in the fading evening light, Cate took in the spectacular views of the hinterland and ocean, the sparkling city below.

Not bad, she thought. Not bad at all. And all at once the view, the room, the balmy evening made her suddenly wistful. I should be here with a lover, she told herself. Someone to share the spa bath with, to sip champagne with, before succumbing to the tempting expanse of the bed.

With a sigh she turned away and began to unpack her overnight bag. Only in rare moments like these was she forced to admit that the longing hadn't died, that the desire for love was still there. Yet to dwell on the fact would, she knew, only make her unhappy. She absolutely refused to be one of those pathetic women who still lived in hope, who breathlessly checked out every man who crossed their path as if he might be the One.

She might have been like that once, right at the beginning, but she wasn't now. Otherwise she'd already be fantasising about Dr Donohoe. Imagining the future. But she wasn't that crazy. Cal Donohoe was attractive enough; she liked his sense of humour; she had a night with nothing to do in a strange town.

Simple as that.

Saturday was the sort of day they describe in the travel brochures. Warm and sunny, not a cloud to spoil the intense blue of the sky. But Cate had no time to play the holiday-maker.

Her day began as soon as she finished breakfast with the first of a series of appointments with the local celebrities who had agreed to appear on *Live!*

Penny Jacklin was the petite and vivacious publisher of a glossy local magazine which featured the hottest gossip in town. As they sipped their coffees in one of the many cafes edging the Broadwater, she giggled and rolled her eyes. 'Oh,

God, sweetie, I can't tell Leanna all the *really* juicy bits about this place or I'll have the knickers sued off me!'

The publisher would be great talent and, Cate had no doubt, was shrewd enough to use the exposure to enhance the profile of her magazine. No problem with that. Most of the guests on *Live!* were selling something.

For the rest of the day, Cate was kept busy meeting a diverse cross-section of talented locals: an English actor who spent four months of the year at his holiday home, a well-known singer, an award-winning movie producer. Cate's job was to spend some time with them, tapping into the areas of their lives that would make for the most interesting television. From her notes she could then formulate the precise questions for Leanna to ask on air.

It was almost five-thirty when she returned to her hotel. Plenty of time to get ready. As she let herself into her room, Cate decided to fill the spa bath. So what if there was no one to share it with?

As she relaxed in the warm, pulsating water, she found herself admitting that she was quite looking forward to the evening ahead. Hell, it was almost a real date. And she couldn't remember how long it had been since she'd had one of those. Certainly the snatched clandestine meetings with Tom Gillespie didn't count.

She let her mind wander to her ex-lover. What would he be doing this Saturday night? Home with the wife he so easily deceived? Playing the devoted husband at some dinner party with long-time friends?

Or had he already found someone else to provide the novelty to offset his wedded boredom?

What a cynic I've become, Cate thought as she stepped out of the water and reached for a thick white towel.

Given what little she'd packed, the decision about what to wear was easy: a simple white shift and high-heeled sandals. She made a couple of vain attempts to pin up her dark hair, made wilder by the humidity, but gave up and left it to wave around her face as usual. It wasn't as if she had to impress some guy she'd never see again.

She was ready when, on the dot of seven, the phone trilled on her bedside table.

'I've come for the princess in the tower.' His accent sounded stronger over the phone, but she found it attractive.

'As long as you're not the white knight,' she joked back. 'I'm not looking for one of those.'

It had been a spontaneous response but, as she picked up her room key, Cate thought it might at least give a clue to where she was coming from. Strong. Independent. Needing no man to make her life happen . . .

If she had been expecting some up-market restaurant, she was certainly surprised.

'It's fabulous!' she enthused. 'Totally inspiring!'

The restaurant was in a quiet street right across from the beach. Two walls were completely open to the air, and the high ceiling consisted of crossed canvas sails which offered glimpses of the night sky.

As she took her seat at the candle-lit table, Cate could smell the salt air and hear the soft boom of the waves.

'Worth the drive, you think?' Cal Donohoe raised a teasing dark eyebrow.

'The drive! All of twenty minutes. You'd hardly get out of your own suburb in Sydney in that time.'

'We-ell, you've found something to like about the place, I see.'

'Look, I'm not buying into that one tonight. Truce, okay?'

He grinned. 'Sure, truce, for tonight at least.'

She wasn't quite sure what he meant by that.

Over dinner, she asked him about his work. He ran a practice with two other GPs, he told her, at Mermaid Beach.

'I always wanted to be a doctor. My parents made lots of sacrifices to help make it happen for me. My mother still makes sure she mentions her son's a medico whenever she meets someone for the first time.'

'They live in Dublin?'

'No, my mother's here now. She came out five years ago, after my dad died. I couldn't believe it. I never dreamed she'd ever leave Ireland.'

'You're an only child then?' A rare event among the Irish, Cate thought.

'No. I have two brothers back home.'

'So you must have been her favourite.'

She had spoken lightly, but for the first time that evening, Cate sensed Cal Donohoe's withdrawal.

He made some self-deprecatory comment and almost immediately deflected the conversation from himself by asking where she lived in Sydney. Cate told him, enthusing about her apartment above Balmoral Beach. 'It's small, but it's all mine. And if I stand on tiptoe at one end of the patio, I can see the water.'

'You live alone?'

Cate nodded at him over the top of her wine glass. 'And love it.'

His expression turned fleetingly serious. 'I don't.' For a moment he seemed to be on the verge of saying something more, then changed the subject again, this time to Cate's work.

They lingered over coffee, enjoying the guitarist who played softly in one corner. When the man began to play a Van Morrison number, Cal noted Cate's reaction.

'You like Van's music then?'

'Love it. Caught him in concert when I was living in London. No frills, no gimmicks, just the man and his awesome talent for words and music.'

'A woman with taste — I like that. Next you'll be telling me you're a Yeats fan as well.'

Cate looked into Cal Donohue's blue eyes. 'He's one of my favourite poets,' she said.

He smiled at her. 'Well, that gives us even more in common, doesn't it?'

She tried to argue with him over splitting the bill, but he told her he was 'far too old-fashioned' to agree to that. In the end Cate gave in.

Outside the restaurant he surprised her again by reaching for her hand and leading her across the dark street to the beach.

78

'I hope you agree it's a perfect night for a walk.' As he spoke, he bent down to slip off her sandals and the intimacy of the gesture caught Cate unawares.

Leaving their shoes by the path that led through the dunes, they continued on until they hit the firm, damp sand by the ocean's edge. The air was balmy, the sky clear and starry, and Cate suddenly felt a million miles from Sydney. How long is it since I've done something like this? she asked herself. Something as simple as walk on the beach in the moonlight with a man I actually find attractive?

For it was true, as the evening had progressed, she'd felt a growing sense of ease and connection with Cal Donohue. Certainly she was drawn to the Irish charm and humour, the intelligence and quiet self-confidence, yet she also sensed a depth and complexity that intrigued her.

Their conversation had been wide-ranging but not really personal. Cate had resisted the sorts of questions that might have given the impression she was attempting to assess his eligibility. For her, those days were over.

Now they walked for a little while in companionable silence until she gazed up at the stars and said, 'It's hard to believe we can be truly alone in this universe, isn't it?'

For the third time that evening, Cal Donohue surprised her. 'Believing in anything is difficult, I think.'

She gave him a quizzical sideways look. His comment had struck a jarring note. 'You don't strike me as a cynic.'

In the moonlight, she saw him shrug. 'Life batters you.' And then, softly, he began to quote: '"Then he struggled with the heart; innocence and peace depart."'

'Yeats?'

'Of course. The great Irish recorder of disillusion.'

Cate made no reply. Without warning Cal Donohoe had revealed a new side to himself, and she was filled with the urge to ask him more. But she knew it wasn't her role to probe.

Suddenly squeezing her hand, he lightened the mood again. 'The Irish go strange in the moonlight,' he laughed, 'let's get me out of here.'

As they turned and headed back to the car, he started to speak of something else, and the odd moment was gone.

As they drew up at the hotel, he asked what time she was leaving the next day.

'My flight goes at five-ten.'

'So you'd have to be there about four-thirty or so.'

'About that.'

'Would you let me drive you?'

Cate felt an emotion rush through her that she didn't try to analyse. 'Well, thanks, but there's no need to do that. I can —'

Cal Donohoe had turned off the ignition, and the doorman was walking towards them. 'I know there's no need. I'd just like to have the pleasure.'

'Well ...' There was something so delightfully old-fashioned about him. 'Thank you ... If that's what you'd like to do, I'd appreciate it.'

The doorman was smiling as he opened the passenger door.

Cate moved to get out, but Cal caught her hand and raised it to his lips.

'Until tomorrow then. Around four.'

Cate stared back into those intense eyes.

She nodded. 'Yes.' Then sliding out of the car, she walked briskly into the hotel. She didn't look back.

But she knew he was watching her.

CHAPTER FIVE

As she scraped plates and cleared away the remains of the meal she'd rushed home to make, Judith could hear the loud bursts of laughter from the living room. Three bottles of wine, followed by the opening of a prized fifteen-year-old port, had put Greg and his interstate colleagues in a decidedly raucous mood.

Certainly no amount of alcohol could have brightened her own mood. But in actual fact, the evening had been little different from what she had expected — which was why she did so little entertaining these days. Even in the company of their friends, Greg treated her much the same way: as if she were invisible, as if her opinions weren't worth listening to.

Half a dozen times this evening, when one or other of his guests had politely tried to involve her in the conversation, it was Greg who had responded, talking over her, talking for her, as if she were incapable of offering an opinion on business or politics or anything else that mattered.

As she stored the left-overs in vacuum packs and thrust them in the fridge, Judith felt tears of angry frustration fill her eyes. How dare he! How dare he treat her with such contempt! Nor was it any easier to bear knowing that he didn't even realise what he was doing. He'd grown so used to treating her that way he didn't notice any longer.

It had started in the early years of their marriage when she'd been so shy and lacking in confidence that she'd been happy to let him do the talking for both of them. Only Greg didn't seem to notice that she'd done a lot of growing up since then, that she now held down a demanding job, was responsible for dozens of staff and was fully capable of holding her own in any company.

He still treats me like the child I was when I married him, she told herself bitterly as she filled the dishwasher with detergent. There were times when she felt like screaming at him to look at her, really *look* at her, see the person she'd become. A grown woman who wanted to be treated as an equal, shown respect, listened to.

They'd had arguments about it in recent years. Inevitably, he'd accused her of turning into one of those 'man-haters', 'those bloody feminists who want to cut off a man's balls'.

Frustrated and teary, she'd try to make him understand that it wasn't like that, but she could see that nothing she said was getting through to him.

Nothing had changed. And now, to her utter dismay, her sons also treated her with the same disdain and lack of respect.

When had she lost the boys? she wondered. When had they switched camps? Once they had been her friends, her only emotional outlet in a marriage where she was never allowed to express her feelings. As a result she had poured all her love into her children and done her best to encourage them to be open to their own emotional needs. But obviously, in the end, their male role model had proved the stronger.

'Here, Sari.' The Siamese came running as she placed a saucer of meat scraps on a newspaper on the kitchen floor. Greg hated her feeding the cat inside, but tonight she didn't feel like giving a damn about that.

The cat finished its snack and began to lick its paws. Bending down, Judith picked it up. Cradling it in her arms, she began to stroke the warm animal body, listening to the contented purrs.

The crazy thought ran through her mind that she got more love and pleasure from her pet than from anyone else in the house.

It didn't surprise her that her husband was ready for sex when they finally got to bed. The drink, the success of the evening — in his terms, at least — had clearly put him in a good mood.

'Come on, Jude.' He reached out a hand to where she lay curled away from him.

Judith knew there was little point in resisting. The same way she knew she could expect little pleasure from the encounter. As always, Greg expected her to turn on just as quickly as he did. There was never any attempt to put her in the mood, no sweet or erotic talk or flattery.

As she felt her husband's hands slide up under her nightdress, Judith wondered resentfully why men didn't realise that foreplay started before they got a woman near a bed. That intimacy was best established through conversation and a sense of togetherness before either of them took off their clothes.

It was another one of the many things they had argued about over the years. But Greg had never got it, had never understood what she was really asking for. Instead he'd taken her suggestions as an affront to his manhood, a criticism of his capabilities as a lover.

'It's not that, Greg.' Hiding her exasperation, she had tried to explain. 'I'm just trying to make you understand that it'd be better for you, too, if I were more turned on, if I were as ready and eager as you. But I can't do that from a cold start!' She could hear herself getting wound up. 'I need affection. I need to know I'm special to you. Not just a body that's offering you relief. I want to feel that you're aware it's *me*. Can't you understand that?'

But she could tell by the resentful and uncomprehending expression on his face that he had no idea what she was talking about.

Finally she had given up trying and avoided sex whenever she could.

But tonight he was determined, she could tell, and

she let him pull her towards him, opened her mouth to his and tasted the unappealing combination of toothpaste and port. With the perfunctory kisses soon out of the way, he mounted her and she opened her legs without protest, knowing she was still too dry.

As she steeled herself for the pain that had nothing to do with love, Judith wondered again about those women who proclaimed that they enjoyed sex. Were they lying? Or were there men out there, different from her husband, who really understood how to make a woman happy?

Of one thing she was certain. She'd never know.

Judith parked her car in the visitors' parking lot and walked through the well-tended gardens to unit 24. After her father's death three years ago, it had taken her months to convince her mother to move into the safety and convenience of a retirement village.

Marjorie Grant had been determined to remain in her too-large home filled with the mementoes and memories of forty-six years of married life.

'I can't,' she had protested tearfully. 'I can't leave here, Judith. It'd be like losing your father all over again.' Her mother had dabbed a damp hanky to her welling eyes. 'Don't you understand? While I stay here, I can *feel* Frank's presence. He's still with me.'

Judith had been torn between her mother's despair and the sheer practicalities of the situation that confronted her. Even when her father was still alive, the large house and garden were becoming too much for her parents to manage. It was Judith they called on whenever they needed help. And now, alone and with her health worsening, Judith had known it would be impossible for her mother to cope.

'But you and Richard can help me,' her mother had pleaded when Judith had tried to make her see reason. 'Between the two of you, I'll be able to manage, I'm sure of it.'

Richard? Judith had felt like retorting, you expect Richard and Lauren to put themselves out? They'd barely bothered to visit even when her father was alive. Why would they suddenly feel the need to share the burden of caring for a now dependent mother and mother-in-law?

Her brother and sister-in-law had the perfect excuse, of course, in the successful nursery they ran on the city's edge.

'This business is seven days a week, Jude,' Richard had justified himself. 'You know how it is. We never escape.'

Except, Judith told herself dryly, to Fiji or Dunk or Noosa.

When she'd been suddenly widowed, her mother, traumatised by grief, had been incapable even of shopping for her weekly groceries. That task, along with a myriad others, had fallen to Judith. Her own few spare weekend hours had been spent at her mother's doing housecleaning, changing the bed linen, seeing to the laundry, taking the extra ironing home, cooking meals for the freezer.

And while her mother had been suitably appreciative, that hadn't prevented Judith from growing resentful. She had her own full-time demanding job and a home of her own to run, so why should she alone have to make the sacrifices? It wasn't even as if her sister-in-law had her own parents to worry about. They lived in Perth close to their other two daughters.

In the end, doing her best to fight off her guilt, Judith had managed to persuade her mother to make the move. Then had come the mammoth task of sifting through rooms of furniture and knick-knacks, cupboards and shelves full of clothes, books, papers, stacks of fading photo albums. A lifetime of possessions that had to be ruthlessly sorted and discarded for the shift into the one-bedroom garden unit.

Very quickly, Judith had recognised that it was better to face the task alone than share it with her mother. For a tearful Marjorie Grant had merely hampered her efforts, swooping on boxes of extra blankets or superfluous pots and pans, insisting they were still needed.

In the end, Judith had sent her mother out of the house while she alone filled the boxes that would go to St Vinnies and other charities.

That didn't meant the task wasn't emotionally difficult for her, too. What did you do with the dozens of framed photographs, the collection of menus souvenired over forty years, her father's fishing rods and suits, her mother's out-of-date evening gowns?

As she worked, she had found herself questioning the point of acquiring possessions. Why are we so hell-bent on endless acquisition, she wondered, when in the end it comes to this — stuffing boxes to send off to strangers who neither know nor care about the sentiments attached to their anonymous booty?

Greg, the quintessential consumer, should be here, she thought bitterly, to see what it feels like to pack away a life.

Now, as she pushed the bell on her mother's door, Judith wished she could feel other than dutiful about her visits. But she and her mother had never been close, that privilege having been reserved for Judith's father. There had been times when she had actually felt like an intruder in her parents' life, so exclusive had their relationship appeared. Not that they hadn't been good parents, interested and kind, but their passion had been for each other rather than for their children.

She wondered sometimes if that was the reason she had married so young. To be loved exclusively, to share her life with someone who would be there solely and totally for her. Certainly, when she'd married Greg, that's what she had longed for.

But she'd had plenty of time since to despair at her youthful naivety.

She spent an hour with her mother, drinking tea she didn't feel like, eating a biscuit her hips didn't need, her eyes straying often to her watch. There was still so much for her to do at home.

When they finally walked to the door together, her mother was pathetically grateful for her time.

'It's always so good to see you, love. I don't know what I'd do if I didn't have you to cheer me up.'

Despite Judith's encouragement, Marjorie Grant had made few friends among the other residents.

'You should ask people in, Mum,' she repeated now. 'Sometimes you have to be the one to make the first move.'

Standing by the open door, her mother looked at her with dull eyes. 'I just can't seem to be bothered to make the effort.' Her voice caught. 'Your father was my whole life, you know. My whole life.'

As she looked back into her mother's glistening eyes, Judith recalled with a sense of disbelief that she, too, had once dreamed of finding total fulfillment in the strait-jacket of marriage.

❄

Rory could still remember what Saturday mornings used to be like. Sleeping in, lazing on the back patio over the newspapers, going out for breakfast to one of their favourite cafes where there was always the possibility of bumping into someone they knew.

Now, Saturdays meant early starts and two or three loads of washing while she fed and dressed Cam. It would have been unthinkable, of course, to expect Deb or one of the sitters to come in when she was home herself, but making the switch from career woman to weekend mother was never easy.

As she sat by the high chair spooning food into her son's mouth, Rory looked around the room with irritation. The place was littered with Cam's toys and bits of newspaper he'd pulled out of the basket and torn up. Last night she'd had to attend a book launch for one of her authors, and Ian had been left to babysit. Obviously it hadn't occurred to him to put anything away.

He came into the kitchen now, hair damp from his shower, dressed in jeans and a shirt.

'You could have made some effort with this, couldn't you?' she said shortly, nodding at the mess.

'Come on, Rory, don't start. I was marking papers till eleven.'

She was surprised at his testy response. Normally easy-going, he usually let her have her grumble, then teased her out of her bad mood.

He started to fill the kettle, then turned to her. 'You've almost finished there, haven't you? Why don't we have breakfast out for a change? It seems months since we did anything like that.'

Rory remembered exactly. Only once since Cam was born — and then they'd had to rush home because her breasts had started to leak.

'Oh, God, look at me.' She gestured at the tracksuit pants and slippers, her unmade-up face. 'I'm not —'

'Doesn't matter,' he insisted. 'Stick something on, and let's just do it. Pretend our lives haven't really changed.'

It was the last statement that resonated. And the familiar feeling of guilt flooded through her. Having a baby had been *her* idea, and she couldn't bear for him to be regretting it.

'I'll finish that,' he said, taking the spoon from her hand. 'You get ready. And be quick.'

Her best jeans were in the wash she hadn't got around to yet, and when she pulled on another pair of pants, they were tighter than she would have liked. With another stab of guilt, Rory recalled her vow about starting an exercise program. In the meantime, a long, shapeless T-shirt would have to hide the way her backside looked in the too-tight pants.

No time for the full make-up, just a smear of lipstick and a brush pulled quickly through her hair, which could do with a wash. God, she hated going out like this, but something told her today wasn't the time to keep Ian waiting. She could shove on dark glasses, and hope she didn't bump into anyone she knew.

'He's been perfect, hasn't he?'

Rory spoke over her shoulder as she pushed the stroller with their dozing son. They were walking single file through the Saturday crowds, Ian festooned with bags of groceries, heading for the car park.

'Excellent gene pool's the way I look at it.'

Rory smiled. A ham omelette and a double shot of caffeine seemed to have restored her partner's mood.

She started to make some jovial response when suddenly she was interrupted.

'Ian! Hi!'

Rory stopped and turned to see Ian greeting two young women. One was a petite, pretty blonde dressed in a sheer mini, the other had waist-length dark hair and cut-off denim shorts that showed off long, tanned legs. Rory guessed they must be students.

She couldn't hear the clearly enthusiastic exchange, but she saw with dismay that Ian was beckoning her to join them. Oh, God, no.... All at once she was even more acutely aware of her unmade-up face and lank hair, the wet patch on her T-shirt where Cam had burped after his bottle. The last thing she needed right now was to be introduced to two attractive young women.

But she knew she had little choice. Waiting for a break in the flow of pedestrians, she reluctantly turned and pushed the stroller toward them.

With a smile Ian made the introductions. 'This is my partner, Rory Hudson. Belinda and Sara. Students in my Lit. 2 class.'

The young women smiled politely enough, but Rory sensed their disinterest. It set her teeth on edge to think that to them at this moment she was just another sloppily dressed middle-aged woman with a child.

'So, have you finished marking yet?' The one called Sara tossed her dark hair over one slim shoulder as she turned her attention back to Ian. 'I hope you realised that I spilt *blood* over that Hardy research.'

'The very least I'd expect.'

Rory saw Ian's grin, and something in the girl's too familiar tone irritated her.

'D'you have time for a coffee?' inquired the blonde, looking from Ian to Rory.

'Well ...' Ian hesitated, looking at Rory. But Rory was utterly determined that no way was she going to sit down with these two young girls looking the way she did now.

'I really don't think so, darling,' she demurred. 'Cam's going to need his lunch any minute.' She fixed her eyes on his, her expression warning him not to disagree.

'Kids really tie you to a schedule, don't they?' It was the dark-haired girl again.

'Maybe, but they're worth it,' Rory managed with a tight smile.

She noted the girl's expression — as if she'd admitted to something indecent.

'So they say.' The reply was delivered with such insouciance that Rory felt her face flush with irritation.

'See you later then, Ian.' The blonde turned to Rory. 'Bye. Nice meeting you.' And flashing their smiles, the two perfect creatures moved off.

She was short-tempered for the rest of the day.

Ian noticed, of course, but when he asked what was wrong, she curtly brushed him off.

'Nothing. Why should anything be wrong?'

'Well, you're in a hell of a mood for someone who's so content with the world.'

'Oh, pack it in, will you? I work hard. I'm tired. That's all.'

But Rory understood herself well enough to know that it was more than that.

Much as she hated to admit it, she was forced to face the fact that she was actually jealous of the two girls they'd bumped into that morning, jealous of their youth, their firm, slender bodies, their freedom, the fact that they had their whole lives before them still. But most of all, jealous of the fact that the man she loved spent his days surrounded by females just like them.

While Cam had his afternoon nap, she holed up in her small, book-lined study, but found it difficult to concentrate on the work she had brought home. Surely he must compare us, she thought about Ian. When we're in bed together, he must wish my body were like that. She knew what men were like. They couldn't help themselves. No matter how much they told you they loved you, you knew they still kept fantasising about someone younger, prettier, sexier. But she was forty-two, for God's sake. How was she supposed to compete with women two decades younger?

It was in that mood of introspection that she was finally forced to face the extent of her insecurity. An insecurity she'd never experienced before, but which she now had to admit she'd been fighting for months.

As she finally took the time to analyse her feelings, she realised they had a lot to do with the change in her self-image. As a successful career woman, she had never felt threatened by girls like the two she'd met today. In place of their hard thighs and flawless complexions, she'd possessed status and power, and had felt herself to be the one worthy of envy.

Yet now, even though she still held down an important, well-paying job, in some subtle way motherhood had altered the image she'd once held of herself. She felt weakened, made vulnerable somehow, as if the hard edge that had driven her so far had been softened, diminished.

Still, she did her best to reassure herself, was that such a bad thing? She'd achieved so much. Couldn't she just relax and accept the changes that having a child had brought to her life?

Yet she knew it wasn't quite as simple as that. Ian had been attracted to her because of who she was when they'd first met — ambitious, fearless, confidently in control of her life. What frightened her now was the thought that her role as a mother might have eroded so much of that appeal.

But the dynamics of all relationships change, she tried to comfort herself. Marriages go through all sorts of ups and downs and still survive. Except, she reminded herself, that she wasn't married ...

Her depressing thoughts were interrupted as the door opened and Ian came into the room carrying a mug of coffee. He rarely interrupted her when she was working.

'Thought you might like this,' he said, putting the steaming mug down on the desk beside her.

She looked up at him with a smile, understanding the gesture of reassurance.

'Thanks.'

He kissed her on the head and quickly left, closing the door behind him.

He knew her so well, she thought, her heart warming. That's why she loved him.

At the same time she couldn't help hating the fact that her insecurity had been so transparent.

CHAPTER SIX

'I'm sorry, darling, there was nothing I could do to change the date. I'm afraid it was a matter of fitting in with everyone else.'

David Arnold's voice was full of apology as he faced his wife across the breakfast table.

'That's okay. I understand.' Dressed in pale lemon pants and a pink cotton jumper Leith cupped her mug of tea and tried to hide her disappointment. Her birthday was the coming Saturday, and it would be the second year in a row that David had missed the occasion. Business, as usual, came first.

With a glance at the time, her husband wiped his lips and pushed his chair back from the table. Bending down, he planted a quick kiss on Leith's scented cheek. 'I promise you we'll do something special the night before. Will that help you to forgive me?'

'Oh, David, it's not that important, really. What woman over forty needs another birthday anyway?'

But as he drove away from the house, David couldn't help feeling guilty. He loved Leith. Had fallen for her from almost the very first moment he'd met her. There'd been a child-like quality about her, a vulnerability and gentleness that had made him want to protect her from a world she hadn't seemed tough enough to handle.

He'd sensed a wariness in her, too, and later it came as no surprise when he learned there had been a relationship that hadn't worked out. She'd referred to it only briefly, but even so he could tell that the affair had left its mark. It was one of the things that made him anxious when, a very short time later, he made up his mind to ask her to marry him.

But, to his joy and relief, she had accepted his proposal, and he'd been ecstatic at the thought that this gorgeous creature would be all his. Even the revelation that he couldn't have children hadn't changed her mind. Yet, as they settled into their life together, David came to see that theirs was the sort of relationship that didn't need children. They were sufficient to each other; they fulfilled each other's needs on every level. And he was sure that that was how Leith viewed it, too.

If he had one regret, it was that the pressure of business kept him too busy to spend as much time with his wife as he would have liked. But it wasn't easy getting off the treadmill. He'd never mentioned it to Leith, but the company had faced some very real financial hurdles these last couple of years. In these unstable times, competition was ruthless and opportunities had to be grabbed when they were presented. It was the reason he had to work so much harder. Nor was he getting any younger. He knew he had only a few years left to ensure their comfortable retirement. After that, he told himself, things would be different. Then there would be the time and the financial freedom to enjoy themselves.

And, he promised himself, he'd spend every minute of that time with the wife he adored.

Maybe everything might have been different if his plans hadn't changed yet again.

It was Wednesday morning when he rang Leith to give her the news that the meeting in Hong Kong had been put forward by two days. It meant he'd have to spend most of the evening finalising things at the office before rushing home to pack for his departure the next morning.

'I'm so sorry, sweetheart.' He hated having to disappoint her again. 'Let's do something together when I get back. Maybe even escape up the coast for a couple of days.'

But Leith knew better than to believe it would really happen. After he'd been away from the office for a week, there'd be a million things to catch up on when he got back.

She did her best to put on a brave front. 'Maybe this is just God's way of telling me I'm staying forty-two for ever.'

But her mood changed after she hung up. Depressed, she contemplated the idea of yet another birthday without the company of the one person who really mattered in her life.

As before, she drove David to the airport, dropping him off in the departure bay.

'Goodbye, darling. Safe trip.' Leaning over, she kissed him warmly, catching the scent of Eau Savage.

He cupped her chin in his hand. 'Darling, you know if there were any way I could have been here this weekend, I would be.'

Leith nodded. 'I know.'

She knew he meant it. The same way she knew there was never any possibility of putting real life first.

Rather than go straight home afterwards, she decided to stay in town and do some shopping. The new season ranges were in the stores already and, as she wandered around her favourite boutiques, she found a couple of things she liked. The usual panacea for well-off, lonely females, she thought wryly, as she carried her purchases back to the carpark.

On the drive home, her thoughts returned to the matter of her birthday. She hated the idea of spending it alone. Maybe she should try to get a couple of friends together. The trouble was that on a Saturday evening most of the women she knew would have family commitments. Even a Saturday lunch wasn't an option for the same reason.

As she let herself into the big, empty house, Leith felt overwhelmed by her sense of loneliness.

When Saturday arrived, she couldn't help feeling miserable. She tried to tell herself it was just another day. But it wasn't. Not really. To her it was special.

When David calls, I'll feel better, she comforted herself.

But in the next couple of hours, the only calls she received were from a handful of girlfriends. Trying her best to sound cheerful, she thanked them for their best wishes and laughed at their corny jokes about getting older. She saw no point in mentioning that David was away. Why make her friends feel guilty? None of them could have changed their plans at such short notice anyway.

By eleven-thirty David still hadn't rung and now she really began to feel upset. There was a two-hour time difference between Sydney and Hong Kong; surely he could have found five minutes in his schedule to give her a call. Or, she thought, was he so engrossed in his work that he'd actually forgotten?

Finally she felt the need to get out of the house. Driving to one of her favourite Balmain cafes, she sat in the sun, drank too much coffee and wallowed in self-pity as she watched other couples around her. Couples leading normal lives. Couples who had time for each other.

It was almost one when she arrived home. Her mobile rang just as she reached the front door. Her expression lightened, it had to be David!

'Hallo.'

There was a pause. And then: 'Leith, it's Paul Houston.'

She was caught totally off guard.

'Paul . . .'

He'd been in her thoughts more than once or twice in the fortnight that had passed since their meeting. He'd intrigued her more than any man she'd met in a long time. The quiet, easy confidence. The charm. The sex appeal so often missing from men who looked that good. She was puzzled, too, about where she might have gone wrong that night, why he, unlike all the others, hadn't asked to see her again, hadn't followed through in a way that reaffirmed her attractiveness.

Now, his voice on the phone brought her a certain sense of satisfaction. At least it proved she *had* made an impact.

Before she could say anything, he went on, 'I'd have called you before now, but I've been away. Only got back yesterday.' His voice was as warm and resonant as she remembered. 'Still, I think I've left it to a more appropriate day, haven't I? To wish you happy birthday.'

She couldn't hide her surprise. 'How did you know?'

He chuckled. 'Don't you remember? You mentioned how you hated having a birthday that fell on April 1.'

Now it came back to her. They'd talked about star signs, compatability, the sort of light-hearted conversation that people sometimes make when they meet the way they had.

'Well, thank you. It's very nice of you to remember.' All of a sudden she felt much better. 'A real surprise.'

'I suppose you've got something planned for the evening?'

Again she was caught unawares. 'I —' She couldn't think quickly enough.

'Don't tell me you're not doing anything?' He was clearly surprised.

What could she say? She couldn't mention David. Flustered, she tried to shrug it off. 'Oh, I don't really —'

'Listen,' he interrupted her, 'no woman as lovely as you deserves to spend her birthday alone. I was calling to see if you'd like to get together again sometime, so if you're really doing nothing, then why not this evening?'

She started to make some sort of excuse, but he refused to take no for an answer.

And Leith allowed herself to be persuaded.

At six she took a shower and began to get ready.

Half a dozen times, as the rest of the day passed, she'd made up her mind to call Paul Houston back and cancel their date. By agreeing to see him again, she was breaking her own firm rule about only ever having one date with the men she met this way.

But on each occasion, as she'd started to dial his number, she'd changed her mind, for as the hours passed without any contact from David, her anger and resentment grew.

She couldn't believe that the day was almost gone and he hadn't rung her. Is that how little she meant to him? That he could have forgotten the date? He knew what a fuss she liked to make of birthdays. And he'd either forgotten, or couldn't find five minutes to put through a call.

Tight-lipped, Leith took in her reflection in the bedroom mirror. Paul was right, she thought defiantly, I don't deserve to spend my birthday alone.

While she may have been persuaded to accept his invitation, she had stoutly resisted his offer to pick her up at home.

'Thanks,' she said when he'd tried to insist, 'but really, it's no problem for me to drive myself.'

She was ready in plenty of time and was just walking down the hall to leave when the phone rang again.

This time, at last, it was David, sounding contrite and apologetic.

'Darling, happy birthday — even if it is a bit late in the day. I hope you didn't think I'd forgotten you. We left this morning at the crack of dawn to visit a project in the New Territories. And since we got back, I've been trapped with a roomful of Chinese big wigs and only this minute escaped. Now, tell me, did you organise something for tonight? I don't want to think of you sitting at home by yourself.'

Leith hesitated just a moment. 'I … yes, I'm having dinner with a couple of the girls.'

'Good, I'm glad about that. You have a wonderful night and we'll do something special when I get back.'

They talked for a couple of minutes more, and then David wished her happy birthday again and rang off.

She replaced the receiver, her emotions in turmoil. Of course David hadn't forgotten. How could she have doubted him? He'd rung her at the first possible moment.

And she had been forced to tell him a lie.

Her stomach tightened with guilt, and she cursed herself for her overreaction. Car keys in hand, she stood indecisively in the hall. What was she going to do? Cancel the date with Paul? At the last minute like this? Could she be so ill-mannered? And what excuse could she give him without getting caught up in her own treacherous web of lies?

No, she thought, there was only one way out of this. She looked down at her wedding band. She'd been going to slip it off as she had done before. Tonight she would leave it on and tell Paul Houston the truth. It was the only way to clear her conscience.

They met in the foyer of the Sheraton on the Park. In his dark, perfectly cut suit, snowy shirt and red and black silk tie, Paul Houston looked as handsome as Leith remembered. He greeted her warmly. 'I have to assure you, you know, that birthdays suit you. You look wonderful.'

The compliment pleased her, as did the open admiration she saw reflected in his eyes. But inside she felt nervous at the prospect that lay before her. How would he react when she told him the truth? Would he feel she'd made a fool of him? At least she would pay for her own meal, explain that it was her own weakness that had made her accept his invitation.

He had made a reservation in the hotel restaurant and as they followed the maitre d' to their table, Leith couldn't help noticing the way the other women in the room turned to look at the man beside her. Their obvious appreciation of her handsome escort brought her a small thrill of pleasure.

He ordered an aperitif and when the waiter brought the two glasses of Bollinger, Paul touched his glass to hers.

'Happy birthday to a very special lady. Someone I think I'm going to want to see a lot more of.'

She should have said something right then, but the words stuck in her throat. Instead, all she could manage was a nervous smile. After we've eaten, she thought. It would be better to tell him then.

Too on edge to enjoy her food, Leith only picked at her meal. She waited until their plates were cleared away and finally could put the moment off no longer.

'Paul, there's something I have to tell you. I haven't been totally honest with you. You see —'

'I think I know what you're going to say,' he gently cut across her. 'I did notice the wedding ring.'

She stared back at him and then began to talk too quickly. 'I'm sorry. I should never have come here tonight. It's just that my husband's away. He's often away these days. And when he didn't ring today, I thought, well I thought he'd forgotten my birthday. Only he did call. Just as I was leaving ... but then I felt I couldn't stand you up. Not at the last minute.' Her back felt damp between her shoulder blades from the effort of having to explain her deception. 'I'm happily married, Paul. You've got to believe that. I love my husband. The only reason I agreed to meet you tonight was because I thought he'd forgotten me.' Embarrassed, she looked away from his gaze. 'It was a stupid thing to do. And I'm sorry that I wasn't honest with you earlier.'

They sat in silence for a moment. Then Paul said quietly, 'I'm not quite sure I understand you, Leith. I'm wondering why a woman who says she's happily married makes contact with single men. It doesn't make a lot of sense to me.'

Leith felt sick. Why was he making it so difficult? Why couldn't he just accept what she was telling him?

Stomach churning, she did her best to explain. 'My marriage is important to me. I mean that. But when David's away so often, I guess I get lonely. So many of my friends work, have families ... What I did — how we met — it's just a way of filling in time. I've only done it a couple of times before,' she added quickly. 'And I never saw any of the others more than once. This — this is the first time I've ever done that.'

He was staring at her, and she could sense him weighing up what she had told him. But if she'd expected a critical response, she was surprised.

'A woman as beautiful as you shouldn't ever have to be lonely,' he replied with quiet intensity. 'If you were my wife, I know I'd want you to be anywhere I was. I'd never want to leave you alone.'

Leith couldn't believe it. Paul Houston was speaking the words she longed to hear from her own husband. Then he reached across the table and she felt his hand cover her own. 'Maybe you've got more problems than you're admitting to yourself, Leith. Maybe there's a lot more you need to talk about.' He saw her eyes widen in alarm. 'No, I don't mean here, tonight. But maybe sometime soon, when it suits you. I'm a good listener, you know.'

She hadn't expected such sympathy and under-standing. And in her fragile state, it proved too much. She felt her eyes swim with tears. Oh, God no, she couldn't make an even bigger fool of herself. Picking up her handbag, she pushed her chair back from the table.

'Will you excuse me a moment, please?'

He rose to his feet as she hurried to the ladies room.

Afterwards, he walked her to her car in the hotel parking lot. She was composed again and strangely reluctant now to say goodbye. Instead of being annoyed at her deception, Paul Houston had shown genuine sympathy and understanding. She felt as if tonight she'd made a friend.

As they said goodbye, he echoed her thoughts. 'You know, Leith, not many people are big enough to admit to being lonely. So many of us are, but we hide it in all sorts of ways. Maybe you'll let me call you now and then, and see how things are going. That's all. Just a call to keep in touch.'

She looked at him for a long moment. He'd been so compassionate to her tonight. It had almost been a relief to unburden herself, to admit her fragility and neediness to a man like Paul. What harm could it do to talk to him now and again?

Leith nodded. 'I think I'd like that,' she said.

❊

It was two weeks since Cate's initial trip to the Gold Coast. Now, as she packed everything she'd need for the week they were shooting there, she couldn't help thinking of Cal Donohoe.

As it turned out, he hadn't been able to take her to the airport that Sunday afternoon. At the last minute he'd rung her at the hotel to apologise that he'd got tied up at the surgery.

'One of my weekend staff had an accident with his own motor mower, so I'm having to do his session myself. There's a full waiting room at the moment and no chance I'm going to get away.'

'No problem. I'll take the shuttle as I was going to.'

'So when's the program locating up here?'

'In two weeks.'

'You'll be up for that, then?'

'Without me they're nothing.'

She heard his chuckle. 'I like a confident woman.'

'That's me.'

'Well, I don't know how busy you're going to be, but if you have a spare hour or so, I'd love to see you again. How can I get in touch? Will you be staying at the Marriott again?'

She couldn't remember meeting a man who was so direct. And she liked that, after all the jerks who played their endless ego-destroying games.

'I guess so. Why don't I give *you* a call when I know I'm going to be free?'

'Sure. Whatever suits.'

They had exchanged numbers and she'd put the phone down feeling a sense of excitement she hadn't felt in a long time.

And that worried her. A lot. A helluva lot.

The *Live!* team flew into Coolangatta airport on Sunday afternoon, but with everything that needed to be set up for the week, there was no chance for Cate to escape.

On the Monday morning she was up bright and early, ready for the last minute hiccups that were all too much the norm whenever they did an OB. But apart from the late arrival of one of the interviewees, everything ran like clockwork. Leanna was pleased, and by five o'clock Cate was able to call it a day.

She knew she should ring Cal Donohoe then as she'd promised, but she'd begun to ask herself what was the point. He seemed a really nice guy and she'd certainly found him interesting, not to mention sexually appealing, but that was exactly why she was reluctant now to re-establish contact. What good would it do her to go out with him again and perhaps find herself more attracted, when they lived a thousand kilometres apart?

No, Cate thought, she didn't need that sort of emotional complication in her life. She'd done her fill of waiting by the phone, of changing her schedule, her plans, her life, to accommodate a man. So why the hell should she bother to open that particular can of worms with Dr Donohoe?

Yet she couldn't help thinking of him as she did what she had to do each day, especially when, by Tuesday evening, she'd got tired of drinking too much after work with the crew. The idea of a quiet meal with someone like Cal was growing more attractive.

Yet she resisted the impulse to call.

'Cate! It's Cal. You didn't keep your part of the bargain, so I'm calling you.'

Oh, Jesus. It was four-thirty and he'd called her on her mobile. She was in Leanna's suite in the middle of a meeting about the next day's program.

'I can't talk now,' she said quickly. 'Can I call you back?'

'Sure. Try me at home. I'll wait in till I hear.'

Well, that put her on the spot. Now she had no option.

Finally, with her meeting over, she called him back around six.

'Sorry about that. I was in a meeting.'

'My apologies too. But I thought you were a woman of your word.'

She felt a moment's irritation at being held to account. But then she remembered guiltily how she'd felt when men had done the same to her, had said they'd call and hadn't.

'Well, I am. I was going to call you,' she lied.

'And now you have, so I forgive you,' he said with assured good humour. 'So tell me, what would you like for dinner?'

He surprised her again. He'd told her to dress casually and when he picked her up from the hotel, she saw a picnic basket and rug on the rear seat of his Prelude.

'You are going to eat the best fish in town,' he promised.

Five minutes later they stopped in front of a small wooden shopfront that looked incongruously out of place, situated as it was opposite the marble and glitz of the Sheraton Mirage hotel.

Inside, Cate saw they were in a mini fish market. Customers were choosing their fresh fish or shellfish from the refrigerated display and having their selection cooked to order.

The shop was busy and they had to wait a short while for their whiting and prawns and calamari, but as on that first occasion, the conversation between them never flagged.

When they finally received their warm, paper-wrapped meal, Cal drove a little further down the road and, with food and rug and picnic basket in hand, they walked over the dunes to the beach.

He spread the rug on the sand, and from the basket produced two shortened bamboo flares that he stuck in the sand beside them and lit with a match.

'You think of everything,' Cate said in amazement.

'It's an Irish trait.'

From the same basket he brought out a chilled bottle of wine, two glasses and an opener, and while Cate unwrapped the seafood, he poured them each a wine.

Then he raised his glass to hers in a toast.

'To confident women.'

'To Irish imagination.'

And they both laughed out loud.

It was a magic night. The food was every bit as delicious as promised, the moon silvery on the water, the lights of the high-rises strung along the coastline outlined the scene.

'Do you know I've never done anything like this ever before?' Cate said.

They were lying on the rug and she had her head pillowed against his chest, a glass of wine in her hand.

'Not mixing with the right people, were you?'

'Maybe not,' she answered.

After a moment of silence he said, 'I'm trying to figure out how old you are, Cate.'

There was something in the way he asked the question that made her avoid a joking or evasive reply.

'Well, I'm brave enough to tell you the truth. Forty-two.'

'Same as me. And you've never been married?'

'No.'

She hesitated, wondering just how much she wanted to reveal. Then, with deliberate succinctness, she continued, 'I spent five years with someone. Thought it might happen, but it didn't.'

It was a short-cut reply that revealed nothing of her pain, her anger, the shock of having to start her life over again.

'No regrets,' she added, with defensive bravado.

There was a pause and then he said, 'I envy you. Having no regrets in life.'

She realised he was completely serious now. Rolling over, she propped herself up on her elbows and looked down at him.

'Are you going to expand on that?'

He sat up and stared out at the ocean before replying. Then he said quietly, 'I was married. Almost seven years. My wife and four-year-old son were killed in a car accident.'

His voice was carefully neutral.

'Oh, Cal ... I'm so sorry for you.' Putting her glass down in the sand, she sat up beside him. 'How long ago did it happen?'

'Six years. Not far from home.'

'It — it must have been unbearable.'

'It was.'

She sensed some change in him, a sort of relief, as if he'd unburdened himself, as if he'd needed her to know, to understand him.

She knew then that something indefinable had suddenly changed in their relationship.

When he dropped her back at the hotel entrance he gave her a light kiss on the cheek. The brightly lit foyer of the hotel was hardly the venue for anything more ardent.

'Thanks, Cate. I enjoyed it.'

'Me too.'

He knew she couldn't make a late night of it and that solved the difficulty of whether to invite him in or not. However, she had expected that he'd say something about seeing her again. But he didn't, so with a final thank you and goodbye, she stepped out of the car and entered the sliding glass doors.

That night she found it difficult to get to sleep. Her self-protection system was sounding its shrillest alarm. Because she knew she was more attracted to Cal Donohoe than she dared to admit.

Cate didn't know whether to be relieved or upset when she didn't hear from Cal again for the rest of that week. But if she were being honest, she'd have to admit to the latter. That night on the beach had established a new intimacy for her, and she'd been so sure that he'd felt it, too.

Despite herself, she couldn't help wondering why he hadn't called. Was he playing the game so many men played? she asked herself in growing annoyance. Pulling you close, so that they could enjoy the power of thrusting you away?

Except that in the short time she'd known him she'd seen nothing to indicate Cal Donohoe was that sort of bastard.

The note was handed to her as she was checking out, late on Friday afternoon. Moving a little away from the clamour of the rest of the *Live!* team who were clogging the foyer, Cate pulled the single sheet of paper out of the envelope addressed with her name. Her heart beat faster as she read his message.

Dear Cate,

I enjoyed our time together so much. For a confident woman you're one of the best. There's no one I'd rather sit by the sea with and quote Yeats to than you. Take care, and know I'm thinking of you,

Cal.

Standing stock still, she read the note through again. The message was clear. Cal had 'enjoyed' her company. But had no intention of seeing her again.

They had to call her name twice before she realised the airport shuttle had arrived.

CHAPTER SEVEN

Judith was excited as she grabbed her notebook and bag and locked her car. This was the first time in years that she was actually doing something for herself.

She remembered the surprise on the boys' and Greg's faces as she'd gathered her things together after dinner and told them she was off.

'I've got to be there by seven, so I'm sorry but I haven't got time to clear the kitchen.' She'd addressed her comments to Greg, who was slumped in front of the television. 'Make sure the boys give you a hand,' she added. Then she'd turned and walked out before any of them could protest.

On the short drive she'd felt her excitement growing. This was something she'd promised herself she'd do for years, but she had never had the time — or rather, never *made* the time — for it previously. In an indirect way, it had been attending the reunion that had finally pushed her into action. The news that two of her former classmates had succumbed to breast cancer before their fortieth birthdays had finally forced her to face the fact that time wasn't infinite. She'd realised then that she couldn't put her dreams on hold any longer.

The application form had been in the local paper four weeks ago, and she'd taken the first step by cutting it out. It had taken her a week to eventually get around to filling in the details, writing the cheque and sending the whole lot off. Then she'd worried that she'd left it too late. She was bound to miss out, she told herself anxiously. She should have done it at once.

But to her delight, she'd been informed by letter ten days later that her application had been successful. She was one of the fifteen lucky people who'd been accepted onto the next creative writing course.

The two-hour classes were held on Tuesday evenings over eight weeks, and now, with a sense of anticipation, Judith pushed open the door and entered the brightly lit library.

From behind the counter, a middle-aged woman with a too-tight perm smiled at her. 'You after the writing group?'

'Yes.'

'The room right at the back,' she pointed. 'You're on time. Mr Kendall hasn't arrived yet.'

With a murmured thank you, Judith hurried past the shelves where borrowers were browsing and found the open door to a room that was glassed from midway up the walls. A mixed group of men and women ranging from late teens to sixties were sitting around three tables that had been pushed together.

Some of them smiled at her, others said hallo and Judith returned their greetings. There was a spare seat beside a spectacled, dark-haired girl who looked to be in her early thirties. As Judith pulled out the chair beside her, the girl gave her a smile and introduced herself as Lyn.

'Have you done any writing before?' she asked, as Judith burrowed in her handbag for a biro.

'No, not really.'

It was so long ago that her one short story had been published she didn't think it worth mentioning.

'Neither have I, but I'm determined I'm going to have a novel published by the time I'm thirty-five. I've promised myself that.'

Judith heard the utter determination in the young woman's voice and was amazed at such an openly declared ambition. It was hers too, except that she was already years late in trying to achieve it.

As she waited, Judith studied the class brochure again. Their teacher was a Tony Kendall, the author of four 'well-received mainstream novels'. It was a name Judith hadn't heard of, nor was she quite sure what was meant by a 'mainstream' novel, but she was looking forward to learning what she could from anyone lucky and talented enough to be published.

Tony Kendall arrived at seven on the dot. Tall and well-built, he wore baggy corduroys and an open-necked, checked shirt. His greying hair was thick and unruly, and there were deep creases around his friendly brown eyes. Judith guessed he was in his early fifties, and she found him quite attractive in a dishevelled sort of way.

With friendly informality he introduced himself and filled them in on his relevant background. He'd been a teacher, a sports store owner, had run a yacht chartering business in Vanuatu for two years and, somewhere along the line, had decided he was going to write a novel.

'I spent three years thinking about doing it, and it took me another eighteen months to actually do it. What I hope to do in this course is inspire you to boot up those computers *now*, not to let anything put you off, to get started as soon as possible.'

As she listened, Judith found herself nodding and smiling. Oh yes, this is was she needed. This was the stimulus that would help her to realise her dream. Whether she had the talent or not, she'd never know unless she finished something. And Tony Kendall was going to inspire her.

The two hours flew by. Judith felt as if she'd been put into some sort of trance. That first evening they ran through the basic elements of the course, and Judith hung onto Tony Kendall's every word. He explained how ideas were everywhere if you learned to develop the skills to spot them. He told them ways to test if an idea had the potential to be turned into a fully developed plot. He spoke about style and dialogue and exposition, and Judith couldn't scribble down her notes quickly enough.

When nine o'clock arrived, she was disappointed that the lesson was over. And from what she could hear of the chatter around her, her fellow students felt the same.

'He's a great teacher, isn't he?'

Judith saw the glow in Lyn's eyes as the younger woman tucked her pen and notebook away in a shabby canvas shoulder bag.

She could only agree.

As the room emptied, Tony Kendall was wiping the white board and cheerfully responding to the chorus of thanks and 'goodnights'. High on what she had learned, Judith felt she had to stop and say something more.

'I really enjoyed that. You know how to explain the process so that amateurs like us can understand.'

Duster in hand, he smiled at her over his shoulder. 'Thank you. I'm glad you got something out of it. And there's plenty more to come.'

'I'll be here,' Judith promised.

They'd put the dirty dishes in the dishwasher, but that was the full extent of their efforts. The frying pan stood caking by the sink, and the benches were littered with crumbs and vegetable peelings. Upstairs, she could hear the shower running in the ensuite. Greg was getting ready for bed.

As usual, Luke was stretched out on the sofa, an empty can of Coke beside him, the floor strewn with chocolate wrappings. 'You're back early,' he said, eyes barely moving from the TV screen. 'Where'd you go?'

'I told you. I'm doing a writing course.' Judith was filling the sink with hot, soapy water for the frying pan. 'For eight weeks,' she said tartly. 'So you lot are going to have to do a better job than this.'

But her son's attention was already re-rivetted on the screen.

After that, Judith couldn't wait for Tuesday evenings. She didn't even care that the mess was always waiting for her when she got home. As she cleaned up, she went over in her mind everything she'd learned that evening: how and where to start a story, the essential facts that needed to be given to the reader at the beginning, how to introduce the main character, subplots, dialogue, point of view.

As the weeks passed, she knew she was putting together the jigsaw that would help her create her own story. She'd had the idea in the back of her mind for years, it seemed, but had lacked the confidence and knowledge to take the first step. Now, the idea began to take shape in her mind as a storyline, not fully developed as yet, but with the bones she needed to help her coat them with flesh.

A couple of times when the class was over, she managed to hang back so that she and Tony Kendall walked out to their cars together. There were so many questions she wanted to ask, but she knew she couldn't intrude too much. Still, he was invariably approachable and seemed happy enough to stand and chat for a few minutes in the library car park.

'What are you working on now?' she asked him one evening, hoping he wouldn't mind talking about his own work.

He gave a half smile. 'I'm taking a little break at the moment. It happens like that sometimes. You can't force creativity.'

Judith nodded, but for her it was different. 'I'm brimming over with ideas. The moment this course is finished, I think I'm going to be ready to start.'

Immediately she worried that he might think her silly or naive. 'Of course, I don't want to be too premature about it and end up losing my confidence.'

'Well, the piece you wrote for me last week was excellent. It's always good to find a student with a fresh eye.'

His words of praise sent her home in a daze of happiness.

But already in the sixth week of the course, Judith sensed a readiness in herself to begin the novel she was planning in her mind. She had awoken one morning infused with a compelling inner force, a sense of vibrant anticipation, the certain knowledge that the time was right for her to begin.

That day at work her mind was miles away. She couldn't wait to get home. A quick pasta dinner, the laundry thrown in the tub, the kitchen given a perfunctory clean, and then she hurried upstairs to the spare bedroom, which she had claimed as her workplace.

After the first class with Tony Kendall, she'd gone out and bought herself a second-hand computer. Naturally Greg had raised an eyebrow at that. Why couldn't she use the boys' PC? he'd asked. And of course she understood his implication. The way Greg saw it, she was wasting money on some passing phase.

But after a lifetime of spending the money she

worked damn hard for on everybody else, this time Judith was going to spend some of it on herself. She needed her own computer, one she could have access to on a regular basis, and now, as she switched on the machine, her lips set tight with determination. She'd prove to Greg and all of them that they were wrong. Totally wrong. For no matter how many rejections she might get, no matter how many times she had to try, she was never going to give up. And one day she was going to have a novel published. It would sit on the bookstore shelves with her name on it and would bring her more joy and pride than anything else she'd ever done in her life.

Tingling with anticipation and drive, Judith double-spaced her page and in capital letters typed CHAPTER ONE.

Then, heart beating a little faster, she wrote her opening sentence:

When she woke on the morning of her fortieth birthday, Jo Sullivan knew she was about to change her life ...

Only when she realised it was past midnight did Judith finally switch off her PC. But she felt alive with excitement and, when she went to bed, she found it impossible to fall asleep.

I've done it, she told herself, smiling in the dark. I've finally started.

And it felt totally wonderful.

She didn't speak about her work to any of her fellow students. It was far too early for that. She was still feeling her way, and everything seemed too fragile yet to actually talk about. But she was dreading the end of the eight weeks. There was only one lesson to go, and Judith knew it was going to be a terrible wrench when it was all over. The two hours every week inspired her and gave her the courage and faith to keep going. She knew she was going to miss Tony Kendall's encouragement and advice.

And she wasn't the only one feeling that way. It was clear that most of the others were as reluctant as herself to see the course end. A sense of cameraderie had grown up in the time they'd all been together. Tony Kendall had encouraged openness and honesty. Good writing, he proclaimed, could only flow from that. As a result, her fellow students had opened up about themselves, in both their writing and their contributions in class. They were going to miss each other.

Someone had suggested that they should have a formal end to the course and proposed a dinner at some local restaurant. The idea was enthusiastically endorsed, and they booked a cheap and cheerful Italian place for the Friday evening following their final class. Naturally Tony Kendall was invited too.

Meanwhile Judith persevered with her work. As soon as her basic chores were finished in the evening, she would hurry up to her room and, with Sari curled at her feet, address the challenge of bringing her heroine to life. Jo Sullivan, trapped in a loveless marriage, but determined that it wasn't too late to change her life.

It hadn't taken Judith long to realise that her heroine was drawn from so many aspects of herself.

Jo Sullivan's desires — freedom, respect, a lover who was considerate, romantic, and emotionally open — were exactly what Judith longed for herself.

Wish fulfillment, Tony had told them, was a valid impetus to creativity. When Fredrick Forsyth or Tom Clancy wrote about their action heroes, he explained, they were just as surely tapping into that part of their male selves that desired adventure and freedom from the humdrum. And so, each evening, Judith wrote about her protagonist's courage as she confronted the difficulties in leaving her loveless marriage.

For Jo Sullivan, Judith knew, had the courage that she lacked herself.

At the farewell dinner that Friday evening they packed themselves around their teacher at one long table. Judith found herself selfishly wishing that everyone else would disappear so she could have Tony Kendall to herself, so they could spend the whole evening talking about the joys and difficulties of writing.

As the platters of steaming pasta arrived, the wine glasses were filled again and the group grew noisier. Afterwards, while they were waiting for their coffee, one of the men stood up and proposed a toast, thanking Tony on behalf of the group for 'all he had so generously given them'.

As she looked around the table at the raised glasses, the smiles and nods of agreement, Judith couldn't help wondering how many of her fellow students would actually find success. For how many of them would the momentum of the last eight weeks endure so they would actually fulfill their dream and see their work published?

Tonight, for the first time, she had to admit to her own uncertainties. Over the last week or so, she'd struck a difficult patch and could feel herself losing confidence. As she reread what she'd written, the words didn't seem to ring true, her characters appeared shallow and dull and unconvincing. Trying to solve the problem, she wrote and rewrote, struggling for improvement. But because of her inexperience, she couldn't be sure if she was succeeding.

Yet she couldn't give up, she told herself. She mustn't let herself panic.

At last the evening was over. They were the last to leave the restaurant, reluctantly, and it was almost midnight when they streamed out into the chilly night air. Addresses and telephone numbers had been exchanged, and now people hugged each other, shook Tony's hand, thanked him again.

Judith lingered, but it was clear she couldn't have a word about her problem with Tony tonight. She was on her own now. Somehow she'd have to get over her hurdle alone.

As she said a final goodbye, she was surprised when he took her hand in both of his. He smiled at her. 'Don't give up, Judith, and keep that fresh eye.'

She was warmed by his encouragement but at the same time ached to talk to him about her difficulties. Instead she smiled, thanked him again, and walked to her car.

While the others drove away around her, Judith began to rummage in her handbag, searching for her keys. It took her a couple of minutes to realise that they were sitting in the ignition of her locked car.

Oh, no, she groaned inwardly. It was late and getting colder by the minute.

Helplessly she looked around. The restaurant had already put out its lights, and the front door had been locked behind them. But surely someone would still be there to help her. Or, she wondered, should she use her phone and pray that the roadside service wouldn't be too long?

While she stood there indecisively, she heard someone call her name.

'What's up, Judith? Anything wrong?'

A car had pulled up beside her. It was a beaten-up Commodore and Tony was at the wheel.

She shook her head in exasperation. 'I can't believe I've been so stupid! I've locked my keys in the car.'

'Let me see what I can do.'

He manoeuvered the Commodore so its headlights shone on her driver's door, and when he got out, Judith saw he was carrying a length of wire.

He grinned at her. 'With a car like mine, you're always ready for anything.'

He crouched down beside the door and carefully poked the wire into the lock, jiggling it for a few seconds. To Judith's amazement, it snapped open.

'Is *that* how easy it is? No wonder cars disappear off the streets all the time.'

He smiled again. 'Rat cunning beats high-tech most times.' He gestured at the open door. 'You okay now?'

'Oh, sure, fine. And thanks so much. For the course too. I learnt so much.' And then she blurted it out. 'I — I've even started my novel.'

He looked pleased. 'That's great. How's it going?'

'Well, I'm working at it every spare moment and, until recently, I was really firing along, but suddenly I seem to be floundering. And I'm having trouble working out exactly why.'

Oh, Judith, she admonished herself, you're as obvious as all hell. But what did she have to lose?

'Well, that's par for the course when you're just starting out.' He seemed to consider something for a moment, and his next words made her heart leap. 'Look, I don't do this for everyone, only very occasionally for those I feel have some real promise. Send me what you've written, and I'll have a read of it. I'll give you a call and tell you where things might be going wrong.'

Judith stared at him in delight. 'Do you mean that? I'd *love* it. I'd just love to have your feedback.'

He was scribbling on a small notebook he'd pulled from his pocket. 'Here's my address, and I'll take down your number.'

Eyes shining, Judith repeated it for him. She couldn't hide her happiness. 'I really appreciate this, Tony. Very, very much. I can't tell you how much of a boost the course gave me. For the first time, I've really started to believe I might be capable of finishing something.'

He looked at her and said softly, 'We're all capable of much more than we give ourselves credit for.'

And with a final smile, he got back into the dilapidated Commodore.

✽

Rory loved the time she had with Cam before she left for work. Ian had had an early meeting, so she was alone with her son. Sometimes she preferred it that way, felt less tense and inhibited without Ian looking on. She had enough doubts about being a 'natural' mother without sometimes getting the feeling that she was being judged.

Now she changed her son in his small, cheerfully decorated bedroom, smiling and cooing at him just like those perfect mothers in the ads you saw in magazines and on TV. Cam giggled back at her, his face still rosy with sleep, and Rory thanked God that he'd always had a sunny temperament. She didn't know how she would have coped with a difficult baby.

Carrying him through to the kitchen, she lowered him into his highchair and filled a pan with water for his egg. When it was ready she sat and fed him, but now her eye was on the clock. If Deb had got held up in the traffic, she'd have to fly to be on time for work.

A few minutes later, she felt a sense of relief as she heard a key in the front door.

'Hi, Rory ... Hi, darling, have you eaten up all your egg?' Unbuttoning her jacket, Deb walked into the kitchen and gave Cam a kiss on the head. He laughed and beat his teaspoon against the tray in front of him.

Rory wiped her hands on a tea towel. 'Hi, Deb. I've cut more toast, it's in the toaster.'

'Fine.' The girl slipped her coat onto the hanger behind the kitchen door. 'Just leave it to me.'

'Thanks.'

As she hurried away to get ready, Rory felt the familiar sense of guilt seeping through her. Much as she adored her child, she didn't think she could possibly cope with spending seven days a week at home with him. In the end she felt sure she'd go crazy — not only at the mindless slavery of it all, but at the thought that she had sabotaged her career, was wasting her skills, might never get the chance again to make her mark.

No, she told herself as she turned on the shower and quickly stepped under the spray, this was the way that worked best for her. With Deb's help, she could still have a life.

She was collecting her notes after the morning's editorial meeting when she was told that Colin Rikard wanted to see her in his office.

As she made her way down the corridor, Rory wondered what the MD wanted. She worried about everything these days. Was she choosing the right authors? Bidding too high? Not paying enough to keep them? Picking the trends in the market? Once she had felt unassailable. More recently she seemed to have to agonise over every decision.

But Colin Rikard had a surprise for her.

'We've got a problem, Rory. A big one. The master chefs project.'

Of course Rory had heard about the project. The idea had originated from their Australian office: an expensively produced cookbook consisting of recipes donated by some of the world's leading chefs. It had been enthusiastically received by the international marketing managers, and production was being handled by their Melbourne office.

But, she thought, puzzled, what did it have to do with her?

'We had Elizabeth Clark working on it,' Colin Rikard continued. 'Our best editor down south. Except that she's suddenly had to drop out. Hep B. From what she says, it'll keep her at home for months.'

He tapped the end of his pen on the desk top. 'The material's all there — the text, photos; it's just waiting for the lay-out. But there's no one else with the experience down there to pull it all together. It's the sort of project that needs an all-rounder like yourself. And the deadline is tight.'

Rory said nothing. She could guess what was coming.

'What I'm asking is if you might be prepared to put in a three-day week down there for a month, maybe six weeks, to ensure we're still able to publish on schedule.'

She felt her mouth go dry. On the one hand she'd just been handed the reassurance she so badly needed regarding her abilities. On the other, she felt ill at the prospect of what going away for three days a week would do to her finely tuned routine at home.

Her mind raced. It was a major opportunity. Could she possibly consider it? So much depended on what she could ask of Ian and her nanny. And she knew she was already pushing Ian to the limit. Would he go that bit further to help her, just this once?

'If I could do it, when would you need me to start?'

'As soon as you can get away. Next week, if possible. I know it might be difficult for you at home, but this is too big and important for me to entrust to someone less experienced. I'm not asking you to make a decision on the spot. Just think it over and let me know in the morning.'

For the rest of the day, Rory agonised over her options.

Because of the international exposure such a book would receive, it would be a real shot in the arm for her career. The sort of opportunity that didn't come along every day. At any other time in her life, she'd have jumped at it, loved the challenge and the kudos. But how could she leave her child for whole days at a time? She wasn't sure if she could do it. And even if that were possible, the reorganisation it would mean to their domestic routine was another major stumbling block.

She tossed the options back and forth, driving herself crazy in the process. God, she wanted to do it so much, but at the same time she knew it would make everything else so difficult. By the time she left the office, she realised the only way she was going to be able to come to a decision was to discuss it all with Ian.

'And you really want to do this?'

They had eaten dinner and were finishing the bottle of red they'd opened with their meal.

Rory tried to explain. 'Look, I know I shouldn't. I know I should just go into Colin tomorrow and tell him it's impossible. But to answer your question, I'd *love* to do it. It's a chance to make my name with a really high profile international project. And anyway, I know Colin wouldn't have asked me if he didn't really expect me to step in. That's what makes it so touchy.'

'Have you talked to Deb? It'll depend on her as much as on me.'

Rory nodded. 'She said she'd be able to stay over on two of the nights. But not Thursday, she does a ceramics class then.'

She saw he was weighing it up. In her own mind she had finally come down firmly on the side of wanting to accept Colin Rikard's offer. With Deb available, Cam would be all right, she felt sure. Now it all depended on whether Ian would support her.

He finished his drink and put the empty glass down on the polished timber table in front of him. 'Well, it won't be easy, but I guess we can manage if it's only for a month.'

He was obviously less than enthusiastic, but Rory felt her heart leap that he wasn't going to stand in her way. Slipping an arm around his shoulder, she kissed him warmly on the cheek.

'Oh, darling, thank you. It's wonderful of you. I promise I'll organise everything as best I can so you'll only have the minimum disruption.'

The next morning, when she gave a relieved and happy Colin Rikard her news, she did her best to push away the guilt she felt at leaving her child.

The night after he arrived home, David took Leith to their favourite restaurant for a belated celebration. She knew there must have been a million things waiting for him to catch up on at the office, but he had kept his promise.

It was a delight to have her husband all to herself for a change. As the waiters handed them their menus, she wished it could be like this more often. Time, unrushed, a chance for intimacy. What a difference it would make!

She felt guilty now at the thought of that evening a week ago with Paul Houston. She knew she should never have seen him again, should never have weakened and broken her cardinal rule. It disturbed her, too, that she'd revealed so much of herself — her loneliness, her neediness. It had been a mistake to have encouraged him. Even as a friend. If he did ring again, she'd make it abundantly clear that there was no possibility of any sort of relationship continuing between them, that her marriage was important to her and no one was going to change that.

When they'd given their orders, David produced a slender package wrapped in burgundy paper and tied with gold ribbon.

'Happy birthday, sweetheart. I hope this will help make up for our not being together.'

Leith undid the wrapping and opened the flat, velvet box. Inside lay a slim gold bracelet, its clasp made of glittering emeralds.

'Oh, darling...' She looked up at him in delight.

'It's absolutely beautiful.' Then, putting the box down, she reached across the table, cupped his face in her hands and leaned forward to kiss him. 'Thank you, my darling. Thank you so much. You're so good to me.'

'Try it on.'

She did as he asked, and the bracelet fitted perfectly.

'I measured one of your others before I left.'

'With everything else you had to think of?' She looked at him, shaking her head in disbelief.

He stared at her for a moment, then said quietly, 'Things are a bit tough at the moment, Leith. I know it's hard for you to be alone so much. But I love you. You know that, don't you?'

Reaching across the table, she squeezed his hand and nodded without speaking. But her guilt made it hard to look her husband in the eye.

They didn't make too late a night of it. David was as eager as she was, Leith felt sure, to catch up on the nights they had spent apart. In her softly lit ensuite she undressed and washed her face clean of make-up. Her skin looked luminous in the glow reflected off the bronzed marble, and her hair hung loosely around her shoulders.

She slipped on an ivory silk negligee that clung softly to her breasts and hips. Underneath she wore skimpy matching knickers. The outfit was new, David hadn't seen it before, she had bought it with this evening in mind. To surprise him. Excite him. Welcome him home. She was eager to feel him inside her, to renew the sense of belonging and fulfilment that was for her so much a part of their lovemaking.

With a sense of anticipation, she walked back into the bedroom. The room was lit only by the pink glow of the bedside lamps, and David was already lying beneath the sumptuous quilted cover of the wide bed.

Leith saw at once that he was asleep.

On bare feet she moved closer, hoping he was merely dozing and that his eyes would blink open and he'd smile and welcome her in beside him. But as she stopped and looked down at him, she could hear the rhythmic sound of his deep breathing.

A crushing disappointment welled inside her. It seemed so long since they'd made love, and the evening together had established such a perfect mood. She'd been relishing the prospect of slow, tender lovemaking.

As she moved around to her own cold side of the bed, she did her best to console herself. It wasn't that he didn't want her. He was jet-lagged, that was all. He couldn't help it.

Maybe tomorrow night would be a possibility. After he'd had a good rest. If he was home on time. If the phone didn't ring all night. If they could recapture the mood.

In the dark, Leith lay listening to her husband's breathing and fought against her frustration. And resentment.

CHAPTER EIGHT

Three weeks after returning from Queensland, Cate was still dealing with the emotional fallout.

She hadn't heard another word from Cal. The note he'd left for her had been clearly the kiss-off. Nice couple of nights. Thanks a lot. Over and out. On closer inspection she obviously hadn't measured up to whatever impeccable standard he expected in a woman.

Oh, God, Cate, she tried to rationalise with herself, give it a break. Why the masochistic put-down? So what if the guy hasn't called? Who the hell cares?

Except that, much as she hated herself for admitting it, she did care. Cal Donohoe had got under her skin. She found herself thinking about him at the oddest times, replaying the time they'd spent together, especially that evening on the beach, and trying to figure out how she could have got him so wrong. He'd seemed so *interested*, so *nice*, so bloody *normal*.

What really pissed her off was the disruption that meeting him had caused to her emotional equilibrium. Everything she had vowed never to let happen to her again was happening. It was a replay of what she'd gone through with Tom, only ten times worse. Suddenly, too, she was more aware of her *aloneness*. She wasn't exactly lonely, but she kept remembering how it was to be with someone whose company she had really enjoyed.

But she wasn't going to let any man stuff her up. She'd get over it, she knew that. And next time, she vowed, she'd be even more damn wary than she was now.

It was nine p.m. when the phone rang. She was finishing off a pepperoni pizza, one of the usual staple of take-aways that saw her through the working week.

'Hallo.' She wiped her greasy lips as she put the receiver to her ear.

'Cate, it's Cal.'

Her heart thumped as if an electical current had been shot through it. She felt a flush heat her cheeks.

'Well...' For once she was at a loss for words, torn between a desire to return the rejection by slamming down the phone, and her need for an explanation. As well she sensed some other undefined emotion she didn't at that moment want to examine too closely.

She gathered herself. 'A most unexpected pleasure.'

'You're angry at me, and I can't blame you.'

'Why should I be angry?'

'Because you think I'm a bastard. That I was playing with you.'

'Oh, please ... I read your note. I got the message, okay? Why the postscript?'

She couldn't help the sarcasm. All the rejection and confusion she'd felt for the last few weeks came spilling out.

'Cate, I'm coming to Sydney next weekend. The next part of the course I was doing when we met.'

'And you'd like to fill in a little time again, is that it?'

'Cate, please. It's not like that. I'm not the bastard you think I am. It's just ...' He cut himself off and she heard the pleading in his tone. 'Look, I can't talk about it like this. Please, will you say you'll see me? Just to let me explain?'

She knew she should tell him no, draw on her anger to make it clear she didn't need any man screwing up her emotions, put the phone down and forget she'd ever met him.

But curiosity, and that same indefinable emotion, made her hesitate.

'So what did you have in mind?' Her tone was still surly.

He told her. He was persuasive, insistent — in the nicest possible way — and by the time she hung up, she'd agreed to meet him the coming Saturday evening.

Afterwards she sat and stared at the phone. It had become an object of hope again, instead of her tormentor. She felt light-headed, as if the oxygen had been sucked out of her lungs.

When he arrived, he rang her from his hotel in North Sydney.

'Why don't we have a drink in the bar first?' he suggested. 'I think we need to talk. It'll be better for both our digestions.'

She could only agree.

This time it was her turn to pick him up, and as she left her car in the hotel car park and took the lift to the foyer, she was trying to decide which of all the emotions she was feeling was predominant. Anger? Hurt? Confusion? Curiosity? ... Excitement?

By the time she spotted him sitting in a corner of the almost-deserted cocktail bar, she still hadn't made up her mind.

'Cate.' He stood up and reached for her hand, enclosing it in both of his own. 'Thanks. Thanks for coming.' It was a strangely old-fashioned gesture.

He was wearing chinos, a blue button-down, and a blue-grey tweed sports jacket. Doctor Cal Donohoe was as attractive as she remembered — and that helped to prioritise her emotions.

Before she could do more than return his greeting, a pretty uniformed waitress came to take her order. Cate glanced at his beer. 'I'll have a vodka and tonic, thanks. Lots of lemon.'

Then it was just the two of them, staring at each other, trying to read what lay behind the other's eyes.

Cate asked some totally meaningless question about his course and for a couple of moments they made desultory conversation. Then, abruptly, she got to the point. 'I'm really not sure what I'm doing here.'

'I'm just glad you're giving me the chance, Cate. I had to see you again. I couldn't leave things as they were.'

At that precise moment, the waitress arrived with her drink and neither of them spoke until she'd left them alone.

Cate could feel his eyes on her as she raised her glass and took a long sip. He waited until she'd placed her drink back on the table.

'Cate,' he was speaking very softly, 'I told you — what happened to me. My son Jack, my wife. The last few years haven't been easy. I've changed. I'm wary, careful. Very careful. I don't want any more loss in my life. Until I met you I felt — well, *numbed* is probably the right word. In a way, that didn't matter, because it also meant safe. But after that night on the beach with you, I didn't feel safe any longer. That's why I wrote that note.'

He reached for her hand again. 'Do you understand what I'm trying to tell you? I thought I could stop what was happening to me, but I tried and I couldn't.'

His intensity and sincerity were obvious, and Cate stared back at him, her breathing suddenly quickening. This is crazy, she thought. She understood what he was trying to tell her. Only because she felt the same — frightened, aware of how dangerous it can be when you decide to open your heart. She had felt it starting to happen for her that evening on the beach. And almost right away, she'd paid the price in pain and rejection.

Yet here was Cal Donohoe, sitting beside her, admitting that he'd found the courage to let down his defences.

She looked at him. 'Maybe it's impossible for any of us to stay safe,' she answered softly.

She saw the wave of relief pass over his features as he nodded in agreement. 'Yes ... because sooner or later someone might come along who's worth taking the risk for. And that's how I feel about you, Cate.'

Her mind spun. She hadn't expected anything like this. And now that it was happening, she wasn't sure it was really what she wanted.

'But Cal, it's crazy — in practical terms, I mean. You up there, me here. I just can't —'

'Look,' he interrupted gently, 'why don't we worry about that after we've eaten? I'm always more optimistic on a full belly.' He scribbled his signature and room number on the check and stood up, reaching out for her hand. Cate got the impression that he felt he'd dealt with the most troublesome problem, and the rest would be easy. Without a word, he walked her to the elevators but, as the doors closed behind them, he pulled her close and kissed her. The kiss lasted until they came to a stop at the basement car park.

'I'm not as hungry as I thought,' he whispered breathlessly in her ear. 'What about you?'

Still dizzy from the kiss, Cate felt her heart skip a beat. He was holding her so close she wondered if he could feel it against his ribs.

She knew this was crunch time. If she slept with him now, the emotional risks were multiplied a hundredfold. She knew what her answer should be. But the scent of his hair, the pressure of his hard body against her own made rational thought impossible. Because she wanted to sleep with him. Her body was yearning for it. Ever since that night on the beach, she

142

realised, she'd been fantasising about making love with him.

Now she sensed the intensity of his expectation as he waited for her reply.

'I can manage.' Her voice sounded as breathless as his had. 'Only I'm worried about your optimism quotient.'

He smiled down at her, and she saw the relief and pleasure in his eyes. 'Suddenly I'm feeling okay in that department, too.'

Reaching over her shoulder, he pushed the button for his floor. As the doors slid together, his lips found hers again.

In the end they ordered room service at midnight, sitting up in the rumpled bed devouring soup and toasted cheese and tomato sandwiches.

Cal brushed crumbs off the sheets. 'I don't like this restaurant, it's far too formal.'

'You're right,' Cate agreed, 'let's find somewhere more casual and cosy next time.'

Their eyes met and they burst out laughing. Then he pushed the tray aside and pulled her close again.

It was after one in the morning by the time she left, and he escorted her down to her car.

His hair was rumpled, his shirt creased and smudged with her make-up, and Cate guessed she was probably just as dishevelled-looking herself. But what the hell.

Leaning her against her car, he linked his hands behind her. 'It was wonderful, Cate. And thank you again for understanding — and for everything.'

Her lips were sore from the pressure of their kissing, her chin chaffed from his emerging beard, but their last kiss was as long and hard as all the others.

As she drove home, her thoughts were full of the amazing night. They'd made love over and over until only sheer exhaustion had beaten them, and Cate had felt an intensity in Cal's desire that was every bit as powerful as her own. She knew they had both let go of their safety lines.

They had managed to talk a lot too, and she'd told him about Simon. The anguish of the break-up, her struggle to make it on her own. 'It was so damned hard, Cal. It almost broke me. But in the end it made me stronger.'

'You're a survivor, Cate. We've both made it on our own. But now we've been lucky enough to find each other.'

Yet, as she drove through the darkened streets, Cate felt her old fears returning. Was this really what she wanted? Did she really want to turn her life upside down again for a man? Was she going to let this thing happen with Cal Donohoe? Or should she walk away now before it was too late?

Too exhausted to make any rational decision, she decided that, like Scarlett, she'd think about it tomorrow.

Cal was tied up with his training course all the next day, but he'd booked his flight as late as possible on Sunday evening.

'Just in case a miracle happened and I managed to talk you round,' he'd told her with a smile.

So they had plenty of time before his plane left to share satay and red curry over a bottle of white wine.

'I'm not getting on that plane until you let me know when I can see you again,' he said as he spooned more rice onto his plate. 'Are you going to be free this coming weekend?'

For a moment Cate didn't answer. She'd checked her diary. There was nothing she had to do that she couldn't change.

'Look, Cal,' she began, 'this has all happened so quickly. Last night was wonderful, but I really don't know. I really don't know if I'm capable of another full-on relationship.'

His gaze met her own, and he put down his fork and knife. After a moment he said carefully,

'Cate, I understand what you're saying. It's all happened like a bolt out of the blue. Neither of us was really expecting it. But do you know how very, very lucky we've been? There are no guarantees in life, you know that. All we can do is have the courage to see where it goes from here.'

He was watching her intently, trying to judge how his words were being received. 'Just let me say this to you,' he added, 'I think I know where *I'd* like it to go.'

Cate looked back at him in silent wonder. He was the most honest and direct man she'd ever known. He'd laid all his cards on the table, and now it was up to her.

So what was she going to do? Walk away just because, as Cal said, there were no guarantees, and she might get hurt again? Or plunge in and take the risk, and perhaps find a happiness she'd almost given up believing in?

She looked back into his eyes. How could he entrust his heart so openly after all he'd been through? How could he dare?

She thought of the pain that had lasted such a long, long time after Simon had left her. How could she believe that that wouldn't happen again? And how could she cope with it a second time?

She swallowed and said quietly, 'I'm not as brave as you, Cal. I'm sorry. I need — I need time to think about it.'

❇

'I thought the course was finished?' Greg was frowning at her as she picked up her car keys.

'It is. But my tutor's read my work, and he's offered to give me some help with it. We're meeting at the library. It's only for an hour or so.' Judith's even tone belied the excitement she felt at having Tony to herself for the first time.

Her husband gave a short disdainful laugh. 'I don't know why you're wasting your time, Judith. What makes you think you're capable of writing the great Australian novel?'

Judith forced herself to ignore his goading. 'My aspirations aren't that high, Greg. I just want to finish what I'm working on, and my tutor thinks what I've written is quite good.'

Tony's exact words were imprinted in her mind. He'd rung her four days after she'd sent him her completed pages. And her heart had leapt with joy at his appraisal of her work.

'I think this has a lot of potential, Judith. I'm really quite excited about what you've written so far. There are problems, of course, but nothing that can't be fixed.'

And they'd made an appointment to meet this evening at the library. 'I'll talk it through with you and tell you where I feel it needs some work.'

Now, without looking at her husband, Judith said, 'I'm going. I'll be back by nine or so.'

As she walked down the hall he called after her, 'I hope you've ironed the shirt I wanted for tomorrow. My green stripe.'

As she let herself out of the house, Judith worked out what her heroine would have said in reply to that.

Tony was sitting in one of the library's low chrome and vinyl chairs and had another pulled up beside it in readiness. As she walked towards him, he rose to his feet with a smile of welcome.

'I've tucked us away in this quiet corner.'

'Fine.' She sat down and saw the manila folder she'd sent him with her pages on the floor beside him. Again she realised how lucky she was to be spending a couple of hours or so with a published, experienced author. It was wonderfully generous of Tony to offer her his time like this.

'Well, now,' he reached down for the folder, 'shall we get right down to it?'

An hour and a half later, Judith felt as if she'd imposed long enough. But the time she'd spent with

Tony had left her elated. He'd read the passages that were troubling her and quickly grasped the problems.

'Too much dialogue that does nothing to move the story onwards,' he suggested, pointing to the relevant section.

Or, tapping his pencil on the paper, 'Jo's attitude here needs to be stronger. We need to know exactly why she's made this decision.'

And: 'I think you can develop this scene further and show the contrast between the emotional support she gets from her women friends and the remoteness of her husband.'

As he explained and offered solutions to the parts of her writing that had caused her such difficulty, Judith felt herself emerging from the worrying fog that had gripped her over the last couple of weeks. As she listened to Tony, suddenly everything was made clear. She could see at once where she was going wrong and what she had to do to fix things.

He'd had lots of positive things to say, too. 'You're really getting into the heart of this character, Judith. You're standing right in her shoes and making us feel her pain, her unhappiness, her inner conflict.'

Judith had only nodded, afraid to answer in case he might have guessed that so much of her own life and problems had gone in to creating her heroine. 'I really appreciate this, Tony. More than you can know.' He had walked her to her car and they were talking in the glow from the carpark lights. 'I was so frightened I was going to run off the tracks, completely lose my way. Your advice has helped so much.'

'I'm glad. As I said, I think you've got what it takes.'

'You don't know how much that encourages me. I really feel nothing can stop me now.'

They chatted for a moment longer, but before they parted, Judith unlocked her car door and reached over for the bottle of wine that was on the passenger seat.

With a smile she handed over the wrapped bottle. 'This is just a small thank-you for your time. I hope you like a good red.'

He grinned. 'Oh, you could twist my arm. Thanks, Judith. This is sweet you. Though certainly not necessary.'

'I had to repay you somehow.'

'Well, thanks a lot. I'm sure I'll enjoy it.'

They said goodbye and he waited until she'd slid in behind the steering wheel. Then he bent over and leaned in at the open window. 'Look, don't think I'm trying to fill my cellar, but you know I'm quite happy to do this regularly, if you feel it would help. Why don't you send me your pages in batches of twenty or thereabouts? That way I can make sure you're on track.'

She looked at him in delighted surprise.

'You'd *do* that? Oh, Tony, that'd be *great*. But are you sure? I mean, I'd be happy to pay for your time.'

'I'd see it as helping someone I believe in, Judith. You give it some thought, and send those pages through when they're ready.' She felt his hand pat her shoulder, and then he drew back and walked away.

That amazing parting offer captivated her thoughts as she made her way home. She was blown away by Tony's generosity. He believed in her. He really believed in her. Already she could feel her confidence soaring after the time they'd spent together. And not only had the evening been enlightening and encouraging, but she'd felt so comfortable being with someone who loved books and writing as much as she did. A man who understood about sensitivity and feeling and human relationships.

A man so very different from the one she had married.

It was only later, as she lay in bed still thinking about Tony Kendall's offer, that a new slant on his generosity suddenly occurred to her. Was there any possibility that this could be a come-on? Could he be using the excuse of helping her with her work to try to get her into bed?

But the next second Judith had dismissed the crazy thought. Oh, please, she chided herself, enough of the jokes. If Tony Kendall were after a roll in the hay, it certainly wasn't going to be with an overweight, forty-something married woman.

❊

'Clare's good, isn't she?'

'Too good for me,' Leith admitted, watching the four players on court from behind her sunglasses. 'She ran me ragged in that last set.'

The two women were relaxing in the shade of the cabana next to the tennis court. Not long after moving into her home, Leith had established a regular Tuesday game with the handful of her friends who didn't have full-time jobs. She'd never been a good player herself, but she enjoyed the exercise and the chance to socialise.

Now, she glanced at her watch. 'I'll bring lunch out in a moment. They're almost finished.'

'Need a hand?' Heather Anderson lolled beside her in a director's chair.

'No thanks, Heather, everything's under control.'

The other woman put down her empty glass with a tinkle of melting ice cubes. 'So how's David these days? Still as busy as ever? Ben says he hasn't seen him on the golf course for months.'

'Oh, it's business. He's been away a lot. Interstate. Overseas. I hate it, to tell you the truth.'

Heather widened her eyes in disbelief. 'You're kidding! I *love* it when Ben's away, mainly because I don't have to go anywhere near the kitchen. The kids and I live on take-away. And I can read all night if I want to, with no one grumbling that the light's keeping him awake.'

'Well, I wish I felt like that. I really miss David when he's away.'

'So why not go with him? You've got no kids tying you down like the rest of us.'

Leith shook her head. 'I tried that. A couple of times. But it wasn't much better. David was gone twelve hours a day, the evenings usually meant dinner with clients, and I was stuck in the hotel with nothing to do.'

'Then what about a job?' Heather suggested. 'I mean I know you hardly need the dough, but it'd give you something to occupy your time.'

'I've thought of that too, believe me. But then I didn't know what I could actually *do*. I worked as a stewardess. What does that qualify you for?'

'Being rude to people and producing the sorts of meals nobody can eat?' Heather grinned to show she was joking. 'Listen, I can think of half a dozen restaurants that'd snap you up.'

Leith smiled. 'I'll ignore that, I think.' She stood up. 'Anyway, he's promised me faithfully that we're taking a three-day break this weekend. Peppers at Terrigal. I can't wait.'

Heather was squinting up at her in the sunshine. 'You know what I'd do if I had no kids and a workaholic for a husband? '

'Tell me.'

'Amuse myself with a lover.' She nodded and smiled. 'A young lusty stud. The perfect distraction.'

Leith smiled and shook her head. 'You're a bad influence, Heather. Good thing I'm not easily corrupted.'

But her smile changed to a frown as she walked towards the house. She certainly wasn't looking for a lover. But in the last ten days, she'd had two phone calls from Paul. And for all her resolve about cutting things off, she had found herself enjoying speaking with him again. He had a way of really listening to her, of making her feel good about herself, a charm that was hard to resist.

He'd told her more about himself too. Had spoken about his two married sisters, his nephews and nieces, his parents. The latter were still alive, and he saw them regularly. There was something very reassuring, she thought, about a man who was so close to his family.

To her relief, the conversations hadn't led to any complications. Both times he'd rung off without any mention of wanting to see her again. And Leith could reassure herself she had nothing to feel guilty about.

It was Thursday morning, the day before she and David were due to leave for their break, when Paul rang again.

Leith was in the bedroom, her eyes aglow with anticipation as she packed the suitcase she'd dragged out from the storeroom as soon as David had left the house.

There was still a chill in the air, so she'd need a couple of warm cardigans, she had decided. And then something nice for the evenings. A pair of good walking shoes, too. She had found herself humming as she folded and packed. God, it was going to be wonderful! Three whole uninterrupted days. It'd be heaven.

When the phone rang, she had picked up the extension on her bedside table.

'Hallo, Leith speaking.'

He didn't need to say his name. She recognised that deep, modulated voice at once. And David rarely had a spare moment to call her during working hours.

'Paul ... how are you?'

'I'm fine. But I rang to find out how *you* are. Tell me what you're doing right at this very minute.'

She explained about the weekend at Peppers guest house.

'He's trying, Paul. He's trying to make it up to me. Even just three days will be good for us.'

There was a moment's silence before Paul Houston replied.

'A marriage needs nurturing, Leith, you're right about that. It's a continuing process. And it's good when both parties recognise that.' It was a strangely formal response, but then he changed the subject.

'Look, I'm really ringing to ask you a favour. I'm dying to see the Flemish exhibition at the Art Gallery. Only I hate to go alone to something like that. I'm wondering if I can persuade you to come with me one morning next week. A couple of hours out of your day, that's all.'

Leith fell silent with indecision. She'd made it clear, she thought, that she didn't want to go along that path, that there was no way she wanted to continue their meetings.

But then, she reasoned with herself, was there really any harm in merely spending a couple of hours, as he'd said, viewing an exhibition with a friend?

She took a deep breath, flipped a mental coin. It came down the way she knew it should.

'I'm sorry, Paul. I really wouldn't feel right about that. I told you the way I wanted to leave things between us. I hope you understand.'

'I'm a very understanding guy.' She heard his chuckle. 'Just thought I'd ask. If the answer's no, then I'll have to live with that, won't I? But listen, you have a great time this weekend. I'll be thinking of you and wishing you all the best.'

They said goodbye and, as she hung up, Leith

realised that he hadn't mentioned anything about talking to her again.

She didn't know whether that made her glad or sorry.

David had been dreading the moment, but better to tell her in person, he'd felt, than on the phone.

He'd made it home in time for dinner and waited until they'd finished eating. Now he faced her across the dining table and told her the bad news.

She stared at him in disappointment and disbelief.

'But you *promised*. You told me nothing could stop us going.'

'Darling,' he sighed, 'you know if there were any way I could get out of this I would. It's just impossible.'

'But there *must* be some way. Surely there's someone else who can handle it.'

'It's my company, Leith. The buck stops with me. And if I've got an angry client demanding to see me, then I've just got to wear it. The guy's flying in from WA. I've got to be here. I can't afford to let this deal fall through.'

She pushed herself up from her chair and looked down at him. 'And what about me, David?' Her voice was tight. 'Can you afford to let your marriage fall through? Do you realise how many nights I sit alone in this house? How many weeks I've had to spend by myself while you're somewhere out of the country? Don't you know how much I was looking forward to this weekend? To have you to myself. Just for once!'

He stood up, tried to take her in his arms. He'd expected her to be upset, but her vehemence took him aback.

Leith shrugged him off. 'You don't know what you're doing to me, David. I've tried to tell you but half the time you aren't even here to listen. Do you know what you're doing to this marriage?'

'I'm just asking you to be understanding, Leith. Just a little longer. Times are tough out there. I can't risk giving my competitors an inch. And I'm doing it for us. It's a sacrifice now so we can reap the benefits later.'

She swung round on him, her eyes dark with hurt and anger. 'Later? Do you know how patient I've tried to be because of *later*, David? But what if there is no *later*? Did you ever think of that?'

She swept past him and out of the room.

The next morning she was awake before he left the house. Unwilling to face him, she stayed in bed until she heard him drive away. Even then she didn't get up at once. Lying beneath the covers, Leith allowed the anger and disappointment of the evening before to seep back.

It wasn't fair, she thought bitterly. After all the days and nights she'd spent alone, how could he possibly have let anything change their plans? Three lousy days. Was that asking so much?

The problem, she told herself, was that lately David had started taking her for granted. That was the crux of it. She was always there when he came home, always the devoted wife, ready and available for whenever it suited him. But what about her needs? Why did everything else in his life have to take priority?

Still upset, she got up, washed her face and pulled her yoga mat out onto the patio. But even that couldn't relax her today. She was brimming over with resentment, with the unfairness of it all.

And she could think of only one way to make herself feel better.

She rang his mobile and could tell she'd surprised him.

'I've changed my mind, Paul. If the invitation's still open, I'd love to go with you to that exhibition.'

'Leith, that's great! You've really made my day.'

She could hear the delight in his voice. At least one man looks forward to my company, she thought with bitter satisfaction.

They made their arrangements. They'd meet outside the State Gallery at eleven the following Wednesday.

'What about lunch afterwards?' he suggested. 'Would you have time for a quick bite?'

Leith didn't hesitate. 'I've got all the time in the world.'

She wasn't sure if she'd managed to keep the bitterness out of her voice.

CHAPTER NINE

Although she hadn't had time for breakfast, Rory shook her head at the tray being offered by the cabin attendant.

'Just coffee, thanks.'

She felt too uptight to eat. Her belly was churning with guilt because she had made the decision to leave her baby son for three days in a row, because she'd sensed Ian fighting to hold back his resentment as he drove her to the airport.

When he'd lifted her suitcase out of the boot and set it beside her on the footpath, they'd looked at each other and she'd seen the disapproval in his eyes.

'Darling, it's only for a month.' She'd wanted their parting to be on a positive note. 'And I'll make it up to you, I promise.'

'Hopefully we'll manage.' She couldn't miss the lack of conviction in his voice. Then he'd lightly kissed her cheek. 'Good luck with the project.'

'Thanks.'

'I'll pick you up Friday, then. Seven fifteen, right?'

'Yes,' she'd nodded.

And she'd stood and watched as he'd quickly slipped into the driver's seat and headed back into the traffic. He hadn't turned to wave.

Now, as she sipped her cup of black coffee, Rory could imagine what he would have been thinking as he'd driven away. That it was she who had wanted a child, she who had insisted that their lives didn't have to change that much, that with the right sort of planning and organisation, a child would slot into their daily routine with the minimum of disruption.

She could only look back on her naivety in bewildered disbelief.

And all Ian would be able to see now was the fact that she'd shifted the responsibility onto him, had asked him to do more than his share so she could take up this major option in her own career.

With troubled eyes she stared out at the clouds. God, how she hated this burden of guilt! She felt as if it had attached itself to her like a carbuncle almost since the day Cam was born — because she'd been the one who had made the choice, wanted a child so badly that she'd eventually talked Ian into accepting the idea.

In recent months there had been more than one occasion when she'd doubted the wisdom of what she'd done. Having a child had changed their relationship in myriad ways. But what could she have done? The desire had welled inside her, impossible to ignore. She'd been ambushed by biology, and the ache for fulfilment had been almost physical in its force. What it meant was that, unlike every other major decision that had faced her in her life, this one had been made via her hormones, not her head. All that mattered was to fulfil the longing that gripped her with such startling fervour. To bear a child, a child by the man she loved, their own flesh and blood.

And for all the difficulties, she knew that Ian loved his son as much as she did. Things would get better, she reassured herself, when Cam was a little older, less dependent. Ian would enjoy him more when they were able to interact. Until then, it was a matter of patience and managing to cope.

She looked up as the chime sounded and the seatbelt sign came on. They were were approaching the landing in Melbourne.

With an effort, Rory pushed her troubled thoughts away.

It was a crisp, clear day, much colder than Sydney at this time of the year. From Tullamarine, she took a taxi straight to the office overlooking Albert Park. As she paid off the driver, Rory couldn't help remembering the last time she'd been in Melbourne. It had been before Cam was born. Looking back, she could hardly recognise the person she'd been then. Focused, confident, energetic. Her career and personal life both under control.

And at once she admonished herself for such negative thoughts. With the pressures and responsibilities waiting for her here, she couldn't afford to let herself go down that track.

She'd been expecting some reservations, resentment even, on the part of the local staff. It was only natural that they wouldn't be overly keen on having their prestigious project taken over by someone from head office.

One or two of the team were certainly cool, but the person she had to work most closely with, the art designer, appeared to have no problem with Rory as a replacement for the absent local editor.

'Look, I just want to bring this project in on deadline and make it the huge success I know it can be. That's all that matters, as far as I'm concerned.'

Antonella Grasso was short, with dark, curly hair and an intense, forthright manner that Rory warmed to at once. Her dedication to the project was obvious, and Rory guessed that she wasn't the sort of person to let inter-office politics damage the publication process in any way.

For the rest of the day the two of them tucked themselves away. They sat at a computer terminal and Rory was shown exactly how far along the line the project had progressed.

'I know you'll want to go over it again, but the text is mostly completed,' Antonella explained. 'It's a matter of lay-out now, making decisions on order of inclusion and on photographs, headings, captions, feeding the right stuff through to marketing. Elizabeth and I had only just started on all that when she fell ill.'

Rory nodded, suddenly very nervous as she began to comprehend the volume of material that awaited her attention.

Whatever happened, she told herself, she *had* to finish this in a month. She couldn't bear to imagine what Ian's reaction would be if it took any longer than that.

She was booked into a nearby hotel, and it was after six before she checked in. Antonella had offered to drive her, and she dropped Rory under the portico.

'Thanks a lot,' Rory smiled in at the car window as a porter took her suitcase from the boot.

'No problem.' The art designer leaned over from the driver's seat. 'You have a good night's rest, and I'll see you in the trenches tomorrow.'

Rory laughed. 'Don't worry, I'm heading for a shower, room service and an early night.'

'Try a double vodka as well, and tomorrow'll be a breeze.'

Still smiling, Rory walked into the hotel foyer. She was going to enjoy working with someone like Antonella.

Her room was on the tenth floor and, for a moment after she closed the door on the porter, she simply stood and absorbed what had become such a rare experience. Solitude. She had almost forgotten what that felt like. To be completely alone. No noise, no clutter, no demands.

It felt wonderful.

She unpacked her small case and, instead of a shower, opted for a bath, relishing the fact that she would actually have time to lie and relax. Sighing with pleasure, she slipped into the warm water. It was exactly what she needed after a day like today.

162

There was a telephone on the wall beside her and, for a brief moment, she thought about phoning Ian, but then decided against it. Not yet. She didn't feel ready to scratch her guilt straight away.

Afterwards, wrapping herself in one of the oversize towelling robes provided, she scrutinized the room service menu and ordered a light meal. While she waited she switched on the TV and found herself a drink in the well-stocked bar, smiling as she remembered Antonella's advice — only it was a G and T she opted for instead.

It was still only nine when she was finished eating and, dusting the crumbs off her hands, she finally picked up the phone and dialled home.

'It's me.'

'Hi, how'd it go?'

'Not too bad. The woman I'm working with seems fine. She spent the day giving me an overview of the project. I'm pretty sure we'll make it happen by deadline.' But she didn't want to dwell on that particular topic. 'How's Cam?'

'No dramas. Deb's been great. I spent half an hour with him before she put him down. I had a meeting tomorrow evening but managed to change it to Friday.'

'So you're not hating me too much?' She kept her tone light.

'As long as Deb doesn't come down with the flu or run off with a boyfriend to Queensland, we'll manage. I told you that.'

She laughed, glad he could make a joke of it. 'Deb's not that sort of girl ... thank God. Have you eaten yet?'

'Just making something now.'

'Then I'd better let you go. Kiss Cam for me. I'll save yours for when I see you Friday night.'

'That sounds like an eminently good idea.'

She rang off, pleased with the way the conversation had gone. He wasn't going to give her a hard time about it. Everything would work out fine.

She cleaned her teeth and decided to have an early night. Today was the easy part, the pressure would be on tomorrow. As she pulled back the covers and slipped into the cool, tightly tucked sheets, she realised how strange it felt to be alone in the vast bed. Much as she might relish this short interlude of solitude, she knew she would hate it as a permanent condition. She'd been with Ian too long now to ever be able to imagine how it would feel to be alone, to miss his love and companionship, his body next to hers every night. The idea was too awful to contemplate. She had seen what break-ups and divorce had done to several of her friends. If the same thing happened to her she'd be devastated, she thought, as she switched off the bed light.

But she felt totally secure with Ian, even without the legal sanction of marriage. The relationship, she knew, meant as much to him as it did to her, and a piece of paper wouldn't make any difference to that. All that really mattered was keeping each other happy. And that meant in bed as well as out.

For months after Cam's birth, sex had been the last thing on her mind. Poor Ian had had to be patient then, she knew. Even when they'd started doing it again, a lot of the time she had pretended

164

more interest and enjoyment than she'd really felt. But she realised the dangers of leaving a man unfulfilled. Especially a man as attractive as Ian still was. Tennis and running and windsurfing had kept him trim; his body was as lean and toned and muscular as a man fifteen years his junior.

And of course, she frowned in the dark, her own lack of discipline in that direction still worried her. The longer she put it off, she knew, the harder it was going to be when she finally got around to doing something about it.

Rory sighed. Well, didn't love mean acceptance? Until she found the time to do something about getting into shape again, Ian would just have to love her despite her loose thighs and softening breasts. After all, she wasn't twenty two, was she?

Without luggage to worry about, she realised the next morning that her hotel was within walking distance of the office.

Thankful for her warm jacket against the early chill, she walked through the gardens and stopped at a crossing on St Kilda Road, waiting for the lights to halt the stream of cars and the procession of crowded trams. The wide road, lined with soft green trees, reminded her of some European boulevard and suddenly, as she stood there, her blood quickened. She felt heady with a sense of freedom she hadn't experienced in too long a time, as if she'd been given her old life back again when she'd relished new experiences, new challenges, had confidence in her abilities. With greater eagerness she began to look forward to the day.

The hours passed quickly. The work was every bit as challenging as she'd envisaged, and she and Antonella worked with focused concentration, trying various lay-outs, rejecting others, sometimes each insisting on the merits of their own approach. The designer was every bit as forceful as Rory herself, yet they were always able to reach a compromise. It was one o'clock before they stopped for a quick snack at their desk, each loath to break the momentum of their task.

'I was worried, of course, but after this morning I can see you're definitely the right person for this.' Antonella gave her a considering look as she reached for another brimming sandwich. 'Decisive, great eye for detail, and that magic extra — instinct.'

'Well ... thank you.' Rory hid her surprise at the compliment. Such open and positive acknowledgement of a peer's talents was hardly an industry norm.

But then, she was coming to realise, Antonella was hardly someone who fitted that norm. Even the way she dressed, for example. Instead of the uniform black that was *de rigeur* in most publishing houses, she was dressed today in an attractive cream linen suit and high heels. Her dark hair hung thick and curly past her shoulders, and her make-up was perfect. Very feminine and glamorous, like some European princess, Rory thought, and it made her feel boringly cliched in her black pants and sensible shoes.

At seven-thirty they finally called it a day.

'God, I'm starving!' Rory exclaimed as she zipped up her briefcase.

166

'Me too. What are you doing for dinner?' Antonella was shutting down the computer.

'Hadn't thought about it.'

'Want to grab a bite? There're a couple of good places near where I live.'

'Where's that?'

'South Yarra.'

'Sure.' Rory was pleasantly surprised by the invitation. A second night of eating alone didn't have quite the same appeal, she realised.

'But only if it's not putting you out,' she added. 'You don't have to look after me.'

'No problem.' Antonella stood up, smiled at her. 'Come back for a drink first, and we can freshen up.'

The apartment was an eclectic mix of styles as interesting as Rory might have expected. High ceilings with ornate cornices, polished wooden floors overlaid by old, richly coloured rugs, walls covered in some mulberry-hued fabric, a sofa that was a carved Indian wedding bed strewn with large tassled pillows, an antique English writing desk next to a Javanese sideboard.

There were books and paintings everywhere, and Antonella left Rory to wander around as she prepared their drinks.

'What a wonderful place!' Rory exclaimed as she took the proferred glass. 'How long have you been here?'

'Almost three years. I don't think I'll ever shift,' Antonella answered as she dropped into a saggy wing chair.

'Looks like you've done a lot of travelling.'

'Soon as I graduated I took off. London, Europe, India, Nepal. The whole youth trip. My parents were horrified. They were the typical Italian immigrants who wanted their daughter to pass her time in some job for the year or so it would take to find a husband and "settle down."'

Rory noted the ironic emphasis.

'Not your plan?'

'God,' Antonella rolled her eyes, 'far from it! I wanted a *life*, not an existence in some genteel Melbourne suburb.'

'But you're back here now,' Rory pointed out.

'Without — note — husband or kids in tow.'

'Not part of the future plan?'

'Look, I'm thirty-seven. I've got a job I love, a home in my name, a good salary. Best of all, I've got freedom. No one trying to control my existence. I'm in charge of my own destiny, and that's the way I want to keep it.'

Rory was intrigued by the intensity of her response.

'And boyfriends? How do they cope with that?'

Antonella gave a wry, light laugh. 'They hate it. Because you know what? The less you need men, the more determined they are to prove you do. As long as a woman knows that, she can always call the shots.'

And on that rather ambiguous note, they finished their drinks and went out to eat.

On Friday evening her flight was late getting into Sydney. Ian brushed aside her apologies as he reached for her briefcase and kissed her warmly.

'Doesn't matter, you're here now. Let's just get you home in time before Cam goes to bed.'

'I can't wait to see him.'

It was true. Her arms ached to hold her son. She'd thought of little else as the plane neared home. As if she were stepping out of the compartment labelled 'career woman' and back into the one labelled 'mother'. Maybe, she mused, being away from home made the transition easier.

The traffic in and out of the domestic terminals was the usual Friday night catastrophe. Ian forced the Audi in front of another driver and was immediately subjected to a blast of horn and a gesture of abuse.

'It just gets worse, doesn't it?' she said.

'Yeah, let's just give it all away. Move to Tasmania tomorrow.'

'Or Port Douglas.' She joined in the joke they played out regularly in Sydney's snail-like traffic.

'Or Byron Bay.'

'What about Oodnadatta?'

He flashed her a grin. 'Now you're talking.'

Filled with contentment and relief, Rory gave a small smile as she looked out at the busy streets. What really mattered was the fact that he wasn't bearing a grudge.

❅

'Do you have to rush off now? What about a coffee?'

It was Judith's third meeting with Tony Kendall. As before, they'd spent a good hour and a half discussing her work and, by the end of that time, she felt her usual sense of inspiration. She looked up now as she fitted her manuscript pages back into their manila folder.

'Well...' She thought quickly. It was only just past eight-thirty. Greg was playing his usual Tuesday evening game of indoor cricket, and the boys wouldn't miss her.

'Sure,' she replied with a smile. 'Why not? Let's have a quick one.'

They found a corner table and a bored-looking waitress took their order.

Now that she was actually there, Judith started to feel nervous. She realised that she'd never been in this situation in all her years of marriage. Alone in a social situation with a man who wasn't known to both Greg and herself. It felt alien, strange. But, she told herself, she wasn't doing anything wrong. Her motives were totally innocent. Tony was merely a friend, someone with whom she shared a common interest. And she felt sure he had no ulterior motives either.

'It's coming along very, very well,' he said as he poured a sachet of sugar into his coffee. 'I can't believe the pace you're working at.'

Judith smiled at him over the top of her cup. 'Having your ongoing input has made all the difference. It keeps me focused, gives me the discipline to keep going.'

'Well, I have to say I can't help being envious. For me, the process of putting words on paper is painfully slow.'

Judith looked at him in surprise. He'd never

talked much about his own writing process. 'I — I never realised that. I thought it happened the same way for all writers.'

He gave her a wry grin. 'Unfortunately not. Otherwise, I could have written three times the number of books.'

'But your books sell well?'

He shook his head. 'Not well enough. It's taken a long while, but I've finally resigned myself to the fact that I'm never going to be good enough to make it to the next level.'

Judith stared at him in dismay. 'Oh, Tony, you can't think like that. I'm sure it's not true.' She didn't want to hear him talk like this. He was a *published* author. In her eyes he'd made it. She realised she didn't want to think of him as anything less.

'It's reality, Judith. I can't kid myself.' Then he smiled at her. 'That's why I get a thrill when I see the potential in some of the people I've taught. People like yourself. You don't know how much satisfaction it's giving me to help you.'

What she liked about Tony Kendall, she thought, was his utter *niceness*. She'd never met a man quite like him before. As she placed her cup back in its saucer, she said, 'Well, I really don't know how to thank you for all your time and interest. You've been amazingly generous to me.'

He gave a lazy grin. 'Oh, I might have helped a little, but I can see in your writing how driven you are with this story. It's pouring out of you.'

He paused for a moment, then added, 'I hope you won't think I'm being too personal, but there's a lot of you in Jo, isn't there, Judith? A lot of the same frustrations and yearnings?'

She felt her cheeks grow warm and, for a moment, didn't trust herself to answer. Was she that transparent? If her work were ever published, would everyone guess what Tony had guessed? That she longed to escape from the cage of her own home, to find the courage to begin her life again, to run away from a place where she was treated as invisible and not worthy of respect or concern or understanding.

Aware of her discomfort, he went on as if he'd read her thoughts. 'Don't worry ... it's only because I'm experienced. I know when writing is coming straight from the heart.'

She finally found her voice. Looking down into her empty cup, she said hesitantly, 'You're right, of course. I've drawn a lot from my own life.'

He put out his hand and she felt it cover her own. 'And don't ever lose that ability, Judith. Don't inhibit your emotions. Use them. All of them. The good and the bad. That's what'll keep your writing special.'

It was his gentleness that made the sudden tears well into her eyes. She couldn't remember a time when Greg had ever treated her with such utter tenderness.

Over a second cup of coffee, the conversation grew more personal and touched on the subject of their respective marriages. Tony had been divorced for eight years, Judith discovered. His wife, it seemed, hadn't been prepared to endure the scanty earnings of a struggling writer.

'She told me I'd never make it — and I guess time has proved her right. But I had to try. The desire to create just ate at me. I couldn't ignore it. If I had, the marriage would probably have died, anyway — I'd have been so resentful and frustrated.'

'Well, Greg hasn't ever tried to stop me. But he sneers at my efforts, at the time I'm putting into it, and tries to make me feel as if I'm neglecting him and the boys or my chores. But that's not true,' she said emphatically. 'I do what needs to be done around the house. The place isn't falling apart. What really irks him, I think, is that my writing is something he can't control. Something I do that he has no say in. The first time that's ever happened in all our years of marriage.'

Tony nodded. 'I've seen that happen before. When a woman starts to bloom in a new direction a lot of men are threatened. But I guess every relationship has its own pitfalls and difficulties. I know if I were ever tempted in that direction again, I'd be very, very careful.'

And, Judith said silently to herself, the woman who'd get you would be very, very lucky.

It was almost ten-thirty by the time she arrived home. She didn't need to use her key to let herself in. Greg was waiting for her by the open front door.

'Where have you been?' he demanded.

'You know where I've been. Working on my manuscript.' She moved past him into the hall, trying to fight off an irrational guilt. Why should she feel guilty? She hadn't done anything wrong.

'Don't tell me the library's open till this time of night!'

Her heart was thumping as he followed her into the kitchen. She should have kept an eye on the time, avoided a scene like this, but the conversation with Tony had totally engrossed her.

'We had a coffee later. There's nothing wrong with that.' A note of defensiveness had crept into her voice.

'Nothing, except the little crisis around here.'

Eyes widening in alarm, she swung around to face him, immediately thinking of the boys. 'What's happened?'

'Sari. I found him bleeding in the gutter. Saw him in my headlights as I drove in. Somebody'd obviously hit him and not bothered to stop.'

'Sari!' Her relief that nothing had happened to her sons was replaced by her anxiety for her pet. 'Is he okay? Where is he?'

'I took him to the vet. He was in a bad way.' His voice lost a little of its edge. 'You should have been here, Judith.'

She took a step towards him. 'Well, is he going to be all right?'

'There was no option. He had to be put down.'

Her hand flew to her mouth. Oh, no. Not Sari, who sat by her feet every night as she worked on her dream, whom she'd brought home as a tiny mewing ball of fluff five years ago, and who so often seemed her only source of comfort in this house of indifferent male strangers.

'But there must have been something they could do!'

Her husband wouldn't meet her gaze.

'His leg was broken in two places. D'you know what that would have cost to fix? The vet told me. Almost five hundred dollars.'

A third of the cost of your golf clubs, the incongruous thought occurred to her.

Her breathing had grown very rapid. So Sari might have been saved, except that Greg hadn't wanted to spend the money.

Reaching out, she gripped her husband's arm, her fingers biting into his flesh with a strength she could never have imagined as her own. As she stared with loathing into his startled face, she managed to force the words past the anger that strangled her throat.

'I'll never forgive you for this. *Never*!'

Then, releasing her grip, she pushed past him out of the room.

That night Judith slept in the spare single bed in her work room. Except that she was too agitated to sleep.

She knew she was at a turning point. Two events that evening had finally brought to a head all her years of frustration, loneliness and resentment. Firstly, there had been the closeness she had felt with Tony, and then Greg's callous indifference to how much Sari had meant to her.

The comparison between the two men, the difference in how she felt in each one's presence stood in stark relief. I can't do it any longer, she told herself. I can't waste my life like this. You only get one chance, and I've already squandered too much of my allotted time.

She had gone into marriage with such high hopes, never dreaming for a moment that the love for her husband would ever die. But tonight she had hated Greg. The incident with Sari had been only one more piece of cruel evidence of how little he cared for her or her feelings. But it had tipped the scales, forced her finally to face the fact of her own cowardice. How much longer could she go on turning a blind eye to the way he treated her? How much more self-respect did she have to lose before she said, 'Enough!'?

As she lay sleepless in the dark, Judith knew that she had to get out, even though the practicalities seemed insurmountable. Other women managed to do it and survive, and she would too.

Even if the thought of being alone terrified her.

CHAPTER TEN

'Leith, I'm sorry ... I didn't mean to barge in on you like this, but I didn't know who else to turn to. Everyone else I know is a friend to both of us. It — it just didn't seem right to put them in that position.'

Concerned by her old schoolfriend's obvious distress, Leith laid a soothing hand on her arm. 'Jude, please, you don't have to apologise. I'm just glad you thought to call me. You know I'll do anything I can to help.'

Judith had rung that morning from work, praying Leith would be at home. She was desperate to talk this out with someone, but loath to confide in those friends who were close to both her and Greg. Not only because it would make it awkward for them, but because she wanted to speak to someone who would be truly objective, who could give her impartial and unbiased advice about the enormous step she was considering. It was then she thought of Leith. She would understand. Leith would help her.

Barely able to make it through the day, she'd left work early and was now sitting in her old schoolfriend's perfectly coordinated sunroom, her coffee growing cold in front of her as she poured out her misery. She wasn't normally a weeper, had grown used to keeping her emotions to herself over the years, but now, in the face of Leith's quiet sympathy, that control had finally deserted her.

'I've tried, Leith ... For so long. I told myself it didn't matter how much everything had changed. That the important thing was we were still together, had two healthy kids, a nice home, everything we needed materially ... But, I'm not going to lie to myself any longer. I need *more* than that! I know that now. I can't go on like this. I just can't!'

Leith waited as Judith reached for a tissue and blew her nose. Then she asked, 'I guess it goes without saying that you've tried to talk to him?'

Judith rolled her damp eyes in response. 'Oh, God, tried and tried and tried. Made absolutely no bloody difference. Because he doesn't *see* there's a problem! As far as Greg's concerned, life is great. He can't understand why I'm not happy or what I'm going through.'

Leith nodded in sympathetic agreement. 'I know what you mean. You try to tell them what's wrong, what it's doing to you, but men often have absolutely no idea how far they're pushing you.'

As she spoke, Leith couldn't help thinking how ironic it was that Judith should have turned up today.

Twenty-four hours before she was due to meet Paul, keeping the date that she had justified to herself on the grounds of her own husband's neglect. It made it easy to empathise with her friend's situation.

'It's taken me far too long,' Judith was speaking again, 'but I've finally realised that Greg isn't going to change. Which means it's up to me. And I've made up my mind. I'm getting out. I just wanted to talk it all through with someone, get things straight in my head, decide what to do first.'

'What about money, Jude? Is that going to be a problem?'

Judith's expression tightened. She had her job, of course, and her name was on the deeds of the house. But when it came to everything else — their investments, life insurances, superannuation — she felt certain it would come to a fight. She knew Greg too well to imagine that he would agree to play fair, despite the fact that she'd contributed all her working life to building up their assets.

She said as much now to Leith. 'I guess it'll come down to a face off with the lawyers,' she shrugged. 'In the meantime, thank God, I've got my job to fall back on.'

'What about the boys? How d'you think they'll handle it?' Leith felt she had to make Judith consider the situation from every angle.

'The boys?' Judith's voice took on a hard, sarcastic edge. 'Apart from needing their creature comforts provided, they're just as indifferent to me as their father. If you want to know the truth, they'll probably be glad to get me off their backs.'

Leith was touched by pity at the bitterness in her friend's tone. Poor Judith. Not only had marriage disappointed her, but it seemed her children had, too. At least, she told herself, she didn't have that to face as well.

'Well, are you sure *you* want to be the one to leave the house?' she asked. 'From what I hear, it's not always the smartest move.'

Resolutely, Judith shook her head. 'Do you know how much I hate that huge place? It's what Greg wanted, a show-piece to impress his mates. I've done more than my share of paying it off, but believe me, it was never my idea of a home.'

Leith heard the vehemence in her friend's voice. It was clear that no matter what the risk to her future financial security, staying put was not an option. Leith only hoped it was a decision Judith wouldn't come to regret.

'If that's how you feel, then the first thing you've got to do is find somewhere to live.'

Judith shook her head and gave a small, mirthless laugh. 'Can you believe it? I'm forty-two and this'll be the first time in my life I'll have lived alone.'

Again Leith felt her heart squeeze in sympathy. Poor Judith. No doubt she was making the right decision, but how must it feel to start all over again after so many years of marriage? She couldn't begin to imagine herself in the same position.

Forcing a smile, she gave her friend a quick hug. 'Don't worry, darling, I'll help you. We'll find you somewhere nice as soon as you decide you're ready to look.' After all, she thought, she had all the time in the world for helping a friend in need.

With a glance at the time, Leith saw it was almost six. 'Now listen,' she said more cheerfully, 'what about staying for dinner? David's going to be late as usual, so it'll be just you and me. I'll make something light. You can stay, can't you?'

Judith thought of Greg and the boys coming home and expecting their dinner on the table as usual. Well, damn it, she told herself. They'd have to start getting used to waiting on themselves.

'Thanks,' she replied, 'I'd really love to stay. Talking like this has helped me so much. It really has.'

All she had to do now was keep her resolve and make her plans for escape.

Leith made cheese and ham omelettes with a tossed salad. For dessert she cut up fresh fruit.

'No wonder you stay so slim,' Judith said as she speared another slice of kiwi fruit. She felt calmer now. Talking everything through with Leith had really helped her to straighten things out in her mind. She was glad now she'd made that spontaneous call.

'Well, I've always preferred to eat four or five small meals a day rather than sitting down to something massive,' Leith answered.

Judith gave a resigned sigh. 'When I'm home alone, I nibble all the time. Or maybe nibble's not the right word for it. I wolf down chocolate, biscuits, ice cream. I don't have to be hungry, there's just this urge to fill myself up.' She wiped her fingers on the Laura

Ashley napkin. 'Of course, I've figured it out by now. They're always writing about it in those women's magazines. One of the major reasons females stuff themselves is for emotional comfort. Food becomes a substitute for all that's missing emotionally in their lives. Look at poor Princess Diana for the perfect example.' Judith sighed. 'But it's one thing to understand the reasons, another to do something about it.'

'But you're not that much overweight, Jude.'

'Six or seven kilos.' Judith grimaced. 'Just enough to make me feel blah and matronly.'

'Then,' Leith said brightly, 'maybe making this change in your life will help shed the weight, too. A new beginning all round.'

Judith made no response. Her eyes met Leith's and she finally said quietly, 'But it's not really going to be easy, is it, Leith? Any of it?'

She knew the answer, yet somewhere in the back of her mind, she took comfort from the fact that someone like Tony Kendall was in her life.

They were just about finished tidying the kitchen when they heard David's car pull into the garage.

'Nine-thirty...' With a frown Judith glanced at her watch. 'Is he always this late?'

'Sometimes later.' Leith kept her voice neutral. The last thing Judith needed was to be confronted with someone else's problems.

'I guess that's how it is when you run your own business. It can't be easy on him.'

As she wiped her hands on a tea towel, Leith

found herself momentarily irritated by Judith's reply. What about some sympathy for *her* situation?

Before she could reply, the kitchen door opened and David walked in, jacket flung over his shoulder, a heavy file under one arm. He smiled a welcome as he dropped both on a nearby chair.

'Well, hallo, am I interrupting a girls' tete-a-tete?'

Judith noticed how he slid an arm around his wife and kissed her warmly on the lips.

'I was just about to leave,' Judith answered with a smile.

Leith made the introductions. 'This is Judith Burton darling. Remember I told you? My old schoolfriend from the reunion?'

'Of course.' David put out his hand. 'Delighted to meet you. I hope you're not going to rush off before I can find out all about my wife's schoolgirl antics?'

Judith noted the expression in his eyes as he grinned back at Leith. He really loves her, she thought in envious admiration. It was written all over his face.

'Sit down and I'll make some more coffee,' Leith suggested as she picked up the kettle. 'You can stay a bit longer, can't you, Jude? I'd hate him to think he'd missed out on digging up some of my dim, dark secrets.'

When Judith agreed, Leith was filled with a sense of relief. Somehow, with what she had planned for tomorrow, she didn't want to spend too much time alone this evening with David. Didn't want to look into her husband's eyes and remember that the next day she was meeting another man, a man who made her feel special and wonderful.

Judith stayed for another half hour. She found Leith's husband easy to like. He was attractive, of course, but what impressed her so much more was his warmth and good humour, his obvious feeling for his wife and his interest in a woman he'd never met before. It was clear he'd had a long and demanding day — the lines of tiredness were etched on his face — but he could still find the energy to sit and chat.

Judith couldn't help making comparisons. She couldn't imagine Greg ever taking the time to do the same with any of her friends, unless of course — she corrected herself — there might be some business connection to his advantage.

When she finally said goodnight, both David and Leith walked her to her car. As she drove away with a final wave, her last image was of the two of them standing together arms around each other's waists.

There are some happy marriages, she thought.

Leith was one of the lucky ones.

❋

Her bed was covered in discarded clothes. Leith had changed half a dozen times before finally settling on the pale blue linen suit and ivory silk shirt.

All morning her belly had been tight with a mixture of excitement and nerves. When David had asked what she had planned for the day, she'd been unable to meet his eyes.

'Nothing much. Lunch in town. With a friend.'

Even to her own ears, her voice had sounded tight and strained, but he hadn't seemed to notice.

'Enjoy yourself then, darling,' he had replied,

giving her a goodbye kiss. As he'd headed for the door, he'd added over his shoulder, 'I'll be home for dinner. Hopefully around seven.'

Leith had sat immobile at the breakfast table until the sound of his car had disappeared down the drive.

She knew she should pick up the phone at once, call Paul's number and tell him that she wasn't going to meet him today. Or any day.

But then the memory of those days and nights of rejection and loneliness returned, as well as her anger at David's refusal to do anything to change things. Why *should* I feel guilty? she thought defensively. If David neglects me, why shouldn't I amuse myself any way I can?

There was no harm in having lunch with a friend.

She took a cab into the city, saving herself the worry of parking. Paul was waiting for her by the gallery entrance, smiling as she walked towards him, looking drop-dead handsome in a dark suit and patterned yellow silk tie.

'Leith.' He took her hand in his. 'You always look wonderful. I'm just so happy you could make it.'

His lips brushed lightly against her cheek, and she felt herself blush like a schoolgirl. Not so much at the compliment, as with trepidation that somewhere among the people in the foyer, there might be someone who knew her.

'I was looking forward to it,' she replied, still flustered.

He didn't seem to notice and, unselfconsciously keeping hold of her hand, he led her inside.

'I've already bought us a program. They've got about a dozen Vermeers. I've always been fascinated by those scenes of domestic life.'

Paul had called a cab on his mobile, and it was waiting when they emerged from the gallery close to two hours later. They drove only a short distance before pulling up in front of one of the city's better-known restaurants.

'One of my favourites,' Paul said as he helped her out onto the sidewalk. 'I eat here at least three times a week,'

Leith was feeling a lot more relaxed. The exhibition had been interesting, and she couldn't help but be impressed by Paul's knowledge of art. She'd learned a lot as they'd slowly made their way around the Flemish masters.

'How do you like living in the city?' she asked as they stepped into the restaurant's cool foyer. He'd told her he lived in a restored art deco building just behind Macquarie Street.

'Love it. The convenience is wonderful, everything I want right at my front door.'

The next moment they were being greeted by a short, dapper man with jet black hair and a neat moustache.

'Ah, Mr Houston, how nice to see you again!' The accent was European, the manner effusive and welcoming. 'You and the beautiful lady come with me, please. Your favourite table is ready for you.'

'Thank you, Costa.'

Their table was by the window and offered a glimpse of the harbour and gardens. Leith ordered a main course only, veal limone, while Paul chose the more hearty osso bucco. While they waited, he talked her into a glass of Dom Perignon, and then ordered a bottle of wine to accompany their meal.

Leith was careful to restrict herself to only two glasses of the semillion but, even so, combined with the champagne, she could still feel the effects.

'Thank God, I came in by cab,' she said as the waiter cleared their plates. 'I hardly ever drink at lunchtime, it goes straight to my head.'

'So,' Paul gave her a teasing look, 'you're already accusing me of leading you astray?'

'Of course! You're totally guilty.'

'But you're enjoying yourself, aren't you?' His fingers began to gently caress her hand, where it rested on the starched white cloth.

She was. It had been a wonderful few hours. Paul was so attentive. His focus was only on her, as if no one else existed for him, and Leith couldn't help feeling flattered.

'It's been wonderful,' she said, smiling at him. 'I guess it's really helped me to forget my troubles.'

His expression changed and she saw his frown.

'Is it still difficult for you?' he asked. 'At home, I mean.'

She sighed and nodded, then found herself telling him how she had felt about the long weekend break that had never happened.

'I just can't seem to make him understand what it's doing to our marriage. Every time it happens, every time he lets me down like that, I feel less and less important to him — as if everything else has priority but me.'

Paul shook his head, and she felt his fingers tighten on her own. 'I can't believe any man could treat you like that. Doesn't he know what a prize he's got? If you were mine, I'd make you feel the most important woman in the world. I'd never let anything get in the way of our time together.'

She stared back at him, saw the intensity in his eyes. And her own reaction frightened her. This man makes me feel utterly beautiful and desirable, she thought. He makes me fly . . .

'Look,' Paul gave a quick glance at his watch, 'it's only just on three. Would you have time for a quick look at my apartment? It's just around the corner. I'd love you to see the place.'

He looked at her expectantly and, for a moment, Leith hesitated. She was aware of some instinct deep inside her that told her she should refuse the invitation. It wasn't that she didn't trust Paul. They were friends. But that didn't mean she would feel right about visiting his apartment.

Yet the lightness in her head, her feeling of warm contentment and enjoyment of his company made it too easy to ignore that instinct.

'Only for a little while then,' she answered with a smile.

'It's fabulous!'

Leith stood in the middle of the spacious living room and took in the high, creamy ceilings and the grain of the dark, polished floors, the exquisite ornate lamp sconces and the warm glow of the walnut cabinets. In actual fact, she found the place too stark for her liking, but she could appreciate the taste and skill that had created it.

'*And* you can see the harbour!' she exclaimed. As she moved over to the row of windows, she still felt light-headed from the alcohol. Another coffee would do her good.

'I knew you'd like it.'

Paul had come up behind her and she was intensely aware of his closeness. The next moment she felt his hand slide under her hair and begin to gently stroke her neck.

At once Leith tensed at the intimacy of the gesture. Her breath quickened and she knew she should push him away, but the gentle touch of his fingers was irresistible.

'Do you know how wonderful it feels to touch you?' His mouth was close to her ear and she felt his warm breath as he whispered the words.

Her every nerve seemed to come alive, and suddenly she realised that in some dark, subconscious part of her, she had been yearning for this moment.

Only now that it had happened she knew she had to get away from here at once.

'Please, Paul —' She began to turn around, but his arms encircled her from behind, and his words were softly seductive against her hair.

'Leith ... oh, Leith, I really meant it when I said I only wanted to be friends. You've got to believe that. But every time I speak to you, it's harder and harder to ignore what's happening to me … I think about you constantly, you're always in my mind. You can't imagine how I was looking forward to today. I haven't slept, could barely eat. All that mattered was getting through the time in between so I could be with you again.'

Releasing his hold, he slowly turned her around to face him. 'I can't help it, Leith.' His eyes were dark with emotion. 'You're everything I've ever dreamt of in a woman. I want to protect you, care for you, do anything in my power to make you happy.'

She forgot to breathe. Overcome by the sheer intensity of his emotion, she stared mutely back into his handsome face. In that instant she felt totally loved, in awe of her own sense of utter completeness. This is how it is meant to be, she told herself in wonder. This is what she longed for, what David had once given her and, for too long now, had denied her.

Tears welled into her eyes. She felt as if she were drowning in emotion. Oh how she needed to be loved like this! She needed it so much.

Then he was drawing her close, and her heart fluttered wildly in her chest as she felt the length of his body against her own. His lips crushed on hers, and she opened her mouth to share the savagery of desire.

When she awoke, the dying sun was striping the room through the slanted wooden shutters.

For a moment, as she blinked awake, Leith had no idea where she was. Disoriented, all she knew was that her mouth felt as dry as old paper, and her right temple was throbbing. She felt awful.

But not as awful as she felt a second later when she suddenly realised where she was and what had transpired. With her heart racing, she stared wide-eyed at the sleeping man beside her. Paul lay on his back, one arm flung backwards. The rumpled sheet had fallen to one side, and she could see he was completely naked. As naked as herself.

Oh, dear God... With frightening clarity, she recalled the feverish kisses, the move into the bedroom, the swift discarding of their clothes.

And how truly wonderful it had felt when he'd made love to her ...

With an involuntary moan of distress, she swung her legs out of the bed. Her head throbbed more painfully as she bent down to grope for her underwear on the floor.

Standing up, she began to dress in frenzied haste. She had to get out of here. If she were lucky, she'd manage it without waking him.

But she wasn't going to be lucky ...

'Leith ...' The low murmur made her pause and turn to look at the man in the bed.

Paul was smiling at her sleepily. 'You weren't going to rush away, were you, sweetheart? Not before I told you how wonderful that was?'

Leith could barely trust herself to speak.

'It should never have happened, Paul. I should never have come here.' Breathless with agitation, she turned away, grabbing up her jacket that hung over the back of a chair. She had no memory of placing it there, she realised, as with fumbling fingers, she pushed her arms into the sleeves.

'Leith . . .' She saw his smile disappear as he swung out of bed and reached for his trousers.

Crossing the room towards her, he attempted to draw her into his arms, his expression soft and understanding.

'Oh, my darling, you mustn't feel guilty. There's no need for that. Not when two people love each other.'

But guilt was exactly what she felt. And shame. And confusion. Avoiding his embrace, she pulled away, hurriedly trying to finish buttoning her jacket. Vehemently, she shook her head. 'This is never going to happen again, Paul. Never.'

She wouldn't let him drive her home, and the ten minutes she had to wait for the taxi to arrive seemed endless.

'Look, you're upset now, I can see that,' he said quietly as she stood by the window, keeping an impatient eye on the street below. 'I'll give you a call tomorrow, we'll —'

She swung on him in alarm. 'No, Paul . . . you mustn't. You mustn't call me. Ever again.'

A horn sounded in the street below. With relief she grabbed her handbag and headed for the door.

'Leith, we can't leave it like this.' He was following her across the room.

She didn't answer. All she wanted was to escape, to be left alone to face the enormity of what she had just allowed to happen.

As she reached for the door handle, he clutched her arm and she was forced to look at him, view the anguish that marred his perfect features.

'Leith, listen to me. What happened here this afternoon was something very, very special. Neither of us can pretend it wasn't.' His eyes were locked on hers. 'Remember what you're going home to. You deserve so much more. And I can give it to you, everything you're looking for. All I'm asking is that you give me that chance.'

For a long silent moment, she stared back at him. Then the impatient beep from outside made him release his hold.

'No, Paul ... no...' All she could do was shake her head in anguish.

She pulled the door open and was gone.

She couldn't believe she'd let it happen, was appalled at what she'd done.

As she stood under the showerhead in her own bathroom, her tears mingled with the flow of the warm water. She knew now she should never have gone to Paul's apartment. It had been a terrible mistake, especially given the fact that she'd been drinking. At the best of times, she had a low tolerance for alcohol, and the wine, she knew, had served to loosen her inhibitions.

But if she were being totally honest with herself, she knew she couldn't sheet all the blame in that direction alone. Her attraction to Paul had been strong from the start, and she'd willingly and recklessly exposed herself to the danger by agreeing to see him again.

Never, never, never would it happen again, she vowed fiercely as she stepped out of the shower and wrapped herself in a satin-edged towel. If he ever dared to ring her again, she would make that utterly clear.

With one hand she wiped away the mist on the bathroom mirror and studied her bare face in the glass. Her eyes were red and swollen, and she felt that her tension and strain were frighteningly obvious. Her belly clenched in panic. Why, tonight of all nights, did David have to be coming home early? Would he be able to tell that something was wrong? Would he sense her betrayal?

In the bedroom, she slipped on a pair of slim-fitting pants and a light sweater, then did the best she could with make-up. Somehow she was going to have to act as if nothing were wrong. As if what she had done had never occurred.

Automaton-like, she prepared a meal, but the moment she heard David's car in the drive, she felt her nervousness increase and knew she couldn't face the evening that lay before her. How could she calmly sit across from him, eat her meal, ask him about his day — all the while dreading any questions about her own? They'd been married too long for David not to guess when something was wrong.

She took the only way out that was open to her.

Her heart squeezed as she accepted his welcoming kiss on her cheek.

'Something smells good,' he looked over her shoulder where she stood at the range top, a deliberate ploy to avoid his eyes. 'I could do with a home-cooked meal for a change.'

'Darling,' she busied herself stirring a pot that didn't need to be stirred. 'I hate to tell you, but I've got a splitting head. It's just come on me this last half hour or so. I think I'm going to have to lie down.'

'That's not like you.' She could hear the concern in his voice. 'What brought that on?'

'I don't know.' Still she kept her back to him. 'Everything's ready here,' she said, lifting the pot and turning off the hot plate. 'I'm just sorry I'll have to leave you to eat alone.'

'Don't worry about me. What about you? Shall I bring you an aspirin?'

Finally she had to turn and face him. 'I've already taken a couple.' She wiped her hands on a tea towel, trying to avoid making eye contact. 'I think if I lie down, I'll be okay.'

'Maybe you should have an early night.'

She nodded, relief seeping through her. For tonight, at least, she would escape his scrutiny.

'Yes, I think I will.'

The next day was Friday. Leith stayed in bed until she heard the sound of David leaving for work. Her sleep had been restless; her guilt and emotional turmoil had made sure of that. Again and again, her thoughts kept returning to what had happened. How could she have been such a fool? Why had she allowed herself to go to the apartment of a man she was so attracted to? It had been asking for trouble.

Thick-headed with fatigue, she finally rose and dressed and, after a cup of tea, left the house to pick up some groceries. Her mobile rang just as she was unpacking her trolley at the checkout.

Her throat tightened. It was Paul.

He didn't bother with a preamble. 'Leith, I know you told me not to call, but I have to talk to you. I know you're upset, but we can't just —'

Quickly she interrupted, trying to keep her voice steady. 'Paul, I can't talk now. And, anyway, there's nothing to talk about.' She was acutely aware that the young checkout girl was listening to her every word. 'I meant what I said yesterday. So, please,' she said with emphasis, 'don't call me again. Please.'

With shaky fingers, she switched off her phone.

It was half an hour later and she was stowing away her groceries in the kitchen when the phone beside her rang.

'Leith, please...' She was taken aback to hear his voice. 'Don't hang up. I need to talk to you. We've got to talk this through. Both of us.'

'Paul, please, I said —' Her voice shook.

'Listen to me, Leith.' He was speaking quickly, urgently. 'Yesterday was nothing to be ashamed of. For you to do what you did, I know you can't love your husband. But you're longing for love, Leith, I've always seen that. Only he can't give it to you.' She heard him draw a deep breath. 'You *can't* go on living like that, untrue to yourself. If you let me, I'll make you the happiest woman in the world. Nothing and no one will ever come between us.'

The sheer forcefulness of his tone stunned her into a momentary silence.

She finally found her voice. 'Paul, you don't understand. I've told you how I feel about David. I could never leave him. We might have our problems, but ...'

He interrupted her, his voice low and intense. 'Do you know how much I hate hearing you fool yourself like that? You're beautiful, sweet, sensual. Do you really want to waste your life with a man who'll never appreciate what you're offering him? I can't force you to change your mind, but I want you to know I'm always going to be here. Because sooner or later, I'm sure of it, you're finally going to let me show you what real love is. I'm surer of that, Leith, than I've ever been of anything in my life.'

And before she could begin to reply, he said a soft goodbye and hung up.

Her nerves were stretched to breaking point for the rest of the day as she fought to put those confronting words out of her mind.

But the more she tried, the more confused and upset she became. Could Paul be right? Had she really stopped loving David? Is that why she had ended up in bed with another man? The most disturbing aspect of all was that, much as she might try to deny it to herself, she was forced to admit she had found a deep and sensual pleasure in the lovemaking she had shared with Paul. Could she really have responded like that if she were still committed to her marriage?

Her doubts continued to plague her, and for the rest of the day, every time the phone rang, she feared it might be Paul. It was tempting to let the machine answer, for today at least, but she knew she couldn't do that if his calls continued. Sooner or later, David would be bound to catch one of the messages.

It was almost one when the phone rang again, and she picked it up with trepidation, only to hear her husband's voice.

'Oh, David ... how are you?' She let out her breath in a sigh of relief.

'I'm ringing to see how *you* are, darling. Headache gone?'

'Yes, yes. I'm fine.'

'Good. I'm glad about that. And listen, I'm trying to make it home early again. We're seeing the Barneses tonight, aren't we?'

Leith realised that in all the turmoil of the last twenty-four hours, the dinner party with friends had completely slipped her mind.

'Yes.' She checked the desk calendar beside the phone where she had written the details. 'Seven-thirty they're expecting us.'

'I'll get away as soon as possible.'

✳

As it turned out, he made it with just twenty minutes to get ready. Leith had his clothes laid out in readiness on the bed and, as he entered the house, he kissed her on the lips and handed her a soft, flat, beautifully wrapped package.

'For you, darling. To make sure you're feeling better.' He smiled at her. 'Now let me get at that shower.'

Left alone in the bedroom, Leith unwrapped the expensive paper. There, folded in gold-edged tissue paper, lay a beautiful silk and lace lingerie set.

As she stared at the gift, she felt her cheeks grow warm with guilt and confusion. She knew David would have sent his secretary to buy it, but still it meant he had thought of her. He often surprised her like this.

Slowly refolding the expensive gift, she wished she could make him understand. Of course she appreciated the thought, but it was her husband's time and company that were the gifts she longed for most of all.

Although she tried her best, she knew she wasn't very good company that evening. She was too much on edge, too distracted, to enjoy either the meal or the company. She longed to get away, but it was close to midnight before they finally said their goodbyes. In the car on the drive home, David made it clear he'd noticed that she wasn't herself.

'You seemed very quiet tonight, darling. Are you feeling all right?'

'Just a bit tired, I guess.'

'Perhaps you're coming down with something.'

Leith looked out at the quiet, suburban streets and nodded. 'Maybe that's it.'

At home as they undressed and prepared for bed, she felt sick with tension. She was dreading the possibility that David might want to make love to her. How could she bear to feel his hands, taste his lips, accept his body into her own while the memory of her betrayal was etched with such painful clarity in her mind?

Stalling as long as she could, she finally slipped into the bed beside him. At once David moved towards her, curling his body against her own.

'I know you're tired, my sweet,' he whispered against her hair. 'We'll leave it until some other time.'

In the darkness, she almost cried with relief.

It was four days later when he phoned her again.

'I'm missing you so much, Leith. I can't concentrate on anything. All I can think of is how I long to be with you and take care of you.'

'Paul ... don't,' she said desperately. 'Don't talk to me like that.' Cordless phone in hand, she paced nervously as she spoke. 'And please, you mustn't call here. It can't go on. You've got to understand that. I'm not walking out on my marriage. It might take some work to fix it, but I'm not walking out.'

Still he was insistent. 'I hear what you're saying, Leith, but all I want to do is keep in touch, to let you know how I feel, to remind you that there's a man who really does understand everything you're longing for, someone who will always put you first.'

Her fingers tightened around the receiver. God, what was happening to her? She knew she should hang up. Yet another part of her wanted him to keep talking to her like this. Why did he make her feel this way? Why?

'Paul, please don't do this to me. It's over. It can't go on. You have to accept that.'

As soon as she hung up, she burst into tears.

For the rest of the day, her thoughts were preoccupied with what she had to do to escape the dilemma that now threatened her marriage.

Tonight, whatever time David came home, she

decided, she'd sit him down and *make* him listen. She'd do everything in her power to convince him that things had to change. That he couldn't leave her alone so much. That they had to get their lives back in balance. That there were more important things in life than clients and deals and making money.

She'd make him see that the bond in a marriage was kept strong by communication and intimacy, and that theirs had been seriously eroded by his constant absences.

She would even hint at the fact that living separate lives could pose a serious threat to their marriage. And hope that he would heed her warning.

Then she would insist that they take a holiday, a proper holiday — two weeks at least, and as soon as possible. To get their relationship back on track, to rekindle the spark they were so close to losing. Because she was rational enough to see that a large part of her attraction to a man like Paul was due to her feelings of neglect and rejection. If David had taken notice of her before this, made a real effort to change the things she'd begged him to change, the situation with Paul would never have occurred.

As well, the two weeks away would also keep her out of Paul's reach, show him that she meant what she'd said about sticking with her marriage. And with the problems between herself and David resolved, she'd come back stronger, more able to resist any temptation that would endanger her marriage.

Only it didn't work out as she'd planned.

When David came home, she waited for him to change, pouring them both a drink, but before she could begin to say what she had sorted out in her mind, it was David who got in first.

'Darling, I know it's not going to make me popular, but something's come up.'

He stood, propped against the kitchen bench, his expression apologetic.

'What is it?'

With a sigh, he put his glass down beside him. 'I'm afraid I've got to spend some time on that project in Perth.'

Leith felt her heart grow cold.

'How long?' She couldn't believe it. It was happening again. Before she'd even had a chance to talk things through with him.

'Three months, I'm afraid. And it's urgent. I've got to leave sometime next week.'

His eyes pleaded with her for understanding, but he saw her expression change. Standing up, he moved towards her, put a hand on her arm. 'Darling, I'm sorry. I know how awful it is for you. I hate it, too. I'll try to get home when —'

With an abrupt, vicious gesture, she shook off his hand. The sudden contradiction to how she had envisaged the evening acted as a trigger to all the months of her pent-up hurt and anger.

'*Three* months!' She faced him with blazing eyes. 'How *can* you? How can you do this to me? How long do you expect me to go on living like this? Don't you *see* what you're doing to this marriage?'

'Leith, please, darling. I've got no —'

But she continued as if he hadn't spoken. 'No, David, *you* listen! Just for once you listen! And let me tell you exactly what you're doing to this relationship.'

She took a deep breath. 'Last week I slept with another man.' Her voice trembled with emotion. 'A man who has time for me, who pays attention to me, who tells me I'm wasting my life with a husband who's forgotten I exist!' Angry tears filled her eyes. 'A husband who puts me after every other damn thing in his life!'

For a long moment he made no reply as the significance of her words sunk in. Then, with a pitying look, he shook his head. 'Leith, darling, you don't have to lie to me, to try to scare me. I know how difficult it's been for you. If there were anything —'

'I'm not lying!' She was furious that even in this he was refusing to take her seriously. 'It *happened*, David. I've tried to warn you. Over and over. I begged you not to keep neglecting me. That's why it happened. That's why I ended up in bed with another man!'

She stopped then, her chest heaving with emotion, aware that the colour had drained from his face.

In the silence that followed, he stared at her, his eyes never leaving her own. The pain and shock distorted his features and, in that instant, Leith felt her anger ebb away. The hurt and disbelief she saw on her husband's face made her wish with all her heart that she could suck back her angry, impetuous, wounding words.

'Who ...? Who is it?' His voice was raw and unsteady. Now that he was convinced of the truth of what she was telling him, he wanted to know the details. No matter how unbearable.

'David ... it's not important.' Oh God, she couldn't endure him looking at her like that. 'It didn't mean anything. I was lonely ... I missed you ... I just wanted you to —'

'I've been lonely too, Leith.' He interrupted her coldly, in a voice she'd never heard him use before. 'I've missed you too. There were ample opportunities to do something about that I suppose, but the idea would never have occurred to me.'

'David, please,' she pleaded, 'try to understand how it was for me.'

She moved forward, her hand stretched out to him.

'No!' He flinched. 'Don't touch me.'

Shocked by his rejection, she stopped dead. God, what had she done? ... How could she have hurt him like this? ...

There was a terrible brittle silence before he spoke again.

'Do you know what you've done to me, Leith? I was always so proud of you. Despite what you might think, you were the focus of my life. If I was working hard it wasn't going to be for ever. I'm not a young man — if anything happened to me, I wanted to make sure you were well looked after.'

He paused, and his voice grew more intense. 'I put you on a pedestal. I idolised you. But I see now that I was kidding myself.'

She was looking at him with stricken eyes.

'David, I'm so sorry ... Please, believe me, it didn't mean anything. It happened only once. Because you weren't there for me, not the way I needed you to be, not the way it used to be. I've tried to tell you so often.'

For a tense, silent moment he stared back at her.

'You don't understand, do you, Leith? You just don't understand.'

Then he walked out and left her alone.

They slept apart, David in the guest bedroom, and, the next morning, he was gone before she awoke. Unable to sleep, Leith had swallowed a sleeping pill sometime before dawn.

When she finally opened her eyes, the sun was streaming in through the drapes she'd forgotten to close the night before. For a moment or two, she had no idea why she had awoken with such a heavy heart. But then reality returned, and with a sense of desolation that was as acute as a physical pain, she recalled the devastating confrontation of the night before. Worst of all was her memory of the expression on David's face when she'd moved to touch him. His obvious disgust and abhorrence had shaken her to the core.

How were they ever going to get over this? she wondered fearfully. What could she possibly do to make him trust and love her again?

Finally, she forced herself to crawl out of bed, dressed in the first thing she put her hand on and dialled the number of David's office. She felt incapable of doing anything else until she had some inkling of his state of mind.

His secretary answered cheerfully and, a moment later, David came on the line.

'You should have woken me,' she said.

'I thought it better not to.' He sounded stiff, remote.

'David, what are we going to do?' She could hear the desperate pleading in her voice.

There was an agonising pause before he finally replied. 'I'm not sure, Leith. I don't think I'm capable of making any decisions at the moment.'

Decisions? What decisions? she felt like asking. She didn't want him to make decisions. She wanted him to forgive her, to tell her he still loved her and that they'd get through all this.

Fighting to stay calm, she replied, 'I can't bear to have hurt you, David. Please, darling, let's try and work this out.'

But his reply offered none of the comfort she was so desperate for. 'I can't talk now, Leith. I'll see you tonight. Late. Don't worry about dinner.'

The rest of the day passed in a blur of despair. She couldn't settle to any of her normal chores, and the thought of eating made her stomach heave.

I've got to make him understand, she repeated to herself. He's got to see I was at the end of my tether, that it wasn't *what* I did that matters, but *why* I did it. Once he understands that, we can start to put this marriage back together again.

It was after nine when he finally came home. Leith saw the strain and tension on his face as she greeted him awkwardly. For the first time in as long as she could remember, he didn't kiss her.

'Have you had something to eat?' She did her best to sound normal.

'A working dinner.' He was shrugging off his jacket. 'I wasn't very hungry.'

'What about a drink?'

He nodded. 'Okay.'

He went to change and when he returned in jeans and T-shirt, she handed him a glass of wine.

He swallowed a mouthful, and there was a tense silence as they looked at each other.

His first words made her feel weak with relief.

'I'm going to try, Leith.' He spoke without emotion. 'I'm going to do my best to come to terms with it.'

She felt as if the blood had been poured back into her empty veins. 'Oh, David ... I'm so —'

But he hadn't finished. 'Maybe I can. Maybe not. Either way it's going to take me time to work it all through.'

She was clutching the stem of her glass so tightly it was in danger of snapping off in her fingers.

'In the meantime, until I leave for Perth, I think it's best I continue to sleep in the spare bedroom.'

Over the next eight days, they existed in a strange vacuum of polite remove, like strangers forced to share the same house.

Leith did her best to get through each day, her nerves on edge as she waited for some sign that it was going to be all right, that David had forgiven her.

But as the days passed with no clear evidence of any thawing in his demeanour, her tension increased. She found it almost impossible to believe that the David she had known all the years of their marriage had retreated to somewhere beyond her reach. For although he had resumed his evening greeting, the fleeting touch of his cold lips against her cheek did nothing to reassure her, and his usual good humour had been replaced by a polite remoteness.

Each night, alone in the bed they'd once shared, she lay unable to sleep, her body rigid with despair, wondering what she could do to make everything as it once had been.

And then, one morning, not long after her devastating revelation, the telephone rang, and it was Paul.

Her stomach clenched as she listened to his affectionate greeting. The contrast with David's coldness made her wince with pain.

But before he could go on, she broke in. 'Paul, I've told him. I've told David what happened.'

'You have?' Surprised, his tone leaped in excitement. 'That's wonderful, sweetheart! Then we can —'

'No, Paul,' she interrupted abruptly. 'You don't understand. David and I are working things out. We're getting back on track.' It was what she wanted to believe. It *would* happen, she vowed to herself. 'So don't ever call me again. If you do, all you'll get is the machine.'

She put the receiver down on his response.

It was the evening before David was due to leave for Perth, and nothing had yet been resolved.

Leith dared to let herself think that maybe he was prepared to allow the subject to drop, without any further need to confront what she had done. Perhaps, she thought hopefully, it would mean that when he returned, their relationship could slip back into its old ease and intimacy.

But she soon discovered how wrong her reasoning had been. That evening, when they'd finished dinner, he told her they would have to talk. With her heart beating faster, she took a seat opposite him in the living room.

He looks so tired, she thought, noting with guilty remorse the deep lines around his eyes and the pallor of his complexion. It was the first time she had ever thought of David as old . . .

He began to speak, and his carefully neutral expression gave her little clue as to what to expect.

'Leith, these last few days have been the hardest of my life. Almost my every waking hour has been spent trying to analyse my own feelings. And they seem to have run the gauntlet from shock, to hurt, to anger and resentment. What I'm feeling now is a profound sadness.'

Her every nerve screamed for him to get to the point, to give her the assurance she was praying for.

'I've told you how I felt about you, Leith. You were everything to me. I not only loved you unreservedly, but I admired and respected you as well. Over this last week or so, I've done my best to find some comfort in your excuses — that it happened only once, that it meant nothing, that you were lonely.'

He paused, and when he spoke again, his voice had an edge of utter despair.

'What I've found is that I just can't reason myself through this. I've tried, but I can't put out of my mind the thought of you with another man. You've destroyed something very precious to me. And I can't see how we can ever make this marriage work again.'

The blood drained from her face. She finally understood what it meant to be 'paralysed by shock'. She felt as if ice had been injected into her veins. Oh, God, no. Please. Don't let this be happening.

'When I get back from this trip,' he went on, 'I won't be moving back into the house. If you want it, it's yours, and of course I'll ensure you'll be well taken care of financially. You won't have to worry about that side of things.'

At last, she managed a choked response, forcing the words past the painful tightness in her throat.

'David . . . what are you saying to me?'

He looked at her, his expression stricken.

'I'm sorry, Leith. I can't pretend. I've tried, but I just can't. It's over.'

CHAPTER ELEVEN

'So come on, Cate, just let me get this straight ... You find him attractive, he's good in bed, he's smart, funny, kind, *but* you're not sure whether to get involved.' Jessica Wilson rolled her eyes. 'Yeah, I can see your point. Hell, you're only forty-two, you've got years ahead of you to meet another great guy. Especially in Sydney, they're thick on the ground, every place you go: dozens of eligible males all looking for a committed, honest relationship with a forty- something woman.'

Cate couldn't help smiling. Jess was one of her best friends. They'd been at school together, shared gossip, confidences, clothes. It was Jess who'd been there for her during those first terrible months when Simon had left, when her world had split apart. Now, sitting in their favourite wine bar, Cate was explaining how confused she felt about her feelings for Cal Donohoe.

'It's not as simple as that, Jess,' she answered. 'Apart from anything else, he lives a thousand kilometres away, on the Gold Coast, for God's sake. What am I going to do? Spend my life in the air?'

'Look on the bright side. There'll be no one cluttering up your life from Monday to Friday, and exciting, romantic weekends to look forward to.'

'And what about if it goes further than that? What if I really fall for this guy? What do I do then?'

'Oh, God, the usual female glass-ball prophecies. Well, one of you'll just have to move, won't you?'

'That's my point exactly. It won't be *him*. Not only has he got a business up there, but an elderly mother to tie him down as well.'

Jessica reached for a handful of nuts from the glass bowl between them. 'I've always loved Surfers,' she said, popping them one by one into her mouth. 'Clean air, clean water, semi-naked men. Think about it as a change for the better.'

Cate shook her head in exasperation. 'All right, then, what about my work? Can you ever see me getting a job like this anywhere else again? People would kill for it. I'd be mad to give it up.'

Her friend dusted peanut shells off her fingers, and this time her response was more serious. 'Okay, sure, work and who's going to make the move are issues, but that's not what's really worrying you, is it, Cate? It's the emotional bit, isn't it? You're terrified of letting go, so fearful of letting yourself fall in love with someone in case it's a repeat of the Simon scenario. With poor little Cate out on her arse again. Nowhere to go, all vulnerable and betrayed and wounded and facing the world alone yet again. Well, just stop and think about it a moment. Look how far you've come since Simon. Do you think anyone could ever destroy you like that again? Don't you see how much stronger, self-reliant, independent you've become since then?'

With greasy fingers, Jessica reached for her wine glass. 'You want my advice? Stop trying to predict the future. You could be dead next month. Until then, go with the flow and stop worrying about what *might* happen. You survived Simon. If this keels over, you'll survive this as well.'

She gave Cate a grin. 'And, anyway, you know I'll always be around to pick up the pieces.'

He'd rung her every day since she'd left, but not once had he tried to pressure her into making a decision. They talked about anything and everything except the one topic that was on both their minds. Cal was charming, witty, good fun, and afterwards, when they finally hung up, Cate felt as if she'd been talking with an old friend, someone she'd known for years.

He sent flowers to her work on a couple of occasions, and that put her on the spot to offer some sort of explanation in response to the inevitable curious and teasing comments. While one part of her wished Cal hadn't made the romantic gesture, she also had to acknowledge the pleasure of knowing there was someone out there to whom she meant something.

On each occasion she took the flowers home and, in her solitude, she'd look at them and think about Cal, driving herself crazy wondering what she should do. Start a long-distance affair with all the possible repercussions, good and bad? Or call a halt to everything before it got complicated? Crawl back into her safety zone and never let Cal or anyone else tempt her out of it again?

It took her three weeks to finally admit to herself that she had always known the answer.

He made no secret of his delight when she rang to ask him if he were free the following weekend.

'Free? I'm pathetically, abysmally free! So free I'll give up medicine, sell the surgery, cut off all the phones so that I can spend every second with a wonderful woman called Cate Tremain.'

What else could she do but laugh and book her flight?

She flew in on Friday evening. When she walked into the arrival lounge at Coolangatta airport, she spotted him at once, and saw his face light up with pleasure as he pushed his way through the crowds to her side. When he reached her, he folded her in his arms and before saying a word, kissed her fiercely on the lips.

When at last they drew apart, he looked down at her and grinned. 'I should sue, you know.'

'What?' She gave him a puzzled frown.

'You landed four minutes late. They robbed me of four full minutes of your company. That's got to be a crime.'

His apartment was in a recently completed high rise at the northern end of Surfers.

'Everything's recently completed around here,' he explained, as he opened the door to a spacious living area with floor to ceiling windows that offered panoramic views of the ocean. 'I moved in three months ago. A good investment, my accountant assured me.'

The place showed evidence of a Mediterranean influence, a style that was popular, especially on the coast, Cate had observed. The walls were lime-washed and there was abundant use of terracotta floor tiles, and wooden shutters. It still smelled new.

'Take a look around. Not much Vogue decor, I'm afraid. I've been too busy to go looking for furniture.'

Cate saw what he meant. There were the usual bachelor's necessities — a long, comfy-looking sofa, a pile of stereo equipment stacked in one corner, a TV. Only the dining table was out of place. Waxed, light wood — oak, she thought — with wonderfully carved legs and six matching chairs. To Cate's untrained eye, it looked like a genuine antique.

'This is beautiful,' she said, walking over and running her hand gently over the grain of the timber.

'It's my mother's. A family heirloom. The only thing she couldn't bear to leave behind when she left Ireland.'

Cate turned to him with a smile. 'I can't imagine my mother transplanting herself thousands of kilometres to live close to me. You really must be the favoured son.'

There was a fleeting change in his expression and, for a split second, she thought he was going to say something more, but he merely gave a half smile and carried her suitcase into the bedroom she could see at the end of the hall.

He'd bought a platter of fresh seafood and they peeled and ate the prawns and bugs and spanner crabs at the table on the small patio. Afterwards, sated, they finished the wine and listened to the soft thud and murmur of the surf. The silence between them was one of contentment and ease, a silent connection that needed no words.

It's perfect, Cate thought, and her verdict included everything: the night, the view, the sea air, the pleasure of the company of the man beside her. Quite perfect. And because it was, she felt the prickle of familiar anxiety. I'll remember this later, she found herself thinking. When it's over. When what happened with Simon happens again.

'You look impressively serious.' He glanced over at her. 'Anything you want to share?'

Cate shrugged. 'Nothing important.'

But she felt his eyes still watching her. A second later his hand reached out and found hers.

'I'm so happy you came, Cate. Really, really happy.'

Mutely, she squeezed his hand.

Don't go too fast, she begged him in silent warning. Be careful with my fragile heart.

It had been so long since she'd had to share her privacy that the most difficult part of the weekend, she figured, was going to be using the bathroom and loo. Cleaning your teeth and having a widdle in close proximity sure had to take some of the romance away. But Cal, like the gentleman he was, left her the ensuite, while he took himself off to the guest bathroom.

She had just slipped into the satin, low-cut nightie she'd rushed out specially to buy before leaving Sydney when he gave a tap on the bedroom door.

'It's okay. Come in.'

He entered the room and stood still for a moment, taking in the sight of her.

'That's lovely,' he murmured.

Moving closer, he slid his hands down the smooth length of her. 'Only I wouldn't get too attached to it if I were you.'

If anything, Cate enjoyed their lovemaking even more than the first time. She felt more at ease, more open to the emotional experience as well as the physical.

As Cal's lips and hands explored her body, she became slick with desire and, when he finally entered her, she gasped with both the sting of momentary pain and the pleasure of having him in her at last. Wrapping her legs tightly around him, she drew him deep inside, greedy for him to fill her, to connect them as closely as it was possible for two humans to be.

I've missed this, she told herself, I've really missed this. Her throat tightened with emotion, and she felt the tears prick behind her closed eyelids.

She couldn't remember the last time she'd felt so completely happy.

The next morning they went out to breakfast. The weather was perfect, and they were lucky enough to land a table in the sunshine at one of the busy sidewalk restaurants not far from the apartment.

From behind her sunglasses, Cate took in the passing parade of fashionable pedestrians and the continual stream of prestige cars, many open-roofed as they drove past with casual deliberation.

'Not everyone wears King Gees and singlets then,' she observed with a teasing smile.

'Only the millionaires,' Cal replied with a grin.

As they chatted and waited for their meal, Cate felt totally relaxed. You did need to get away from Sydney now and then, she thought. A break like this was great, although she could never imagine herself living permanently at this pace. To feel truly alive, she knew she needed the urgency of deadlines and pressure, constant stimulus to her adrenalin levels. But for a couple of days, she was perfectly happy to unwind.

'Now, I guess this is yours?' The waitress, a slim-hipped ash blonde, had arrived with their breakfast and was placing the brimming plate of bacon and eggs in front of Cal.

'No,' Cate corrected her. 'I'm the one who needs the fat injection.'

'Oh, sorry.' Looking surprised, the girl swapped the plates around.

With a wry smile, Cate picked up her knife and fork. 'Guess women like her only serve food, they don't eat it.'

Cal lifted an eyebrow as he poured milk into his bowl of muesli and fruit.

'You're hardly overweight. Your metabolism must be great.'

'Yeah, I'm one of the lucky ones. Live on junk food and don't put on an ounce.'

'What about exercise?'

Cate stopped midway through cutting the thick strip of greasy bacon. 'What about it?'

'Well, there's more to good health than staying slim.'

'Sorry,' she pierced a piece of bacon with her fork, 'my idea of exercise is carrying out the garbage. Of course, I forgot I was out with a descendant of Doctor Kildare. Which reminds me,' she added over Cal's chuckle, 'I, uh, might need to actually consult you in that particular role.'

'Yeah? What's up?'

'Can you write me a prescription? I'll pay you of course. No abuses of the system. It's just that these surroundings beat a consulting room, and I guess I'm sort of desperate.'

He looked at her curiously. 'What is it?'

Cate felt the heat creep over her cheeks. Oh, God, surely she wasn't going to blush. Not at her age.

'Well ... let's just say the virgin bride is starting to pay the price for her abandon.' She cocked an eyebrow at him. 'You know what I mean?'

He stared at her for a moment, and then the penny dropped. He couldn't hide his amusement. 'Oh, hell! You mean a little wear and tear down below?'

She nodded. 'You got it. It's been a long time between ... uh, drinks.'

He chuckled. 'I'll get you something to fix that. And then it's just a matter of more regular ... uh, drinking patterns I guess.'

Cate picked up a slice of toast. 'You know what I like about you?'

He shook his head.

'I reckon you're the sort of doctor who would take his own good advice.'

As soon as they'd eaten, they dropped in at the surgery so Cal could write a script.

'Come on in,' he invited, 'I won't be a minute.'

Three or four people were in the waiting room, and behind the reception desk sat an attractive, forty-ish woman with fair, wavy hair. She gave Cate a smile of welcome when Cal introduced them.

'Vicky's been with me eight years. She knows all my foibles. So I won't leave you with her a moment longer than necessary.'

'Hey, you pay me,' Vicky said over her shoulder as he moved away. 'My loyalty is above question.'

With a chuckle she turned back to Cate. 'Take my word for it, he's a great guy. So how are you enjoying the Coast? Must be good to get out of Sydney for a couple of days.'

Cate hid her surprise at the receptionist's knowledge. She hadn't expected Cal to confide the details of his personal life to an employee. But then, she remembered, they had known each other a long time.

Cate nodded. 'A nice break, but I'm an adrenalin junkie, I guess. Need the pace of a big city.'

The other woman looked at her and nodded. Cate got the vague impression that she was being sized up.

'I thought that once. But I made the move from

Melbourne, and I've never looked back. I can't imagine living anywhere else now.'

At that moment the glass door from the street slid open, letting in a gust of warm air, and with a final smile at Cate, Vicky turned to attend to the new patient.

It was a perfect weekend. On Sunday morning they took a long walk along the beach and, later, drove up to the Runaway Bay marina, where Cal kept his small runabout.

'Do you know how long it is since I took this thing out?' he asked, as the engine spluttered into life amid belches of blue smoke. He looked up at her and grinned. 'Guess I just needed a good excuse.'

He was stripped to the waist and Cate was enjoying the sight of his strong, tanned torso. 'That's me,' she quipped back. 'Nothing more than a simple excuse for fun.'

With the engine running smoothly, they headed out through the Broadwater towards South Stradbroke Island. Various craft of different sizes sailed around them through the deep, clear water.

Cal explained the various markers and safety regulations and, a little later, invited her to take the wheel, but Cate preferred to sit back and enjoy the view. With the green hills of the hinterland on one side and the ocean on the other, it made for a delightful contrast.

They were heading for the island to have a picnic lunch, but on the way Cal showed her the new Couran Cove Resort with its apartments and facilities built right over the water.

'It's the baby of Ron Clarke, the former Olympic runner,' he explained as he cut the engine and drifted into the pristine bay. 'Supposed to be one of the most ecologically self-sustaining resorts in the world.'

'Looks fabulous.' Cate was impressed. The natural bush was a wonderful backdrop to the pastel-painted timber dwellings that edged the water. 'Can't see how it can lose.'

As he slipped the boat back into gear, Cal said with feeling, 'I love this country. I've seen a bit of the world, and I wouldn't want to live anywhere else.'

From behind her sunglasses, Cate shot him a glance. She wondered how he felt about Sydney. And at once she heard Jess's voice telling her off about trying to predict the future.

They'd hoped to drop anchor somewhere secluded, but it seemed as if every Sunday boatie had headed for Stradbroke's beaches that weekend. Instead, as soon as they'd finished lunch, they headed back to the marina earlier than planned and made love in Cal's bed rather than amid the glories of nature.

'I only did that for your sake, you know,' he said afterwards as she lay with her head against his chest. 'Doctor's orders. Keeping you in training, so to speak.'

Without opening her eyes, Cate teasingly tweaked a tuft of his chest hair. 'For someone making a sacrifice, you seemed to be having a bloody good time.'

With time running out, they took a quick shower and headed down the highway to the airport. For the first time that weekend, they barely spoke, each lost in their separate thoughts.

It's been total bliss, Cate thought. They'd spent every moment in each other's company without the slightest sign of friction or discord. Yet she couldn't help feeling nervous now that the moment of departure had arrived. What happens next? she wondered. Do I ask him to visit me? He'd *seemed* to enjoy her company, but perhaps he was only being polite. Maybe at the last minute he'd tell her that it hadn't worked, that he didn't think a long-distance relationship was feasible, that they should call it quits before it went any further.

The thought churned her stomach. She was made frighteningly aware that, in just a very short time, she had already connected to the man beside her more deeply and dangerously than she'd thought possible.

The final boarding call for her flight had just been announced. By the security exit, Cal held both her hands in his own.

'You realise you've changed everything, don't you, Cate?' he asked softly. 'You've brought me to life again. I was only pretending before, going through the motions. But meeting you has made all the difference.' He paused, squeezed her hands tighter. 'You will see me again, won't you? As soon as possible?'

Her heart felt as if it were swelling in her chest. She nodded, and for some crazy reason, her eyes felt moist.

'Sydney rock oysters next time. My shout,' she said.

'Next Friday night? Rendezvous Big City?'

She nodded again, aware she was taking the next big step, setting a pattern. But sensing also, that she could trust this man.

'I'll call you with the flight details,' he replied, and his voice, his manner, his expression revealed his utter happiness. Then he was kissing her passionately until, reluctantly, they finally broke apart, and she hurried through the security check-point towards the boarding gate.

A crazy grin stayed on her face all the way to Sydney. She'd found it at last, she told herself in wonder. Even though she hadn't been really looking.

Cal was the man of her dreams.

Her wildest dreams.

✳

Exhausted, Rory let herself into her hotel room. It was almost ten. She and Antonella were working as hard as possible on meeting their deadline, but it wasn't looking good.

They weren't going to make it, even at the pace they were going at now. And she felt sick at the idea of having to tell Ian that she'd need another two trips to Melbourne to finish the project.

She'd admitted as much to Antonella when they'd nipped out for a quick bite earlier that evening. Perhaps it was the pressure and intensity of the work they were doing that made it easier for her to open up to someone she'd known for so short a time. But there was a passion and honesty in Antonella that short-circuited the usual superficialities.

'Oh, come on, you're not frightened of him, are you?' The other woman was looking at her in bemused wonder. 'A strong, successful lady like yourself? Surely he has to understand. I'm sure you'd do the same if the shoe were on the other foot.'

Rory found herself explaining then about Cam. About her unexpected and overwhelming obsession with having a child and Ian's reluctant acceptance of fatherhood.

'I guess that's why I can't help feeling guilty all the time. *I* made him do it. *I* talked him into it. So I suppose it isn't really fair to ask him to do more than his share.'

'Fair!' Antonella's dark brows shot up. 'We're supposed to be talking about two mature adults here, aren't we? Two people who love each other and can shoulder the burden for each other when they have to?'

Rory sighed. If only it were as easy as that.

She shook her head. 'Look, no matter what, there's no way I can tell him that I'm going to need a further two weeks. But what I have been thinking is that maybe I could stay on this weekend and the next. We could work flat out and I'd go back Sunday evening. Perhaps he'd accept that as an easier alternative.' She looked pleadingly at Antonella. 'I know it's a big ask of you. Virtually non-stop from Wednesday morning till Sunday night. Do you think you could possibly consider it?'

Antonella stared back a moment, her mouth set in an irritated line. 'I think I'm damned happy that I'm not married.'

Then, in the face of Rory's obvious anxiety, she added quickly, 'Sure, okay, let's work the whole weekend and get this wrapped up as soon as possible. And after that,' she said with feeling, 'I'm taking off. A week or two in Tahiti, or five-star Bali maybe. Anywhere to keep the stress-induced wrinkles at bay.'

Rory didn't answer. She could still remember a time when she too had lived that sort of spontaneous life.

Ian's reaction was predictably cool when she rang to tell him of the change of plan.

'I'd better bring Cam to the airport with me Sunday night then; at least that way he'll get to see you.'

It wasn't so much what he said, but the tone in which he said it. Rory felt her cheeks flush with annoyance. It was clear he wasn't going to make it any easier for her. She knew she should have left it at that, but she couldn't help herself.

'Ian, I've got enough on my plate. I don't need to be made to feel even more guilty than I already do. It's just two weekends, that's all I'm asking. Is that so impossible? To look after your own son for two bloody weekends? It's not like I'm sunning myself in Noosa, for God's sake!'

There was a moment's pause, and then he replied with the same cool evenness of tone. 'I'll talk to you later, I think — when you've calmed down.'

She heard the click of the receiver as he hung up.

They worked late again on Friday, and on Saturday morning were back in the office by eight a.m. Rain ran down the window panes but, cocooned inside, Rory and Antonella barely noticed. At six they decided to call it a day.

'God, my neck!' Rory turned it carefully back and forth as they took the elevator down to the ground floor. 'It's so stiff.'

'Well, I think tonight we should treat ourselves unmercifully at company expense.' Antonella stood beside her, briefcase in hand. She was wearing caramel-coloured pants with a cream polo neck jumper and looked as fresh as she had first thing that morning. 'Why don't you take a nice relaxing bath and I'll pick you up at -' she glanced at her watch, 'how does seven-thirty sound?'

'Fine. Where are we going?'

'Leave it to me.'

While the bath was filling she picked up the phone to put a call through to Ian. She deliberately hadn't rung him yesterday and there'd been no message from him either. Now, as she dialed the number, Rory made up her mind to apologise. Maybe that would help to clear the air.

But to her surprise, it wasn't Ian who answered.

'Oh, hi, Rory.' It was Mandy Asher, one of the young girls they occasionally used as a weekend babysitter.

'No,' she responded in reply to Rory's question, 'Ian had to go out. Some uni function, I think he said. I'm sure he's got his mobile with him.'

'Thanks, yes, he probably has.' She wondered what function Ian had gone to. He hadn't mentioned anything to her. Usually, after her days away, they made no plans for the weekends.

'And how's my little darling?' she asked.

A couple of minutes later, having been assured that her son was just fine, she hung up and tried Ian's number.

'It's me, darling. I rang home and got Mandy ... Where are you?' In the background she could hear loud music.

'It's a farewell for one of the retiring staff. I wasn't going to go, but then I thought it was probably good politics to show my face.'

And much more fun than staying home looking after baby, she couldn't help thinking.

'Well, it sounds like fun.'

'A lot of noise, but I wouldn't go that far.'

The music made it difficult to talk properly, but she was determined to try.

'Look, I'm sorry about the other day. I didn't mean to snap. I —'

'Listen, I really can't talk now.'

She was taken aback by his abruptness.

'I'll let you go then,' she answered, her voice chilling.

'Okay. See you tomorrow night.'

And that was it. He rang off. No endearments, no tenderness, no enquiring how she was, how the work had gone. As much emotion as if he'd been talking to the checkout chick at the supermarket, she thought resentfully as she walked through to the bathroom.

Her resentment grew as she lay and soaked in the warm water. Was she supposed to be made to feel guilty again? Was that what it was all about? God, she hated that sort of game playing.

Trying to shrug off her mood, she dressed in a pair of red tailored trousers and a black silk sweater. When Antonella rang from the foyer a few minutes later, she grabbed her black Armani jacket and headed for the elevators.

The restaurant was somewhere in Armadale. On two separate levels, it had stark white walls with soft lighting and polished wooden floors. Judging by the number of times the young female waiting staff went up and down the steep staircase, the place was obviously as crowded upstairs as it was down. Watching them hurrying by in their black pants, black polo necks and ankle length white aprons, Rory wondered how they avoided tripping as they made their perilous journey with fully-laden plates.

Antonella had told her that the restaurant was one of Melbourne's best.

'How the hell did you manage to get us in at such short notice?' Rory asked.

The designer looked up from reading the small, handwritten menu. 'Corruption is best not explained,' she answered with an arch smile. Then, with a decisive flourish, she placed the menu down on the starched white cloth. 'I recommend the risotto.'

The meal was excellent, and best of all, they avoided talking about work. Instead, the conversation ran the gamut of movies, music, politics and industry gossip.

Then, over coffee, Rory told Antonella about her earlier telephone conversation with Ian. It was still on her mind, and it seemed easier to talk through her feelings with this woman who wasn't in her normal circle of friends.

'Do you see yourself ever marrying this guy?' Antonella asked.

Rory tilted what was left of the wine in her glass. 'You know once I didn't give a damn about marriage. It was the absolute last thing I wanted, but having a child changed all that. For Cam's sake, I'd really love us to marry.'

Antonella stared at her a moment, then said perceptively, 'But for your sake too, right, Rory?'

Rory looked back at her and nodded mutely.

Later, when they were driving back to the hotel, Antonella returned to the topic.

'Why is marriage so important to you?' she asked. 'You're a clever, interesting woman, self-supporting. Why do you need a man to validate your existence, child or no child?'

As they stopped behind a tram, Rory tried to explain. 'It's not really a matter of validation. It's more a sense of feeling complete, of somehow taking the next step.' She lifted one shoulder in a shrug. 'Growing up, perhaps, accepting the confines and limitation of marriage because of the sense of belonging it offers.' But not security, she told herself. She wasn't going to utter aloud that particular word.

'Believe me,' she went on, 'it's only since Cam that I've felt this way. It was having a child that changed everything for me.'

Antonella gave her a reflecting look. 'And maybe not for the better, it would seem.'

Rory opened her mouth to protest, but the words died on her lips. This woman seemed to understand her so well, to see the truth she'd barely admit to herself.

'Yes,' she said finally. 'It's been hard. I constantly worry about whether I'm short-changing my child, about where my career's headed, if I've lost my edge, how I'm going to balance the whole bloody show. And Ian doesn't make anything easier by making me feel guilty so much of the time.'

'Ah yes,' Antonella nodded with a tight smile, 'men have a great way of making women feel like that, don't they? You know,' she tapped a long, perfectly manicured red fingernail on the steering wheel, 'when I see women going through what you're going through, I can't believe they let it happen. And I'm talking about strong, educated women, women who should know better. How can they let men pull them down like that?'

'I don't know. I really don't know how it happens,' Rory said with disquiet. 'I *was* strong. I always felt equal in the relationship. We always got on so well. And I know Ian loves Cam, but there's still this refusal to become fully involved. You know, I've started to wonder if he feels that having a child means he's no longer young. Maybe being surrounded by young people all the time has made him reluctant to face the truth about growing old. It's as if he's hanging onto the image of youth, and being a father somehow distorts that for him.'

It was the first time she had ever put into words the thought that had been steadily taking root in her mind. And the more she pondered it, the more it seemed to make sense. The obvious signs lay in Ian's obsessiveness with staying slim and fit, his enduring wardrobe of jeans and casuals, his interest in the latest music and fads. Recently, she recalled, he had even begun to think about dyeing the grey that was starting to appear in his dark hair. On the one or two occasions when she'd teased him about his refusal to face the fact that he was hardly going to be competition for Brad Pitt, she'd been taken aback by his sensitivity on the issue. It was clear she'd struck a nerve.

They were drawing up at the hotel. Antonella switched off the engine and turned to look at her. 'And so you feel you have to be the one to hold everything together, right? Your career, child, home, the relationship?'

It was a question that didn't require an answer and, in the silence, she reached out and laid a cool hand on Rory's arm. 'And it's all too much at the moment, isn't it, Rory? I can see what it's doing to you.'

It was the first time in all the months of strain and worry and confusion that anyone had offered her any sympathy or understanding. Rory felt as if some pressure valve inside her had suddenly been released. For so long she'd done her best to pretend that she was holding it all together, living her perfect life, coping with all the changes and tensions of motherhood as easily as she had always coped with everything else.

But somehow Antonella had helped her to open up and admit the truth, that, beneath the competent exterior, she was frightened and vulnerable and insecure, that the image of herself she'd once held was shattered into a thousand pieces and she didn't know how to put it back together again.

With a soft sob, she dropped her head and covered her face with her hands.

'It's awful...' she cried. 'I hate my life. I feel so *helpless*. As if I'll never be able to cope. And it's tearing me apart.'

She felt Antonella's arm slide around her shoulder. 'It's all right, Rory. It's all right to cry.' The other woman spoke with quiet sympathy. 'Come on, I'll come up with you. We'll have a nice, strong coffee, and you can let it all out. I've got pretty broad shoulders.'

Ten minutes later, Rory was beginning to feel a little better. Room service had brought them a pot of freshly percolated coffee, but Rory allowed hers to grow cold as she poured out the emotional turmoil she'd kept to herself for so long. Her insecurity and inadequacies about motherhood, her relationship, her career. For the first time, she was able to be completely honest about everything that was causing her such anguish.

Antonella let her talk and didn't make the mistake of offering her own opinions or advice. When Rory finally ran out of steam, all she said was, 'Well, now that you've admitted the extent of the problems, you've taken the first step to doing something to solve them.'

Then she'd gone into the bathroom and found some moisturising lotion, insisting that a neck and shoulder massage would help Rory to relax and get a decent night's sleep.

'The neck is easier to fix than the head. But we've got to start somewhere,' she joked.

Making Rory sit on the edge of the bed stripped off to her bra, Antonella kicked off her high heels and knelt down behind her. Rory was surprised at how strong the other woman's hands were as they rubbed the cool lotion into her skin.

'I could have run home and found you a gram of coke, but that would've done nothing for your neck.' Rory could tell she was smiling. 'How's it feeling?' she added.

'Wonderful. *You're* wonderful. The best part is having someone listen to you, to assure you you're really not going crazy.'

'Of course you're not. You've just got a few things to straighten out. First of all, you have to stop trying to do everything, and trying to do it perfectly.'

Rory knew she was right. Just as she knew Antonella was right in saying that she now had to do something to solve her problems. When she got home she was determined to sit down with Ian and talk to him as she'd talked to Antonella. Ever since Cam had been born, she'd driven herself crazy trying to keep her promise that nothing in their lives would really change. But now it was time to face the truth. So much *had* changed and the two of them would have to work out a way to balance those changes in both their lives.

'That's the beauty of living alone,' Antonella said, breaking into her thoughts. 'You never have to please anyone but yourself.'

Rory felt more lotion being added to her back. The massage felt wonderful.

'Don't you ever see yourself getting into another relationship?' she asked.

Antonella gave a short laugh. 'With a man you mean? You've got to be joking. I gave up on men a long time ago.'

There was a momentary pause, and then Rory felt herself stiffen as the truth dawned on her.

Slowly, she turned and looked at the woman kneeling behind her. With a smile, Antonella dropped back on her haunches. 'I thought you might have worked that one out already.'

Rory shook her head. 'No. No, it never occurred to me.'

'Does it upset you?'

'I — no, I don't think so.' But in a subconscious movement she reached for her blouse.

Looking amused, Antonella put out a hand and stopped her. 'Come on, calm down. What do you think I'm going to do? Attack you? Sure, I find you a very attractive woman, but it has to work both ways, you know. So, come on, turn around and let me finish what I was doing.'

Tentatively, Rory did as she was told, and as the massage began again, she did her best to examine her reaction to Antonella's admission. Was she shocked? she asked herself. No, not really, it was just that the revelation had come as such a complete surprise.

Antonella was the epitome of femininity, the sort of female men would avidly pursue. But she didn't want them, didn't need them, obviously didn't seem to think she was missing anything in having made her choice.

But now, confronted with this unexpected knowledge, Rory found herself reacting to Antonella's touch in a completely different way. All at once there was a sensuality, an eroticism to their contact that hadn't been present moments before. Her senses were heightened by the softness of Antonella's hands, the proximity of her lush body, the faint scent of her perfume. And before she could stop it, the unbidden thought flashed into her mind. What, she wondered, would it feel like to have a sexual encounter with a woman?

A moment later, she wondered if Antonella had read her thoughts.

'Have you ever wondered how a woman can please another woman, Rory?' Antonella asked softly.

Rory's breath caught in her throat as she felt the other woman's fingers slip under her bra strap. Her heartbeat was suddenly throbbing in her ear, and her flesh caught fire with an excitement that shocked her.

'Let me show you. Let me show you how wonderful it can be.' Antonella's voice was husky as she unclipped the bra and slipped the straps gently down Rory's shoulders. Rory couldn't move or speak. The breath felt frozen in her throat. The next moment she felt the other woman's soft, small hands slip around to cup her breasts.

Then Antonella kissed the back of her neck. 'I told

you I found you very attractive ... I couldn't help myself,' she breathed.

Rory felt her nipples blossom into taut knobs. To her surprise, she found the sensation of another woman's touch every bit as stimulating as a man's — with the added excitment of the taboo.

'Let me see you. I want to see as well as touch.'

Fluidly, Antonella moved off the bed and went down on her knees in front of Rory. Gently, she began to fondle each pale globe of breast, and Rory was mesmerised by the gleam of excitement in the other woman's dark eyes.

'To me, a woman's breasts are the perfect symbol of her femininity,' Antonella whispered. 'The softness, the shape, the beauty of the nipple ...'

Lifting her head, she parted her lips and her tongue began to circle Rory's jutting nipples.

Involuntarily, Rory found herself arching her back, her senses reeling as if short-circuited. Suddenly she realised that the hang-ups she felt about her body with Ian didn't matter in this different context. For once she didn't feel as if she were being judged, as if she had to live up to some unreal standard, the fantasy woman of most men's dreams.

Her mouth opened in a soft moan as Antonella sucked more forcefully and her long, soft hair brushed against Rory's bare skin. Rory closed her eyes in pleasure. It felt so wonderful ... more wonderful than she could ever have imagined ...

It was the sudden noise outside in the corridor that disturbed the mood. The sound of conversation and laughter as other guests passed by. And the distraction instantly brought Rory to her senses. Her heart pounded. Oh, God, what was she doing? How could she have allowed this to happen? How was she going to face working with this woman again?

Putting a hand on Antonella's shoulder, she forced her away.

'Please, Antonella, no ...'

The other woman sat back on her haunches, her dark hair cascading down her back as she looked up at Rory. Her eyes were glazed and unfocused and her breathing shallow.

'I'd never want to force you, Rory. That's not what it's about.' Her voice was unsteady as she got to her feet and left Rory to hurriedly pull on her blouse.

It was Antonella, poise regained, who broke the awkward silence. 'Don't look so embarrassed. You don't have to worry. This will never go further than you or me.' She gave a low chuckle. 'And I promise I'll still respect you in the morning.'

Rory shifted her gaze to stare up into those amused dark eyes. Suddenly, she couldn't help herself, her mouth spread in a smile. 'And I won't give the gory details to my mates in the pub.'

Suddenly they were both laughing out loud, their shared amusement helping to dissipate the nervous tension. But Rory knew it would never happen again. The same way she knew she would never tell Ian.

CHAPTER TWELVE

Judith knew she had only one option but, after almost a quarter of a century of marriage, the idea of taking the enormous step of leaving her husband and children still frightened her. It was the thought of walking out on her sons that really upset her, but she would see them often, she promised herself. She wasn't abandoning them and, in the end, they might come to understand that she had done it for the best, for all of them.

Meanwhile she sought solace in her writing and in her now regular meetings with Tony. Over the months he had become more than just a mentor to her, she realised. He'd become a friend as well.

They had fallen into the habit of having coffee together after they'd finished reviewing her latest efforts with her manuscript, and as the conversation between them had grown more personal, Judith had gradually begun to confide her growing frustration with her marriage. Yet she wasn't quite ready to admit that she was seriously thinking of leaving.

Greg had grown used to her weekly outings. Occasionally, he made some sarcastic put-down about her continued literary efforts, but he never bothered to show any real interest in what was absorbing her. As long as the house was tidy, there was food on the table, and Judith contributed her share to the mortgage and other expenses, he paid little attention to whatever else she did to pass her time.

Judith found herself more and more reluctant to bring the evenings she spent with Tony to a close. She enjoyed his company so much. He was everything Greg was not: kind, warm, unselfish, interested in other people. Money and possessions seemed to count for little to him.

He'd told her that following his divorce eight years before, he'd given his wife the home they had shared.

'I figured all I really needed was one room to write in and another to sleep in,' he'd commented with a dry smile.

And now he lived in a rented apartment somewhere overlooking the bush in Lane Cove. 'I've been there six years,' he explained. 'It's quiet and I can look out at the bush and think.'

'I guess if I were a full-time writer, I'd prefer to live alone, too,' Judith replied.

Except, she told herself silently, if I were living with you.

It happened when she was about half way through her novel, the night Tony was stuck without his car.

He'd rung her as she was driving home from work to apologise for not being able to make their meeting that evening.

'Gear box packed it in. Probably cost a packet. But if I can get a bank loan to pay the bill, I'll be back on the road next week, they assure me.'

Judith was aware of the sharpness of her disappointment. Whether she wanted to admit it or not, her meetings with Tony had become a real highlight of her week.

Making a quick decision, she suggested tentatively, 'Well, it'd be no trouble for me to pick you up. That's if you can still make it tonight.'

When he accepted her offer graciously and without demur, Judith realised he was probably only being polite, not wanting to ask for a lift, but grateful when it was offered. It gave her a warm feeling to think that he might enjoy their meetings as much as she did.

It was a quarter to seven when she drew up outside the small block of eight apartments in the quiet cul-de-sac. Tony was waiting for her on the footpath, and she leaned over to unlock the door.

'Thanks a lot for doing this,' he smiled, as he slid in beside her.

'Listen, it's you I've got to thank. I hated the thought of missing my weekly inspirational "fix".'

Tony chuckled. 'Is that how you see our meetings?'

'Partly,' she replied.

She was grateful that he didn't ask her how she viewed the other part of their evening together.

Because she barely dared to admit the truth to herself.

It was a ten-minute drive to the library. They were almost there when Judith suddenly threw him a sideways glance and exclaimed, 'Listen, are we crazy or something?'

'What do you mean?'

'Well, I'm wondering why we didn't just stay at your place? Why we felt we had to drag ourselves all the way over here!'

Then, she caught herself. The words had popped right out of her mouth before she'd given them any thought. What was she saying, for heaven's sake? It wasn't up to her to suggest that Tony's place might have been an option.

'Oh, I'm sorry,' she added hurriedly. 'I didn't mean to assume —' She was glad it was dark so he wouldn't see the blush creeping over her cheeks. 'I mean —'

He gave a light chuckle and patted her shoulder. 'Don't worry about it. I know what you mean. To tell you the truth, it did occur to me, but I wasn't sure if you'd feel comfortable with that.'

'Oh, Tony, of *course* I would have,' she shot back. Then quickly caught herself again. God, she'd sounded so full on. 'I mean,' she forced a more measured tone, 'we know each other well enough now.' She shot him another quick look. 'Don't we?'

'Well ... yes ...'

She hadn't been expecting the doubt in his tone and immediately felt something tighten inside her.

'I *think* I could trust you,' he added.

And then she realised he was only teasing, and she

covered the relief that flooded her by laughing too loudly.

It seemed only natural after that to have their usual post-work coffee at his place when she drove him home that evening.

Judith parked at the kerb and followed Tony up the dimly lit concrete stairwell that led to the second level of apartments. Although it was only just past nine, their footsteps were the only sound to be heard.

'Most of the other tenants are elderly women,' Tony explained as he fitted his key into the lock. 'They're all in bed by eight-thirty.'

For a fleeting second Judith got an image of herself as one of those women: alone, vulnerable, her life wasting away. A woman without a man — just like her mother. The way she'd be when she left Greg ...

'Take a seat.' He switched on a table lamp as they entered the small living room. 'Now, just remind me, yours is white, one sugar, right?'

'Thanks.'

While Tony busied himself in the outdated kitchen, Judith took in her surroundings. The living area opened onto a tiny patio that had a view of the bush. The room itself was lined with shelves that overflowed with books of all shapes and sizes. There were books stacked in corners too, under chairs, on side tables — in fact, everywhere she looked. It was the sort of room she would have loved, a place in which to dream and read and write. Greg hated mess and clutter.

As she took a seat on the ancient sofa, its dark leather worn and stained, Tony reappeared with a tray. Pushing aside a jumble of newspapers, he found a place for it on the glass- topped coffee table.

Judith felt the sofa sink deeper as he sat down beside her.

'I'd love a room like this,' she said as she accepted the mug of steaming coffee. 'How long did it take you to amass such a huge collection?'

'The books? God, this is just part of it. I couldn't move them all into this shoebox. The rest are stored in cartons all over the place, mainly with my poor suffering friends.'

Judith was silent a moment. Is the same thing going to happen to me? She wondered. Bits and pieces of her life stored wherever? The thought made her remember her mother and the painful hours spent sifting through the accumulations of yet another lifetime. Why, she asked herself, did human beings feel such a pressing need to acquire and possess?

She took a sip of coffee and asked, 'Was it hard? The divorce, I mean. Starting over.'

He pursed his lips, considering the question. 'The hardest bit, I guess, was breaking the habit of being a couple. Even when you're not getting on with your partner, you're still used to their presence. It takes a while, but eventually you get used to being by yourself, too.'

'You've got no regrets?'

He shook his head. 'No. It was never going to work. Better to cut your losses, lift the stone from your back and get on with being happy again.'

Lift the stone from your back ... Yes, she told herself, that's how it might feel for her, too.

'And are you happy now?' She couldn't stop herself from asking the question.

She saw his lips widen in a gentle smile. 'Sometimes I'm very happy. Like now, for instance.'

His answer, so unexpected, made her pulses leap. In the silence that followed, they held each other's gaze. Then she was aware of Tony sliding closer over the worn leather, of his arm slipping behind her shoulders. Hardly able to breathe, she felt his hand cup her chin, and then his mouth was closing on hers in a gentle, tantalising kiss that lit a tinder of excitement in her veins. When he drew away he looked down at her, then traced a gentle finger over her cheek.

'Judith ... Oh, my dear, sweet Judith ...'

She looked back into his eyes, unable to speak, trembling with excitement and desire. And then, as if something had been suddenly released inside both of them, he pulled her even closer and, in a natural response, she slipped her arms around his neck, buried her fingers in his hair and opened her mouth to his now hard and eager lips.

The kiss seemed to last forever and, when they finally broke apart, it was only to shed their clothes. As she lifted her buttocks to help him undress her, there was a small part of her mind still objective and lucid enough to stand back from the heat of her passion. I'm betraying Greg, she told herself with a sort of fearful awe. For the first time in her life, she was breaking her marriage vows. And she knew it was an enormous step. Maybe the first step towards lifting the stone off her back ...

And then nothing else mattered but the weight of Tony's body on her own and the pleasure of his hands and mouth. She felt as if she'd been brought to life in a way she had almost forgotten was possible. When she was ready, he slipped inside her wetness and she moaned with joy. Curling her legs about him, she tightened herself around the unfamiliar thickness, and finally, as she abandoned herself to the rapture of making love with her body, her mind and her heart, the words sang in her soul: I love him. I loved him from the very start.

Judith's only fear was that somehow Greg would be able to look at her and know, as if what had happened with Tony might be revealed in her face, her actions.

But in that regard at least, little seemed to have changed. Her husband paid her as scant attention as always.

What *had* changed, though, was something inside her, for the unexpected intimacy with Tony had brought her not only emotional joy and physical pleasure, but had also filled her with a new confidence about herself as a woman. With a sense of dazed pleasure, Judith realised that although she was no longer young, her body far from perfect, a man had found her attractive and wanted to make love to her. The assurance she had found in Tony's arms made her feel so much stronger, so much more sure of herself.

After that first night together, there was no drawing back. The next time they met, it was a mutual decision that they would work at Tony's flat and finish the night in bed.

'See how disciplined we are,' he joked as he slipped her growing manuscript back inside its folder. 'Business before pleasure.'

The affair with Tony suddenly made everything more urgent. By the time another fortnight had passed, Judith had finally made the firm decision to pull the pin on her marriage. Having Tony in her life had given her the courage to face Greg and tell him it was over.

Her first step was to find somewhere to live. And she decided to settle on a place before surprising Tony with the news. During her lunch hour she began calling on rental agents. All she was looking for was a small, one-bedroom place close to work. Even so, she was shocked at the rents being asked for even the most basic of places. It wasn't going to be easy, but she was determined to keep looking.

Meanwhile, at home, she began surreptitiously to sort through her belongings. If Greg made any comment, she would tell him she was spring cleaning, she decided. But again, he took no notice of what she was doing.

The task proved momentous and drove her to despair. What was she supposed to do with the cupboards-full of fine china? With her linen and silver? Her wardrobe of clothes? How did you split up photo albums and wedding presents? What did you do about paintings and sewing machines and pianos? To make it worse, there was also the overflow of her mother's life: family heirlooms, framed photographs, her father's much loved — and probably valuable — jazz collection. How could she leave all that behind?

Judith began to understand why the storage shed had become such a necessary accompaniment to the overflow and detritus of modern life. It would have to be her solution too, she decided.

In the end, she was forced to compromise on a place to live. The apartment was larger than the norm and fairly up- to-date, but located close to the railway line. Maybe, she told herself without much conviction, she'd get used to the noise in time.

Only when the rental agent slid the six-month contract in front of her did Judith feel seized by a split second of last-minute doubt. Even with Tony in her life, could she really go through with this? Walk out on her marriage and her children? Take this frightening step into the unknown at her age?

Then she thought of the years she'd already wasted, the years of indifference and lack of love, being the invisible woman, taken for granted by those who should have cherished her the most. She had faced the fact long ago that Greg was never going to change. There was no chance of ever finding the love, the serenity and consideration she longed for with the man she had married. Her fingers tightened on the pen and, with a fluid gesture, she signed her name. She would set herself free and have a man like Tony to love, instead.

She planned to make her move on the weekend she knew Greg would be away on a golfing trip with his mates.

He left after an early breakfast, eager to be gone, and she wasn't worried about Luke or Brent. The boys were typical teenagers; most Saturdays and Sundays she was lucky if they emerged from their bedrooms before noon. And they inevitably slept like the dead.

The removal van arrived at eight on the dot. The two men quickly loaded the few items of furniture she'd decided she was going to need: the double bed from the guest bedroom, her writing desk and chair, her computer, the small bar fridge from the billiard room, the patio furniture that would serve as a dining table and chairs, and the antique dressing table that had belonged to her mother. As well as her suitcases of clothes and boxes of linen and kitchenware, there were the cartons she'd packed over the last few weeks, which she would drop off in storage.

As she'd hoped, the task was finished and neither of the boys had put in an appearance. Judith doubted that they'd even notice anything was missing. The two of them seemed to live in some totally self-absorbed teenage universe that barely acknowledged the existence of anyone or anything else. But she had no intention of leaving them in the dark about the decision she had made. They were still her sons, her own flesh and blood, and she owed them the truth. Later that day, she planned to return to the house and tell them exactly what was going on. She wasn't going to leave it to Greg to distort the facts.

Leaving the van to head to her new address, she called in at the rental agency to pick up the key, her heart beating with a strange mixture of excitement and anxiety. Ten minutes later, when she finally pulled up outside the block of less than prepossessing apartments, she felt another moment of panic. The home she'd just left might not have been what she would have chosen for herself, but at least it was modern and clean and set on a block large enough to ensure privacy. Now she was going to have to adapt to a ten-year-old flat where she'd live cheek to jowl with her neighbours, and with the sound of passing trains to add to her comfort.

Of course she knew she could have found somewhere a bit more up-market if she'd wanted to share. But that had never been an option. She wanted to be alone, to have the peace and quiet to work. After a lifetime of sharing her space, she was suddenly longing for solitude. And that was different from loneliness, she reminded herself, as she walked up the narrow, concrete path to her new home. Having Tony in her life was what made all the difference.

Not long after the removalists had left, Judith headed back to the house. She couldn't concentrate on making any real order in the flat until she'd faced the boys with the truth of what was going on.

She found both her sons in the family room. Brent was sitting at the table finishing off a bowl of cereal. Luke was lying on the carpet in front of the TV, hypnotised by the flicker of music videos.

Judith walked over to the TV and switched it off at the set.

'Hey, *mum*!' Luke sat up, frowning angrily at her.

'There's something I have to speak to you both about. It's important. And I want your full attention.' She looked over at her elder son. 'That means you too, Brent.'

Grudgingly he turned to look at her while Luke, muttering, maintained his angry frown.

Judith sat herself down on the ottoman. She didn't want to feel as if she were delivering the Gettysburg Address.

'It's difficult for me to know where to begin. But I guess you might have sensed that things haven't been as good as they could have been between your father and myself for quite a while now.'

'Oh, shit,' Luke lay back again and rolled his eyes at the ceiling. 'Don't tell me we're going to hear the D word.'

Her sons' diffidence unnerved her. Was her announcement of the family break-up just another boring event to be endured before they could switch the television back on? she wondered. Is that what the world had come to?

'Maybe it doesn't have to be that,' she said carefully. 'All I know is I have to separate myself from the situation for a while. Maybe neither of you realised it, but I haven't been happy in this house for a long time. There were too many occasions when I felt all I was good for was cleaning up after the three of you and keeping you fed. I tried to talk to your father about it, but he wouldn't listen. It seems as if I was fit to work to pay the mortgage, your school fees, your father's green fees and everything else, but not quite good enough to be shown a little respect or appreciation.' She tried to keep the bitterness out of her voice.

'Well, I've made up my mind that I don't need to be treated that way any more — by any of you. Which doesn't mean,' she added, 'that the three of us, at least, can't still try to be friends. You've got my mobile number. I hope you'll feel you can ring me at any time. I'm your mother and I'll always care dearly for you, the only difference is that I won't be here to play the role of chief cook and bottle washer any longer.'

'But what about cricket this afternoon? Who's going to drop me at the game?' Brent looked at her with a worried frown.

'If you're ready in ten minutes, I can drop you over there now. But you'll have to get someone else to bring you home.'

'What about next week?' he asked, his voice close to a whine.

'Talk to your father,' Judith replied curtly.

'When are you going to tell dad?' Brent was looking at her uneasily, as if she were someone he didn't recognise.

'Tomorrow evening when he gets back.'

She spent the rest of the weekend unpacking and finding a place for things in her new abode. Yet looming over everything she did was the thought of having to confront Greg with the news of her departure.

She found herself trying to imagine his reaction. Shock? Anger? Disbelief? If she knew Greg, it'd probably a mixture of all three. Would he try to bully her into coming back? Or would the shock of what she'd done actually make him realise the extent of his neglect? It was that second premise which worried her the most. If he pleaded with her to come back, promised that things would change, would she be tempted to weaken, to give him a second chance? She really couldn't be sure.

Greg was due home about six on the Sunday evening. By late afternoon, too nervous to concentrate on much else, she paid a visit to her mother, who would have to be told the news too.

And perhaps, Judith told herself as she drove to the retirement village, by announcing the situation as a fait accompli, she would be more able to withstand Greg's reaction, whatever that might be.

Marjorie Grant sat in her over-furnished living room and stared at her daughter, her pale eyes wide in disbelief.

'Oh, no, Judith! You can't! You can't walk out on your husband, on all those years of marriage. And what about the boys? How can you possibly think of leaving your children?'

Judith had been prepared for her mother's reaction. With her own happy marriage cut short, it would be very difficult for her to understand how her daughter could deliberately walk out on her relationship. Not only that, Judith thought, her parents belonged to a generation who believed in sticking with a marriage, no matter how bad, until the bitter end.

'Mum, the boys are almost grown up. They're young men. And to tell you the truth, they barely notice I'm around, unless they want me to do something for them.'

'But it's not —'

Gently, Judith interrupted, and did her best to explain.

'Mum, this isn't something that's happened overnight. I haven't wanted to upset you, so I never really told you how things were between Greg and me. The marriage has been dead for a long time. I want to get out now while there's still time to follow some of my own dreams.'

She could see the incomprehension in her mother's face. It was clear that the idea of a woman pursuing any other means of fulfillment than that provided by marriage and motherhood was beyond her.

Marjorie Grant shook her head. 'I really don't understand you young women. Look at you, Judith,' she gestured with a frail, age-spotted hand, 'you've got everything any woman could want: a lovely home, a faithful husband, two healthy children — and it isn't enough. What more could you possibly want?'

A soulmate, Judith said in silent reply. Someone who understands me, who listens when I talk from the heart, who thinks of my happiness before his own.

Someone like Tony.

As if reading her thoughts, her mother's expression suddenly changed. 'There isn't someone else, is there?' she looked at Judith sharply. 'This isn't to do with another man?'

Judith shook her head. 'This is about Greg and me, mum, about finishing something that isn't working for either of us so that both of us might have a chance of making the rest of our lives happier.'

At this stage it was the nearest she could get to making any reference to Tony.

She could see by the expression on Greg's face that the boys had already told him the news. But her sons were nowhere in sight as he confronted her angrily in the living room. He was still dressed in his golfing gear, designer T-shirt and expensive slacks.

'Are you crazy? What the hell do you think you're doing?' His anger deepened the colour of his sunburned face. It was patently clear he wasn't about to discuss the topic amicably. 'Do you really think I'm going to let you simply walk out of here, just like that?'

Judith faced him, her heart thumping with nervousness. She struggled to keep her voice steady. 'It's not a matter of you "letting" me do anything, Greg. I've found myself a flat. I've gone. That's it.'

He gave a choked, angry laugh and swept out his arm in a wide gesture. 'A flat? You're leaving a bloody mansion like this to move into some dump of a flat? Have you taken leave of your senses, Judith? What the hell's wrong with you?'

She'd been so determined to remain calm, but his aggressiveness inflamed her and also helped to dissipate her nervousness.

'I'll tell you what's wrong with me, Greg. And maybe for the first time in our life together, you might listen. For years I've endured living with a man who thinks only of himself, who treats me like some unpaid servant, one who, just luckily, is capable of bringing in some money as well. For the things *you* want, Greg. For the fancy houses and boats and cars and restaurants that are meant to impress your so-called friends.'

His face tightened with temper. 'You're talking crap, Judith! Absolute crap. You don't —'

But, emboldened now, she talked on over the top of his interruption. 'When was the last time you had a thought about what I might like, Greg, about what might make *me* happy? I've tried to talk to you about how I felt, so often, but you never bothered listening. And finally I realised that you were never going to listen. I was never going to get through to you. That's why I'm leaving. I'm getting out while I'm still young enough to have a life.'

He stared back at her and gave a humorless laugh of cynical disbelief. 'So that's it, is it? Had enough of the marriage, so let's just walk out on the responsibilities. The kids, the mortgage, the car payments, everything else we're hocked to the eyeballs with.'

It dawned on her then. The truth hit her in the face like a bucket of iced water. Of course, he was shocked and angry, probably hated the idea of what his friends might think, but what was really upsetting him about her leaving, she realised, was the loss of her regular income. It shouldn't have hurt. But it did.

'The money side of things will have to be worked

out,' she replied, speaking more calmly. 'But until then I'm quite happy to go on paying my share of the mortgage. For one thing, I don't want to disturb the boys during the school year. When that's over, we can think about selling the house.'

'Oh, we can, can we?' He shook his head at her, his face a mask of anger. 'You've got it all worked out, haven't you, Judith? Well, maybe it won't be that easy. Just wait till you see what it's like being out there, a woman on your own.'

Judith stared back at him. She knew him so well, had predicted his reaction. Locked in his own selfish world, it would never occur to him to examine their relationship, to wonder if perhaps he could be in any way to blame for driving her away. No, Greg's strategy was always to attack. Intimidate. Play on her insecurities.

Only this time it wasn't going to work.

'I intend to see, Greg. And no matter how tough it is, I know it won't be as bad as spending the rest of my life with a man as selfish and as emotionally retarded as you.'

And, turning on her heel, she walked away without another word.

But the confrontation had shaken her all the same. Over the next two days, she found the best solution was to keep busy: putting things away in the flat, setting up her computer in a corner of the living room and getting back to her writing. For so long now she had found the art of creation a salve. In an attempt to escape her own life, she would put herself into

Jo's universe. And in solving her heroine's problems she gave herself hope that she'd solve her own.

She saved her surprise until the night of her next meeting with Tony, hugging the secret to herself, imagining his pleasure and delight when she told him she was free, that her life was now her own.

But as it turned out, Tony had a surprise of his own. As soon as she entered his apartment, he shared the news with her.

'I've mentioned your work to an agent I know, Judith. She's one of the best. She said she'd be happy to look at the finished manuscript.'

Her face lit up with excitement as she took her usual seat on the sofa. 'Oh, Tony, that's fabulous! I'm so grateful. Who is she?'

He carried through their coffee and, in answer to her eager questions, filled her in on the details. Annie Selkirk was a well-known agent who specialised in women's fiction. She had liked the sound of Judith's work.

'But let's keep our feet on the ground,' Tony cautioned. 'she's a businesswoman first and foremost. The commercial nature of the work has to appeal to her.'

'Oh, God, Tony, if only she likes it.'

'The important thing is you've got an intro. She actually agreed to look at it. And that's a great start.'

'Oh, yes, yes!' Judith couldn't hide her delight.

As Tony pulled the typed pages out of the file, she decided to keep her own exciting news till they were in bed.

Their lovemaking left her sated, drugged with happiness. When she was with Tony like this, she thought, she felt so secure, so safe. And now she was going to be able to see him so much more often.

Lying in her lover's arms, she smiled a lazy, contented smile and drew a finger gently through the greying tangle of his chest hair.

'I've got a surprise too,' she said teasingly. 'I wanted to tell you straight away when it happened, but I decided to save it until now.'

'A night for surprises.'

She could hear the langour in his voice as he ran his hand lightly down her bare back.

She couldn't suppress her emotion any longer. 'I've actually done it, Tony. I've left Greg, moved out, got a flat of my own.'

His hand stopped moving, and she felt his body stiffen. There was a long silence before he answered.

'You've left him ...? When?' It wasn't the spontaneous response of delight she'd been anticipating.

'Last weekend. I've taken a six-month lease on a flat. I know exactly how it feels to have lifted the stone from my back.' She moved her arm to his waist and hugged him tight. 'And the best part of it is that we'll be able to see each other much more often.'

'Judith...' He drew away from her, and she lifted her head to look at him. The way he spoke her name, his lack of enthusiasm, sent a warning spasm through her.

He gave a heavy sigh, looking embarrassed and uncomfortable. 'Look, I'm not sure if there are any wires crossed here, but ... oh, God...' He pushed himself up and swung his legs out of the bed. Judith lay still and silent, watching him, the sheet now pulled up under her chin.

Over his shoulder he glanced back at her. 'What I'm trying to say is that I find you a very attractive woman, Judith, of course I do, but it never occurred to me — I didn't think you were looking for a future with me.'

She felt a cold hand squeeze her heart. Her eyes were fixed on him, and she opened her mouth — to say what, she had no idea — but nothing came out. Her throat felt as if it had been clamped off.

'You misunderstood me, love.' His expression revealed his discomfort. 'I'm very fond of you, I enjoy our time together, but I'm not looking for another relationship. I know you've told me how unhappy you are in your marriage, and for that reason I'm glad you've made the move to leave. But if … if you've left because you hoped for some future with me, I'm sorry, but you've got it wrong. I really can't offer you that.'

She felt rigid with the shock of his response, and the embarrassment she had caused them both. How could she have got it so wrong, made such a terrible mistake? But they'd been so close, she'd felt so sure that Tony was looking for something more too, and that he'd found it with her.

But then, she reminded herself now, he'd never said anything outright, had never told her he loved her. Not that that had worried her. It was the way he'd treated her that mattered, the sense of rapport and companionship that had existed between them. She'd been so sure, so stupidly, naively sure …

All she wanted now was to get away, remove herself from the humiliation, shield herself from the pity she saw in his eyes.

Suddenly, too, she was ashamed of her nakedness, of her less-than perfect body. Where before she hadn't let it worry her, now she felt as if she were undressed in the presence of a stranger. But she couldn't bear to get out of the bed and get dressed while Tony was in the room.

'I think I should go.' Her voice was tight. 'If you'd just let me get dressed ...'

'Of course,' he said gently as he stood up. 'We'll talk when you're ready.'

Picking up his own clothes, he closed the door behind him and she dressed hurriedly. There seemed something so pathetically sad and obscene now about the rumpled sheets that still held the imprint of their bodies. Her urgent, desperate need was to get out of his apartment as quickly as possible.

When she emerged from the bedroom, he was sitting, fully dressed, on the sofa, waiting for her.

'Judith, love, I can't let you go just like this.' But the last thing she wanted to do was talk. Refusing his offer to take a seat, she picked up her handbag and folder from the coffee table.

Rising to his feet, Tony followed her to the door and moved in front of her, barring her way.

'I had to be honest with you, Judith.' His eyes pleaded with her to understand. 'I had to tell you the truth. But that doesn't mean we still can't go on being friends. I've enjoyed so much helping you, seeing your talent bloom. There's no reason for that to finish.' He shook his head and spread his hands in a gesture of helplessness. 'Probably we should never have ended up in bed. That always complicates things.'

She turned her face away, not wanting him to see the hot tears of self-pity that stung her eyes. 'I guess it does,' she managed.

But he put a gentle hand on her arm, and she was forced to look at him. 'You're a wonderful woman, Judith, please believe that. Maybe knowing me has given you the courage to take this first step. But I promise, if you do it alone, standing on your own two feet, in the end you'll find yourself stronger than you could ever believe right now.'

He tightened his grip and his eyes searched her own. 'Will you believe me? Will you believe me when I tell you that?'

Judith couldn't bring herself to answer. Instead she nodded mutely, barely taking in what he was saying. Because escape was the only thing that mattered.

She felt so small. So vulnerable. A total fool.

CHAPTER THIRTEEN

It was almost a week since David had left for Perth. Despite the terrible finality of his words, Leith still didn't believe that her marriage was over. While he was away, she reassured herself, he'd have time to think things through, understand what he was doing to both of them, realise that the blame lay not only with her. When he got his head together, she felt sure he'd ring and assure her that they could work everything out.

Meanwhile, she did her best to get through the empty days. But she had little energy, or interest in her usual pursuits. It was hard to concentrate on anything else when her mind was so distracted by her problems. More than anything, she wished she had bitten back her words that night, never revealed to David what had happened with Paul. It was desperation that had forced her to confess, the overwhelming desire to try to make David understand how far he had pushed her.

Until the last two or three years, their life together had been close to perfect. David had always worked hard, but not the crazy hours he worked now. Nor had he spent so much time away from home. If things had stayed the same, she knew she would never have looked at another man. Even one as exciting as Paul Houston.

But as the days passed and the call she was waiting for never came, Leith began to feel increasing panic. Surely David would get in touch with her. Surely he wouldn't let her suffer like this for too long.

By the end of ten days she couldn't bear the suspense and tension any longer. That evening she put a call through to his mobile.

As she waited for him to answer, her heart thudded painfully against her ribs.

'David ... darling ... It's me.'

There was an uncomfortable pause.

'How are you?' There was no warmth in his response.

'Darling, I feel terrible. I thought I'd have heard from you by now. I'm missing you so much, I just want to talk to you, to get all this terrible mess sorted out.'

She could hear his breathing in the silence that followed. 'Leith, I thought I made it clear.' He sounded as if he were speaking to a stranger. 'I'm not interested in getting into emotional discussions. What I'm doing now is trying to get things sorted out in my head. It doesn't help to have you call me like this.'

She felt sick as she listened to his cool goodbye.

For the first time she started to face the fact that her husband had meant what he'd said. That their marriage was over. He wasn't coming back.

By the end of two weeks, she'd lost more weight than she could afford to, and needed pills to put her to sleep. When she woke she had to drag herself out of bed to face another endless day in the silent loneliness of the house. And for the first time in her life, she didn't give a damn about how she looked. Her face, bare of make-up, looked drawn and haggard. Her hair was lank and in need of a tint. But none of that seemed important now.

In a state of increasing despair, Leith began to realise that this was real loneliness, not what had gone before, when it had been a matter of filling in time, knowing that eventually David would arrive home.

If I could only talk to him, she told herself as she paced restlessly around the empty house. Talk properly, make him listen to my side of things. All she wanted was a chance to bring him round. To convince him that they could get through all this.

Finally, her desperation growing, she ignored his direction and tried his mobile again — and again. All she got was his message bank and he never returned her calls.

Meanwhile she did her best to keep the news of what had happened from their friends. There were a couple of dinner invitations for the weeks ahead which she managed to sidestep with the excuse that David was in Perth, and she wasn't quite sure when he'd be back. She couldn't bear for anyone to know what had happened, to admit that there was anything less than perfect with their marriage. How could she reveal her infidelity, or the fact that David had walked out on her?

On other occasions she turned down requests to meet girlfriends for lunch or a movie. It was hard enough to lie over the phone, and she knew it would be totally impossible to carry off face to face. That was the reason, too, that she'd cancelled her regular tennis morning with the excuse of having 'put her back out'.

The resulting isolation made everything worse to bear, but Leith felt she had no option. There was no one she could turn to for solace and comfort.

But finally, as the days passed and her desperation grew, she thought about calling Judith. Judith would understand.

When she rang, it was one of the boys who answered, mumbling something about 'mum not living here any longer'. In her own confused state, Leith hadn't the energy to try to piece together the disjointed explanation.

And then one morning the note arrived in the mail. With a small frown of curiosity, she opened the expensive creamy envelope, addressed in a handwriting she didn't recognise.

Dear Leith,

I'm respecting the fact that you asked me not to call you again, but I hope you won't be angry that I'm dropping you this short note.

The last time we spoke, you said that you'd told your husband about us. Since then, I haven't been able to stop worrying about you. In just the short time we knew each other, I think I got a very good idea of the sort of person you are. Your honesty was one of the virtues I most admired. My only hope is that you haven't been made to pay too high a price for that honesty, because you certainly don't deserve that.

If you need to talk — about anything at all — please know you can call me at any time. I will always be here to help you in any way possible.

Warmest love,

Paul.

For a long while, Leith stared down at the neatly written words from the man who had been her confidant and lover. Finally, she crumpled the piece of expensive notepaper in her nervous fingers. Much as she longed to talk to someone about the terrible situation, she knew it could never be Paul.

Not when she was still hoping and praying for David to change his mind.

She spent hours sitting by the phone, hopelessly willing it to ring. The television flickered in the background, but she saw and heard nothing. Fearfully, she tried to imagine a life on her own, without David. It seemed impossible. How would she manage? she asked herself. What would she do with the rest of her life?

But she didn't have any answers. Her only response was to crawl back into bed and take another sleeping tablet, hoping that when she woke up, a miracle might have happened and David would have returned.

The second note arrived a couple of days later, among the usual pile of bills and catalogues and bank statements. She recognised the same expensive envelope and, this time, Leith knew who it was from. Struggling with herself, she knew she should throw it away, but her loneliness and need got the better of her.

She slit the envelope open and pulled out the single sheet of paper.

Dear Leith,

Believe me, I don't want to intrude on you against your wishes, but last night I ate at the restaurant where we first met and all I could think of was you. My darling, I never wanted to cause you any pain. All I could see was a woman crying out for love, one who deserved to be loved more than anyone else I have ever known.

You have my number. Call it if there is ever anything I can do to make you happy.

With all my love,

Paul.

She read his words again, and then once more. On a rational level, she knew she should disregard this letter too, but, in her fragile state, she felt assailed by the torment of her confused emotions. She had told Paul to leave her alone, yet the sympathy and concern he had expressed in both notes beckoned to her like a lifeline. The temptation to get in touch was great. Just to talk, she assured herself, just to retain her sanity.

She could hear the delight in his voice.

'I'm so glad you got in touch, Leith. I've been so

worried. All I wanted to hear was that you were all right.'

Struggling for control, she took a deep shuddering breath. 'It's been awful, Paul ... He won't talk to me, won't try to understand.'

And then she couldn't hold back any longer and, in a raw, anguished voice, she poured everything out. The trauma of the last few weeks, her disbelief, her shock. By the time she had finished, her tears were flowing freely.

'Oh, Leith... I can't believe he's done this to you. You'd think if he truly loved you, he could forgive this one indiscretion, or at least understand that you're not the only one to blame.'

'I can't believe it either,' she whispered tearfully.

'If you were mine, you'd never have been in this position. I swear that.'

And she knew he was speaking the truth.

'I wish I could be there to comfort you properly, but I know that's not what you want. I just hope that you'll at least let me call you from time to time and see how things are going.' He paused a moment. 'Will you let me do that, Leith?'

The conversation, the outpouring of emotion, had left her drained, but had also offered the release she had craved. Paul had listened, *comforted her*, agreed that she could not be expected to shoulder all the blame. Talking to him again would do no harm, she assured herself. It would help her to sort things out in her own mind so that when David finally came home, she would be strong enough to convince him that they could still get their marriage back on track.

In a low, choked voice, she answered Paul's question in the affirmative.

And then, a couple of days later, Leith felt her prayers had been answered. The telephone rang around seven, and it was David.

Her heart leapt with hope as she heard his voice.

'David ... oh, I'm so glad to hear from you ... How are you? How's the work going?'

After waiting all this time for his call, she'd now been caught completely off guard.

'No real problems ... but I haven't rung to discuss my work, Leith.'

She heard him take a deep breath. He's going to tell me it's all right, she told herself, that he's forgiven me and we're going to put this nightmare behind us.

'Leith, we've been apart almost three weeks now, and I've had plenty of time to think about all that's happened. It hasn't been easy, I can assure you. There's still a part of me that loves you and maybe that'll never change. But what I am certain of now is that our marriage is over.'

Her breathing stopped, and she felt as if a steel band were being tightened around her heart. But he hadn't finished.

'It just won't work for me, Leith.' His voice was edged with despair and regret. 'Every time I close my eyes, all I can see is you with someone else. I just can't forget it. If we tried to keep things together, it'd poison every day ... I'm sorry, more sorry than you can ever understand. But I don't want you clinging to some useless hope. There isn't any future for us.

When I get back, I'll move my things out as quickly as possible so each of us can start to get our lives back on track.'

Ice threaded through her veins. She felt her belly turn to water. This couldn't be happening ... She had to make him see ...

'David, listen to me!' she pleaded. 'I made one mistake. *One* mistake. If you truly love someone, is that so much to forgive?' Subconsciously she found herself quoting Paul's words.

'Forgiving is different from forgetting, Leith, and I'm not —'

Fear and despair made her rush on blindly. 'But I'm not the only one to blame! Why can't you stop and see that for a moment?' Her voice rose shrilly. 'Can't you understand that it's your fault, too? It would never have happened if you'd been the husband you should have been. It's not all my fault, David! You can't put all the blame on me.'

She was sobbing now and, in the pause that followed, he made no response.

'It's past being a matter of blame,' he finally offered, his voice full of weary resignation. 'It's the fact that I can't live with you any longer, Leith. I can't live with just the memory of love.'

And before she could say anything more, he quietly replaced the receiver.

She had no idea how long she sat there still listening to the sound of the disconnected line, as if she could somehow keep hold of that last link to him, keep him with her a few moments longer. In a

271

stupor of anguish, she tried to absorb the finality of David's words.

He wasn't coming back. It was over. All those years of memories swept away because he couldn't forgive her, because he wouldn't accept the fact that he'd been in any way to blame.

Raising a hand to wipe away her tears, Leith finally replaced the receiver.

What was she going to do? How was she going to survive this?

If Paul was shocked by her loss of weight, her haggard appearance, he managed to conceal his reaction as she let him into the house.

'Paul, I'm sorry...' Her breath was shallow as she fought for control. 'To get you out like this...' And then words failed her, and the next moment she was in his arms, sobbing against the fine wool of his jacket, clinging to the sense of comfort and protection.

'Oh, Leith ... my poor, poor Leith ...'

He held her close, stroking her hair, murmuring gentle words until her tears finally eased. Then he led her down the hall, his arm around her waist.

'Come on,' he said gently, 'let's sit down. Where can I find you a tissue?'

He left her sitting on the sofa and returned a few moments later with a box of Kleenex and a glass of water. Taking a seat beside her, he waited while she wiped her eyes and blew her nose.

'I must ... look awful,' she stammered, as she reached for the glass with shaky fingers.

He ignored the remark. 'I'm going to stay with you tonight. In the guest bedroom,' he quickly assured her. 'I'm not leaving you alone in this state.'

He sat beside the bed, holding her hand, stroking her face, until she at last fell into an exhausted sleep. But it was the first night in weeks that she hadn't needed to take a pill.

The next morning she awoke to find him sitting on the edge of the bed. He smiled down at her and brushed a strand of hair off her cheek.

'The kettle's on. I'll pop on some toast while you wash your face. And how does an egg sound? Perfectly fried in a smidgen of butter?'

She surprised herself by managing both the egg and the tomato he'd fried with it. She realised it was the first real food she'd eaten in days.

The weather was warm enough, and they ate on the patio overlooking the water. He refused to let her dwell on the subject of her marriage. 'Not now, Leith,' he asserted. 'It won't do you any good to rehash it all at the moment.'

And he was right, she found. Before too long she felt a sort of calm settle on her. She realised that just being in Paul's presence made her feel stronger. His gentle assumption of control offered her the comfort and security she was longing for.

She'd forgotten it was Saturday and was surprised when he suggested that they spend the day on the water.

'Much better for you than moping round here all

day,' he ordered kindly. 'My boat's moored at Pittwater. We'll pack a lunch and make a day of it.'

She hadn't expected to enjoy herself, had hoped only for a distraction from the trauma of the last few weeks. But the hours spent on the water in the fresh air proved a real tonic.

They'd dropped in at Paul's apartment so he could shower and change, and pick up the keys to his cruiser. Then, on the way, they'd stopped at a deli and bought a selection of nibbles for lunch. To Leith, it had seemed more than they could ever eat but, after two hours on the water, she had amazed herself by actually feeling hungry for the first time in weeks.

Paul was so right to bring me here, she thought. The warmth of the sun on her arms, the breeze off the sea, the gentle movement of the boat had done so much to restore her equilibrium. But it was more than the change of scene and the beauties of nature, it was Paul's company, too, that had helped to lighten her mood.

He did everything to please her, thought only of her needs. He gently rubbed sunblock on her face and arms, fetched an extra pillow for her back, filled her glass with wine. Then, when they dropped anchor in a shady bay, he prepared her a tempting lunch from the bits and pieces they'd brought with them.

'You're spoiling me,' she said with a grateful smile as she accepted the plate of food.

He looked at her from behind his Ray Bans. 'And I'm never going to stop,' he said seriously.

Not like David. She couldn't help the thought that

sprang into her mind. And for the first time that day, she let herself dwell on everything that had happened. To her surprise she found her grief being supplanted by anger as she began to question David's role in the breakdown of their marriage. Why had he let everything change? Why had he taken her for granted? Why couldn't he have appreciated her as Paul did?

It was almost seven when they drove back over the Harbour Bridge.

As they neared the city, Leith grew more silent. Her thoughts were taken up with trying to face the return to loneliness after such a wonderful day.

It was the touch of Paul's hand on her knee that brought her back to the present moment.

'I don't think it's a good idea for you to sleep alone in that huge house tonight, Leith.'

She felt as if he'd read her thoughts.

'I suggest we go and get your things and you can spend the night at my place.'

She saw later that that was the turning point, the moment when she still could have avoided everything that happened afterwards.

CHAPTER FOURTEEN

It was almost midnight when Judith finally switched off the computer.

She'd set up a workspace for herself in the tiny alcove that passed for a dining room off the kitchen. It was better than being cramped into the second bedroom with only a view of the railway line. Her desk took up the entire space, but that didn't matter. She had no intention of entertaining anyone. She'd done more than her share of all that during her life with Greg.

With a yawn she stood up, stretched, then went into the kitchen to make herself a final cup of tea. She was already in her pyjamas. One of the great pluses about a writer's life, she'd found, was that you could dress as comfortably as you liked because nobody ever saw you. She couldn't help wondering if Jackie Collins or Danielle Steel or Joanna Trollope worked in their dressing gowns. In magazine articles she'd only ever seen them at their writing desks wearing designer gear and looking as if they'd stepped out of the beauty salon. But she'd take a bet they didn't do their real work like that. Still, she supposed it all had to do with maintaining their public image.

After the humiliating scene with Tony, she'd found it difficult to get back into her work. Even now, whenever she allowed herself to recall that evening, she felt her cheeks flare. How could she have made such an idiot of herself, assuming he was as keen as she was, daring to imagine that he could truly have been interested in a future?

The feeling of rejection had been compounded by the realisation that at almost forty-three, she'd burned all her bridges. Walked out on her marriage and family, left her home for a man who didn't want her. She had taken the chance to escape, and now she was totally alone.

To begin with, she'd been overwhelmed by fear and panic, but then she'd forced herself to try to think the situation through more calmly. She'd been unhappy with Greg long before she met Tony. Thoughts of leaving him had crossed her mind on many occasions, except that she'd never had the guts to do it until she'd met another man. It was Tony who had given her the courage to take that huge step, even if he wasn't there for her afterwards.

Now, as she waited for the kettle to boil, she couldn't help remembering what he'd said about standing on her own two feet and finding herself stronger than she'd ever believe. At the moment she couldn't quite imagine it. But maybe it was true.

And she had to admit that the flip side of being alone was the newly found freedom of having only herself to please. It didn't matter if the laundry piled up while she worked, if she didn't make the bed, or played music at two in the morning. And after a lifetime of cooking meals for three hungry males, she was now free to eat whatever she felt like whenever she pleased. Sometimes that meant muesli at midnight, or cold baked beans straight out of the tin with a spoon. It gave her a certain wry pleasure to think that she'd never have to peel a potato or look at a recipe book again if she didn't want to.

But that didn't mean she wasn't worrying about how the boys were managing. A lot of the time they were ungrateful, selfish little b's: but still it had torn her apart to leave them. It was true what they said, she thought, once you were a mother you never stopped worrying or caring about your kids. She hated to think of them struggling to cope without her but, she did her best to console herself, this had to be a lesson to them, too, a chance to understand what could happen when respect and consideration were missing in a marriage. If they wanted their own marriages to last, they might see that they'd have to treat their own wives a hell of a lot better than their own father had treated her.

In the meantime, she determined, they would have a chance to see how things ticked over at home without her. Maybe then, they'd have some idea of just how much they'd had done for them.

Greg had called her, of course. Angry and abusive on the phone, he'd demanded that she 'stop all this crap' and come home at once. But she didn't need a degree in psychology to know what was really bugging him. It had nothing to do with missing Judith, the person. Rather, it meant that he was running out of clean, ironed shirts, that the sheets needed changing, and that he was the one who now had to stand in the supermarket queues on his way home from work.

He'd done his best to frighten her again, emphasising once more how half of Sydney was full of lonely, impoverished, sex-starved women, all desperate to find a man to take care of them.

Judith had put the phone down before he'd finished. All his call had managed to do was convince her that, no matter what the reason that had finally spurred her to leave, she had made the right decision. Better loneliness, she told herself, than a two-minute 'quickie' once a fortnight, and nothing but domestic drudgery in between.

She couldn't help missing Tony. They'd always got on so well, and she'd looked forward to their meetings so much. It crossed her mind to give him a call, but she didn't feel comfortable about that. He'd think she was chasing him, and she'd hate to give that impression. All she wished was that things could go on as they had before the complications of sex had made them messy.

She was still writing, of course, but a seed of doubt had taken root in her mind. Considering what had happened, she began to worry that perhaps Tony had encouraged her work only to get her into bed, had told her she had talent, made her think she could really write, when his only goal had been to have sex with her.

Somehow she couldn't quite believe it, however. The two of them had spent a lot of time together, and she'd always considered herself a better judge of people than that. But then, she reminded herself dryly, what experience had she had with men? Tony had seemed so honest, so open, but if he'd been spinning her a line, would she really have known?

The doubt delivered a serious blow to her confidence. There were a few days after the shock of Tony's rejection when she hadn't been able to write at all. Without her usual salve and distraction, she'd felt herself start to panic. Not only had Tony rejected her, she'd also lost faith in her ability to write.

With an effort, she had done her best to rationalise the situation to herself. She'd worked so hard already, was so near to finishing, she'd be a fool to stop now. And, even if she never got published, the sheer act of creating brought her so much pleasure. Finally, too, she remembered the agent. If Tony had only been trying to seduce her, surely he wouldn't have bothered mentioning her work to an agent? Unless, of course, that was a lie as well.

But her instincts told her that Tony Kendall wasn't that sort of man.

It was two weeks and three days after it happened that he got in touch. Judith had just finished a dinner of egg on toast followed by strawberry yoghurt and was watching the seven o'clock news when the mobile rang on the table beside her.

Her heart turned over when she heard his voice.

'Judith, it's Tony. I hope you don't mind that I'm calling. I'd have rung earlier, but I wasn't sure if you ever wanted to hear from me again.

Even though he couldn't see her, she shook her head in vigorous denial. She was so happy to get his call. 'Oh, no, Tony. You mustn't think that.'

'I want to apologise. I didn't mean to upset you that night. I handled everything badly, I know. I'm truly very sorry if you think I was being dishonest with you. It was never meant to be like that.'

'Tony, please, I was at fault too.' Somehow, at a distance, it felt a lot easier to discuss the situation. 'Reading too much into things, I guess. Needing something to give me the courage to get out of my marriage.'

'But you've done it now, haven't you? On your own. And in the end, that'll be the best way to grow, Judith.'

'I think I know now what you meant about lifting the stone off your back.'

'You're strong, Judith. You'll make it.'

She was surprised at that. The fact that he thought her strong. Maybe with all she'd endured over the years, she was. Only you never saw yourself as others did.'

'There's something else I want to make clear, too,' he went on. 'As far as your writing goes, you must believe that I had no ulterior motive in praising your work. You've got talent, Judith. Real talent. I would never have lied about that. Please believe me.'

She could hear the sincerity in his voice and knew with certainty now that her fears had been totally misplaced.

'I couldn't help worrying that you might have got the wrong idea about that.' There was a pause, then he asked, 'Are you still writing?'

'Yes. Yes I am.'

'Then, would you let me work with you again like we used to, Judith? I miss that. And I miss you too. I've realised these last couple of weeks that I'd really hate to lose our friendship.'

Her throat tightened. 'I'd love that.' Then she added softly, 'I've missed you too.'

❅

'He's asked you to meet his mama?' Jessica Wilson widened her eyes in mock amazement. 'Now, that's what I call *serious*.' She cocked an eyebrow at Cate. 'How long have you guys been seeing each other now? Three months? Must mean you've passed the third month crunch time.'

Jessica put her empty wine glass down among the remains of the Thai takeaway that littered Cate's coffee table.

'Need I ask what *your* verdict is on *him*?' she enquired.

Cate took a moment to reply. She was remembering the last twelve weeks and the pleasure with which she had looked forward to each weekend. When Cal came to stay, they rode the ferries, visited the zoo, the museums, the Rocks — all the things you never bothered to do when you actually lived in a place. It was like renewing her acquaintance with the city all over again. And being in Cal's company made everything so much more fun.

He had a restless nature, she'd discovered, was full of boundless energy, enthusiasm and curiousity. Everything he did, he did at full throttle, but she liked that about him. She was at the stage where she was liking everything about him ...

Yet it suited her to have her own space, too. She had her life to herself during the week and the excitement of being with Cal almost every weekend — the best of both worlds she figured.

'Don't bother to answer.' Jessica waved a hand, dismissing her own question. 'It's written all over you. True love hits home.'

Cate smiled. 'Let's just say it's been the happiest three months of my life.'

'So you've actually stopped worrying and started living?'

'Someone should write a book with that title.'

'Well,' Jessica responded, 'I always say, there's nothing like a bit of regular sex to turn a hard-nosed career woman sweet and docile.'

Cate couldn't help smiling. They were joking, of course, but she knew for certain that something inside her had changed. If she had to find a word for it, she'd say she'd found peace. Since coming to know Cal she'd felt a sense of being complete, of having found whatever it was that she hadn't admitted was missing in her life.

As the weeks had passed, she'd come to trust what was happening between them, had peeled back the safety wrapping on her heart and let herself feel again. The night Cal had told her he loved her, she'd been suffused with joy, and all need for caution had finally disappeared. She knew then that she was truly loved. And that made it so much easier to love in return.

Jessica broke into her thoughts. 'D'you know when I realised it was the real thing between you two? When you told me about the jogging. That *really* clinched it. I figured anybody who could up your heart rate, in the vertical position that is, had to be a cert.'

Cate chuckled, remembering the weekend when Cal had presented her with a pair of brand new joggers. She'd stared at them in their box with a sort of horrified amazement.

'Are you kidding?'

'Every girl needs one pair of comfortable shoes,' he'd joked.

But he hadn't let her off the hook. They'd begun with long, fast evening walks along the beach, and gradually he'd encouraged her into a short jog. No more than five minutes at first, with her complaining every step of the way, but gradually finding it easier. He never pushed her till it hurt. And somehow the combination of fresh sea air, the sight and sound of the surf, the forgiving surface of sand beneath her feet began to convince her that there might be something worthwhile in her efforts.

'You're right,' she grinned, 'I'd never have got up a sweat for just anyone.'

'Yeah, well, just let me know if you sweat when you meet mum,' Jessica retorted.

'She's very independent,' Cal explained as they pulled up in front of the small apartment complex overlooking the sheltered inlet of the Broadwater. 'Wouldn't hear of it when I tried to talk her into a retirement village. Insisted she was quite capable of looking after herself.'

'How old is she?' Cate asked as they got out of the car.

'Seventy-eight. Arthritis is her worst complaint, but I still don't like her living alone. I keep a close eye on her which, of course, suits her, doesn't it?' He grinned as he held the squeaky entrance gate open for Cate. 'Gets to see me for dinner once a week.'

The apartment was on the ground floor, and when Cal pushed the buzzer on the front door, they were greeted by a wild frenzy of barking and scuffling from the other side.

'Oscar,' he explained over his shoulder. 'World's largest Pomeranian.'

'It's open!' came the call from inside.

As Cal pushed the door open, a huge bundle of black and white fur shot out and immediately began to sniff furiously at Cate's feet.

'Call off the hounds, mother,' Cal grinned as they entered.

Maude Donohoe was standing in the small living room. She waved her walking stick in the direction of her pet.

'Oscar! You come here right now! Remember your manners.'

She gave Cate a reassuring smile. 'Don't worry. He's all noise. He'll be making up to you in a moment.'

Maude Donohoe's voice had a stronger lilt than her son's. She was frail and a little stooped, but her wide blue eyes were still bright and alert, and her high cheekbones and fine complexion made it clear she'd once been an attractive woman. She'd obviously taken some pains for the evening. Her white hair was deftly arranged in a soft french roll and she was wearing lipstick and blush, while down the front of her tailored linen dress hung a single row of pearls.

Cal kissed his mother's cheek and then, putting an arm around Cate's waist, made the introductions. 'Mother, I'd like you to meet Cate Tremain, a very special friend of mine.'

Cate was aware of the scrutiny in those Irish eyes. Stepping closer, she held out her hand. 'How do you do, Mrs Donohoe.'

But the old lady ignored the gesture. Instead she opened her arms and, still holding her walking stick, gave Cate a hug.

Drawing back, she looked at Cate, a twinkle now in those blue eyes. 'That's the way we Irish welcome special friends,' she said with a smile.

From that moment, the ice was broken and Cate felt herself relax. It was clear Maude Donohoe wasn't going to be some crotchety old dragon.

The evening turned out to be a lot more fun than she'd been anticipating. Cal's mother, she discovered, had the same wicked sense of humour as her son, and over dinner she had Cate laughing out loud at some of her stories of life in Ireland.

'I think it's amazing that you transplanted yourself so late in life,' Cate offered once in reply.

There was a split second pause, and Cate only just caught the fleeting exchange of glances between mother and son.

'It wasn't all that difficult,' came the soft answer.

Overiding his mother's objections, Cate and Cal insisted on tidying up after the meal.

'I'm sure you two have much better things to do,' the old lady protested, the twinkle in her eye obvious again.

'Better things are worth waiting for,' Cal replied with false solemnity as they carried the dirty plates into the kitchen.

'She's hardly what I expected,' Cate whispered, scraping the plates while Cal filled the sink with soapy water.

'And what was that?'

'Oh, you know. Rigid. Old world. Handmaiden to the parish priest.'

Cal couldn't contain a chuckle. 'No, you couldn't say that about ma. Always too skittish for dad. He had to learn to live with it.' He slid the plates into the hot water. Then, turning to Cate, he added, 'But she likes you. That's the important thing.'

Cate could see how much that pleased him.

They didn't stay too late. It was clear Maude Donohoe was used to early nights. With the help of her stick, she walked them to the door, and Cate watched as Cal gave his mother a warm kiss. All evening she had noted his small kindnesses, his consideration and gentleness with her. It told her a lot about the man she loved.

Then the old lady turned to her, and this time the hug was accompanied by a warm kiss and a quick whisper in Cate's ear.

'I'm glad he's met you, Cate. He needs someone to bring a little happiness into his life.'

It was, Cate realised, the certain seal of approval.

And it made her both happy and nervous.

It was two weeks later, her next trip to the Coast, when Cal made the suggestion that turned her world upside down.

They'd just made love and were relaxing in each other's arms. Through the open patio door, Cate could hear the sound of the ocean. With a sigh of pleasure, she ran her fingers gently over Cal's chest. 'Do you know how wonderful that was?'

For a moment he didn't answer, and she thought he mightn't have heard her. But then he responded.

'Wonderful enough to indulge in a lot more often?'

It took her a second or two to catch the significance of his words. Slowly, she lifted her head to look at him.

'What do you mean by that?' Her heart had begun to beat faster.

'I mean,' he was staring into her eyes, 'I'd like you to think about moving in with me.'

And then he was silent for a moment, letting his words sink in, or maybe waiting for her to reply.

When she said nothing, he went on. 'I miss you, Cate. So much it hurts. I'm on automatic pilot Monday to Friday. It's only the weekends when I come alive.'

There wasn't enough light to see his face properly, but Cate could hear the depth of feeling in his voice.

'I've been thinking of putting the idea to you for a while,' he continued, 'only I know how big an ask it is. Giving up your job, your flat, your friends. I know it's something you can't make a decision on immediately, but all I can say is that if you make the move, my darling, I promise you won't regret it.'

Cate was doing her best to come to terms with what he was asking of her. Of course she'd realised that it might come to this. But not so soon. And in some vague way, she'd managed to convince herself that it was Cal who would move in with her, instead of vice versa.

But, of course, when it came to the point, she could see that was impossible. There was not only his business to consider, but his mother too — which meant the only logical option was for her to make the move.

Only she couldn't imagine how she could ever do it. She loved her work. What in the world could she ever find to replace it up here? And what about her independence? Her own flat? Her own *life* . . . ?

Cal broke into the silence.

'Cate, I'm sorry. Maybe I shouldn't have said anything so soon. Or,' the thought seemed suddenly to occur to him, 'maybe I've not judged things right. Between you and me, I mean.'

She heard the note of concern enter his voice and quickly put a finger to his lips.

'No, no. Of course it's not that. There's no question how I feel about you, Cal. It's just — I guess it's so soon ... And maybe I knew it had to come, but I didn't really want to face all the ... complications.'

Gently he brought her head down to rest against his chest.

'I know, Cate, I know. If there were any way I could be the one making the sacrifice, I would. But a business like I've got ties you down. And then there's my mother. I don't feel I could ask her to move again. But I miss you, my darling. So much. I so want to make my life with you.' He ran his hand over her hair, stroking her gently. 'Maybe if you just think about it. Give it some consideration. That's all I ask. And if the answer is no right now, then I'll just have to be patient.'

But it was clear that with the question now out in the open, it would plague her thoughts until she'd made a decision.

It wasn't only a matter of leaving Sydney, her friends, her work. How would she feel about living full-time with someone again? Of fitting her life into Cal's on a daily basis? She was used to making her own decisions, being in charge of her own destiny, never having to consult anyone else. Maybe, she thought, she was past adapting to such a radical change.

If so, what was the alternative? To continue as they were? But how long could they keep on doing that? She knew that sooner or later Cal would make the same suggestion again, and maybe then it would come attached to an ultimatum. And if it reached that stage, could she really walk away, turn her back on a future with a man she loved and respected, because she couldn't give up her independence? And, she reminded herself, would that independence be just as attractive when she was facing her sixtieth birthday alone?

Even sidestepping her propensity for melodrama, Cate still couldn't escape the anguish of wrestling almost constantly with her decision. It stayed at the forefront of her mind, refusing to go away.

When the weather in Sydney stunk, when she couldn't get a cab for love nor money, when the polluted air stung her eyes, or the rates notice arrived for an amount that made her weep, she would wonder what was keeping her from ringing Cal at once. But then there were those days when she pulled off some major coup at work, when she sat in the Belvoir and watched the latest experimental production, when a girlfriend suggested lunch at the Rockpool and the sun was shining and the harbour glistening, and she couldn't ever imagine herself leaving the excitement and stimulus of this wonderful city.

Finally, when she was totally and utterly confused, she sat down with Jessica to talk through the situation.

'It's driving me crazy,' she said. 'One moment I think I'm capable of actually doing what he's asking, the next it seems totally impossible.'

Jessica gave her a considering look. 'Okay, let me ask you the important question. How do you feel about this guy, Cate? Really feel? I mean, when you strip away all the romantic novel stuff of airport welcomes and sex binges, and not having to clean the bath, or pick up his dirty socks.'

Cate didn't hesitate. 'I love him. I've never felt like this about anyone else.'

Jessica waved her hands in a gesture of finality. 'Then I can't see your problem. There *is* no decision.'

'But what about my job? I'll never find anything as exciting or stimulating up there.'

'Don't tell me someone like you can't find another job. What about all the movie production on the Coast? Didn't you always say you wanted to try that side of things eventually?'

'Wanting to, and actually doing it, are two different things, Jess.'

'Sure. And how long have you been at *Live!* now? Close to four years? Cate, I *know* you. Odds are you *will* get bored with it in time and be looking for a change. And in the meantime you'll have thrown away this wonderful opportunity for happiness.'

Cate sat hunched on the sofa, her hands clenched tightly between her legs. 'Jess, I'm forty-two. Maybe I'm past handing over control of my life to someone else.'

'Oh hell, woman, where do you get your crazy ideas? It might have felt like that with Simon, but that's a decade ago. You're a different person now. And from what you've told me, we're talking about a mature human being here, a man who has no desire to absorb you or take over your life. Cal fell in love with you *because* you're independent. He's not going to want to change that.'

But Jessica could see by the expression on her friend's face that she still wasn't totally convinced.

In a softer voice, she tried to reinforce her argument. 'When it's the right person, it helps you to grow, Cate. What you've got to try to do is think about this from the perspective of what you're gaining, not what you're losing.'

There was a long pause before Cate answered. Sighing heavily, she said, 'I'm just not *sure*, Jess. I'm just not sure if I can take the gamble.'

'Then to be really sure, you'd better ring your psychic hotline', Jessica answered sarcastically.

He didn't try to hurry her into a decision. In fact, Cal barely mentioned the subject again when next they saw each other. He's leaving it up to me, Cate told herself. He's not going to try to sway me.

But still she remained plagued by indecision.

❈

Rory could hardly believe it was over. Somehow they had done it. By the end of the second weekend, they had managed to complete the project. It would get to the printers by deadline. A couple of months down the track, there would be the proofs to review, the finishing touches to decide on, but she and Antonella could do that from their respective offices.

By the time they finally wound up on the Sunday evening, she hadn't stood a chance of making her flight. When she'd realised that was how it was going to work out, she'd rung Ian in plenty of time to warn him.

'How did he react?' Antonella had left her alone in the room to make her call.

Rory frowned. 'Wasn't home. I spoke to the nanny and then had to leave a message on his mobile.' She didn't bother to hide her annoyance.

'What's wrong?'

'Well, *he* was supposed to look after Cam. Deb's with him all the rest of the time. Is it such a big deal to spend a few lousy hours with your son?'

'Forget it,' Antonella advised. 'Don't let it worry you now, or we'll never finish here.'

But finally they had. Tired, yet elated at having completed their mammoth task at last, they cleared their desks and got ready to leave the office.

As Antonella began to switch off the lights, she made a suggestion. 'Look, I know we're both dead on our feet, but I'm too charged up to think of sleep. What about you?'

Rory had to agree. She wasn't in the mood to go back to the hotel and crash.

Late as it was, they found a bar somewhere and drank far too much champagne, celebrating their triumph, high on the relief of having accomplished their task by the deadline. They laughed too loudly, interrupted each other, and were bitchy about most of the people they knew in the industry. It didn't matter much, as there were few other customers around at that time on a Sunday evening to overhear them.

'Do you know how much envy this is going to provoke?' Antonella, propped on her elbows, gave her a weary smile. 'When this book's a runaway winner, we're going to be the most hated duo in publishing.'

Rory gave an exaggerated shrug. 'Hey, the price of success. I can live with that.'

Both finally giving in to exhaustion, they decided it would be safer to leave Antonella's car where it was and catch a cab.

When they drew up at the hotel, Rory turned to say goodbye. And now that the moment had come, she felt a strange pang of loss. She realised she was going to miss this woman to whom she'd grown so close during the past intense weeks.

'Thanks, Antonella. For everything. You were the best to work with.' In a spontaneous gesture, she reached out and gave the dark-haired woman a hug.

In response, Antonella held her tight, and next moment Rory felt herself being kissed on the mouth. It didn't feel that strange.

'I enjoyed it. Every minute of it.' Drawing back, Antonella still held Rory in her embrace. 'Working with a real professional is always a buzz.' Then she added softly, 'Personally, it mightn't have worked out quite as I would have wished, but I hope you'll always think of me as a friend, Rory.'

Rory knew she meant it. There had been an intensity between herself and Antonella, she realised, that she'd never felt with any other woman. Whether it had anything to do with what had happened between them physically, she wasn't sure. Yet she had opened her heart and soul in a way she'd never allowed herself to do with anyone else. She and

Antonella had communicated at a depth she had never managed with Ian, and probably never would.

She nodded in reply. 'It was special, Antonella.' Her voice was husky with fatigue, with drink, and something else. 'Really special'.

She had a restless night. The alcohol made her heart race, and her sleep was shallow and unsatisfying. The wake-up call made her jolt awake and, gritty-eyed, she took a quick shower before throwing everything into her suitcase. There was no time for breakfast, but it was the last thing she felt like, anyway.

In the Qantas Club at Tullamarine, she grabbed a cup of black coffee and took in the passing parade. It was the businessmen who interested her. She wondered about their marriages. If they loved their wives. If they took notice of their children and spent time with them. If they were happy or just pretending.

She knew she should feel pleased about going home, but as the time to board her flight grew closer, her depression deepened. She had a sense of being stifled, of a noose tightening around her neck. In Melbourne, working on the book with Antonella, she'd felt competent, assured, confident. But she knew that as soon as she returned to the situation at home, the familiar sense of guilt and helplessness would torment her again.

Her flight was called and, as she made her way to the boarding gate, Rory found herself having crazy thoughts about escaping, of catching a plane that would take her far away from the problems that awaited her.

But then she thought of Cam and hated herself for her weakness.

Ian was at work, of course, and she caught a cab home. Deb greeted her with the news that Cam was 'a little off-colour' so she'd put him back to bed.

Dropping her suitcase by the bedroom door, Rory hurried through to see her son. He was sleeping on his tummy, his face turned to one side. She could hear his heavy breathing and see the heightened colour in his cheeks. Guilt washed over her in an uncompromising wave. And suddenly she felt like crying. She couldn't cope with *this* ... She didn't *want* this responsibility, the endless worry about another helpless human being who was so dependent on her, the uncertainty of knowing if she was doing the right thing, bringing him up the right way, or if he was already damaged by her fear, her absence, her incompetence.

With an effort, she tried to pull herself together. I'm exhausted, she told herself. Too emotional. It'll all seem better once I've had a decent sleep.

Telling Deb to wake her if she became worried about Cam, Rory stripped off her clothes and climbed under the covers. She couldn't remember the last time she'd ever taken a nap during the day. Only lazy women did that. Women with nothing better to do. Women who'd lost the plot.

But even her guilt couldn't keep her awake.

'And this is to celebrate.' With a flourish, Ian pulled the bottle of Yellow Glen out of the fridge. 'The end of the project, and having you back home.'

Rory did her best to look pleased. The thought of more alcohol made her stomach turn over, but she wasn't going to refuse and spoil the mood. It was more than she'd hoped for to find Ian in such a good humour. She hadn't seen him so light-hearted in a long time.

He popped the cork and filled two flutes. Handing her one, he tapped its rim with his own. 'Welcome home.'

'Thanks, darling.' She smiled, and lifting the glass to her lips, took the tiniest of sips.

She'd awoken mid-afternoon. Cam, thank goodness, was fine, and she'd played with him a while before bundling him into the car with her for the trip to the supermarket. After too much takeaway, not to mention his own limited culinary efforts, Ian, she knew, would be looking forward to a home-cooked meal.

Now, with Cam in bed and Deb gone home, they were finally on their own. Rory had made one of his favourite meals, and they ate in the dining room for a change. It had seemed appropriate, somehow, to make a fuss, and she'd even lit candles and put something classical on in the background.

As they ate, they filled each other in on the days they'd been apart, and slowly Rory felt herself relax. The sleep had done wonders, and there was the relief, too, that Cam had recovered, and Ian was in such a pleasant mood.

She told him about her boozy last evening with Antonella, laughed as she described their noisy, acid commentary on the publishing fraternity.

Ian filled his glass. Given her restraint, he'd had to finish most of the wine himself. 'She sounds like a wonderfully corruptive influence. I'll have to meet her sometime.'

No, Rory found herself thinking quickly. I'd never want you to meet her. In some way that would spoil what was special between Antonella and herself . . .

She changed the subject. 'What about you? Why did you have to go into the office yesterday?' When he'd returned her call, he still hadn't been at home.

'Actually, I was looking for some journals I'd laid aside somewhere. Needed them for a tute I'm presenting next week.'

'Very dedicated of you, rushing in on a Sunday.'

She hadn't meant it to sound accusing, but he obviously took it that way.

'Deb was here with Cam,' he said with a hint of defensiveness. 'It was okay, you know. I wasn't away that long.'

She let the subject drop. The mood was too good to spoil for no reason.

She was looking forward to making love. It seemed so long since they'd really had a full-on session together. Usually it was one or other of them who was too tired, but tonight Rory felt rested and eager to make up for lost time.

While Ian was in the bathroom cleaning his teeth, she slipped on one of his favourite outfits, a black lace teddy that cupped her breasts provocatively, and lace-topped black stockings.

When he entered the bedroom, she had thrown the covers back and was waiting for him. In the dim glow of the bedside lamp, she saw his expression change. Almost as if she had caught him unawares ... as if he hadn't been expecting such a blatant invitation.

She smiled at him. 'You look surprised.'

He shook his head. 'No ...'

'Then why don't you come over here?' she said softly.

As he moved towards the bed, she could see the swiftly growing bulge in the front of his briefs. Suddenly, she realised how much she wanted him. It was a depth of desire she hadn't felt for a long while.

Without saying a word, he sat on the edge of the bed, and his eyes moved slowly over her provocative attire. Rory felt her excitement grow sharper with the anticipation that he was going to tease the moment out.

Raising a hand, he trailed his fingers lightly from the dip at the base of her throat, over her right breast and down the length of her torso to where the teddy fastened between her legs. Closing her eyes, she let out a long, low sigh of pleasure. Oh, God, how long had it been since she'd wanted him so much! Her excitement was almost unbearable. The best response of all.

Breathing shallowly, she opened her eyes and putting out a hand, touched the hardness between his legs. Gently, rhythmically, she began to stroke and heard his quick intake of breath, saw him arch his head back in pleasure.

A moment later she hooked her fingers around the elastic of his briefs and pulled them down as far as they would go. He stood up and quickly slipped them the rest of the way, and then, with fumbling fingers, he was unsnapping the studs between her legs, rolling the black lace down over the length of her, tossing it aside.

Aching with desire, she felt his body cover hers, and then his mouth was closing over her own, his tongue eager and probing.

The kiss left her breathless, her mouth burning, as he raised his head and moved his attention to her breasts. She thrust herself against him, desperate now for the feel of him inside her. Finally she could bear it no longer. Lacing her fingers in his hair, she drew him upwards again, kissing him wildly, parting her legs, letting him know she was ready.

With her excitement at fever pitch, she felt the thick knob of him begin to part her flesh. The exquisite pain and pleasure of the moment of entry made her gasp and she wrapped her legs around him more tightly, holding him prisoner within her.

Head thrown back, she began to move, finding the rhythm that suited them both, eagerly anticipating the ecstasy to come.

It took her a moment or two to realise what was happening. The fact that the thickness inside her had diminished, that Ian had changed their rhythm, begun to move faster. The distraction spoilt her concentration. They had long ago established a pattern that suited them both, that was nearly always a sure fire means of achieving mutual satisfaction. But now, she realised, Ian was losing his erection and his frantic pumping was an attempt to restore it.

She did her best to help him. Squeezing tighter, quickening her own response, doing all she could to return them to where they had been a few minutes before. But it soon became clear that nothing was going to achieve that.

Sweating, breathing heavily, he rolled onto his back beside her.

'I'm sorry, darling ... I — I guess I must be tired.'

She could hardly talk. Her body was screaming for release, her nerves drawn tight with unrelieved tension. But she knew better than to reveal the extent of her frustration, aware of the damage that could do to the fragile male ego. These things happened sometimes, she told herself.

But she couldn't remember the last time it had happened to them.

'Don't worry ... it's okay.' Her mouth was dry and parched, her pelvic area felt as if it were on fire. Reaching out a hand, she patted his thigh and forced herself to answer calmly. 'Next time'll be fine, I'm sure.'

Then to further reassure him, she snuggled up close, cradling her head in the crook of his arm.

But, try as she might, she couldn't get to sleep for a long time afterwards.

And she sensed that he was still awake, too.

CHAPTER FIFTEEN

It was Paul who helped her get through it. He was there for her in every way and kept her so busy that she barely had a moment to brood or feel sorry for herself. They met for lunch, dinner, drinks; went to the movies, concerts, the theatre. His near constant company and loving attention made it easier for Leith to accept the fact that the break with David was final.

It was only when she finally reached that conclusion that she permitted herself to sleep with Paul again. She was grateful for the fact that he'd made no move to pressure her in that direction, had left the decision and timing entirely up to her. Yet the first time they resumed their love-making, she found her pleasure was also tinged with regret at what she had lost and what might have been.

But then she made herself remember David's hasty rejection, his uncompromising lack of forgiveness of her one mistake, and the bitterness these thoughts aroused made it easier to surrender to Paul's devotion.

He pampered her in every way, making her feel as if she were the centre of his universe, telling her that he would do anything to keep her happy. 'I love you, Leith,' he said one night after they'd made love. 'I loved you by the end of that first evening, wanted nothing more than the opportunity to offer you the happiness I could see you were crying out for.'

And as the days passed, as Paul proved his devotion over and over, Leith opened herself to what was happening between them. This was meant to be, she told herself. Her life with David was over. There was no reason for her to resist what Paul was now offering her.

She was still living in the house, but had begun to spend three or four nights of the week at Paul's apartment. He'd made it clear he was uncomfortable in the home she had shared with her husband and Leith could understand that. The house, with its memories and reminders of her marriage, was beginning to have an effect on her, too. She really didn't feel as if she could continue to live there in the long term.

It was just one of the many issues she'd have to talk to David about when he returned home, she realised, but she wasn't looking forward to facing any of that. Dreading it, in fact. It was on Paul's advice that she went to see a lawyer recommended by someone he knew. 'Leave it to the lawyers to talk, my love,' he'd insisted. 'That's the best way, believe me.' And she felt sure he was right.

Then, one Sunday afternoon, about three weeks before David was due home, she realised how sensitive Paul was to her state of mind. They'd had lunch at Watson's Bay and were driving back towards the city when, without explanation, he turned off New South Head road.

'Where are we going?' she asked, looking at him in surprise.

He gave her a quick smile. 'Wait and see.'

Suppressing her curiosity, Leith said no more as they drove through quiet back streets and finally turned into a leafy avenue.

Paul pulled up in front of a handsome villa, complete with ivy covered chimneys and a charming front garden.

'What do you think of that place?' he asked, leaning over and gesturing out of the passenger window.

'It looks lovely.' Leith looked out at the home, still not understanding. Were they visiting someone? Did Paul know the owner of the house?

'It's ours,' he said simply.

She turned to face him, her amazement clear. '*Ours*? You mean you've bought this place? For us? This beautiful house?'

He was grinning now, obviously pleased with the success of his surprise.

'I thought it was for the best, darling. My apartment is a man's home, I realise that. And I was beginning to sense that you weren't happy staying where you were. I thought somewhere completely new for both of us would be the best solution.'

Still overcome, Leith shook her head. 'You're an amazing man, you know. An absolutely amazing man.'

With a soft laugh, he leaned over and kissed her. 'And don't you ever forget it.'

Then, pulling the keys out of the ignition, he added, 'Come on. It's vacant and I've got the keys. Let's take a look.'

In the end it was harder than she had imagined to face the packing up of the home which she and David had bought with such happy expectation. And it was a job she had to do alone. Clearing out cupboards and wardrobes, sifting through the accumulated possessions of more than two decades of marriage, deciding what to take and what to leave behind.

She had no intention of doing the wrong thing by David in splitting their property and, in the end, it was mainly her clothes, a few treasured pieces of furniture, some favourite paintings and what she thought was her fair share of their photos and memorabilia that she took away. They'd buy things new, Paul said. It would signify the beginning of a fresh start for both of them.

And then at last, the packing was done and the removalists booked for the next morning. As Leith did a final check of the rooms, the emotional impact of the moment hit her sharper than ever. It was really over. She was leaving the life she had known and beginning another. The time with David would be part of her history.

And then, as she walked through the bedroom they had shared, she saw the row of suits and shirts and jackets left hanging alone in the walk-in robe. They still held the faint scent of David's aftershave.

For a moment she felt overwhelmed with panic, and her eyes filled with tears. Oh, God, was she doing the right thing? Could she have done anything more to patch things up? If she'd persisted, was there a chance David might have forgiven her?

But again she recalled the cold finality of those last conversations, his unshakeable conviction that their marriage could never be rescued, her own anger and frustration at his inability to forgive or to accept any blame.

Dropping onto the bed they had shared as man and wife for so many years, Leith covered her face with her hands and began to sob.

It was strange to see her bits and pieces in their new surroundings, but Paul encouraged her to get to work on the house, and together they picked out furniture, rugs, curtains, accessories.

'It won't take long before it feels like home, my darling,' he promised as they returned from yet another shopping expedition. 'It'll be fun doing it together.'

And it was. The loneliness she had felt in her marriage had been banished by the comfort of Paul's presence. He spent as much time with her as possible, working most mornings in his study at home before going into his office. It made her feel good just to know he was in the house with her. This is what I've always wanted, she told herself, happily. A friend and lover who's there for *me* Who understands what companionship is all about.

Yet she wasn't stupid. She knew Paul had a successful business to attend to, other interests in his life. While he might be doing his best to reassure her now, she'd let him see that she didn't want to monopolise his company to the extent that he'd feel deprived of breathing space.

As the days passed, Leith couldn't remember when her life had been so hectic. Thanks to Paul's contact with wealthy clients, he received a never-ending stream of invitations to first nights and cocktail parties, movie premieres and charitable functions. Almost every evening they had somewhere to go, and sometimes Paul would arrive home with three or four beautiful dresses he'd bought for her. His taste was excellent and, with shining eyes, she would try them on for him, so he could choose the one he liked best. He made no secret of the fact that he liked showing her off. 'You're my dream woman, darling,' he smiled, 'and I want everyone to know it.'

No matter what time they returned home, Paul was always eager to make love to her, to whisper how much he adored her, to make her senses sing. Sometimes it seemed to Leith as if she were living a dream.

The only disturbance to this new and exciting existence came with the letter from David passed on via her solicitor. Leith opened the envelope with a feeling of unease, resistant to any disruption of her new contentment. Despite half expecting what she might read, she felt her heart go cold as she scanned the contents.

He was making contact, he said, to make sure everything was fine with her and to say that he quite understood about her not wanting to stay in the house. He also wanted to let her know, before she got the official correspondence from her lawyer, that he had initiated divorce proceedings.

'A quick clean break is for the best, for both of us, Leith. I'm sure you'll agree. And you don't have to worry about the money side of things. I'm not sure of your present circumstances, but rest assured that you'll be well taken care of financially. We had many good years, and I wouldn't want to be anything but fair.' He finished with the hope that she was happy now and that 'whoever you're with is able to give you everything I seemingly couldn't.'

The letter upset her. Of course she knew that divorce was the next logical step, but it had been better when she hadn't had to think about it, when David was still away and she could try to forget what had to be faced to put a formal end to their marriage.

It was then, in a split second of insight, that it occurred to her she was thinking like a child. A child who didn't want any unpleasantness. Who wanted everything in her life to go exactly the way she desired it.

Abruptly, she refolded the letter. Well, she told herself in justification, wasn't it only natural to feel like that?

With the new sense of order and contentment in her life, Leith felt ready to see her friends again, pick up a tennis racquet, have people around for lunch or dinner. It seemed ages since she'd seen anyone and now there was no need to go into the humiliating details. All she would say was that there was a new man in her life, and she was very happy.

Heather Anderson, one of her old tennis friends, was surprised and pleased to get her call. 'Leith! We wondered what had happened to you. When you called off the tennis mornings and we didn't hear from you, we thought you must have persuaded David to take you on a real holiday at last.'

'Not quite.' It wasn't something Leith wanted to get into over the phone. 'I'll tell you all about it when I see you. Are you all still playing?'

'Sure. D'you want to join us? I'm sure we could fit you in.'

Leith took down the details and promised to appear at the suburban court the following week. She was smiling as she put down the receiver. Paul would be happy to learn that she wasn't going to be living in his pocket.

Finally she tried again to get in touch with Judith. This time when she talked to one of the boys, Leith understood what had happened. Judith had left! She had finally plucked up the courage to walk out on her marriage. How incredible that they'd both done it at almost the same time! ...

Later that evening she dialled the number she'd scribbled down.

Judith was home and delighted to hear from her.

'You make me feel guilty, Leith. I should have rung you, I know, and told you what had happened.

But I just got selfishly bogged down in my work. I'm almost there! And there's an agent who's said she'll look at my manuscript when it's finished. It's just amazing.'

Leith could hear the excitement in her friend's voice. It was clear that there were more important things on Judith's mind than the breakdown of her marriage.

But, holding back her own news for the moment, she persisted in probing Judith on that particular topic.'

'So, how does it feel? To be on your own, I mean.'

'I should have done it years ago,' Judith answered passionately. 'You have no idea how it feels to be free, Leith.'

And now at last it was her turn. 'Yes I do, Jude . . . You see, I've left David.'

Her old friend's reaction was even more forceful than she might have expected.

'You've left *David*? But *why*? He so obviously adored you. I saw it with my own eyes. What earthly reason would you have to leave a man like that?'

Leith was taken aback by Judith's amazement and found a defensiveness creeping into her tone as she described David's obsession with work, the late nights and long absences, his neglect, and disregard for her loneliness.

'I just couldn't take it any longer, Jude. And he wouldn't listen, didn't seem to understand how terrible it was for me.'

'So where are you now? Still in the house?' Judith still sounded disbelieving.

Leith hesitated. 'No ... I'm actually living with someone. Someone wonderful. His name's Paul Houston, and I'd love you to meet him. How are you placed for dinner some time next week?'

That evening they were invited to a charity dinner at an inner city hotel. It was in the car, as they were driving into town, that Leith told Paul about making contact with her old friend.

'I've asked her over for dinner one night next week. She can make any night but Thursday. Do you think we can keep an evening free? She's just left her husband, and I thought she might be a little lonely.'

For a moment Paul made no reply. Then, as they pulled up at a red light, he glanced over at her and said, 'I must say I'm a little surprised at you, Leith.'

It was hardly the reply she'd been expecting and, with a puzzled frown, she returned his look. 'What do you mean?'

'Well, you know the house isn't quite finished. Do you really want to ask people over before it's ready?'

She understood then and gave a light laugh. 'Oh, God, that wouldn't matter to Judith. She doesn't care about things like that.'

The lights had changed and they were moving again. 'I still don't think it's a good idea, darling.'

There was a note in his voice that she didn't understand.

'But the place is almost finished, Paul.' She gave a confused chuckle. 'It doesn't have to be perfect.'

He kept his eyes on the road and his tone was

firm. 'I just think it would be better to wait, that's all ... darling.'

It wasn't worth arguing about, Leith thought.

'Okay. I'll let Judith know. Put it off till we're picture perfect.'

He turned to give her a quick smile and, taking his hand off the wheel, patted her knee.

It was a week later, and as they ate breakfast together, she told Paul about her plans for tennis.

'It's all the women who used to come to my place. They've found a spot for me back on the team.'

He put down the coffee cup that was halfway to his lips. 'You mean today?'

Leith nodded. 'Yes. This morning.'

He was staring at her. 'Where are you playing?'

She told him and saw his frown.

'That's too far for me to take you before my meeting.' He had a rare early meeting in his office with an out-of-town client.

Leith was touched by his thoughtfulness. With a fond smile, she reached across the table and patted his hand. 'Darling, it's very sweet of you to even think of it, but you don't have to drive me. I'm quite capable of driving myself.'

'What you don't understand is that I'd *like* to drive you, Leith. It's the sort of thing I'd enjoy doing for you.'

She couldn't help being flattered. 'Well, maybe another time.' She gave him a teasing smile. 'And then I can show you off to the girls.'

With a glance at her watch, she pushed back her chair.

'I'd better get ready.'

'What time do you have to be there?'

'About nine.'

'How long do you usually play for?'

She gave a self-deprecating grin. 'We take it easy. None of us is much competition for Monica Seles.'

'How long?' he persisted.

Leith lifted one shoulder in a shrug. 'Oh, maybe three hours. Nothing too strenuous.'

He left just before eight, coming in to say goodbye as she sat on a towel on the bedroom carpet doing her yoga. She hadn't hit a ball in a long time. Some stretches would help protect her against injury.

She got to her feet and coiled her arms around his neck.

'Have a wonderful day, darling.'

'You too, my sweet,' he replied. He kissed her as warmly as usual, and Leith felt a shiver run down her spine.

'What time are you home?' Her voice was a little breathless.

'Early. We're due at the Landmann's at seven, don't forget.'

They were important clients, and Leith was looking forward to the dinner party at their Bellevue Hill mansion.

'Don't worry, I'll make sure I'm ready.'

It was almost noon as Leith came off the court, breathless, hair stuck damply to her forehead. She patted her partner's shoulder in apology. 'Sorry,

Anne. I cost us those last couple of points. Shows what the break did for me.'

'Forget it. It'll be my turn to blow it next week.' Reaching for her towel from the back of a seat next to the court, the other woman wiped her face. 'It's stinking hot for this time of the year, isn't it? Coming for a drink?'

Leith nodded and together they crossed the lawn to the small kiosk that supplied refreshments for the players on the six busy courts.

She had almost reached the welcome shade when she caught sight of a familiar figure leaning against one of the kiosk's wooden pillars. She stopped dead in her tracks, her eyes widening in surprise.

'Paul! What are you doing here?'

Pushing himself upright, he walked towards her looking totally out of place in his dark business suit. 'Just wanted to make sure you got here okay.'

She gave him a puzzled smile. 'I'm *fine*. You didn't have to do that.' Then, as he slipped an arm around her waist, she pulled away, saying quickly, 'Oh, God, don't touch me, I'm dripping with sweat. It's hotter than you'd think out there.'

His only response was to pull her closer, his fingers tightening around her bare arms. Looking into her eyes, he said softly, 'Do you think I care? When I adore you like I do?'

And then he was kissing her, not caring who was looking at them.

The evening with Paul's clients was pleasant enough. Ivan and Monica Landmann were an urbane, elegant couple in late middle age. Three other couples besides themselves had been invited, and the food was light and stylish, but Leith wasn't really enjoying herself.

For the last couple of hours, she'd endured a throbbing headache and was reluctant to spoil the mood by asking her hostess for an aspirin. It was probably the sun today, she thought. It had been dreadfully hot. Next week she'd have to wear a hat.

She struggled to concentrate on the conversation, which was mainly to do with the state of the sharemarket, but her thoughts kept drifting to that morning and Paul's unexpected appearance at the courts.

She was still amazed to think that he'd gone into his meeting, then left the office to cross town to find her and 'make sure she was okay'. Afterwards, he'd even insisted on following her back home.

A frown puckered Leith's brow. It was such a strange thing to do ... Almost — the thought occurred to her now — as if he couldn't bear to have her out of his sight.

CHAPTER SIXTEEN

By the light of her torch, Judith peered into the meter box and nervously surveyed the row of switches. Hell, which one was it? Which fuse had tripped and plunged the flat into darkness? She'd never had to cope with this before, but she hated the idea of knocking on a neighbour's door to ask some strange man for help.

Then she noticed that only one switch in the row was not in the same position as the others. Gingerly, she moved it back into place.

Nothing happened.

Swearing under her breath, she studied the switchboard a moment longer. Then she tried again, different switches this time, and suddenly the lights in the flat came back on.

With a small smile of triumph and relief, Judith closed the meter box door. Another job accomplished without the help of a male! In the last few weeks she'd also managed to unclog the insinkerator, as well as fix a dripping toilet. She was learning fast.

As she walked back into the kitchen to store the torch in its drawer, she wondered if her sons were coping as well. For the first month after she'd left, the phone had rung endlessly as they questioned her on how to operate the washing machine or microwave, how to clean their cricket gear or where to find the spare vacuum bags.

Things had tapered off a bit since then, but the last time she'd talked to Brent, he'd mumbled something about never realising how much there was to do around the house. Then he'd added, 'I don't know how you coped, mum — and working too.' It was the obvious awe in his voice that had knocked Judith for six.

Her other surprise had come from Luke. She'd made it clear that the boys were welcome to visit her at any time, but she'd never expected to have her youngest asking if he could come in and spend some time with her after she picked him up from his cricket training.

Of course, the television was the inevitable accompaniment to their conversation as she made him a snack. But at least there *was* conversation: everything from the latest group he was following, to his growing interest in a possible career in computers.

Judith was barely able to hide her surprise at this gradual change in her sons. Maybe, just maybe, they were beginning to appreciate her. The only shame was that it had taken them so long.

She never asked about their father, but each of

them told her enough for her to get the picture. Greg, it seemed, was enjoying a dynamic social life. Dressed up, reeking of cologne, he went out most evenings. And women had started calling him at the house. If he was home, he always took the calls in another room.

'As if we're interested,' Luke spat contemptuously.

Judith felt absolutely nothing at the thought of her husband's busy social — and, no doubt, sexual — life. Whatever she'd felt for Greg had died long ago. If he found happiness with someone else, then good luck to him.

The only time they communicated was to discuss the boys. Judith had been quite amenable to Greg's request to collect Luke once a week from his cricket training. It was the full-time sole burden and being taken for granted that she'd objected to.

As well, true to her promise, she was still helping to pay off the mortgage and the boys' school fees. It made things tough when she had her own rent and keep to pay as well but she was determined to manage, despite the difficulties.

As far as doing anything about a divorce, neither of them had made any move in that direction. Maybe Greg's reason was the same as hers. Too busy. At the moment, all her energies were concentrated on finishing her manuscript. It was all that really mattered to her. She'd seen what so many of her friends had gone through when they started fighting with their husbands about settlements and the splitting up of assets. She didn't feel like inviting the sort of emotional upheaval that might affect the concentration she required for her writing. And as well, she was thinking of the boys. If things got nasty between herself and Greg, it would only bring more disruption into their lives. The longer they had to adjust to what had happened, the better.

Tony had resumed working with her again and, as before, his encouragement and input were her inspiration. At the same time, they had picked up the reins of their friendship more easily than she might have imagined. When he'd first come to see her in her flat, she'd expected to feel a little awkward. But, somehow, he'd made it easy, treating her with the same warmth and good humour he'd always shown.

Judith knew, however, that what she had felt for him hadn't gone away. Could tell by the way her heart quickened when she hurried to open the door to his knock. When he smiled down at her and said hallo. When he walked into her sparsely furnished living room and said with quiet sincerity, 'It's good to see you again, Judith.'

If she could have wished for anything at that moment, it was that he would pull her into his arms, kiss her as they had kissed when they'd lain close in the dark. She longed to feel his touch again, to lay her head against his chest, to wrap herself in the full force and comfort of his masculine presence.

The memory of their lovemaking was painfully sharp, but she did her best to ensure that she gave no outward sign of her emotions. Tony's friendship was too important to her. She had no intention of risking it again.

Without the distraction of family and housework, she was making good progress on the manuscript. Her biggest worry was that the agent who had expressed an interest might change her mind if she took too long to finish. With that fear always in the back of her mind, she rose early each morning and, after a strong cup of coffee to stir her brain into life, did as many pages as possible before getting ready for work. In the evening she was back at it again as soon as she'd finished a simple dinner. Only when exhaustion finally overcame her did she head for bed.

Even so, she figured, it was going to take her another couple of months to finish. But Tony had warned her about the dangers of rushing. 'Those last chapters are so important, Judith. The various threads of the story have to be tied up with great care and effectiveness. You want to leave your readers totally satisfied, so they'll be looking forward to your next novel.'

She'd looked at him then, eyes widening in wonder. It had never occurred to her for one moment that she might write something else. Her entire focus had been on completing the story she had worked on for so long and with such pleasure, on taking that first step to fulfilling her dream of getting published. She'd never dared to think that this could be just the beginning.

Tony responded to her reaction. 'Why not? If you can write one book and get it published, why not another? You've enjoyed the whole process, haven't you?'

She nodded emphatically. 'Oh, yes. It's been the most satisfying experience of my life.'

He gave her a knowing smile. 'Let me tell you something. Once you discover the sheer joy of creativity, it's like being hooked on a drug. You need your fix regularly. That's why even an old hack like me can't give the game away. As long as they keep paying me even a pittance, I've got to do it.' He gave a wry chuckle. 'Even if they didn't pay me at all, I guess I'd still feel the drive to write. For the sheer pleasure of exploring lives you'll never live, of trying on personalities different from your own, of selecting and polishing words to tell your story in the best way possible. And hopefully, if you do it well, if your writing is driven by the force of your own passions, you'll end up touching something important both in your readers and yourself.'

As she listened to Tony's words, Judith realised she could relate to much of what he was saying. But for the moment, she was too afraid to look that far into the future. First of all she had to finish Jo's story.

And then came the first shock with the letter that arrived just one week later.

❋

It took Cate another month of agonising to make up her mind, to finally decide that if she told Cal 'no', she'd regret it the rest of her life.

Once she had made her decision, she couldn't understand why it had taken her so long. Suddenly it felt so right. She was in love with Cal, and she wanted to be with him always. That was all that really mattered in the end.

'You've just made me the happiest man in the country,' he said joyfully when she rang that evening and told him of her decision. 'I promise you won't regret it, my darling Cate. All I want is to have you always. To make you happy forever. Do you understand what I'm trying to tell you?'

She understood.

After that, there seemed so much to do in such a short time.

Firstly, she called on all the contacts she could think of to sniff out any possibilities of work. As soon as she'd started that ball rolling, she felt more confident about what she had to do next. But it was still tough to face the actuality of handing in her resignation.

Afterwards, as she walked back to her office, Cate felt a moment of gut-wrenching panic. She'd done it. Given a month's notice. There was no going back. She'd severed the umbilical cord that had connected her to a steady income and security, that had given her the best freedom of all: financial independence. The thought made her light-headed. She was almost forty-three. When she left Sydney she'd have no job, no network of contacts to call on . . .

But, remembering Jess's words, she forced herself to think positive. She'd find something, maybe never as good as this, but there had to be another job out there that would offer the challenge and stimulus she needed.

Her only security now was the apartment. At this stage she had no intention of selling. It had taken her years of hard work to scrape up a deposit for a roof of her own and, as she kept reading in the newspapers, a stake in well-positioned Sydney real estate was an excellent investment.

While she hated to admit it to herself, the thought that she still had a bolthole, a place bought in her own name, made her feel less vulnerable. It was her insurance if things didn't work out. But at once she pushed that idea away. There was no risk with Cal. She had no doubts at all or she wouldn't be taking this enormous step.

In less than a week, the agents she'd contacted had found her suitable tenants and Cate began to spend her evenings packing the amazing amount of stuff she'd fitted into such a seemingly small space. Most she'd put into storage until she needed it and, while there were all sorts of ways of reading that, she wasn't ready to map out her future too accurately. Living together was more than enough for her to contend with at the moment.

With only a month before they were to be permanently together, she and Cal agreed that it would be only sensible to sacrifice their weekend visits in the interim. Apart from anything else, Cate was going to need every moment to get herself organised. Cal had offered to come down to help with packing up the flat, but she knew it was something she had to do on her own.

'I couldn't think of a bigger passion killer,' she'd informed him, 'than having you clean out my bathroom cupboards, thanks very much.'

But she did let Jess give her a hand, and very soon the flat was almost emptied of her personal possessions. Her busyness made the time pass quickly, and suddenly it was her last day at work. Leanna and the rest of the crew toasted her over drinks when Friday's program was wrapped up. After a short, very funny speech, peppered with anecdotes about some of the near mishaps they'd all shared on *Live!*, Leanna lifted her glass in a toast. 'You were one of the best, Cate. I hope you find someone to appreciate you up there just as much as we did.'

Amid the chorus of 'hear, hears', Cate accepted the kisses and cuddles from the people she'd grown close to over four years. What am I doing? she asked herself, her throat tight with emotion. What the hell am I doing?

Jessica drove her to the airport. They dragged her two heavy suitcases from the boot and the back seat, and then they were facing each other for the moment of goodbye.

'Thanks, Jess. For everything.' Cate put her arms around her old friend and hugged her tight. 'I could never have managed everything so quickly without your help.' And then her voice caught. 'Oh, God, Jess … I'm so bloody nervous.'

Her friend drew back, gripping her upper arms. Looking into Cate's eyes, she said gently, 'Change frightens us, darling. It always does. But it also makes life exciting. This is going to work out for you. I know it is. Cal's a wonderful guy and he loves you. Totally and utterly.'

Cate nodded. She could feel a tear trickle down her cheek. 'Oh, shit,' she brushed it brusquely away, 'the melodramatic parting scene. Do I really need this?'

Jess grinned. 'No, Meryl Streep does it much better.'

Cate gave a gurgly laugh. 'You're so right.' Then they hugged again, and Cate kissed her friend on the cheek. 'I'll really miss you, Jess. Come and see me when I'm a dried-up old prune in my purple sequin bikini, won't you? In six months time, I mean.'

Jess broke away with a laugh. 'I'll wear one just like it when I'm matron of honour.' She clapped a hand to her mouth. 'Did I say that? Did I dare to imply the M word? Between two modern, self-sufficent women like ourselves?'

Suddenly they were interrupted by a uniformed attendant who frowned and said curtly, 'This your car, lady? Shift it or get a ticket.'

Jess turned back to Cate with a quick, good-natured shrug. 'See what you're missing? Don't it just break your heart? Okay, okay,' she said irritably as the parking officer menacingly flipped open his book of tickets, 'I'm outta here.'

And with a final kiss and a quick wave, she ran around and let herself into the driver's door.

He was waiting for her in the arrivals lounge at Coolangatta airport, holding a bouquet of white flowers.

As the crush of arrivals surrounded them, Cal put his arms around her, holding the flowers precariously

326

behind her back. 'Oh, Cate, oh my darling Cate, this is the moment I've been dreaming of for so long.'

As she lifted her face to kiss him, her heart swelled with love, and all her doubts and fears disappeared. This is what she wanted. With Cal she would be happy for the rest of her life.

CHAPTER SEVENTEEN

It was almost nine-thirty. With a yawn, Rory tossed her paperwork aside. She was too tired to concentrate. The work had piled up even more dauntingly during the time she'd spent in Melbourne and now, more than three weeks later, she was still bringing material home every night trying to catch up.

In a way she was thankful for the fact that Ian's schedule seemed to be just as crazy as her own. At least it saved her from feeling quite as guilty when he was working late, too.

With the end of semester imminent, this was the second time in a week he'd called to say he wouldn't be home for dinner. And while a part of her had been relieved at the chance to work on uninterrupted, she also couldn't help wishing that their lives weren't quite so out of control. It seemed like ages since they'd had time to sit down with each other and just talk and laugh and relax. But then, she reminded herself, she was in no position to complain, not after Melbourne and the sacrifices he'd made during that period.

With a heavy sigh, she pushed herself up from the sofa. Damn it, she decided. Tonight she was going to hit the sack early. A good night's sleep was what she badly needed.

In the ensuite she washed her face and cleaned her teeth, then slipped on her old cotton nightdress. A neck-to-knee job. Comfortable — and less than inviting, she knew. But what the heck. By the time Ian came home, she'd probably be fast asleep. And he'd be too tired to even think of sex. It certainly hadn't been high on the agenda for either of them recently.

Padding down the hall on bare feet, she did a last check on Cam. He was lying on his tummy, sheets and blankets kicked off, so she gently tucked them around him again. Then she stood for a moment looking down at her son.

What had happened, she wondered, to that dream she'd had before he was born? Of the three of them as one close unit, experiencing the joys of family life. Had it been just a fantasy? Had a clever woman like herself fallen for the illusion portrayed in so many women's magazines? And, if so, why did the illusion go unchallenged? Was it because women who'd already been there and knew the truth kept it to themselves?

Reaching out, she brushed a finger gently down her son's warm, perfect cheek. It'll all be worth it, she tried to reassure herself. Everything we're going through now will all be worth it in the end.

As she pulled the door to behind her, she wasn't even sure if she really understood what she meant.

'*Rory*! We're going to be late!'

She could hear the impatience in Ian's voice as he called out to her from the end of the hallway. In Cam's bedroom, she leaned over the cot and gave her son a quick kiss on the forehead. 'Be good for Mandy, sweetheart.'

'He'll be fine.' The babysitter smiled at her. 'He's usually asleep before you've made the top of the road.'

'Thanks, Mandy.' Rory spoke over her shoulder as she grabbed her handbag and headed out of the room. 'I don't think we'll be too late.'

By the open front door, Ian stood frowning with impatience.

'Come *on*! You know I can't afford to be late for an evening like this.'

The English department was playing host to a visiting American playwright and tonight, on campus, the man was giving an address on his work. It was Ian's task to introduce the evening, and Rory was looking forward to both the talk and the cocktail party afterwards.

'I'm sorry. I just wanted to be sure Cam was settled.'

Quickly locking the door behind them, Ian strode after her through the front garden to where his car was parked at the kerb.

'It's open,' he said as he hurried around to the driver's side.

Rory slid into the passenger seat and snapped on her seat belt. As she did, her fingers touched something that had fallen down the side of the seat. A slim, hard-covered book.

'This yours?' she asked, pulling it out.

Ian was turning the key in the ignition, his concentration only on getting to the campus on time.

'What?'

'No ... it isn't.' Rory answered her own question as she flicked the book open and saw the name on the inside cover. 'Sara Trent. A collection of Blake's poems.'

The name rang a bell but she couldn't quite remember why.

'Who's Sara Trent?' she asked. Then, all at once, she remembered and answered her own question 'She's the girl I met that morning, isn't she? She and her friend.'

Rory recalled it clearly now — that Saturday morning a few months ago, the girl with the tiny shorts and the long dark hair. The sexy one.

Ian was moving quickly through the gears as they sped up the suburban street towards Military Road.

'Yeah.' His eyes were fixed on the road. 'I gave a couple of kids a ride to the station a few days ago. She must have dropped it then. I'll give it back to her next time I see her.'

After seven years, Rory knew the man she lived with very well. The slight alteration in his tone was barely there. But she picked it up.

And then told herself she was imagining things ...

The talk was interesting, the American unexpectedly amusing. His plays had been Broadway productions, and his work was often compared to David Mamet's, yet the man had a self-deprecation and lack of earnestness that Rory found appealing.

When the talk ended, Ian stepped in front of the crowded lecture room and proposed his thanks, then led the audience in a round of applause.

The formalities over, people began to edge out of the tiers of seats, and a dozen or so students mounted the podium to crowd around the guest speaker. Ian was still there, too, standing a little to the side and, as she started to move out of her seat, Rory saw a girl with long dark hair break outof the crowd and join him.

She knew at once who it was.

As she watched, Rory saw Sara Trent put her mouth close to Ian's ear, and whatever she said made him smile. Then, still talking, the girl casually lifted a hand to pick a piece of thread or lint off Ian's jacket.

Rory felt her heart freeze.

The subconscious intimacy of the gesture was more revealing than the girl could know.

And then Rory remembered the book in the car.

The next couple of hours were almost unbearable. With a sick churning in her belly, she forced herself to move around the room, making small talk to Ian's colleagues and the other guests.

The evening seemed interminable. As Ian, too, circulated, her eyes followed him, searching his face, watching the way he smiled at and interacted with other women. Her nerves were at breaking point as she waited for the moment when they would finally be alone, when she could confront him with her suspicions. And she prayed his answer would prove her wrong.

They were among the last to leave but, to her dismay, Ian had responded to a colleague's request for a lift.

'You don't mind, Rory? Bill's only a couple of streets away. It'll save him waiting for a cab.'

'Of course not.' She forced herself to answer civilly as the three of them made for the car park. 'Would you like me to drive?'

She could read the signs well enough by now to realise that while he wasn't drunk, Ian had certainly had enough to make him more outgoing than usual.

'No, I'm fine.' Perhaps in his jaunty state, he hadn't picked up the coldness in her tone.

When they reached the car, too agitated for small talk, Rory insisted that the two men sit together in the front.

'Went well, don't you think?' Ian asked his colleague as he slipped the key into the ignition.

'Everyone I spoke to seemed to think so.'

Ian gave a derisive chuckle. 'Did you see the way Stephen was all over the Yank? The guy just can't help himself, can he?'

The two men began to discuss the evening, but Rory wasn't listening. She was still trying to decide the best way of handling this. Was there any alternative to a blunt confrontation? She didn't see how there could be. She wanted the truth. And she wanted it as soon as possible.

Yet there wasn't time to say anything even after they'd dropped off their passenger. She knew she'd have to wait now until the nanny left and they were finally alone.

Somehow she managed to go through the motions of seeing the girl off and saying a polite thank you and goodbye. But as soon as she had closed the front door, Rory hurried through to the bedroom where Ian, wearing only his briefs, was sitting on the side of the bed, setting his alarm.

For a moment she stood in the doorway and looked at him, an image filling her mind of Sara Trent's hands touching that still taut, lean body. It was an image that turned her stomach to water.

'Coming to bed?' He'd finished fiddling with the alarm and looked up, suddenly aware of her scrutiny.

And then she could wait no longer. Abruptly she brought up the subject that had been tormenting her all evening.

'Ian, I want to know what's going on between you and that girl. Sara Trent.'

She saw his expression change. Something that looked like shock was followed by a frown.

'Sara ... ? What do you mean "what's going on"?'

Her throat had tightened with tension, her heart was banging painfully against her ribs. 'I mean, I'm beginning to wonder whether I've been supremely naive about all the late nights you've had to work since I've been back from Melbourne.'

He gave her a hard stare, then swung his legs under the bed sheets. 'I don't know what you're getting at, Rory. And I really don't want to talk rubbish at this time of night.'

It was the quick belligerence in his tone, the abrupt rejection of the subject that heightened her fears. Even affected by alcohol, Ian was the supreme rationalist. If there were really nothing going on, she knew he'd have countered her fears with a lot more reasoned argument.

She moved into the room. 'Ian, listen to me. I want the truth. I want to know if you're sleeping with that girl.'

He threw her a quick, angry glance. 'Are you crazy? How long do you think I'd last in my career if I were sleeping with every bloody female student who came along?'

'I'm not stupid, Ian. Don't treat me as if I am. I know what I saw.' Her voice rose, grew shriller. 'And what about the book in the car? And the fact that you couldn't make love to me when I first got home from Melbourne? Are you trying to tell me that's all just coincidence?'

With a dismissive gesture, he pulled the sheets around him and turned away from her. 'I don't have to put up with this shit.'

His refusal to answer only fed her agitation. 'Ian, I have to know! I need to know the truth. Are you having sex with that girl?'

Abruptly, he swung around to face her again. His expression was tight, his voice challenging and aggressive.

'Well, I'd have plenty of bloody reasons to, wouldn't I?'

She felt her heart thud to a stop in her chest. The blood ran from her face. When she spoke, her voice sounded as if it belonged to someone else. 'What do you mean? What are you telling me?'

'You really don't understand, do you?' He pushed himself up in the bed, his anger untempered now. 'Do you know how it makes me feel to always come last? After your career, your ambition, the kid you were so hell-bent on having? And given that you barely have time for Cam, that doesn't leave too bloody much for me, does it?'

But she didn't want to be distracted by those sorts of issues right now. All that mattered at this moment was to find out exactly what was going on with Sara Trent.

'You haven't answered my question, Ian!' She was almost shouting now. 'Are you screwing that girl?'

He stared back at her, his gaze hard and unflinching. When he finally answered, there was no contrition in his tone, merely defiance. 'You drove me to it, Rory. If things had been right between us, it would never have happened. For too long now, I've felt as if I'm existing on the periphery of your life. Your other, more important life. I have needs, too, you know. For sex, companionship ... someone to talk to who's prepared to give me their full attention just occasionally.'

She felt a trembling begin inside her. What she'd suspected was true. He'd betrayed her, had slept with someone else. Someone younger, more desirable, someone she could never compete with. And now he was using any pathetic excuse to justify himself.

'Oh, please!' she shot back, her eyes wild with anger and pain. 'Don't try to explain away your midlife crisis with all that crap! Why don't you just admit it, Ian? You're afraid of getting old. And having a child makes you feel that way, doesn't it? That's why you're running after a bird young enough to be your daughter. You can't resist the boost to your ego, the chance to prove you're not staring middle age in the face, that you're almost past it. It's as simple as that, isn't it? As simple as that!'

Wearily, he shook his head, looking at her. The anger in his tone had been replaced by resignation. 'You still don't understand, do you?'

'I'll tell you what I understand! I understand that I'm sick to death of being made to feel guilty because I wanted a child. Sick to death of always trying to "make things up to you" for having Cam.' She could feel herself losing control but was incapable of doing anything about it. 'Well, I can't hack it any longer, Ian. I just can't hack it! And screwing around's the last bloody straw. I thought you were different, but now I see you're just like any other middle-aged jerk. And you know what else I think? That Cam and I'd be one hell of a lot better off if you just pissed off! Got out of our lives as soon as possible. I wanted a partner, an equal, I'm not interested in living with two bloody kids!'

❋

Leith gave a quick, anxious glance at the Cartier on her left wrist. 'I'll have to go, Jude. Paul likes me to be there when he gets home.'

The two women had just finished a late lunch. It was Leith who'd got in touch, calling Judith a few days before to arrange to meet. 'The place is still not quite finished here, Jude. Why don't we meet in the city somewhere? Is there a day you usually have off?'

It was then Judith had told her the news. After two weeks, at least the shock had worn off. She gave a brittle laugh at Leith's question. 'Every day from now on. They retrenched me. The kiss off — by letter. Three incisive little paragraphs after eighteen years. Can you believe it?'

'Oh, darling, I'm so sorry.' Leith's voice was full of sympathy and concern. 'What are you going to do? Will you be able to manage?'

'Well, I'm certainly not going back to Greg, as some people have suggested.' Judith spoke with fierce determination. 'In fact, now that I'm over the shock of it, I can see that it might all work out for the better, really. I'll have my retrenchment pay, and now I can work full-time on the book. I'll finish it even earlier than I'd hoped.'

She didn't see any point in telling Leith about Greg's furious reaction when she'd broken the news of her retrenchment and made it clear that she'd no longer be able to keep paying her share of the mortgage or other bills. Listening to him, you'd have thought she'd deliberately got herself retrenched to 'renege on her responsibilities' as he'd so sweetly put it. But she didn't really care what Greg thought. It was only the boys she worried about, the effect of this latest disruption on them. Because she knew now there was no way they could hold on to the house.

'It's going well, then?' Leith asked, referring to her writing. 'Are you still working with the same guy?'

Judith smiled and nodded. 'I told you, didn't I, that he's found me an agent who's interested in looking at the finished manuscript? I can't tell you how much he's done to help me.' That was as far as she wanted to discuss her relationship with Tony.

'But what about after that?' Leith asked. 'When the book's finished, I mean.'

She had no intention of undermining Judith's confidence about getting published, but from everything she'd read, the odds were long shots, indeed. Then again, she reminded herself, maybe not that much longer than finding another job when you were a woman over forty. She said a silent prayer of thanks that she hadn't been faced with Judith's situation.

Judith understood the implication, but also that her friend hadn't meant any offence. She answered calmly, 'You know what, Leith? I've worried about the future all my life. From now on, I'm just taking each day as it comes.'

They met at Darling Harbour, and Judith had had to hide her reaction when Leith walked up to the table. She'd always envied her friend's slim figure, but now Leith looked gaunt rather than attractive, and her face was drawn and tense. The well-cut jacket she was wearing looked too big on her narrow shoulders.

But it was Judith's own weight loss that Leith noticed. As she took a seat, she exclaimed, 'Jude, you've lost weight! You look terrific.'

'Thanks. Don't know how. I haven't really been trying. But I guess my diet's changed now that I don't have to cook for three big eaters. Most of the time I live on pasta and fruit.'

Leith accepted a menu from the waiter, but put it down on the table in front of her without opening it. 'And maybe being happier helps.'

'That's for sure,' Judith agreed with emphasis. 'For the first time in years, I feel — well, I suppose I have to say — grown up. In control of my own life. It wasn't until I left that I realised how much my life was dominated by Greg.'

Leith looked at her a moment before replying. 'And how are the boys handling things now?'

Judith explained about the new respect she sensed in her sons. 'That's been another good thing to come out of all this. I thought I'd lost the boys, I really did, but now I think we might have a chance to sort ourselves out.'

They were interrupted by the waiter arriving to take their order. With barely a glance at the menu, Leith ordered a Caesar salad, while Judith settled on the Thai fish cakes.

While they waited for the food to arrive, Judith switched the subject away from herself.

'Have you heard from David?'

'Only that he's going ahead with the divorce.'

'Oh, Leith,' Judith looked concerned. 'Are you sure that's what you want? I only saw you together on that one occasion, but you seemed so right for each other. Do you really want to walk away from all those years together?'

Leith looked away. 'I was lonely, Jude. And he didn't understand that. I barely saw him. Business was more important than our relationship.'

'But he was working for both of you,' Judith responded gently, knowing she shouldn't interfere but unable to help herself. 'And surely it wasn't going to be like that forever?'

Leith's expression tightened. 'Look, it's over, Jude. I really don't want to talk about it.'

'I'm sorry.' Judith took a sip of her wine and let the awkward moment pass. 'So tell me how things are with — Paul, isn't it? Is everything turning out the way you hoped?'

Leith put down her wine glass. Part of her reason for wanting to meet Judith today was to ask her advice, to talk over how she should handle what was happening with Paul. She knew his possessiveness was only his way of showing how much he loved her, but still she was finding it difficult to come to terms with his need to dominate her life so completely, to know exactly what she was doing when he wasn't there, with his firm views on what she should wear and with whom she should spend her time.

It was only a problem, she told herself, because it was so different from the way things had been with David. She knew it was because Paul was so much more *interested* in everything she did. That was all. It was his way of expressing the extent of his love for her.

But now that the moment had come to say something, Leith worried that by bringing up the subject that was on her mind, she'd sound as if she were complaining. Neurotic. As if she'd changed her life so drastically and still wasn't happy. A bitchy woman who was impossible to please.

She took a deep breath and smiled. 'Everything's wonderful. Paul makes me feel loved. Totally and utterly loved.'

She was almost home when her mobile rang. With one eye on the traffic, Leith scrambled in her bag and pulled out the phone. It was Paul.

'I'm at home, darling, wondering where you are.'

Leith told him. 'Won't be more than ten minutes.'

'Where've you been?'

'Having lunch with a friend.'

There was a pause.

'Who?'

'Judith ... Remember I —'

He interrupted her. 'I wish you'd told me you were going out.'

She caught the hint of disapproval in his voice.

'Well, I ... I wasn't sure ... Judith wasn't certain if she could make it.'

It was a weak excuse, but the only one she could think of quickly. Because she hadn't told him deliberately. Had known he wouldn't have been happy that she was going somewhere without him.

'Well, hurry home, my darling.' His voice grew warmer. 'You know how much I miss you.'

It's only because he loves me, Leith repeated to herself as she hung up. Because he wants me to need only him.

But a little frown appeared between her brows.

✳

Tony was coming to dinner. They'd fallen into a pattern of sharing a meal together about once a fortnight. It was Judith's way of thanking him for all his time and help.

But when he found out that she'd been retrenched, he'd tried to drop their arrangement. 'You've got better things to do with your money than feed me,' he'd protested. But Judith wouldn't hear of it and, in the end, they'd resumed their routine.

As far as Judith could tell, he certainly seemed to enjoy the evenings every bit as much as she did. They still talked about books and writing, but about a lot of other topics, too: politics, the environment, travel, music. Tony was still the most interesting person she had ever met. And even if they'd shut down the sexual side of their relationship, she could still enjoy the way he stimulated her mind.

Now, on the way home from her lunch with Leith, Judith dropped in at her local supermarket. Tonight she'd planned on cooking veal in lemon sauce, followed by fruit salad. But as she moved through the aisles, picking up what she needed, she found her thoughts returning to the conversation with her old school friend.

There was something not quite right there, she told herself. For a woman supposedly madly in love, Leith had both looked and sounded strained. Was she really as happy as she professed? Or was she already having doubts about the step she had taken?

In some ways, Judith mused, Leith had never really grown up. That was apparent even now in her expectation that everything in life should go exactly as she desired, in her need for constant companionship, to be continually flattered, adored, have her ego stroked. It seemed to Judith, that Leith, like a lot of very attractive women, lacked real self-esteem. Her entire sense of self depended on how she was viewed by others, particularly by men. She clearly equated David's commitment of time and energy to his work as a rejection of herself, an was incapable of accepting the fact that she couldn't always be the prime focus in her husband's life.

Women like Leith, Judith figured, as she pushed the trolley out to her car, were still trying to live in the world of romantic fantasy they'd believed in as young girls. That was probably why Leith had allowed herself to be swept off her feet by this Paul, whoever he was. Yet, if Judith's instincts were right, things might not be working out there quite as she'd expected either.

With an inward shrug, she began to load her groceries into the boot of the car. It really was none of her business. All she could do was be there if Leith needed her.

It was an hour later, as she was getting dinner ready, that the phone rang and Judith got another shock.

Much worse than the first.

CHAPTER EIGHTEEN

The adjustment on the professional level was the most difficult. Cate found herself missing her work more than she had ever imagined. Even now, six weeks later, she still had a tendency to wake in the middle of the night and reach for a notebook to scribble down some idea for the program that had occurred to her. And then she'd remember that that life was over. But there were compensations. Like the man sleeping next to her, the man she had grown to love enough to risk changing her life for.

She saw now that she should never have had any fear of adapting to living full-time with someone like Cal. He was so easygoing, so considerate, so much fun to be with. She felt as if she'd known him all her life. It was wonderful to lie beside him every night. To know she had a lover who was never going to go away, someone she could trust with her heart and mind and soul. She had waited so long for this, and she knew she would never take it for granted.

The only shadow on her happiness was the question mark over what she was going to do about work. Nothing had come of her initial feelers, and the situation wasn't likely to get any easier the longer she waited. She'd approached all the more likely sources — the local television stations and the nearby movie studios. As she'd half expected, the former had little to offer and, at the latter, she hadn't made it past a secretary who told her there was 'really nothing around at the moment' but to send in her resume and they'd keep it on file.

When she got a bit down about it all, Cal did his best to keep her positive.

'New productions are slotting in at the studios regularly, Cate. The Americans are using the place a lot now. I'm sure you'll find something right for you in time.'

'But overseas productions arrive with their own producers,' Cate explained. 'They won't be looking for someone like me, and with only TV experience, too.'

'It's a matter of being patient, waiting for the right opportunity, that's all. In the meantime, why don't you just relax and enjoy yourself? You'll wonder why you were complaining when you get thrown in the deep end again.'

Cate knew Cal was probably right. She'd keep looking, and meanwhile try to view the break as an enforced holiday. A chance to get to know the Coast and its environs.

Maude Dohonoe made no secret of her delight that Cate had moved in with her son. 'He needed someone like you, Cate,' she said quietly while Cal was attending to the bill one Sunday afternoon when they'd all gone out to lunch. 'He's been through a lot, my son...' The old woman had hesitated. It was clear she was referring to the accident that had taken Cal's wife and child. Except for that first time, Cal himself had never spoken of it again, and Cate hadn't wished to pry into what was clearly a sensitive subject.

But if Maude Donohoe was about to add something more, she had clearly changed her mind. Dabbing a napkin to her wrinkled lips, she'd merely smiled and said, 'You're truly the answer to my prayers, my dear.'

Another weekend, Cal drove her out to the hinterland, a place of rainforest and national parks, ancient trees and silvery waterfalls. They walked the trails that led through damp, shady canopies of hanging vines and foliage, and Cate breathed an air that seared her lungs with its freshness.

'It's so beautiful here,' she said in awe, as she clambered up the steep path after Cal.

He grinned at her over his shoulder. 'And because you're so athletic these days, you're able to visit these magical places.'

'Oh, shut up!' she retorted with a smile.

The change occurred subtlely. It took Cate a while to realise what was happening. At first she didn't really notice the signs. If anything, she decided it was just the pressure of work that was making Cal quieter, more introspective, more withdrawn. There were always problems in running a business and, on top of that, it was the school holiday period at the moment, so the surgery was busier than usual. No doubt he had plenty on his mind.

They still did everything together, but gradually Cate began to pick up on the changes. A detachment. An edginess. A sense of abstraction. It was clear to her that Cal had something troubling him, and she wished he would share the problem with her. They were a team now. They were there for each other, to offer each other support and comfort.

Finally, one evening when they were lying in bed, she asked him about it, explained that she'd noticed something was on his mind, and did he want to talk about it? Later she remembered the way he'd looked at her. The depth of painful intensity in his blue eyes had been quite startling.

'Are you all right, Cal?' With a frown of concern, she'd put her hand out and touched his cheek. 'Tell me, sweetheart, what's wrong?'

But he'd shaken his head. 'Nothing. Really. I guess I'm just tired that's all.' And then he'd pulled her close against him and kissed her deeply. As her tongue explored his mouth, Cate had felt his body respond and was sure they'd make love. But they hadn't.

It took him another two weeks to tell her the truth. They'd been out for dinner and had stopped in at the surgery on the way home. Cate had got quite friendly with Vicky, Cal's long-time receptionist, and they chatted in between patients while Cal checked up on the roster that had been worrying him all evening.

'Okay,' he said, as he reappeared from the rear office, 'that's done.' He leaned over the reception desk and spoke to Vicky. 'I forgot Ken wasn't going to be here on Friday. Better tell everyone to check the changes, if you don't mind.'

'Sure, no problem.' She smiled up at him.

Back at the apartment, he suggested a nightcap, and they carried their drinks out onto the patio. For a few minutes they sat in silence, sipping their ports and listening to the soft thud of the waves.

Then Cate turned to him with a smile. 'I used to wonder how people could leave a big city for the coast. Now I know. I don't think I could ever enjoy Sydney as much again.'

To her surprise, there was no answering smile. Instead, he looked at her with an expression she couldn't read, and even in the soft patio lighting, she noticed how pale his face had suddenly become.

With a frown of concern, she placed her glass down on the small table by her elbow and reached for his hand.

'Cal ... something's wrong. I know it is. Please, won't you tell me? I'm sure it's nothing we can't discuss.'

For a long moment he didn't reply, and again she couldn't interpret his expression as he stared back at her. Finally, he nodded.

'I — I just haven't known how to tell you, Cate.'

Her heart stopped and her brain went numb. She dropped his hand as if she'd been burnt and stared at him with wide, shocked eyes. Because she knew what was coming, knew that the door to her worst nightmare was opening.

He put down his glass and, clasping his hands between his knees, hung his head and began to talk. 'I'm so sorry, Cate ... so very, very sorry. It's just — it's just not working for me. I thought this was going to be everything I needed, but I can't pretend ... it just isn't.'

She could hear the blood drumming in her ears. Sweat had broken out between her shoulder blades and was trickling down her back. All she could do was stare at him.

He lifted his head and looked at her with tortured eyes.

'I *hate* myself, Cate. More than you can ever know.' His voice shook with the passion of his words. 'For doing this to you. Hurting you like this. But it's got nothing to do with you, who *you* are. It's me, Cate! It's everything that happened. I'm scarred, and pathetic. A weak, hopeless bastard. But I can't fight it. And because I can't do that, I'm useless to you. Absolutely, bloody useless!'

She saw his eyes glaze with tears, but she really understood only one thing from all the words he'd spoken. It was over. He didn't love her. She'd turned her life upside down, given up everything she'd fought so hard to achieve, and it was all for nothing. What had happened with Simon was happening all over again, just when she'd finally let herself trust and feel.

And she couldn't believe it. She just couldn't believe it.

Then, through the numbness of shock, another emotion took hold.

Anger. A terrible, burning anger at her own stupidity. At her childish belief that there could still be happy endings, that even at her age a woman could find love.

Tears of rage filled her eyes. When she opened her mouth to speak, she was choked by her own fury.

'I can't believe you've done this to me.'

'Cate —' His voice was raw, and he put out a hand to touch her. But with tears slipping down her cheeks, she pushed herself abruptly to her feet, out of his reach.

'Oh, my God, Cate, if I could have made everything different ...' He stood up, too, reaching for her again, but she jerked away from his touch.

'*No!* Don't!'

Turning, she stumbled in through the sliding glass doors, hearing him coming after her. He grabbed her arms and turned her round to face him.

'Cate, listen! I know I've done terrible damage to you. I know it, and I'll never be able to forgive myself. I love you. That's the honest truth. But I can't forget. I can't let go! Now that you're here with me like this, it's somehow made it worse. Because you're the only woman I've let touch me so deeply. But I keep seeing my wife's face, my son's. And it feels like — it feels as if I'm betraying them!'

She shook her head. It wasn't excuses she wanted. She didn't need to hear the pathetic reasoning and wretched logic behind it all, not when she was aching

351

with anger and pain and full of self-disgust at her foolish naivety.

Twisting her arms, she freed herself from his hold and gasped out a response: 'Then isn't it a bloody pity you hadn't worked all that out about yourself before you screwed up my damned life!'

Turning away, she ran into the bedroom and slammed the door.

She didn't sleep. Instead, she spent the night replaying the terrible scene, hearing the echo of Cal's words in her ears, 'I can't forget ... having you here has made it worse ... I feel as if I'm betraying them...' Those words refuelled her bitterness, anguish and anger again and again.

She'd trusted him, had truly believed that she'd found the man with whom she'd grow old, had finally overcome her fear and resistance and opened her heart to what she thought was true and everlasting love. And she'd been betrayed.

He knew she'd been hurt before, knew she was wary. And it was he who had taken the first step, made the promises, the declarations, until finally, completely, she had surrendered herself, been persuaded to find the faith and confidence to believe that this time she would be lucky.

That this time it would last.

The next morning he looked every bit as drawn and exhausted as she did.

'We've got to talk, Cate,' he pleaded with her when she emerged from the bedroom just after seven.

'Maybe I was crazy last night. Maybe we can sit down and straighten all this out. I never ever wanted everything to end up like this.'

She didn't trust herself to reply as she opened the hall cupboard to find her suitcases.

'Please, Cate, I don't want you to go. Maybe all I need is more time. A chance to work it all through in my own screwed-up head.'

She turned then, looking at him with angry, swollen eyes.

'And you expect me to wait around, just in case? To lie beside you every night knowing you're weighing up whether it's going to work or not?' She gave a hard, choked laugh as she moved towards the bedroom with a case in either hand. 'Oh, please, Cal ... don't take me for a bigger fool than I already am.'

He followed her, watched helplessly as she opened cupboards and drawers and threw her things back into the suitcases. She knew no other option was conceivable. She would have to return to Sydney and put her life back together again. Find a place to stay until the lease was up on her flat. Start looking for another job. Face the curiosity and pity of her friends.

And never, ever trust any man again.

❋

Greg had arrived at the hospital first. The moment Judith was shown into the brightly lit waiting room close to the ICU, he swung on her and launched his attack.

'I blame you for this! Now maybe you'll see what your own bloody selfishness has done to your kids! This'd never have happened if you hadn't pissed off!'

Judith stood white-faced in the doorway, letting the wave of accusations wash over her. She could barely remember how she'd driven to the hospital so quickly. Her only focus was the information they'd given her on the telephone: that her son had been taken to hospital from a city dance party, unconscious from an overdose of whatever it was he'd taken.

The ICU sister she'd just spoken to had told her they were still trying to identify the drug and were doing all they could to get Luke stabilised.

'What are his chances?' Still numb with shock, Judith had whispered the question.

'It's always best to be optimistic,' the woman replied with professional caution. 'Just be assured we're doing all we can.'

And now it was just a matter of waiting. But not here. Not where she would have to listen to Greg and cop everything he was throwing at her.

Turning on her heel, she walked away, finding a chair further down the corridor. She dropped into it and tried to fight back her panic. Oh, God, she prayed, please let him pull through. Don't let me lose him like this. I couldn't bear it.

Greg's accusations echoed in her head, and she felt choked with a poisonous guilt. Could she really be to blame? Did this have anything to do with her leaving? Had she made a terrible mistake? She'd thought the boys were old enough ... didn't need her ... But did you ever really understand your own kids?

The thought that she might have been to blame tortured her. Too restless to sit for long, she paced the corridor, kept annoying the sister at the desk, begging to know what was happening.

'Doctor will let you know as soon as he can,' came the formal, stonewalling reply.

The hardest part was facing this alone. Surely, no matter what had happened between them, this was a time when she and Greg should have been able to comfort each other, endure the waiting together, but the man who had confronted her in the waiting room would offer her no solace, she knew.

Finally, at some ungodly hour — she had no idea when — the sister found her staring out at the city from the window of a darkened room. The doctor wanted to see them both.

He spoke to them in the corridor outside the ICU, a younger man than she might have expected, but with lines of tiredness under his eyes. As he talked, he had to turn his gaze from one to the other of them, they were standing so far apart.

'He'll be okay, but we'll keep him in two or three days to make sure he's fully recovered. Luckily, someone who was with him had the guts to ring and tell us what he took.'

'And what —?'

'LSD.' The doctor cut across Greg's question.

Judith could only stare at him, stunned.

The young medico nodded. 'There's been a lot of it around lately. This isn't the first case we've seen in recent weeks.'

'Can — we see him, doctor?' Judith pleaded. 'Just for a moment?'

The doctor nodded again. 'Two minutes. That's all.' He looked distracted as if, with this crisis solved, his mind was already on the next.

Judith put a hand on the rumpled sleeve of his gown.

'Thank you.' She looked into that strained young face. 'I just want to say thank you.'

Beside her, she heard Greg mumble something, too.

A few minutes later, when they'd both been ushered away from their son's bedside, Greg barely waited until the sister was out of hearing.

'I'll always blame you for this,' he spat at her. 'And don't think it won't have a bearing on the settlement.'

Ah, yes, Judith thought, the Greg she knew so well. Even now, illogical or not, keeping sight of the bottom line.

Not wishing to give him the satisfaction of a reply, she turned on her heel and quickly walked away.

It was almost midnight when she finally got home. As she crossed the city, she kept seeing the image of Luke lying so pale and still on his hospital bed, the tubes and monitors linking him to the machines that pulsed with soft beeps and sighs around him.

I should have tried harder, she'd admonished herself as she stared helplessly at her younger son. I thought I was doing my best, but I should have been a better mother. I should have found a way to get closer to them and not let them drift away. I should have fought a hell of a lot harder to keep them mine . . .

The note was stuck under her door. The moment she saw it, Judith knew who had left it there.

'Oh, God.'

Tony.

With her focus entirely on the crisis with Luke, she'd forgotten all about their dinner arrangement. Bending down, she picked up the scrap of notepaper and stepped into the hallway reading the brief message.

I waited an hour. Tried your mobile but still couldn't reach you. Give me a call, I'm worried.

Judith looked at her watch. It was far too late to call him now. He was bound to be asleep.

Exhausted, emotionally drained, she dropped her handbag on the floor and sank into the sofa. It had been such a terrible night. The shock of Luke, Greg's cruelty and animosity, her own stifling sense of guilt.

The note was still in her hand, and she looked at it again. Tony had been worried about her. It was that fact she found most affecting, the thought that in all the cold, impersonal world out there, there was one human being who actually cared enough to be concerned about *her*. Judith felt tears prickle behind her eyelids. At this very moment, that counted for one hell of a lot.

And then she knew she just had to call him. No matter what the time. After all she'd been through tonight, she had to speak to someone who would understand. Judith picked up the receiver, desperate for Tony's compassion and kindness.

'Judith ... what happened? Are you all right?' He didn't sound as if he'd been asleep.

She told him then, in a disjointed, jerky way, about Luke. 'I'm sorry, Tony. With all the trauma I just completely forgot about anything else ...'

'Don't be crazy! Of course you did. But Luke — they're sure he's going to be all right?'

'It'll take him a couple of days to recover fully, they said. But yes, thank God, he's going to pull through.' She bit her lip as her voice trembled.

There was a pause, and then he said gently, 'I know it's late, but I think I should come over, Judith. You shouldn't have to cope with this all alone. Would that be all right?'

Her throat tightened and she nodded, even though she knew he couldn't see her. 'Yes ... Oh, please, Tony ...'

The moment he walked in the door, he opened his arms and folded her against his chest. She was past tears now, but she clung to the strength of him, the comforting warmth — and remembered how much she had missed that.

'Thank you,' she whispered. 'Thank you so much for coming.'

He sat her down, put on the kettle and made them each a cup of tea, his bulk filling the flat's poky kitchen.

'Now then,' he said, as he took a seat beside her, 'why don't you tell me everything?'

And she did, more lucidly than she had on the telephone, eventually even revealing how Greg had held her responsible for what Luke had done.

'You don't believe that, do you?' he asked.

'I don't know.' Helplessly, she shook her head. 'How can I be sure? Luke was the one who'd started to come and visit me here. Maybe he needed me, and I didn't see that. Perhaps he just couldn't cope with the fact that I'd left them all.'

'There's no point in jumping to conclusions,' Tony answered gently. 'All you can do is talk to him when he's over all this.'

Judith nodded. And she'd talk to Brent, too. Maybe he could give her more insight into Luke's state of mind.

It had helped to talk, to get things in perspective. Tony, she thought, was a true friend. Their relationship might never be more than that, but she would always value what he offered her.

As they talked, she began to realise it was hours since she'd had anything to eat. And, of course, she'd cheated Tony of his dinner, too.

'I bought a hamburger on the way home,' he told her with a smile, when she enquired guiltily if he were hungry.

'Oh, no! Listen,' she pointed to the kitchen, 'the veal's still in the fridge. Why don't I cook it now? You'll eat some with me, won't you?'

He gave a bemused chuckle. 'At almost two in the morning?'

'I'm starving! And surely a hamburger isn't enough for you.' She was on her feet, looking down at him in expectation. 'It'll only take me five minutes.'

He gave a shrug and grinned. 'Okay, you talked me into it. But you've got to let me help.'

He washed the salad while Judith quickly prepared the veal in the electric frypan. When the meal was ready, she even poured them a glass of wine from a cask in the fridge. They ate at the patio furniture that served as a dining set.

'Delicious,' Tony proclaimed. 'The chef's wasted on the midnight-to-dawn shift.'

For the first time that evening she managed a smile.

Despite her protests, he helped her to clear up, and then she walked with him to the door, trying not to think how terrible she would feel when the door shut behind him and he was gone.

'I can't tell you how much it helped,' she said softly, 'to have you here tonight. Thank you, Tony. Thank you so much.'

Then, instinctively, because it somehow seemed the most natural thing to do, she reached up and kissed him.

What astonished her was the force with which he kissed her back. Breathless, giddy-headed, she read passion in that kiss. Desire.

They drew apart, staring into each other's eyes, and she could hear the quickened rhythm of his breathing. Perhaps it matched her own, but she was far too fearful of making a wrong move.

Then he drew her close again, his kiss as long and deep and passionate as the first. With a sense of bewilderment, it suddenly struck her that he was lonely, too. He mightn't love her, but he needed the same comfort and closeness with another human being whom he respected and cared for, as she did.

Finally, he released her lips and, with a fluttering in her belly, she whispered against his cheek, 'I'd like to sleep with you, Tony … No complications, no expectations. Do you … do you think we could handle that?'

He drew away from her and stared into her eyes. Judith felt as if she'd stopped breathing as she waited for his response. Please God, she prayed silently, don't let me have spoilt things, don't let me have made a fool of myself again. Then she saw his smile, a broad, wonderful smile that made her heart flop crazily.

Hand in hand, they moved towards the bedroom.

Early the next morning, she rang the hospital. Luke was making good progress, they told her.

Next she rang Brent and asked him if he wanted to come with her to visit his brother. Judith was glad when he agreed. He'd be late for school, but that didn't matter as much as trying to get to the bottom of what was happening in Luke's life.

She didn't do more than skirt around the subject on the drive in. That would keep till later.

With relief, she saw that her younger son was out of ICU and had been admitted to a ward. He was still pale and tired, but it was clear to see he was on the way back.

'I'm sorry, mum.' His eyes were big and staring in his pallid face, and they watched her, unsure of her reaction. He barely acknowledged his brother.

'It's okay.' She patted his hand. 'We'll talk about it later.'

But first it was Brent she had to talk to.

They found the hospital canteen and sat facing each other over styrofoam cups of watery coffee.

'Did it have something to do with me, Brent? The fact that I left?' With tortured eyes, Judith put the questions to her elder son.

Brent shook his head. 'Don't hit on yourself, mum. It's not your fault. It was happening long before you left.'

Judith looked at him, aghast. 'If you knew, then why didn't you tell me?' She immediately realised how stupid that question would sound to her son's ears. Of course he wouldn't have told her.

'Well then, *why*?' she went on. '*Why* did he do it? What possible reason could he have for popping some unknown, dangerous substance in his mouth?'

Her son shrugged. 'Because it was there. Because everyone else did. It's just a stage.'

Judith was silent a moment, trying to understand this as a reason.

'What about you?' She had to ask the question. 'Did you ever go through the same "stage"?'

She held his eyes and could see the struggle going on behind them to tell the truth. 'Not hard stuff,' he said at last. 'Never that. Just — well, a bit of dope, you know.' His cheeks had grown pinker.

'But this could have killed him.'

'Yeah,' her son answered pragmatically, 'maybe he's learnt his lesson.'

He dropped his head back and finished his coffee, then began to look edgy as the silence continued.

At last Judith spoke. 'Do you want me to come home, Brent? Is that what you'd both want?'

362

For a moment her son thought about his answer. 'You've got to do whatever makes you happy, mum.' Then, reaching across the table, his hand hovered a second before resting tentatively on her own. 'But don't blame yourself for Luke. It wasn't your fault.'

It struck Judith that a barrier had broken down.

For the first time, she'd received comfort from one of her sons.

CHAPTER NINETEEN

It was two weeks since he'd left.

Rory couldn't believe what had happened to her life. She'd trusted Ian implicitly, never doubting for a moment his commitment to her and Cam, and to their relationship. To discover he was having an affair with a woman almost half her age had shattered her, left her barely able to cope with her shock and jealous rage.

She spent her every waking moment struggling between feelings of love and hate. How could he have done this to her? How could he have thrown aside all the years they'd spent together, left her and Cam alone? And how could she ever forgive him for his betrayal?

But at night, alone in the bed they'd shared, she wept with loneliness and grief. Despite everything, she knew she didn't want to lose him, still wanted to hang on to her dream of how their life together was supposed to be.

Yet she wouldn't demean herself by begging him to come back.

The day after their confrontation, Ian had cleared out his things while she was at work. Later, in a quick, cool phone call, he'd told her where he had moved to: a block of serviced apartments close to the Uni.

'You've got my mobile and work number,' he'd said to her, 'in case you need to discuss anything about Cam.'

The inference was clear: he no longer had any interest in her.

'There's a lot we'll have to sit down and work out,' he went on in that same cool, tight voice. 'But now's not the time. I'll call you to find out when it's convenient to drop by and see Cam.'

'To *see* Cam?' Hurt and angry, panicked by the complete emotional withdrawal she could sense in him, she snapped out the words before she could help herself. 'What the hell for? You never cared a damn about him when you lived under the same roof. Cam was just a nuisance to you, then. Why play the concerned and happy daddy now?'

But Ian didn't respond to her taunts. 'I'm not buying into a brawl with you, Rory. If that's what it's going to be like when I have to deal with you, maybe it's better if I don't see Cam for a little while. Until you're more in control.'

Her cheeks flamed with anger. 'Don't talk to *me* about bloody control! You're the one who couldn't control yourself, you and your sexy little girlfriend.' She took a deep choking breath. 'Don't call me again, Ian, okay? I don't need to hear another bloody hypocritical word from you. Cam and I'll manage just fine on our own!'

Trembling, she slammed down the receiver. Then, covering her face with her hands, she burst into wild sobs.

Oh, God, she still loved him, but she knew that now she'd just driven him even further away ... The pain and grief were driving her crazy.

She told no one at work. She didn't need the pitying glances, or to become the subject of office gossip. But it must have been clear to those who worked closely with her that something was wrong. Her concentration was shot, she forgot meeting times and appointments, was short-tempered and irritable. Like an automaton, she dragged herself out of bed each morning, feeling just as exhausted as when she'd closed her eyes the night before. Somehow, she made it through the day.

She'd given some excuse to Debbie about Ian's absence. Muttered some impossibly intricate story about him having to stand in for another professor, at short notice, at the university school on Fiji for a few weeks. Ludicrous, and she wasn't sure if Debbie bought it, but the nanny didn't question her further.

By the end of the third week, the burden of keeping her nightmare to herself was finally too much to bear. And there was only one person Rory felt she could really open her heart to.

As she had on that previous occasion, Antonella let her talk, let her get it all off her chest, without interrupting.

'I just don't know what to do, Antonella.' She was sobbing softly by the time she finished. 'I thought I was doing everything possible to make us all happy. I bent over backwards. But it wasn't enough. And now I've lost him, to some sexy predatory bitch half my age.'

'Rory...' Antonella was her usual calm, rational self, 'everything's too emotional for you right now. Who knows how this will end up? He might get sick of the girl in another week. But no matter what happens there, you've got to stop torturing yourself. Living in hope, putting your life on hold isn't going to do you any good.' She paused, and her voice softened. 'I can give you all the sympathy you want, my dear friend but, at the end of the day, you have to face the facts and be practical. You know what I think? How long is it since you had a break? You did that massive job in Melbourne with me, and you've jumped right back into it again without coming up for air, haven't you? And now this king hit. If you want my advice, I'd say it's time for you to take a decent break. Time out. You don't even have to go away. Just spend the time with your child and on healing yourself. Be good to yourself for a change, Rory. It's what most women under the pressure of the daily grind deny themselves.'

'But I can't,' Rory protested tearfully. 'Work's the only thing that's keeping me sane at the moment.'

'Rory, I don't hear a woman who's sane. I hear one who's near to breaking point over a situation that she can't do anything about. Remember, darling, no matter how hard we wish or work for the happy ending, it's not guaranteed. The sooner you can accept what's happened and get on with your life, the better off you'll be.'

By the time she hung up, Rory wasn't sure if talking to Antonella had made her feel better or not. The options her friend had proposed seemed impossible to embrace. Could Antonella have any idea how damned hard it was to 'accept' the nightmare she'd suddenly been plunged into? And as for taking a break from work, how could she possibly give up her only lifeline?

But as the days passed, she found her work deteriorating and admitted her inability to make firm decisions, her errors of judgement that cost money and valuable time to rectify. She couldn't help remembering Antonella's words. Yet she succeeded in pushing them to the back of her mind each time. She would cope, she vowed to herself. It was only a matter of getting back on track, not letting this terrible situation with Ian get the better of her.

And then, one evening as she was driving home from work, she was forced to realise just how close to breaking point she really was.

It happened in peak hour traffic, her thoughts were so distracted that she didn't notice the changing lights ahead. Oblivious, she drove on, right into the path of approaching traffic.

There was the sound of tearing metal. The vicious jerk of her seat belt that knocked the wind out of her. A crazy spinning, then a lurch as her car came to rest across the traffic island of the busy intersection.

Dazed and shocked, Rory reacted instinctively. Releasing her belt, she climbed out on shaky legs to survey the damage.

'You crazy bitch! Are you blind or something! Didn't you see the fucking light change?'

The BMW she'd hit had sustained far greater damage than her own vehicle. Its irate owner, a well-dressed businessman, slammed his badly damaged driver's door behind him as he swore savagely at her.

Suddenly it was all too much. Amid the rubble of metal and lost hubcaps, Rory dropped to her knees on the bitumen and began to sob hysterically.

❋

'How'd it go? Any luck?'

Jessica looked up as Cate let herself in at the front door.

They were sharing Jess's apartment. The lease on Cate's wasn't up for another three months and, while she'd been grateful for a place to land when she'd first arrived back, Cate had protested that three months was far too long to encroach, even on her best friend.

But Jessica had insisted.

Now she looked expectant as she waited to hear news of Cate's latest job interview.

With a heavy sigh, Cate threw her jacket over the arm of the sofa. 'Who knows?' she shrugged. 'They told me they'd had more than a dozen applicants for the position. Anyway,' she pulled out a chair and joined Jessica at the dining table, 'I'm not even sure if I want to be a publicity assistant on some crappy woman's magazine.'

'It'll only be until something better comes up,' Jessica comforted. 'You know you'll get back into TV sooner or later. Someone with your talents, it's a dead cert. You've just got to be patient.'

Cate could remember when she'd heard those words before. Cal had said the exact same thing to her just a few short weeks ago.

But she didn't want to think of Cal.

'I don't do "patience" very well,' she replied.

'Then try "drink" instead.'

Pushing back her chair, Jessica walked over to the refrigerator.

'What'll it be? Dry white or vodka? I think there's some lemon left.'

'Maybe I'll just have a coffee.'

'Sure?'

'You don't have to wait on me, Jess.'

'I'm not. I'm exercising. Power walking to the kitchen.'

Cate said nothing while Jessica prepared their coffees, and her friend could tell from her expression that she was brooding again.

'I really can't believe it, you know,' Cate said finally, when the two mugs of coffee were on the table in front of them. 'That I've ended up in this shit of a mess.'

'Cate, you've got to forget it. It happened, for whatever reason, and you've got to put it behind you.'

But Cate went on as if she hadn't heard. 'I'm so damned angry at myself. That's the hardest part to swallow. That I was such a trusting fool at my time of life. To turn my life upside down and then have everything blow up in my face.'

Jessica stirred sugar into her coffee and handed the spoon to Cate. 'Well, it's obvious the guy was still hung up on his wife. He tried to see past that, thought you were the one to help him through it, but it didn't work out that way. Being angry at yourself isn't going to change anything, Cate. To be completely unoriginal, shit happens, and you live on, or you write your farewell note and jump off the Heads.'

'Philosophy's really you, isn't it?' Cate made an effort to snap out of her mood. She'd been back in Sydney for three weeks and was fully aware that she'd hardly been the best of company.

Jessica grinned at her over the top of her coffee mug.

As she spent her days sending out her resume, using every contact she had to secure herself work, trying to fit back into the tempo of the city she thought she'd left behind, Cate fought against a sense of bitterness and loss.

Despite all her promises to herself, she'd opened her heart again and, for the second time, was left to pick up the pieces of her life. She'd trusted Cal totally, felt so sure about their future together, and he'd let her down.

She knew now that she would never take the chance of love again. Never put herself in the position where any man could wound her as terribly as Cal had done. Much as she tried to forget, she couldn't help thinking how good it had been — the excitement and joyful anticipation of falling in love, of having someone of her own after all the years of being alone. The memory of those wonderful months made being by herself again all the harder to bear.

She'd always prided herself on being the sort of person who could find the positive in any situation. But not this time. As she tried to get her life back into some sort of order, she felt unable to shake off her defeat and depression. She'd been through too many changes in too short a time. Her emotions were reeling.

On top of everything else, she was finding it difficult to settle back into Sydney. She realised she was missing the Coast. The lifestyle, the friendliness, the weather — the things that made life worth living. But somehow she had to wind herself up again and jump back into the rat race of the crowded city she'd left behind.

An expensive city, too. Her savings were fast running out, and the situation was looking more serious by the day. Soon she'd have to settle for whatever job she could get.

Swallowing her pride, she'd called the studio, hoping against hope that there might be something available to her on *Live!* But all that did was teach her what she probably knew — no one is indispensable. The girl they'd employed in her old job was well entrenched, and there was nothing else.

'But we'll take your number, and let you know, Cate.'

She wasn't holding her breath.

It was now a month and three days since she'd landed back in the city, and nothing much had changed. Her most recent interview had been with a small video production firm. If she landed the job, she'd hate it. But she'd have to take it. They said they'd let her know by the following Monday. She'd spend the weekend praying.

Jessica gave her the message when she came in from her run that evening. She'd kept up the exercise program Cal had coaxed her into with such gentle skill and cunning. At least it offered some outlet for the energy she'd have expended on a job. But the polluted air of Balmain wasn't quite as invigorating as the fresh air of the wide open beaches.

'A woman rang. With an accent.'

Jessica stopped pushing vegetables into the food processor and turned to look at her. 'Mrs Maude Donohoe,' she said, watching Cate's face. 'Wants you to call her hotel as soon as you get in.'

Still breathing heavily from her run, Cate couldn't hide her astonishment.

'At her *hotel*? Cal's mother? Here, in Sydney?'

Jessica pursed her lips and nodded. 'That's what she said.'

Cate could only stare back into her friend's questioning eyes.

As she showered and changed, she fought her inner conflict. Maude Donohoe was in Sydney. And wanted Cate to call her as soon as possible. Of course it had to be about what had happened between her and Cal.

I don't need this, she told herself, her belly churning with anger and indecision. It was over, and nothing Maude Donohoe or anyone else could say would change that. What was the point of scratching the wound and making it bleed again?

Fifteen minutes later, her hair still damp, she walked back into the kitchen and was met by Jessica's expectant look.

'Okay,' she said resignedly. 'I can't be rude. I'll call her.'

The quick expression of relief she caught on her friend's face irritated her beyond reason.

'Cate, my dear, thank you so much for calling.'

'Maude, I —' She wasn't quite sure what to say. 'How . . . how did you know where to find me?'

'It wasn't easy. Vicky helped me, Cal's receptionist. First she tried your old number, but that was disconnected, as we thought it might be. Then she rang the television place you used to work for. No one there seemed to know where you were, either. At least not until she rang a second time, a couple of weeks later. When she said it was urgent, someone eventually gave her your friend's number.'

Well, if nothing else, Cate thought, she had to admire Maude Donohoe's persistence.

'So urgent that it brought you to Sydney?' she asked. She had no intention of sounding curt, but her heart was too raw and sore when it came to anything to do with Cal.

'Cate, my dear,' Maude Donohoe's voice softened with understanding, 'I'm sure you'll think I'm nothing but an interfering old woman. But all I'm asking is half an hour of your time. I didn't know at first what had happened between you and Cal. When I saw how badly he was taking it, I thought you must have left him. When I finally found out the truth, I knew I had to find you and try to make you understand.'

'Maude, I'm sure you've got the best of intentions, but does it really matter who dropped who? It's over. We both made a mistake.'

There was a pause at the other end of the line, and then Maude Donohoe said with quiet deliberation, 'There's something you've got to know, Cate. I've come here because I want you to hear the truth about my son.'

❋

Leith was nervous. If she thought about it, it seemed more or less her natural condition these days. She had a continual sense of being on edge, of never being quite sure if she was really in charge of her own life any longer.

She should be happy, she knew. Paul adored her, they had a lovely home, they were together almost all the time.

But something wasn't right. Increasingly she felt as if she were some exotic bird trapped in a gilded cage.

She didn't doubt Paul's love for her, but it was a love that extended into controlling almost every area of her life. He brought home books he thought she should read, music he wanted her to hear; if she wore something he didn't like, he gently made it clear that she should change; he chose her perfume, her jewellery; and worst of all, he had isolated her from her friends.

After the day he had turned up at the tennis courts, she had never gone back — because Paul always made other arrangements for that weekday morning. Sometimes it was a trip by sea-plane for lunch at Palm Beach; on other occasions, it was something as simple as taking in the latest hit movie together. But it was always just the two of them.

'You see,' he'd say, squeezing her hand in the dark, 'we really don't need anyone else. Not when two people love each other as much as we do, my darling.'

Yet Leith knew she *did* need other people. Married to David, she had been used to a life of freedom, able to fill her days in any way she pleased. She had never felt smothered or curtailed.

As the weeks passed, she finally admitted to herself that Paul's control of her life, her every move, was not only suffocating, it was beginning to frighten her, too.

Nor was the irony of the situation lost on her. She'd left one man because she felt neglected, for another whose attention was close to claustrophobic. But whenever she attempted to bring up the subject, Paul refused to take her seriously.

'You've just forgotten how it is to be the centre of a man's life, my love,' he had told her with a gentle smile of amusement. 'I want to give you everything you weren't getting in your marriage, and all you have to do is relax and enjoy it.'

But she wasn't enjoying it. And she needed to sort

out her confusion. No matter what Paul said, she thought, she was going to meet with Judith, talk the difficult situation through.

They had arranged to meet for lunch that day at a small restaurant just five minutes drive away. She'd picked a date when she knew Paul would be tied up at the office with interstate clients. By the time he arrived home, he'd never know that she'd been out of the house.

Now, as she dressed, her breathing quickened. This isn't how it's meant to be, she told herself. She shouldn't have to be so deceptive over an innocent lunch date with a girlfriend. It was Paul who was forcing her to act this way.

Dressed and ready, she had just picked up her handbag and car keys from the table in the sunroom when she heard the sound of the front door opening.

Leith froze. It had to be Paul. What was he doing home at this time of day?'

The next moment he appeared in the doorway.

'Darling,' she felt her cheeks flush, 'you surprised me. I . . . I thought you were having lunch with clients today.'

His eyes traced a slow path from her feet to her heated face.

'So it would seem. The clients cancelled, so I thought I'd come home, spend the time with you. But,' he paused for effect, 'I see you have other plans.'

'Yes, I . . .' Leith could feel herself getting flustered. But why, for God's sake? All she'd done was make an innocent arrangement to see a friend.

'I'm meeting Judith,' she said lightly. 'We're having lunch together.'

He was looking at her, his mood suddenly chilly. 'And you didn't think to tell me?'

She shifted her gaze nervously from his. How could she explain the way he made her feel? As if she were ... his prisoner.

'Paul, please. Try to understand ... I need some time to myself. To have a life of my own.'

Frowning, he moved into the room towards her. 'Why, Leith? You're all *I* need. Why should it be any different for you?'

She looked back at him, shaking her head. 'Paul, I need ... to be able to breathe.' There was a plea in her voice. 'I can't be answerable to you for everywhere I go, for everyone I see.'

As if she hadn't spoken, he replied with quiet deliberation. 'I want you to stay home today, Leith. I want you to go and change, and we'll have something to eat together here, at home.'

She stared back at him, her heart beginning to race. Suddenly, as if the scales had dropped from her eyes, she could see what was happening. This wasn't about love. It was about control, possession, owning someone body and soul.

And it wasn't what she wanted.

'No!' She surprised herself by the defiance in her voice. 'I'm not your puppet, Paul. Not some doll you can dress up and control and command and manipulate. It's taken me till now to face up to the fact that that's what you're doing to me. I don't make a decision, don't have a life of my own any more. If we want this relationship to last, things are going to have to change.'

And with that, she made to leave.

But he was too quick, moving to place himself between her and the doorway.

'Where do you think you're going?' he demanded. 'Didn't you hear what I said to you?'

'I'm not doing anything wrong,' she answered, her cheeks flushing again at his tone. 'I'm having lunch with a girlfriend. So, please, get out of my way.'

She went to move past, but he gripped her arm, his fingers biting into her flesh.

'You're hurting me...' Frowning in pain, she tried to twist herself free.

The next moment she felt the sting of his palm against her cheek.

'I said, I want you here with me, Leith.'

Shocked, she stared wide-eyed into his coldly angry face. And suddenly felt a new emotion.

Fear.

Panicked, she tried to break free, but he hit her again as he swung her back into the room. The blow caught her above the right eye, and her head spun with pain and shock.

'No!' She began to fight back, desperate now to escape this violent stranger. She kicked out, her sharp heel catching him in the shin and, for a second, his grip slackened. She lunged away, but didn't see the coffee table that stood in her path. Falling awkwardly, she felt her face connect with the sharp edge of the glass. There was a terrible crunch of breaking bone, and then blood was streaming down her face. She could taste it in her mouth, see it dripping onto her dress, the carpet.

'Leith, darling, oh no!'

Suddenly all concern, he was on his knees beside her. 'Oh, my darling, I never meant to hurt you. Why didn't you just listen to me? Wait, I'll go and get a towel.'

Panting with fear, she watched him hurry from the room. The second he was out of sight, she struggled to her feet.

Snatching up the purse and keys she'd dropped in the fracas, she ran, still dripping blood, down the hall to the front door.

She called Judith's mobile from her own as she drove.

'Judith . . . I can't explain now.' She was breathless with shock. 'Please, I'm going to pull up outside in about two or three minutes. Can you just jump in the car? I'll explain everything when I see you.'

Judith was waiting, and she opened the passenger door as Leith came to a brief stop in the traffic.

Leith saw her friend's expression change as she caught sight of her face. In her panic to get away, she hadn't dared to stop and try to staunch the bleeding.

'*Leith*! What happened? Did you have an accident?'

'I — no . . . Oh, God, Jude . . .' She began to cry, her tears mingling with the blood.

'Pull over! Quickly! Look, over there.' Judith pointed at the next side street, to a spot under the shade of a tree.

As Leith did as she was told, Judith scrambled in

her handbag for tissues, a useless gesture given the amount of blood.

'There's a beach towel. In the boot.' The blood bubbled in Leith's mouth as she spoke. Her fingers found the boot release button by her side.

'I'll get it.' Judith already had her door open. 'You keep your head back. Lean right back over the seat.'

Quickly, she found the towel and slammed the boot shut again. She couldn't imagine what had happened.

Or maybe she didn't want to.

❋

They met in the foyer of the small Surry Hills hotel where Maude Donohoe had made an overnight reservation.

With the help of her stick, the old woman pushed herself to her feet.

'Thank you for coming, Cate. It's more than kind of you. Why don't we go upstairs? It'll be more private in my room.'

She walked with slow deliberation towards the elevator, and Cate could sense how painful it was for her. Yet she hadn't let her affliction prevent her from making the journey to Sydney. Maude Donohoe, Cate realised, was a very determined woman.

In the small, dimly lit room, the old woman insisted Cate take the one easy chair while she sat on the bed. Then, she paused a moment, both hands clasped atop her walking stick, as if gathering her thoughts.

'I want to start by saying that I think you're the best thing that's happened to my son in years,

Cate. You have no idea the difference I saw in him after he met you. For the first time in a long, long time, it was as if he'd had the life breathed back inside him.'

Cate stayed silent. What was she supposed to say? Great, but where had that got them in the end?

'To understand Cal,' Maude Donohoe went on, 'you've got to understand what really happened to his wife and son. Maybe he didn't tell you the truth at the beginning because he'd convinced himself he'd finally got over it all and didn't want to rake up the whole sad and unfortunate business.'

Cate frowned. She'd always thought Cal had been honest with her. What had he held back about his dead wife and son?

'I didn't know till after the accident that my son's marriage was in trouble. Kathleen was a good woman, her heart was in the right place, but I always thought the two of them mismatched. Cal's so easygoing, and she was quite the opposite. A perfectionist, which isn't necessarily a bad thing, but sometimes, I could see, Kathleen didn't seem to know where to draw the line. And she never forgave him for bringing her to Australia. I have to tell you that it was Vicky who filled me in on a lot of what happened. She and Cal became friends, not just employer and employee, and he confided in her when things were going bad. Apparently Kathleen hated living on the Coast and was always nagging at him to go back to Ireland. Of course,' Maude Donohoe gave a dry smile, 'I'd have loved him at home again, but it was his life and none of my business. I knew he loved Australia, had established himself here, but apparently it was a real sticking point between them that he wouldn't return to Ireland.

'Kathleen, on the other hand, would go back for months at a time. It happened before Jack was born. Afterwards, of course, she had a good excuse: to show off the baby to everyone at home.

'As I found out later, it was during one of Kathleen's long absences that Cal met someone else. The relationship became important to him, but he was torn apart at the idea of divorce. Because he knew Kathleen would go back to Ireland, and she'd certainly have custody of Jack. I know my son, Cate, and I can imagine how unbearable he would have found it not to be close to his boy. So, like so many men before him, he stayed in the marriage but kept the affair going on the side.

'Inevitably, Kathleen found out, and it was then all hell broke out. Without going into the details, he told me about the horrific argument they'd had this particular Sunday afternoon and, afterwards, still in a blazing temper, Kathleen had snatched up Jack and driven away to spend the night with a friend.

'It was that afternoon that the two of them were killed. And of course, my poor son blamed himself for the tragedy — because of the affair and because he'd let her leave in such a state. Even when the police reports stated that it was the other driver who had actually ploughed into Kathleen's car, Cal still couldn't help thinking that if she hadn't been so distracted by their row, she might have managed to avoid the accident.'

Maude paused, her face showing the strain of her emotions. 'I didn't need Vicky to tell me that for a long time afterwards he was in a terrible way. The affair couldn't survive what had happened, of course, and it must have seemed as if his whole life were falling apart.'

'Which is the reason you left Ireland,' Cate put in quietly, understanding now.

The old woman nodded. 'I was terribly worried about him. I rang Vicky at the surgery any number of times to find out how he was coping. When I said I was coming out, he tried to protest, but I came anyway. Because I love my son and I couldn't stand back and watch him slowly destroying himself. It's for those same reasons that I've come to see you, my dear. I watched you two together, I saw how good you were for Cal. And I thanked God, because I felt sure he was finally letting go of the past.'

Maude Donohoe paused, her eyes fixed on Cate's face.

'I have to ask you one question, my dear. Do you still love him?'

For a long moment, Cate couldn't answer. She was trying to absorb all Maude had told her, trying to understand how what had happened to Cal had affected their relationship, trying to find a perspective so she could truthfully answer the old lady's question without letting her own pain and anger and disappointment colour her reply.

Finally, she nodded. 'Yes ... I love him,' she said quietly. 'It'll take me a long, long time to get over.'

Maude Donohoe's expression lightened, and her eyes lit up. 'You don't know how happy it makes me to hear you say that, my dear.'

Then, with a plea in her voice, she went on. 'Please, Cate, I'm asking you not to give up, to go back to him and help him take that final step to push away the shadows.'

'But,' Cate protested, 'I can't make Cal forget what happened.'

Maude Donohoe was not to be deflected. 'It's not a matter of forgetting,' she replied fervently. 'It's a matter of getting him to realise that if he doesn't beat the past now, it's going to haunt him for the rest of his life. And leave him a lonely old man. It's a matter of making him see that he *deserves* to be happy. That he can love and be loved again and it won't mean he's betraying Jack. He has to see that he can't drown himself in guilt forever. And you're the one woman in the world who can help him, Cate.'

She paused again and leaned forward on her stick, and Cate could see the same intensity in the mother's eyes that she had seen in the son's.

'Please, come back and be patient with him. Until he sees there's nothing wrong in letting himself be totally happy again, even if Jack isn't in the world any longer.'

From outside the double-glazed windows, Cate could hear the subdued hum of the evening traffic as she felt the old woman's hopeful eyes upon her. Her mind spun. Could she really do what Maude Donohoe was asking? Could she really believe that this time it would work out?

At last she said, 'It's not an easy thing you're asking of me. What if we do try again, and another few weeks or months down the track, he tells me the same thing? That he can't forget. That he can't give me what I need. I'm not sure I can take that risk to my own emotions, my life.'

After a moment, Maude Donohoe nodded. 'I know what you're saying, of course I do. But both Vicky and I believe it's just a matter of time. Cal loves you and needs you like he's never needed any other woman.'

She waited expectantly as Cate sat in silence, pondering what was being asked of her. Oh, God, she didn't want to hurt this old lady. She was genuinely fond of her. But was it really possible that Cal could finally shed the burden of the past?

At last she shook her head in helplessness. 'I'm sorry, Maude. I can't give you an answer right now. I need time to think. I've turned my life upside down once for Cal, I don't know if I'm capable of taking that risk again.'

The older woman nodded, as if she had been expecting the answer. 'I understand you need time, my dear. I can't expect more than that. But at least,' she added, 'I take heart from the fact that you haven't given me a flat "no".'

❋

The rain was pouring down outside. Rory sat in the family room, taking no notice of the television set flickering in the corner. It was Saturday night, and she was alone, no doubt the way she'd be alone for the rest of her life.

Morose, full of self-pity, she took another sip of her drink. The bottle of gin had been almost full when she'd started. Now she saw the level had dropped to almost half. Yet drinking hadn't made her feel any better.

In the end, she'd taken Antonella's advice and asked for early holiday leave. For ten days now, she'd been at home with Cam. Infused with good intentions, she'd told Deb that she'd only need her two mornings of the week. She had been determined to make up for all the time lost with her son.

But somehow, as the days passed, she'd found herself unable to summon the energy to cope with anything more than the basic tasks. By the time Cam was fed and washed and dressed, and she'd made a cursory attempt at tidying the house, she felt overwhelmed by fatigue. Nor did she need a degree in psychology to understand that her physical exhaustion had its roots in the depression that grew more suffocating with every day. It enveloped her like a thick stifling blanket, rendering her almost inert.

And she had no idea how to come to terms with it.

What could she do but keep on going, take one day at a time? Wasn't time supposed to be the best healer? If that were the case, she wished there was a switch she could flick to make the years fly past and free her of this crushing pain and grief and loneliness. But, she mused bitterly grown women weren't granted wishes, were they.

She had only picked at her dinner and could feel the effects of the gin. As if her brain were fuzzy around the edges, but not so fuzzy that she wasn't aware when Cam's piercing cries began again.

He was cutting teeth and, although she'd put him down almost two hours ago, he'd refused to settle. This would be the fourth or fifth time she'd had to try to comfort him.

Pushing herself unsteadily to her feet, she made her way down the hall to her son's bedroom. By the glow of the soft nightlight she always left on, she looked down at his little face, flushed and twisted with distress as he screamed his discomfort.

'Hush, hush, my poor baby.' Leaning over the cot, she ran a finger gently over his hot cheeks. Oh, God, what should she do? Lift him up? Take him in her arms again? When she'd done that earlier this evening, his cries had only grown more insistent.

Nor did her presence appear to do anything to soothe him. Twisting his little head feverishly from side to side, he barely appeared to notice her, and the fact that she could do nothing to calm him unnerved her. How long was he going to keep up these screaming fits? She couldn't give him any more drops. He'd had the maximum allowed in the last few hours.

Why am I so useless? she asked herself in despair. Other women, she felt sure, would know instinctively what to do. Tears of self-pity filled her eyes. She wasn't a real mother, or she'd be able to cope with this.

Fighting for control, she slid her hands under her son's hot body and, lifting him out of the cot, laid him against her shoulder. Patting his back, she rocked back and forth, doing her best to soothe him.

388

'It's all right, my poor darling ... you'll be all right.'

It seemed an age before his sobs finally subsided, and he began to breath deeply in sleep. With a sense of relief she laid him carefully back into the cot, praying that the movement wouldn't rouse him again.

As she tiptoed out of the room, her earlier sense of failure gave way to the opposite emotion. She'd done what any other mother could do. Had soothed her troubled child back to sleep. The thought filled her with an inordinate sense of pleasure, and, back in the family room, she refilled her glass in acknowledgement of her achievement.

It was then, in that state of heightened emotion, that the idea of calling Ian occurred to her. He should know that she'd taken leave from work, she told herself, that she was home with Cam, was coping like a real mother at last. And that was all she was going to talk about, she promised herself. Not anything else.

With quickening heart, she picked up the phone beside her and placed a call to his mobile. She couldn't imagine that he'd be sitting at home on a Saturday night. A moment later as she listened to the message, she was filled with crushing disappointment. His phone was turned off.

Well, so what, she told herself, made suddenly cocky by alcohol and her success in calming Cam. He'd given her the apartment number, too. Maybe he *had* decided to spend the evening at home.

The number rang half a dozen times, and she was just about to hang up when it was finally answered.

'Hallo.'

A woman's voice.

Rory felt as if she'd been kicked in the belly.

'Hallo? Is anyone there?' The arrogant surety of youth was clearly evident in Sara Trent's tone.

With a quiet click, Rory hung up. She didn't know how long she sat there staring at the telephone, imagining them in the apartment together, the man who had once belonged to her having sex with someone else, telling someone else that he loved her, kissing and stroking that young flawless face, that perfect body. Wiping away the past as if it had never existed. Leaving her to bring up their son alone, to face the decline and decay of age by herself ...

It was the screams of her child reverberating in the still of the darkened house that finally jolted her out of her anguished reverie.

Oh, God, no ... Not again ... Not now ...

Suddenly aware of the tenseness in her hands, she realised her fingers were curled tightly into her palms, the nails biting into the flesh. Maybe if she left him, she told herself, he'd cry himself back to sleep.

But the screams didn't let up, and soon she couldn't bear it any longer. Couldn't bear to think of her child in pain. Couldn't bear her own pain ...

Hurrying back to the bedroom, she stared down helplessly at her crying son. No, Cam ... no ... Please, darling. I can't take it any more.

She felt a wave of heat pass through her body and, for a moment, thought she was going to faint. Her mind spun from the noise and the amount she'd had to drink.

And her baby continued to scream.

No ... I can't handle this. I really can't handle this ... *I just can't cope with it any longer!*

It all happened in seconds.

The large down-filled pillow was near at hand on the divan she'd sometimes slept on when Cam was a newborn. When she'd been so frightened that something would happen to him if she weren't nearby ...

With a choking sob, Rory placed the pillow over her baby's flushed, distressed face.

CHAPTER TWENTY

The committal hearing took most of the day.

Sitting beside each other in the public gallery, Leith and Cate and Judith watched with fearful, sorry hearts as their friend went through her terrible ordeal. It was so difficult to believe what was happening.

As the evidence was given, Cate found herself remembering that evening when they'd all met for dinner and the question she had asked of each of them: if they had got what they had wanted out of life.

With painful clarity Rory's answer echoed now in her mind ... 'I wanted it all ... it's too good to be true ...'

Cate was sure the others were remembering, too. And only now were they discovering the terrible truth that had hidden behind their friend's bravado.

But, she asked herself in silent contemplation, hadn't each of them been guilty of less than honesty that night? Talking with Judith and Leith as they'd waited to get into the court she'd learned that Judith had left her husband, while Leith's marriage, too, had had its difficulties. As for herself, she had passionately declared that the last thing she wanted in life was a relationship. She had meant it at the time, or thought she had. It had taken the right man to make her change her mind.

Perhaps, she thought regretfully, if they had all been more forthright, more prepared to admit to less than perfect lives, Rory wouldn't be sitting in front of them now facing the ordeal of her life.

Finally the magistrate had heard all the evidence.

From the operator at emergency services who had reported Rory's hysterical call: 'She said it twice,' the tight-faced woman had stated firmly. 'She said, "I didn't mean to. I didn't mean to do it."'

From the ambulance drivers, whose suspicions had been aroused by the bruises on the neck and cheeks of the ashen-faced child they had rushed to resuscitate. The two men had seen too many cases of abuse not to mention their worries to the police.

From the policewoman who had interviewed Rory: 'She was close to breaking point.' The woman spoke with professional detachment. 'Almost incoherent. But it was clear that Ms Hudson was very concerned that her son was going to be all right.'

When the crown prosecutor was finished, it was the turn of Rory's legal counsel to argue that there was insufficient evidence to put his client on trial.

A small, spry, grey-haired man with pink boyish cheeks, the linchpin of his argument involved calling a medical expert to the stand to elicit if the bruises on the baby's body might have been the result of something other than 'maternal abuse'.

The middle-aged doctor was forced to agree that 'the contusions could have resulted from an attempt to resuscitate the child'.

The lawyer thanked him, knowing he had established reasonable doubt as to his client's intention.

Afterwards, he made a brief and eloquent speech, citing his client's education and good reputation, her desire and love for her child, the trouble she had always taken to ensure he was well cared for.

'My client loves her child dearly, your honour. Like a lot of modern women, she's been used to facing challenges and dealing with them effectively. She admits she has been facing problems in adjusting to her role as a mother, but this is not to infer in any way that she had any intention of harming her child on the night in question. My client is now accessing professional help, which she realises she perhaps should have sought out sooner.'

At the desk behind her counsel, Rory sat with her head bowed. Overcome by a deep sense of shame and guilt, she was unable to meet the eyes of any of those who faced her. All she could do was reassure herself that nothing really mattered except that Cam was all right.

But she would never forget that terrible night. With her nerves already near to breaking point, something inside her had suddenly snapped. All the months of guilt and exhaustion, of struggling to do the right thing by everybody had finally overwhelmed her. Somehow there was a pillow in her hands, and she was holding it over Cam's face. How long for, she would never know. But suddenly she realised that her baby wasn't struggling or crying any longer.

And to her horror, she understood what she had done. It was then she must have bruised Cam as she grabbed him up and slapped at his cheeks, trembling with terror. When no response was forthcoming, she frantically began to breathe air into his tiny lungs.

Finally she had felt a flicker of response. He was breathing again, but she had no idea what damage he might have suffered. Cradling him in her arms, she grabbed the phone and dialled 000, barely coherent with panic.

And then, during those interminable minutes before the ambulance arrived, she rang Ian. Sobbing with relief as he answered the phone, she managed to make him understand her garbled message.

'I'm coming. Straight away.' His voice was sharp with shock. 'Don't say anything more to the medicos than you have to.'

And now he was sitting somewhere behind her, along with Judith and Leith and Cate, and all those curious, prying strangers who filled the public gallery.

Waiting for the magistrate to decide if she should stand trial for the attempted murder of her baby son.

EPILOGUE

Judith savoured the moment. With a smile, she handed the postal clerk the heavy parcel and watched her put it on the scales. Inside the postage bag were the final proof pages of her novel. She had completed the editing only last night, just after midnight. And now at last her task was over.

She paid the amount owed and saw the woman behind the counter drop her precious work into a bulging sack. It was hard to believe that she had finally fulfilled her dream. But she had, and her sense of satisfaction was enormous.

Now, as she walked out into the sunlight, she remembered the days and nights of hard work, the endless hours she'd sat at her computer and created her heroine's story. In the end, she thought, she and Jo had been one. She'd known her as well as she knew herself, and they had gone on their journey of discovery and growth together. It had been a heady experience.

She was still dazed at how quickly everything had happened once the manuscript was finished. Despite her fears that Annie Selkirk might have changed her mind, the agent had been happy to look at her work. For three nail-biting weeks, Judith had waited in an agony of suspense for the verdict. One moment she'd be full of hope, the next, despairingly certain that her work would be rejected. She'd found it impossible to think of anything else.

Finally the agent had rung, and Judith would never forget that phone call. They'd both made the usual polite noises, and then the other woman had said, 'Judith, I'm not going to keep you in suspense a moment longer. I've read your work, and I enjoyed it very much. There are a few areas we can look at, and I've noted down my suggestions for you, but overall I'm very excited about what you've written.'

Judith's fingers tightened around the receiver. She felt almost giddy with relief and joy.

'Oh ... that's wonderful!' she managed breathlessly.

'It's a story that reflects the experience of so many women these days. You've made your heroine so real, with emotions readers will easily identify with. I really loved her.'

'Thank you. She — she seemed to really come alive for me.' Judith could have listened to Annie Selkirk talking about her work in such glowing terms for hours.

'Now, if you'll take a look at my suggestions and see what you think, I'd love to get the manuscript off to a publisher as quickly as possible.'

When the notes arrived, Judith could see at once how Annie Selkirk's input would help to bolster certain areas of the story, and she set to work immediately.

After that, it was a matter of being patient again as she waited for the judgement of the publishing house to which Annie had sent her manuscript.

As the days passed, Judith tried to attune herself to the possibility of rejection, but nothing could have prepared her for the disappointment she felt when she got the news that the publishers had passed on her work.

'Don't let it worry you,' the agent comforted her. 'It's not that they didn't like your work. Only, as it happened, they had just picked up another author with the same target market as you. We'll just try somewhere else.'

It was Judith's first experience of the business side of writing.

'And that's why you need someone like Annie,' Tony had explained in the face of her disappointment. 'So you can stick to being creative, and let her handle everything else.'

Finally, when she thought she couldn't bear to wait a moment longer, she received the news she was so longing to hear.

Her manuscript had been accepted!

If she'd won the lottery, Judith couldn't have been more ecstatic. When she put down the phone, she was jumping out of her skin. With hands clasped to her cheeks, she walked round and round the small living room, speaking out loud to herself, a huge grin splitting her face. 'Oh, God ... I can't believe it ... Oh God ...'

Then she lifted the phone and dialled Tony's number. If there was anyone she wanted to share this wonderful moment with, it was the man who had done so much to help her succeed.

Now, as she drove home from posting off her precious bundle, Judith was still smiling. How amazingly life works out, she told herself. Once she'd thought that at forty-three, her life was over. But all that had happened was that everything had changed. She had left her marriage and home, found a career she loved, and established a much deeper relationship with her sons. She had adapted and grown in ways she could never have imagined, was so much stronger now, so much more in charge of her own life.

Just as Tony had once promised her she would be ...

And as she thought of Tony, she blessed again the day she had met the man who had given her so much hope and support when she had needed it most. One way she had tried to thank him was by dedicating her first novel to him. It would be a surprise when she placed the finished book into his hands.

If she were honest with herself, she had to admit that Tony still had a corner of her heart. But if they were destined to stay just friends, then so be it. Another one of the lessons she'd learned in recent times was that life can't be manipulated, only lived. And she would accept whatever the future held for her, because the only certainty was change.

Yet another change she'd faced in recent times was in her place of abode. When Luke had been discharged from hospital he'd asked to come and stay with her 'for a while'. With Brent a constant visitor, too, it was clear that she'd need a larger apartment. As long as her sons never took her for granted again, they were welcome in her home at any time.

The expense of the move had been made easier by the cheque she'd recently received from her publishers, not only for the manuscript she had just delivered, but for the next book they wanted from her, too.

Still, at this stage of her career at least, the money wasn't going to be enough to allow her to write full-time and it was Tony who suggested that she take her cue from him.

'Creative writing courses are enormously popular now, Judith. Let me ask around. I'm sure you'll find a position that'll still give you plenty of time to write.'

The more she thought about it, the more Judith liked the idea. *She* had done it — written a publishable novel. Ordinary Judith Burton, mother and wife. It seemed fitting, somehow, to give encouragement and inspiration to other women who had the same dream as herself.

And now, with her first novel ready for the printers, she was ready to write again.

The idea of facing another stack of blank pages frightened her a little. Could she really do it again? Could she find inside her heart the essence she would need to create another character who would come to life as Jo had?

Judith gripped the steering wheel, her mouth set in a determined line.

Of course she could. She could do anything.

❄

It was Thursday evening, and Leith was packing her small suitcase. She and David had bought a cottage in the Blue Mountains and regularly got away for weekends.

He had rung a short while before to say he'd be late for dinner, but that didn't worry her so much these days, not when her wonderful husband was back in her life again, not when she had learned the meaning of real loneliness.

She'd done a lot of soul-searching in the months that had passed since that terrible incident with Paul. She understood a lot better now the pressures in David's working life because these days he shared his burdens with her, instead of keeping them to himself. They had both learned from their mistakes.

It had taken a crisis to bring them back into each other's lives. It was Judith who had called David to tell him what had happened and to ask him if he would come to the hospital. Leith had had no inkling of her call and, when David had appeared in the casualty room, it was hard to say who was the more shocked.

She had burst into tears and he had folded her in his arms, oblivious to everyone else around them.

To Leith, it had felt like coming home.

Afterwards, they had done a lot of talking, the sort of talking, David admitted, they should have done many months before. Finally they were both able to acknowledge that there had been mistakes on both sides, but that they loved each other enough to put them in the past and try again.

Now, as she zipped her suitcase closed, Leith realised how the crisis had helped to open her eyes. It had made her understand that what David had always offered her was real love, the sort of love that goes hand in hand with trust and freedom. She had come to realise that she had always wanted more from him than she'd given back, and it shamed her still to think of her selfishness and self-absorption.

Finally, too, she had been able to confront the fact that David was her husband, not her father, and that he couldn't be expected to make up for what had happened in her past. She knew now that to make her marriage work, she had to relate to David as an adult and not as a needy child. It had taken the time she'd spent with Paul to make her see that. He had manipulated her like a child, flattered and controlled her like a child, because that was exactly the role she had allowed herself to play for years.

Now, as she went through to the bathroom to pack her cosmetic case, Leith glanced at her reflection in the mirror. The scars were still visible if you looked closely, but they didn't worry her as much as they once might have. David loved her, she knew, for more than her surface beauty. The difference now was that she didn't have to be a perfect woman on a pedestal in order for him to be with her.

I'm so lucky he forgave me, she told herself as she filled her case with what she needed, so lucky that he gave me a second chance. From the day he'd come back into her life, their marriage had grown stronger. Leith had found that giving brought its own rich rewards. And there was so much she had to make up for.

She'd found other ways of giving, too. These days, instead of trying to fill her time with lunches and shopping, she now spent two afternoons a week at the Children's Hospital. She read to the small patients, helped them with their schoolwork, tried to make them laugh instead of thinking about their pain, and found herself rewarded tenfold.

Now, as she switched off the ensuite light, she thought, I'm at peace with myself. My life is in balance.

It was the greatest reward of all.

❋

She still suffered from nightmares. Dry-mouthed and breathless, she'd jerk awake, her heart racing with fear, her mind full of terrible images of her lifeless child.

Sometimes Ian, disturbed, would wake, too, and he'd take her in his arms and stroke her gently, whispering words of comfort.

And eventually she would drift back into sleep.

On other occasions, when her turbulent dreams woke her, she would slip carefully out of bed and pad down the hall on her bare feet, driven to see for herself that Cam was all right, was sleeping peacefully in his cot, and that he had in fact survived the terrible trauma of his mother's craziness.

Shivering in her nightdress, she would sit on the chair beside him and listen to his breathing, see him twitch in his sleep. And thank God that he was still alive.

When she thought back to that terrible night a few months ago, she felt as if it had all happened to another person. She still found it unbearably difficult to accept that she could have been capable of causing harm to the child she had given life to.

But she *had* been someone else then, a woman in turmoil, a woman who had come so close to the edge that she had almost destroyed everything she held dear.

The day of the committal hearing had been the most frightening of her life. She had been incapable of giving evidence in her own defence. How could she when, in her own mind, she readily accepted her guilt? Irrational though her action might have been, with her mind befuddled by alcohol and grief, she still had to face the fact that, for those few seconds, all she had wanted to do was silence her own son, shut out the screams that, to her ears, had sounded like piercing accusations of her own incompetence and uselessness. Relieve them both of their pain ...

How, then, could she convincingly plead her innocence?

When the long day had finally come to an end and the magistrate had brought down his finding, Rory had taken in little beyond his final sentence, which would be etched in her mind to her dying day: 'The accused may have formed the intention to harm her child, but she did not go through with that intention so, under article 565 of the Act, and given the other extenuating evidence before me, I see no case to answer.'

Rory heard a sharp cry of relief — and realised it had come from her own lips. She began to tremble uncontrollably.

But her guilt and shame did not magically disappear. She felt as if she could never forgive herself for what she had almost done and expected nothing but the harshest condemnation and rejection from those who knew her.

To her amazement, however, she had found, for the most part, support and compassion. From the correspondence she had received, from the responses in the letters pages of the newspapers, it seemed to Rory that there were many, many women out there who understood the pressures and burdens that accompanied modern motherhood. She was assured that she was not alone in her feelings of inadequacy and hopelessness. And the forgiveness of others made it easier in time to begin to forgive herself.

Throughout her ordeal, Ian had been there for her. Perhaps for the first time, he'd realised just what she had been going through. She knew how shocked he'd been by what had almost happened but, instead of blaming her, he'd accepted that perhaps his own short-sightedness had been part of the problem.

'It was my fault, too, I see that now,' he told her during those terrible weeks leading up to the committal hearing. 'I was ambiguous about having a child, you always knew that, but once the decision was made, I should have accepted the changes in our life instead of fighting them. I didn't know, Rory ... I didn't know what I was doing to you.'

She had seen the torment in his face and, with tears in her eyes, had folded him in her arms.

'But we can forgive each other, darling, can't we?' she whispered brokenly.

Now they were taking each day as it came, working at the trust and love they had once shared so deeply.

It made things easier that she had decided to work part-time, at least until Cam was ready for school. Even then she would see how she felt about a full-time career again. Her child and her relationship with Ian, she had accepted, were her first priorities.

At the moment, she was going into the office three mornings a week. And for the first time in a long while, she was enjoying her work again, now that the strains and pressures of trying to cope on all fronts had been relieved.

In particular, she was absorbed by her current project. The book, aptly enough, dealt with the trials and pressures facing modern women as they seek to find a balance between career and motherhood and, in her regular sessions with the woman author, Rory was finding a catharsis of sorts, helping her own recovery. It was Antonella who had suggested she might like to work on the project. Dear, wise Antonella, who had perhaps understood her better than she had understood herself ...

Now, as she sat in the small courtyard of her home, Rory dropped the file she had been reading and smiled as she watched her son playing in the sunshine. She felt suffused with emotions that had eluded her for so long.

Contentment and hope.

❋

The sun was shining. It was one of those perfect days that the Gold Coast expects as its due.

In the bedroom of Maude Donohoe's small apartment, Cate stared at her reflection in the full-length mirror. She couldn't believe it. How quickly life can throw down its new hand, making the impossible suddenly possible! Even the right job had come out of the blue ...

The emotion of the moment got to her, and she felt her eyes well with tears of happiness. Furiously, she blinked them back. It wasn't a day to ruin her make-up.

'Off-white is definitely you, darling.' Jessica smiled over her shoulder, speaking to her reflection in the mirror.

'Yeah,' Cate laughed as she turned to face her friend, her throat still tight with emotion, 'pure white was pushing it a bit, wasn't it?'

Suddenly serious, Jessica looked back into Cate's radiant face. 'I'm so happy for you, Cate. I'm so glad you didn't let this go.'

Cate nodded, the wreath of baby breath that held her veil bobbing around her head.

'Me too,' she said with quiet emphasis.

It was that amazing visit from Cal's mother that had changed everything. After forty-eight hours of agonising indecision, Cate had finally known what she had to do.

She loved Cal and she was sure in her heart that he loved her, so why should they let the past destroy the promise of the future?

Without forewarning him, she caught a plane up north that next weekend. She still had her key to the apartment, and when he walked in that Friday evening, she was sitting on the patio waiting for him.

For a long speechless moment they stared at each other and she saw his stunned surprise.

'Cate...' There was a depth of emotion in the way he spoke her name that made her heart skip a beat.

She stood up and stepped into the living room.

'Cate, what —'

But she had something she'd come a long way to say, and she wasn't going to waste a moment in saying it.

'You have a wonderful mother, Cal, I hope you realise that. She loves her son dearly, and she'd do anything to make him truly happy. That's why she flew to Sydney to see me.'

She saw his expression of astonishment.

'She's seen us together, Cal, and she knew that we had something special. She didn't want you to throw that away.'

She took a deep breath, and her voice became more passionate and intense. 'She told me what happened. Everything. But the past is the past. You can't change anything about that. What you *can* do is forgive yourself, throw off the burden of guilt that you don't deserve to carry. I love you, Cal, and I won't let you destroy both our lives. We'll get through this together. I know we will. Because that's what love is all about.'

It had all come out in a rush, and nervously she searched his face for a reaction.

Would he tell her it was no use?

Or would he step with her into the future?

In the living room, Maude Donohoe was waiting, dressed in a smart suit, her hair and make-up perfect. Her face lit with pleasure as Cate walked through the doorway from the bedroom, followed by Jessica.

'Oh, my dear, you look a picture. A most beautiful, beautiful bride.'

'Thank you,' Cate smiled. 'And for these too. They're just wonderful.'

She touched the rope of pearls around her neck. They were the ones that Maude Donohoe had been wearing the first night they'd met.

'I knew they'd be perfect on you. They were my grandmother's you know. A wedding present from her husband. Now, I'm so glad I have someone special to hand them on to.'

Cate felt the pricking in her eyes again. It was a day for extraordinary emotion.

'You've given me more than I could ever have imagined,' she said softly.

The wedding took place as the sun was setting. A simple ceremony by the ocean's edge, followed by a reception in a riverside restaurant.

It was just after ten when Cal and Cate said their goodbyes to the accompaniment of Auld Lang Syne.

As she moved with her new husband around the thirty or so guests, accepting their kisses and best wishes, Cate thought her heart would burst with happiness. For so many years, she had coped alone. But she had no regrets. Because, step by tiny step, she had acquired a strength and courage which nothing could diminish.

Now she was taking a new journey.

Not with trepidation, but with the joyous expectation that it, too, would bring its own lessons and rewards.

THE END

If you enjoyed *Everything to Lose,*
then you'll love ...

BEST KEPT SECRETS
Jennifer Bacia

Sometimes secrets can be deadly ...

Three good friends – each successful – each facing the crisis of her life.

Cass seems to have it all – spectacular house, lovely children, caring friends and a great marriage to a successful man who adores her. Or so she thought ...

Fran's worked hard to become a leading litigation lawyer, yet she's lonely and longs for a husband and family. When passion ignites with a new client, Fran is overjoyed. But soon she's confronted with the dilemma of her life ...

Angela is the vision of the successful, single career woman. A highly respected television anchor, she's fiercely proud of her independence. Then she faces a crisis too enormous to handle alone ...

Three friends, three secrets, three women whose lives will never be the same.

BEST KEPT SECRETS

CHAPTER ONE

New Year's Eve

SHE couldn't help wondering why it was love that so often taught the true meaning of hate.

Around midnight, after she'd performed the ritual hugs and kisses and clichéd best wishes, the emotion surged through her again, choking off her breath.

But still, Cass congratulated herself bitterly; she was managing the impossible. Keeping her secret to herself. Hiding it behind the fixed smile that made her face ache, and the forced bonhomie of the moment as she moved around the crowded living room. Johnny's friends, mostly. 'Friends' he felt they should know. The city's movers and shakers. The people who knew people who knew people.

She hadn't wanted a party this year. Not after what had happened. But she had known there was little chance of talking Johnny out of something that had become such a fixture on their social calendar. Johnny Dunworth was a party man. Throwing, or going to — Johnny knew how to have a good time. Even at a party for two.

'Cass! Everything wonderful for the year ahead!' She caught a whiff of Giorgio as a tall, attractive strawberry blonde embraced her and planted a kiss on each cheek.

For Angela Kelly, Cass managed to produce a smile that was genuine. They mightn't see each other often but Angela was a real friend — as distinct from a lot of others here tonight. Which was probably why even the smile wasn't quite enough to fool her.

'Cass . . . is something the matter?' Those warm hazel eyes searched her face with concern.

Cass should have known better. Angela Kelly, investigative journo, couldn't be fooled quite that easily. What sign had alerted her, she wondered. Had Angela somehow sensed the anguish and anger behind Cass's artificial stretch of lips and teeth, noted the stress and confusion in her tight, clenched fingers?

'I —' Cass looked away, dreading the sting she felt starting behind her eyes. Suddenly she realised how much she wanted to confide, to pour out her worries. To Angela, who had it all together. Who would tell her what to do, how to handle the nightmare her life had become.

But she knew she couldn't do that now. Not here. Maybe not ever.

'Cass! Happy New Year, my sweet! May all your sexual fantasies come true!' A business friend of

Johnny's, a man she barely knew, had slung a too familiar arm around her neck and was pulling her close, crushing her breasts against his perfectly rumpled Boss linen. Cass could smell the stench of rum on his breath.

Hiding her distaste, she threw Angela an apologetic glance. 'I'll call you, Angie. Soon.'

And Angela Kelly got a hint of something seriously wrong in her friend's bleak blue eyes.

Fran Antoni hated New Year. She hated parties, also. Parties too obviously revealed her as the freak she felt herself to be. If she'd been divorced she could at least have laid claim to fitting society's norms. But there was nothing normal about being a 39-year-old never-married woman.

She stood as inconspicuously as possible in the far corner of the lavish, high-ceilinged living room with its spectacular water views. The glass in her hand was a comforting prop. She didn't drink. Her vices were few. But a selling point? Hardly. So what else? Certainly not her figure, hidden in the expensive crepe pants-suit. Hardly man-catching gear she knew, but what difference did it make when a quick perusal of her assets left on offer only her brain and a six-figure salary? And she'd read enough to know that these days even that hardly counted if it were true that most men were threatened by women more intelligent and better paid than themselves.

Fran took another sip of mineral water and wondered when it might be polite to leave. It was only because Cass had insisted that she'd accepted the invitation for tonight. Kind, generous Cass whom she'd always admired. And envied. Cass who had married the handsome, charismatic Johnny Dunworth, ad man *terrible*. Cass, who was mother to Joanna and Tom and Nicky.

Fran knew that envy was a sin. But she couldn't help herself. Not that she begrudged Cass her good fortune. It was just that Fran wanted her share of it too. The things that made life worth living. The things that really mattered. A husband and a family.

As she watched the happy groups and couples around her she wished again that she'd been strong enough to resist Cass's invitation. A good-hearted attempt, she knew, to keep her from spending this significant evening alone. Yet even being by herself would have been preferable to this.

In the flurry of the stroke of midnight she'd found herself being kissed by half a dozen strangers and felt the stir of a physical sensation she had almost forgotten. How long had it been since she'd felt the pressure of a man's lips against her own? She could barely remember. Four years? The doctor she had met on that Christmas cruise? Breathing passion into her again. Igniting remote memory. Bringing her to life — for a few days at least — before he flew back to somewhere in Perth. Address not offered. She could understand, of course. Not special enough to change his life for. Or hers. But the aftermath had made her almost regret what had occurred. Had left her with an itch impossible to soothe, that clawed at her insides, left her sleepless with unrest. She should have known better . . .

Surreptitiously, she checked her watch. Twenty after midnight. Polite now to leave? It would be easier, she thought, to slip away, avoid the fuss of goodbyes. Cass would forgive her and she'd already mentioned to Angela that she wouldn't be staying long.

Angela . . . She caught sight of her friend across the room, confident, smiling, the centre of attention. Another never-married. The only difference being that the choice was Angela's. Needing no man. Not even one as ruggedly attractive and high-profile as Christopher Tolbert who hovered attentively at her elbow.

Even if her job hadn't made her instantly recognisable, Angela would still have turned heads, Fran thought. Tall and gorgeous, perfect profile, Princess Di legs — the sort of legs Fran would have given ten years salary for. Blessings, taken for granted, she felt sure, by those women lucky enough to be born with them.

With an effort Fran shook off her mood. What good would it do her to get so morose? This was the brink of a new year. Another chance. Another reason to hope. And — another year older . . .

It was time to go. Excusing herself, she moved

through the crowded room and found the small study off the foyer where she had left her handbag. Soft, pale leather. Chanel. One of her compensations for what she really lacked. And there were others. Like the gleaming BMW that awaited her outside. The well-planned share portfolio. The central city apartment where notables such as Angela were her neighbours.

Yet none of it was ever enough to make up for what she longed for so desperately.

Angela Kelly was worried. Sometimes she wondered if it was the natural state for people employed in her fickle industry. Still, she did her best to comfort herself, she had survived longer than most. Twenty years in the business, and now prime time anchor on *Deadline*. The current affairs show everyone watched. Five years, she'd lasted. An eternity for anyone, and particularly for a female of the species.

But tonight she was finding it more difficult than usual to put her paranoias on hold. The party and the anticipated pleasures of Chris Tolbert's sexual prowess were some distraction but she still couldn't shake off her worries.

Because she'd heard the rumours. Because that old line about it being too dangerous in television ever to take a holiday might now be coming true for her.

There was no summer recess for *Deadline*. While Angela took her usual six-week break the program continued to air with a substitute anchor.

In previous years the job had been swapped between a couple of the weekend newsmen. But this year there'd been a change. A serious change. This time Cia Morgan had been chosen to take Angela's place in the chair.

Cia Morgan. Twenty-eight. Bright, brash, intelligent and camera beautiful. From the time eighteen months ago when Cia had joined the program, Angela had known she had something to worry about.

Cia Morgan was ambitious. And it showed. She was also eleven years younger than Angela. And if the rumour mill was as accurate as usual, she was a serious contender for *Deadline*'s top job. The new-blood, fresh-face scenario of the gladitorial ratings game. Especially when those ratings had taken a sudden dip in the last six months.

They would turn it around, of course they would. It had happened before. *Deadline* was the pinnacle and Angela knew how lucky she was to be sitting in that chair. Sure, there was the crap, the pop psychology, the stories geared to the viewing public's short-lived attention spans, but there were important issues as well. Issues she felt passionate about, committed to. And *Deadline* gave her the chance to make a difference. There was no way she was walking away without a fight. Cia Morgan or no Cia Morgan.

'It's almost one-thirty, Angie. Feel like calling it a night?'

Chris Tolbert's dark eyes were as loaded with intent as the plays he wrote to such acclaim. This was their second date and there was still plenty of ground to cover.

Angela switched modes. Easy when you'd had as much practice as she had — and men were such pushovers. She smiled at the attractive playwright. 'Well, it's probably time to do something . . .'

She'd done the asking for this date. Long ago she'd come to the realisation that it takes a certain sort of male to approach a high-profile female. It was the aura of power that men couldn't handle. Particularly those men who were used to wielding it themselves. She had noted with silent amusement their obvious unease and discomfort in her presence. But paradoxically, she had sensed the sexual charge too. Their desire, perhaps, to master that power . . .

But she would never allow that. She was in control of her own life. Exactly as she had always planned.

And so, as daylight broke on the first day of the new year, Fran Antoni lay alone in her hopeful queen-size bed, Angela Kelly rocked passionately in her new lover's embrace and Cass Dunworth lay sleepless beside her handsome, snoring husband.

None of them could know that by the same time next year one of them would be dead.